I0643049

Brighter than the Flames

"Brighter than the Flames," by Stefan Scheuermann.

ISBN 978-1-63868-017-8 (softcover); 978-1-63868-018-5 (hardcover); 978-1-63868-019-2 (eBook).

Published 2021 by Virtualbookworm.com Publishing Inc., P.O. Box 9949, College Station, TX 77842, US. ©2021, Stefan Scheuermann.

Table of Chapters

Preface

ANNA KOOB IS MY TENTH GREAT-GRANDMOTHER. I discovered her during genealogical research and was struck by the words "als Hexe verbrannt" (burnt as a witch). I shared my findings with family and friends. Most responded with enthusiasm. I could not. As I traced my family lines, I was moved by the realization that each generation in my tree was loved by the previous, allowing me to track not only a line of names and a line of blood, but a line of affection, from my own parents to the highest branches in the family tree, so that my own sense of familial connection diluted little as my eyes scanned past those names with which I associated a loving and familiar face, to those whose images and traits I could only imagine.

For that reason, Anna's demise, while intriguing to most, was disturbing to me — deeply and hauntingly. I found myself pitying her and mourning her, though a long life and natural death would still have taken her from this world hundreds of years before my birth. I wanted to know more about her, so I deepened my research. I found little on Anna Koob, but much on the region around Aschaffenburg, Germany, in 1603, the year and place of Anna's death. I learned more about her husband and her child. I found no evidence of Anna's trial but found much on witch trials in the area. As I continued to dig, the work felt familiar. It was reminiscent of the research I do in preparation for a novel.

I don't remember if the idea to write Anna's story into a novel fell onto my head suddenly or crept into it slyly. In either case, research was well underway when the decision was made. But I had to decide on the nature of the story. A great deal of artistic license must be taken to bring to life a figure of whom so very little historical evidence has survived. I battled myself at length on that matter. I wanted to honor Anna and bring to my readers the atrocity of this distant family anomaly, to refresh the humanity of the story in a way that would elicit the same sort of sorrowful compassion I felt. To do so, the tools of fictional character development would have to be employed. Aristotle taught us that literature is truer than history. It is with that rationale that I contented myself with the distances I would have to stride away from the precepts of historical reconstruction to give Anna's story the pungency I desired it to have.

It was not my intention to sensationalize this story, or to make this family tragedy frivolous in any way. I intended a much more scientific approach to the project. But after two months of pondering Anna Koob, of getting to know her, I reminded myself that her blood flows beneath my skin, and I suspect she wants her story told. So, I relinquished my pen to the whims of my imagination, yielding it, I pray, readily and gladly, from my hand to hers.

My morality tells me that all life is equally precious, and all human suffering is to be mourned, though I cannot help but feel that some human pain is *more* tragic, and the loss of some lives is more calamitous to the fortunes of mankind. The extinguishing of *some* lights darkens the Earth more. It is these deaths that burn us, these lives that change us, it is these people that we write about and read about. And it seems to me that a blazingly tragic death is, more often than not, the conclusion of an extraordinary life. With that in mind, it is not so far a stretch of the imagination to place, under the name of Anna Koob, high upon my family tree, a life worth writing about.

I gave the social sciences their due attention in my attempts to capture and bring dimension to Anna's character. There are a few things that even the most disciplined historians must admit. Few people of subtlety die in the flames of execution. For that reason, I may write her as open and forthright. Trials in the courts of the Church have historically featured defendants who have pressed for change, allowing me to add a degree of idealism to Anna's character. Anna's trial was not part of a larger witch trial, like the famous Fulda Witch Trials that occurred in the same year and just a few miles north of Anna's home. There was something singular about her case, not associated with general hysteria. She was hand-plucked from life in a very personal way, suggesting that her individual influence was dangerously profound.

During Anna's life, the earliest rays of the Enlightenment were just beginning to cast the faintest color on the horizon of Western Society. Resistance against the light was staunch. Feminine strength was viewed by most with suspicion and fear. Those women and girls who were free of spirit and sharp of mind were social peculiarities that needed an explanation — a sinister, demonic explanation, as was the sad case of many bright women, including my own dear Anna Koob. Nobody, who is all of these things in such high measure as to draw her fate, deserves to be an obscure fruit, high in the family tree of an obscure author, too high to be noticed even by those nearest the tree.

It would be a grossly inaccurate and irresponsible mistruth to call this work biography in any form. But it feels to me far beyond the hackneyed cliché, "based on actual events." I wanted to pay some honor to a woman that my research and my instincts tell me should be honored. I felt bizarrely in her embrace, haunted in a soft and encouraging way, as I wrote this story, and I hope it is written in a manner that welcomes you to join me there, where her goodness can unite us in familial affection.

The experience often surprised me, delighting me and horrifying me, for Anna's story is one of love *and* tragedy — beautiful and horrid, delicious and putrid. It is with that extreme duality of spirit that I hand it to you, my readers, hoping that you will consume it with an open and compassionate mind, allowing yourselves to be enriched and tortured, and ultimately altered, by the story of Anna Koob.

The story begins in the small village of Kleinostheim, on the River Main, in the modern state of Bavaria, Germany. Kleinostheim was under the care of the city of Aschaffenburg, where the Archbishop of Mainz kept a residence. It was a generation before the Thirty Years War. Tensions between Catholics and Protestants were high, and Kleinostheim was on the front line. Religious zealotry abounded, and those on the lookout for signs of the Devil found them in the actions of the innocent. Anna's story, while riddled with uniqueness, was part of an epidemic, one whose evils linger in various forms to this day.

Stefan Scheuermann

Chapter One:
One Foot in the World

18 January, 1566

IT WAS THE COMMON CRY OF A NEWBORN, yet not common to every ear. Anna Schwarz announced her entry into the world as many babies do. She kicked and writhed in her father's hands while her lungs pushed her voice into the air of Kleinostheim, Germany, for the very first time. The event was well-attended. Of course, they all heard the cry. How could they not? The air carried it jovially around the house, through the walls, and in subtle, muted form, into the neighboring buildings. It was not experienced identically by all. Most heard a baby's cry, with nothing in pitch or tone to distinguish it from any other newborn child. To the discerning ear, however, it bounced with uncommon vivacity, with a crispness and clarity that announced what Anna's parents suspected, that her time on the earth would be extraordinary.

The shrill, yet spritely, cry ended. Anna drew her second inhale of earthly air, but did not use it to force another sound. Instead, she released it slowly and silently while staring into her father's eyes. She looked at Michel like an old friend, meeting by chance for the first time in years. The gaze struck him deeply, pulling his heart into his throat. He believed, as he would describe for many years to come, that her spirit had placed just one foot in the world and kept the other in the Heavens. Anna would have no memory of that first encounter with her father, or of the hundreds that followed shortly behind. But in that first glance, Anna's eyes gripped his with alertness, awareness, and a deep, ancient intelligence — or so he swore at every dynamic recitation of the event.

Anna's mother, Margarethe, received the child from Michel's hands and set her lovingly to the breast. She stared at her daughter, her only daughter, with doting eyes, until she heard the subtle whimper of her husband. She looked at Michel to see a ghostly pale complexion glistening with flowing tears. He tried to explain that first, arcane communication between his and Anna's eyes, but words failed him. Margarethe gestured an invitation to him, and he joined his wife and daughter in bed.

Over the next several weeks, Michel took every opportunity to lock his gaze to Anna's, hungry to recognize the voice in her eyes that had spoken so clearly and intelligently to him in the moments after her birth. Her eyes were bright, but no longer seemed to possess the knowledge of the Heavens. Still, as she grew, her movements and gestures, her giggle and her cry, the occasional inquisitive tilt of her young head, and the way her yellow locks seemed to speak freely with the Franconian breeze, struck each sensitive soul around her as unearthly.

"She is handled by the Angels," her perceptive grandmother once said of her.

Handled by the Angels — some saw her that way. The rest saw a baby, not of striking beauty, with no peculiarities of form, but with a softness of air that seemed to covetously surround her, and with a unique brand of charisma that promised a generous spirit and a faithful heart from the girl and woman that Anna would grow to become.

She was gifted by Heaven as the fifth child born to Michel and Margarethe Schwarz. When Anna was born, her brother Michel was five and half years old, Aulgoin was four, and Martin was little more than two. Martin was born a twin, but his sister died in her first year. Anna was named after her. As the only girl in the house, bearing the name of the lost infant, Anna was coddled by the whole household, but by none more than her father. She was hardly allowed a whimper that went unattended. In her first few years, her brothers entertained her constantly. But soon their tastes and sensibilities drifted away from their little sister, and Anna quickly learned to entertain herself.

Beginning not long after she learned to walk, Anna sought the experiences her village offered. She toddled toward the squawking birds, the barking squirrels, and the honking geese. She was fascinated by the way the loose mud would slowly release the form of footprints and wagon tracks. All of those many hidden things, the minutiae of daily life that hides under foot or goes about its day in the hazy peripheral of a bustling village, received all of its due attention in the eyes of young Anna — and it all delighted her.

Anna's real talent, from her earliest years, was in drawing the attention of others to those delightful little wonders. Once she could speak, she wasted little time in providing that service. When she was three years old, she stood outside of a neighbor's home and stared fixedly at a single rose on a bush. It was morning and the dawn's dew still beaded on the petals. Her neighbor saw her, frozen, as if cursed into living stone.

Slightly fearful for the child, the neighbor asked her, "Anna, what are you doing?"

Anna, barely above knee-height, invited her neighbor to join her in amazement of the rose's beauty. The older woman saw an ordinary dew speckled rose, no more flamboyant than any other flower in the village, until Anna began to describe the rose as *she* saw it. Suddenly, the aged eyes of the neighbor gave attention to the minute beauties Anna pointed out — the deep red veins of the petals, the textures that were magnified by the drops of dew, and the patterns of the overlapping petals, which swayed in the breeze and seemed to churn like the sea. The old woman caught herself holding her breath as the beauties that had sat quite redundantly under her nose for her many years came rushing at her with blazing brilliance.

After that morning, the old neighbor began each morning with a thoughtful, penetrating study of her garden. In the winter, she found other things to anatomize. When she failed, Anna was there to draw her attention to some other natural delight. She gave similar gifts to all who were curious enough to ask her what she was doing. Through her toddler's perspective, she made delightful even those daily annoyances, like the barking of dogs or the sting of an insect, or the muddying of clothes. It did not take long for the folks of Kleinostheim to seek Anna out for her innocent perspective. They did so when they needed it the most.

As she grew into her childhood, she enjoyed wandering about their village. It would be inaccurate to call her boyish, but she was certainly not dainty, preferring dirt and trees to dolls, and flinging herself recklessly in coordination with the wild imaginings that played out inside of her head. Anna had her scrapes and bruises. She had her troubles, which saddened her to no lesser degree than any child her age. What separated her from others was her readiness to recover, to laugh again, and to see the joy and beauty in all that surrounded her. She had a buoyancy of spirit that would have been envied were it not so often the source of other people's joy and recovery from sorrow. Her company was welcomed by all who knew her. Every door in Kleinostheim was open to her. Every dinner table had chairs ready and willing to scoot to one side or the other to make room for the spritely child who had one foot in the Heavens.

Not all of the people of Anna's village took the time to benefit from her. Many passed their eyes over her like they passed over any child or pet, like they passed over dewy roses and muddy wagon tracks. Anna also found it difficult to bond with the other children, yet she was not lonely. She was too delighted with everything that existed around her to mourn her absence of playmates. This continued as she grew, and the affection of those who knew her well also grew as the years passed.

One morning, when Anna was seven years old, she bounced through the village as usual, but with a mind distant from the people and things around her. She had quirks a-plenty, so the villagers thought little of her half-witted answers to their greetings. Her imagination had wings that her concentration was powerless to tame. Nevertheless, those she encountered cherished the lightness of the air around her.

With her mind well beyond the senses of the sharpest eyes and ears, Anna made her way to the river. She removed her shoes and lounged on the bank with her bare heels lightly kissing the water. She was the very portrait of blissful repose. Perhaps repose is a poor choice of words. It tells a half-truth. Her body was at celestial rest, her senses entirely unaware of their surroundings. Her mind, devoid of the incessant bombardment of sensual input, flew at great speeds to the corners of the world, over mountains and across oceans, to the heavens, and beyond. It was everything but restful.

The ordinary riverbank was rendered quite interesting to passers-by, with the sharp contrast between Anna's bright dress and the brownish-gray clay of the bank and the deep green of the surrounding brush. The spectacle drew every person who wandered along the river on their morning walk to a fascinated stop. Anna provided ample entertainment for her growing crowd of spectators. As her musings turned adventurous and thrilling, her chest heaved and her limbs twitched. As they grew tender, she wrapped herself in her own arms and hummed gently, all the time entirely unaware of the captivated voyeurs.

Nobody gawked in astonishment or offense. They all knew Anna, and her peculiarities were not only acceptable, they were endearing and delightful, and had done much to elevate the spirits of those wise enough to allow it. Anna rose from her spot on the bank, soiled of dress and limbs, quite the vision of careless filth. Her appearance bothered nobody as she skipped through the village toward her home. They all knew her and they knew her good parents.

At the skip of a seven-year-old, the distance from the river to Anna's home should be covered in a few minutes. It took much longer for Anna to walk through her door and be cleaned up by her mother. She was stopped, despite her appearance, by any and all who stood to benefit from her authentic "Guten Morgen." And those whose hearts were the heaviest hoarded her for the few extra minutes it took for Anna's contagious spirit to revive them.

Anna was earnestly delighted by everything. She still found pleasure in the honk of the geese, in the wagon tracks in the mud, even in the gnats that pooled about eye level in the heat of the summer. How could one help but to be lifted by such a spirit? Annoyances that were cursed one minute were laughed off within the next minute in Anna's company. The result of this effortless service she provided was that Anna was taken quite personally by everyone in the village. She was an accidental celebrity that brought a swarm of compassion to her every scrape and bruise.

The village repaid her tenfold. Margarethe and Michel stood no chance of tending to their own daughter when she was hurt just a few houses away. Every hand wiped and bandaged her scrapes. Every lip kissed her head and offered their prayers before Anna could approach her front door. In the hearts of the villagers, Anna was both the symbol of all they believed Kleinostheim to be, and a talisman for all they hoped it would become.

Chapter Two:
Maria Echter

ONE MORNING, WHEN ANNA WAS EIGHT, in May of 1574, a messenger came to the house and banged demandingly and repeatedly on the door. Michel answered and could make little sense of the servant who stood at the threshold demanding Anna. The servant panted. His clothes were modest in design but rich in quality. There was an awkwardness to the proportions of his facial features. His nose was too small for his broad jaw, his chin not long enough for his square cheeks. Yet there was a polished refinement in the way he held himself, which took the edge off of his disturbing approach.

As any loving father would, Michel stood in a defensive position and ordered the servant from the doorway. Young Michel was already apprenticed in a neighboring village. Aulgoin and Martin were out of the house. Margarethe, safe in a corner of the room, was free to see beyond the threat to the compassionate desperation behind the shouting. She soothed her husband with a gentle press on his shoulder and shushed the servant.

"How can we help you?" she calmly asked.

"I must take your daughter, Anna, with me!" he shouted.

Michel resumed his fighting stance. The servant stood open, seemingly willing to receive a father's blows to achieve his objective.

Just a slight moment before the scene boiled into violence, the soft voice of Anna broke through from behind her father, "Why do you want me?"

"Go to your bed, Anna," Michel ordered sternly.

Anna ignored the order and continued addressing the servant, "Where do you need to take me?"

"To my master," was the answer, panted between heavy breaths.

Curiosity rose to balance Michel's fury. He relaxed his posture and lowered his arms to his side.

Margarethe had poured a cup of wine and stood behind her husband. "Here, drink this," she forcefully urged the servant with a soft but firmly maternal voice.

She gestured to the table and the servant obeyed, taking a seat. He took the wine and drank half the serving in a single gulp.

"Tell us, now," Margarethe insisted, "who is your master and what does he want with our daughter?"

"I am sorry to come to you like this," he answered after finishing the wine and composing himself, "but the matter is urgent, and I have been ordered to bring Anna immediately."

Michel planted his knuckles into the table and leaned forward toward the man. His throat may not have growled with impatience, but his eyes certainly did.

The servant sat back sharply and blurted, "I work for the Echter family. Their estate is northeast of Aschaffenburg."

"We know of the family," Margarethe spoke, "but Anna is only eight. She is not going to work for them."

The servant sighed and calmed himself. He responded, "It is not my master who demands your daughter. It is *his* daughter, Maria."

Margarethe and Michel both shifted back in confused contemplation.

Anna, whose presence in the room had been forgotten by all, spoke up, "I know Maria. I met her near the fountain in Aschaffenburg, the one near the city square."

"When were you at the city square?" Margarethe asked.

"It was a couple of months ago. I went with Father. He had to speak to a man and I waited by the fountain. I met Maria Echter. She was very pretty and she told me all about her dress and the man who made it for her."

"Yes," the servant interrupted, "well, now she is very ill. She speaks to nobody except to ask for you."

"What does she want with me? How can *I* help her?"

"Please," the servant begged, turning his attention to Michel, "You can all come, but I must bring Anna now."

The younger boys were God-knows-where. Michel and Margarethe could not just lift Anna under their arms and follow the servant away.

Michel asked, "Why the urgency? Why must she go now?"

"Dear Maria is very ill. She is dying and all she wants is Anna."

"Take her," Margarethe instructed her husband, "Take Anna and follow this man to the sick girl."

Maria Echter was seventeen years old. Her encounter with Anna at the fountain struck a deep chord in her, deep enough for Anna's face and Anna's voice to be all she demanded in her illness. Michel lifted Anna onto his horse and mounted behind her. He told the servant to lead the way. The servant wasted no time mounting his own horse and racing from Kleinostheim.

It took a full two hours at a restless sprint to reach the Echter Estate. It was a stately home, yet strangely rustic in design, as if the architect had to get approval from the thick Spessart Forest that enshrouded it. The Echter family was almost as old as the forest itself. Baron Echter enjoyed a degree of local notoriety and prominence that rivaled the archbishop's. The servant led Anna and Michel into a home that spoke nothing of pretension. The home, and everything within, existed for the comforts and joy of the family, without concern for the opinions of others.

Michel followed the servant down a hallway. He gripped Anna's little hand in his. The grasp was tight, but Anna did not mind. She was frightened of the strange house and the mystery of the ill girl, which wreaked havoc with her wild imagination. She squeezed her father's hand with equal force.

They stopped at the closed door of a room, hearing a woman's cry muffled behind it. The door swung open and Maria's mother flew from the room, yelling, "She has left us!"

She bumped into the wall of the hallway, took a few staggering steps farther from the room, and fell to her knees, tugging at her long brown hair and crying, "Oh God, my girl is dead. She is gone. She is gone."

The servant ran into the room. Anna could only see a small portion of the nearest wall from where she stood. The mother rose to her feet and cried as she ran down the hall until out of sight and sound. Anna and Michel stood as they were left, alone in the hallway.

"Anna, please come in," the servant begged from inside the room.

Stone-faced and seeming to be completely free of the fear she suffered as she walked down the hallway, she pulled her hand from her father's and followed the voice. Michel did not move his feet, but bent his body to see fully into the room. Anna stood beside Maria's bed and stared into a face that was a weak imitation of something that lived. The servant backed from the bed and stood at the threshold of the room. Michel watched over the servant's shoulder as Anna took the dying girl's hand in hers. The men could hear Anna whispering but could not make out the words. Anna stood blocking their view of Maria's face.

Anna released the girl's hand and stepped aside, revealing a thin, bluish smile as it lifted the parched corners of Maria's lips. Maria was not dead. Anna jumped onto the bed and sat beside her friend from the fountain. She spoke to Maria, not as a mourner to a corpse, not in terms of loss and death, but of life. With giggling lightness, she told Maria about the silly antics of a cat in her neighborhood. Maria's smile lifted higher. The servant closed the door, took Michel by the hand, and led him to the dining hall, where the men shared food and drink in silence.

Already several hours after Michel expected to leave for home, he remained in the house, separated from his daughter. He began to worry for her. The baron had been conspicuously absent from the happenings of the day and notably neglectful of his guests. Michel had spent most of his day roaming the halls and empty rooms, nervously admiring the art on the walls and antique figurines settled snugly into virtually every cranny in the house. His heart increased its flutter with every passing quarter hour. Despite how well he understood his daughter's character, he still shuddered to imagine her locked in a room with the half-corpse of a dying girl.

The sun set without word from the household, nor sight of Anna. Riding home in the dark was impractical and no nobleman would have turned them out at that hour, but no invitation to remain for the night had been extended. Finally, the baron announced himself with the tap of his heeled boots from the dim hallway behind Michel. He greeted Michel with a degree of warmth and gratitude proportionate to the effort of travel and the loss of the day. He clearly did not weigh the benefit of their presence in the house beyond fulfilling a dying request of his daughter.

The baron's peculiar facial features, with his very high cheekbones, his rounded lips, and his almost disturbingly large eyes, perfectly accompanied the rustic house and the exotic knick-knacks that were placed with obvious care throughout the home. Michel found himself in a mindless study of the baron's face. In his meandering contemplations, he compared the strange face before him with that of the pale and withered face lying in bed, a few weak steps from death, in search of a resemblance. He imagined that the resemblance would be striking in the daughter's bloom. But in her condition, Maria looked nothing like her father, for his eyes were bright and his face unnaturally aglow under the dim light of the candles.

To Michel, the baron seemed inappropriately sanguine in light of the circumstances. He thought vividly how distraught *he* would be if it were *his* daughter being visited on her deathbed. The deeper, hidden pain revealed itself when Baron Echter invited Michel to the dining room, as a distinct brand of sorrow cracked his voice. Michel wanted Anna more than he wanted the hospitality of his host. But that subtle escape of sadness through the baron's words elicited such compassion from a fellow father that he could think nothing at that moment beyond comforting the man.

Michel followed the baron to the dining room, where the servant met them and served them. The mourning baroness was not with them. Her absence was uncomfortably conspicuous, as if her spirit loudly haunted the room. Michel wanted to ask about her. The question knocked violently on the inside of his tightly sealed lips. His only encounter with the baroness was that moment of demonstrative despair as she fell from Maria's room believing her daughter to be already dead. He could not imagine her recovered to any state suitable to welcome guests in the dining room.

Although it had only been hours since he had left Anna in the dying girl's room, he missed her more than he ever had. Had he set aside all courtesy and decorum, and directly followed the mandates of his heart, he would have run through the halls, shouting for Anna until he found her, scooped her into his arms, and run through the dark forest until he and Anna were both in Margarethe's warm and nurturing arms. His courtesy and decorum stood too firmly in place to allow the slightest twitch in that direction.

He was visibly unsettled, and the servant took the liberty of assuring him that Anna had been well fed. The fullness of Anna's stomach was the minutest of Michel's heavy concerns, but he gave a shallow bow and a "Thank you" to the servant, trying to use that little assurance to soothe much deeper woes.

Well into the abundant meal, hardly touched by Michel, the baron relieved one tugging point of awkwardness, declaring that a room was suited up for him.

"For us," Michel answered, "For Anna and me."

"No, no!" the baron retorted rather sharply, "She will remain with Maria."

No thick layers of courtesy and decorum could hold back the shiver that ran through Michel's body and arms, causing an unintended clank of his fork on his plate.

His mind quickly composed a forceful, fatherly rebuttal, but all to stumble through his lips was a choppy, "I..., I..., I..."

He looked to the servant, who simply lowered his eyes and rubbed the back of his head. The baron stood calmly, but with the authority of his position as the area's most prominent nobleman and the master of the house, insisting that Anna must remain with Maria as long as Maria lives and still desires her company. Michel stood much more forcefully than the baron had. Every paternal instinct gathered in his sharply slanted and twitching eyebrows.

Before he could speak, the baron took him by the hand and spoke father to father, "I don't know why Maria asked for your daughter, but with all in my possession, there is nothing I can give my girl that can bring her comfort..., nothing but Anna. Tell me, if your daughter were dying and requesting mine, what would you do?"

The universality of paternal affection ran thickly through both men, and Michel answered after a brief moment of consideration, "I would be serving you dinner and insisting that you and Maria remain with us as long as my daughter lives and desires her company."

The men stared at each other with respect and a strange, budding brotherhood. They shook hands and returned to their meal. When the remnants of the meal were cleared away, and the servant beckoned Michel to follow him to his accommodations, Michel turned back to the baron and asked if he could at least kiss his daughter goodnight.

"Of course," was the answer.

The servant led the way with a massive candelabra that was more than sufficient at its job. Michel walked a few steps behind, with the baron tight on his heels. At Maria's door, the servant stepped aside and allowed Michel to open the door. Anna was sound asleep, snuggled tightly to Maria like sisters at the end of a joyous holiday. Maria's bony fingers rubbed Anna's hair, though she too was asleep. Michel walked to the bed and bent to kiss Anna's head. The baron stayed right behind him.

Michel whispered to Anna, "I love you."

Maria, in her dreamy stupor, believing herself still in conversation with Anna, answered back, "I love you too, Anna."

The weak and whispered response startled Michel, but he understood at that moment the value of Anna's company to the Echter family. He turned to leave the room, and the dim light of the moon that lightly dusted the walls through the window shone rather magically from the tears on the baron's cheeks. Michel gave the baron a gentle embrace, followed by a few pats on his shoulder, before walking around him to the awaiting servant, who led Michel to his room for the night.

Michel had little sleep that night. What he had was uneasy and filled with torturous imagery. He dreamed of Anna, locked in a crypt with a corpse. Her scream for him echoed, distant and hollow, from a direction he could not determine. He had a series of such dreams, loosely tied together between patches of stiff-legged restlessness. In the morning, before a household sound broke the nightly silence of his room, he arose and snuck to Maria's room. His desperation to retrieve his daughter and race her to her mother was urgent. When he opened Maria's door, Anna was not there. Maria rested soundly, with a slight grin and a complexion not nearly so cadaverous as the evening before.

That quick glance at Maria's marked improvement did much to dispel the lingering anxiety of his dreams. There was no ghoulish corpse in Maria's bed, but a sick girl who, from Michel's layman's perspective, was not deteriorating and whispering her last goodbyes to a painful world, but was a recovering girl whose complexion only awaited the morning light from the window to be something quite worth admiring. He even believed he saw some slight inherited resemblance in her features. All of these thoughts occurred in a flash of a moment, overtaken by the fact that Anna was not in the room.

Michel agitated the sleeping halls with a briskness of pace much more suited to a later hour of the day. On his way to the dining room, he found the baron. The poor father appeared as if he had not slept a moment since Michel left him in Maria's room the night before. His cheeks were dry, but his eyes showed all the telling signs of having recently shed tears. Michel asked him if he had seen Anna.

As the baron's mind stumbled upward from half-consciousness, he answered, "Uh, n…, no, no I have not."

He was snapped to his senses by his guest's unveiled distress, and he continued, "Is she not with Maria?"

His concern did not remain on Michel or Anna but jumped quickly and morbidly to Maria. He questioned loudly, "Is my daughter d—, is she gone? Is she d—?"

He could not bring himself to speak his fears.

Michel relieved him, saying in an easy manner, "Maria is asleep, and I must say that she appears improved."

The baron's eyes fixed down the hallway, toward Maria's room. He pushed right through Michel' shoulder, as if his guest had vanished from his senses. Michel continued toward the dining room. He did not find her there, but he heard the scuffling of feet and the clanging of dishes from the kitchen beyond. He followed the sounds and found Anna alone in the kitchen, rummaging through the pantries and collecting fruits and breads. Michel was mortified at the breach of etiquette.

"Anna!" he scolded through his clenched teeth, "put those things where you found them. You cannot help yourself to their pantries."

Anna looked confusedly at her father. They had never been in a circumstance where such a lesson would have been taught and learned. She did not understand why Michel, a moral father who taught openness and kindness, would have such a strong reaction to the gathering of food for herself and her friend. Michel had no time to explain. The baron walked into the kitchen and stood directly facing Anna, while her arms were still loaded down with food.

Michel's poor mind fumbled through words of explanation and apology that his hanging jaw never touched. Anna saw something in the baron that her father could not see. Relief and immense gratitude were written on his face in a language only she seemed able to read. She walked to the baron, leaned into him, extended her neck, and puckered her lips. The baron looked at her for several seconds before lowering his cheek to be kissed. The impertinence, the presumptuousness, and the apparent theft of food deeply mortified Michel. But his nervous and rigid posture loosened when the baron, with blushing cheeks and a broadening smile, tenderly rubbed his face where the kiss had been placed.

"There must be something special in your kiss, young lady," the baron told her with a playful tone.

Michel was correct in assuming that all improprieties were forgiven by a man who had just seen his daughter's improved condition. But there was more at play. Michel did not see that *any* presumptions or liberality of manner by Anna would have been overlooked by their host, with or without the benefit she brought to the sick daughter. Anna had a soft and easy flamboyance, an extreme liberty of spirit that was too generous for ridicule, even from those most staunchly reserved of manner. She brightened people in ways that allowed her to transcend normal social barriers, to walk right through them like a ghost through the walls of its own home. She approached all with familial warmth, and generally received it in return.

During the course of that day, Maria continued her marked improvement. There was nothing the baron or any other mind could attribute the alterations to, except the presence of Anna in Maria's room. With each subtle brightening of the girl's complexion, the baron and baroness were proportionately unwilling to allow Anna to leave. Michel would not leave his daughter alone, despite the growing affections between the families. They spent that night as they had the previous, but in the morning, Michel demanded that the baron send a servant to Kleinostheim, to bring Margarethe and the boys to join them.

Baron Echter complied, with many apologies for not considering it first. By that afternoon, Michel's family was united at the Echter house. Their reception was very different than Michel's. By then, it was not a house in mourning, but a house of hope and immense gratitude. Margarethe met Maria, who by that point was sitting up to eat and converse. No description by Michel, the baron, the servant, or even the baroness could convince Margarethe of Maria's peril and appearance just a couple of days earlier. Margarethe could not understand why she and her family were not allowed to return home.

She and the boys remained for three days, during which time she witnessed, with her own eyes, Maria's continued rate of recovery At the end of the three days, the familial affection between them all comforted Michel and Margarethe enough to return home and leave Anna in the care of the Echters.

Not three full weeks after the servant banged on the door in Kleinostheim, Anna and Maria enjoyed long walks together through the surrounding Spessart Forest. At the end of the third week, the baron escorted Anna home himself, reserving his right to recall her services at any time. Anna readily agreed. To her, it was no service, but a visit to a friend, her dear friend from the fountain.

The prominent figures of the region were well aware of Maria's illness and the imminence of her peril. The astonishment was extreme when she was again seen skipping through the streets of Aschaffenburg in her full bloom. Their curiosity needed satiation, and the entire Echter household spoke freely, and with great animation, about little Anna and the service she provided. The nature of the service was as difficult to express as it was to understand. Nobody could come to grips with how this child could revive, from the far end of the deathbed to that very portrait of health skipping around the fountain where she had first met Anna. Questions were pressing and demanding of answers that could not be given.

Before turning ill, Maria had been engaged to marry a young man from the east, from Old Bohemia. With no expectation of her survival, the engagement was dissolved while Maria lay ashen gray in her bedroom. In her revival, the engagement resumed and Maria prepared to leave her family and the region. The electric air of mystery that buzzed around Aschaffenburg County had a ticket to travel abroad, and it carried with it the name of Anna Schwarz.

Chapter Three:
Father Albrecht

MARIA'S RECOVERY AND SEAMLESS RESUMPTION of her life became notorious. Archbishop Elector of Mainz, Daniel Brendel von Homburg, was determined to understand the phenomenon before Maria left his jurisdiction. He sent a message to a Jesuit House in Frankfurt that the services of Father Albrecht were demanded by the Archbishop. The Pope had sent the Jesuits to the front line of the Counter-Reformation to stave off the spread of Protestantism. The Jesuit order was not subordinate to the Archbishop's religious authority, but the political authority of the Archbishop of Mainz held power over everything in the region.

Father Albrecht was a young priest, perhaps twenty-five or twenty-six when the message found him. He came from Austria and in his few years ordained, he built a strong reputation as a scholar. He was chosen among all religious entities under the Archbishop's influence for his notoriously strict mind and his staunchly academic approach to research. The Archbishop wanted to get quickly to the heart of the Maria Echter phenomenon and put it quietly to rest.

The abbot of the Jesuit House had been a liberal-minded young priest. But years on the front line of the Reformation had turned him suspicious, paranoid, and zealous. The rumors hit his ears no differently than any others, but they ran through soured filters before resting rancidly on his mind. He concluded that Maria Echter had died, and through the unholy practice of necromancy, little Anna revived her for Satan's purposes. Father Albrecht embarked on his assignment under intense pressure from his abbot to bend the evidence in that direction and use Anna Schwarz to make a bold statement for the Church.

Father Albrecht responded to the archbishop's residence in Aschaffenburg, where he soon afterward took his books, papers, and scientific mind to the Echter home. Before embarking for the Spessart Forest, Albrecht spoke to two families in Aschaffenburg. Both had witnessed Maria's decline from health and described, with vivid imagery, the state of the girl's complexion and the utter lack of life within her features as they paid their "final respects" to her at her bedside. This was, of course, before Anna's visit and they did not see Maria again until she was again skipping youthfully through the streets of the city. To them, having not seen the transition, quick as it was, Maria's recovery appeared instantaneous. They described it that way. With only that intelligence, it was natural for the recovery to seem unearthly. Albrecht gathered from the families all that they had heard about Anna. Every rumor spreading through the area, some near the truth and others wildly imaginative, some based on fact and some wrapped in fantasy, reached Albrecht's ear and were scratched into his notebook.

The Echter home was a jovial place indeed. Each exotic figurine seemed to sing its own song of praise. Maria bore every bit of her father's sparkly complexion. The baroness, though sad to lose her daughter to a husband, was relieved beyond expression not to lose her to the grave, so much so that she dedicated two hours in the morning and two in the afternoon to praying the Rosary in the house's little chapel, in thanksgiving to Mother Mary for answering her prayers. She broke from her afternoon prayers when Father Albrecht arrived, and she received him without suspicion.

Albrecht did not have the warm, conversational manner of a country baron. He was awkward in his reception of their hospitality. It became quickly apparent what sort of visit he was paying. He cut through all of the fine niceties of introductions and asked immediately to interview Maria about her seemingly miraculous recovery. Refreshments were offered and refused. Albrecht could see little purpose for them. His academic mind was focused on one task. His actions had been motivated entirely by his orders until his research revealed a mystery that tightly gripped his scientific curiosity. By the time he reached the baron's home, he sought truth for his own sake, not for the bishop's and not for his abbot's.

The baroness complied with Albrecht's demand with a gentle smile, and she sent for her daughter. Albrecht waited in the baron's study, a cozy room with golden drapes pulled back to allow the afternoon sun to fill the room. There was a prodigious amount of stately oak, in the furnishings, the bookshelves, and in the wainscoting that seemed to hold the upper half of the room above its head like a dark hand holding a bright chalice. The mid-afternoon sun was softened by its reflection off of the baron's many books that lined the wall opposite of the windows.

Maria, giddy about her engagement, bounded into the room with more glow than she normally carried about her. Her own internal illumination coupled with the atmosphere of the room to place a heavenly halo around the girl. With his first glance at her, Albrecht's scientific mind abandoned him for a moment and the faithful servant of

God assumed control. Albrecht was first and foremost a man of God. He believed in the Miracles of Christ. He did not come to the Echter home as a religious cynic, trying to disprove a miracle, nor did he come as a fanatic, willing to disregard the precepts of research in order to prove God's or Satan's hand in Maria's recovery. That is why he was chosen for the task. But that first glance, with Maria resembling the paintings of the Saints, struck the priest's faithful heart, and for a moment shocked his mind numb.

Maria greeted Albrecht with a curtsy and a good-day, spoken with a voice that declared the height of youthful health. Albrecht stumbled over a few syllables before regathering his wits and returning to his task.

He closed his eyes for a few seconds and composed, silently in his head, the questions he wished to ask, then spoke, "I have received descriptions of your illness. Tell me, girl, how did you recover so quickly?"

Maria did not expel a single breath before answering, "My little friend Anna came to visit me."

There he had it from the sick girl's mouth. The eight-year-old Anna had healed her.

"Listen closely, Maria," Albrecht interrupted sternly, "and consider your answers mindfully. What did your friend do to you?"

The answer took no mindful consideration. Maria answered quickly and plainly, "She talked to me."

Albrecht began to suspect, as many believed, that unearthly hands were involved.

He pressed her, "How long have you known Anna?"

"I met her just once before I got sick, at the fountain in Aschaffenburg."

Albrecht cocked an eyebrow, which cast a seriousness about the room that had not yet been there.

"So why," he asked, "did you ask for her, a girl nine years younger, when you were on death's bed, rather than asking for an older friend?"

"I don't remember asking for Anna. My father told me that I asked for her."

He lowered his chin and looked at her through his eyebrows, asking, "What do you remember?"

"I remember Anna sitting on my bed and holding my hand."

"And you say she talked to you?"

"Yes."

"Think carefully. Did she speak any incantations?"

Maria squinted her eyes and tilted her head to one side, clearly confused by the question.

Albrecht pressed further, "Did she speak any language you did not understand?"

An involuntary giggle burst from Maria's nostrils, which she followed with a very playful, "Of course not."

To Maria, the last question was so ridiculous that it dissipated all seriousness from the room. In a manner much more like an eight-year-old than a seventeen-year-old, she shook off her rigid posture, walked light-footed to one of her father's chairs, and plopped herself upon it. This frustrated Albrecht, who followed her and pressed his toes against a leg of the chair so that he towered almost directly over Maria. His frustration came out in the form of a series of quick questions that did not permit her time to answer.

Raising his right hand to point down to her and shaking his head, he asked, "What did she talk about? Did her voice sound unnatural? How did it make you feel?" He concluded the line by yelling in frustration, "How did she heal you?"

All playfulness left Maria. She saw where the interview was going, and she grew defensive of her friend. She planted her feet firmly at his, forcing him to take a step back. She stood forcefully, pushing him back another step. The look in her eyes subdued his fervor and brought forth a degree of timidity not normally in his character.

"Anna loves life!" she spoke strongly, "She reminded me that *I* love life."

Maria paused in thoughtfulness. She lowered her eyes to the floor and spoke quietly, as if the realization was new to her, "She made me want to live."

Maintaining his timidity, Albrecht mustered the force to ask, "Did you not want to live *before* speaking with Anna?"

Maria pondered the question for several seconds, having never truly considered it. She sat back in the chair, not like an eight-year-old or a seventeen-year-old, but like a much older person, slowly laying her arms across the rests and folding her legs in front of her, then answering, "I did not want to die, but that is not the same as wanting to live."

She curled herself into a tight ball inside of the chair and wrapped her arms around her knees. She hummed a long, high, calm and steady note, then added, "Anna sees the world uniquely. She shared a bit of that with me. Now everything around me is interesting, exciting, and worth living for."

As she spoke, Albrecht subconsciously inched nearer to the chair, as close as he had been before. But his posture was not as aggressive. He was drawn to her words, by the truth beneath them.

Maria stood from the chair, forcing him backward again. She walked around him and to the door of the study without excusing herself. She opened the door, turned back to him, and added, "You know Father, I think you should talk to Anna. Maybe she can provide a similar service to you."

Maria walked from the room without another word. Albrecht sat on the chair that Maria had occupied. He grabbed his lower jaw, covering his lips with his palm, and stared at one spot on the floor in deep contemplation of his interview.

"Could it be," he asked himself aloud, "that neither God nor the Devil had a hand in this? Could it be that love of life healed this girl?"

The answer he wanted to believe excluded both his scientific and his religious teachings. He only allowed himself the briefest moment to embrace Maria's explanation. Nothing in his study of science could explain the rapid recovery. That left him only two possible explanations — either God or Satan had worked through little Anna to heal Maria. He instinctively reached his thoughts for evidence to the former, for the latter was too vile a thought, and he knew where that could lead. He reminded himself repeatedly that there was nothing in his interview with Maria, not in her words, her tone, nor in her appearance, that hinted at evil.

Albrecht gathered himself. He bid no farewell to his hosts but disappeared quickly and unattended. He made his way to Kleinostheim, determined to seek the hand of God in the words of young Anna and her parents. He took no rest and gave no thought to time of day. He arrived as the sun was setting. He greeted Michel with far more refined cordiality than he displayed at the Echter home. His journey between the two homes was filled to its limits with deep and haunting deliberation. The faith of his childhood crept from beneath the piles of books and manuscripts that had buried it since adulthood. That faith opened the door to Maria's narrative, that Anna's contagious love of life was all the magic needed to recover the ill from death's door. In any case, he prepared himself to meet Anna, expecting something that would redefine his faith and his career.

The Scientific Method, or at least its relative predecessors, had begun to make its rounds within the elite minds of Europe. Father Albrecht was among them. He tried to apply its principles to the task at hand. Being a man of faith *and* science, his determinations on the Maria Echter matter would find acceptance in most circles. He knew that was the reason he was chosen, placing upon his shoulders even more weight of responsibility than the matter already carried. His heart and his mind found themselves in a fierce tug-of-war — and little Anna was the rope.

Albrecht entered Anna's home with none of the focused assuredness that carried him into the baron's study. Michel and Margarethe heard all the rumors about Anna that were spreading across the county. They knew Albrecht was coming. They locked Anna in her room and refused to allow Albrecht to see her until he spoke with them first. The boys stood stone-faced with their backs to Anna's room, like sentries at their post. Albrecht was soft and gentle in his approach. His own uncertainty shone clearly. Compassionate Margarethe poured him some wine and comforted his nerves with the narcotic effect of a nurturing, maternal voice.

Michel, being far less patient, demanded to know his ultimate purpose.

"I have been charged by the Archbishop with getting to the heart of the matter," he answered.

Margarethe, who was not seated at the table, placed her hand on Albrecht's shoulder from behind and asked, "And what have you determined?"

Albrecht told them all Maria had said to him. He was honest about his own difficulties in coming to grips with it. He explained his approach to the research and how all that he had heard so far confused both his mind and his faith.

"Is it really so surprising," Margarethe interrupted, "that a young child, who is so fresh from God, would be Godly in ways that older folks cannot understand?"

Albrecht's only immediate response was to lower his head and fold his hands in prayer. Anna's parents allowed the priest all the time he needed. When he finally raised his head and rejoined the room, he had abandoned all attempts to grip the phenomenon with the fingers of science. His faith still had no tighter grasp, but he resigned to the understanding that the investigation must be conducted in the arena of religion. He had not yet ruled out the hand of the Devil, but he kept that to himself.

The evening was late and Anna remained hidden away in her room. Margarethe made up a bed for their guest. They fed him graciously and saw him to sleep. In the morning, Albrecht awoke to a lively household with a pall of apprehension resting lightly over it. Anna was in the kitchen, helping her mother prepare breakfast.

In a panic, Albrecht made himself presentable for Anna, as if preparing to greet the Pope. At a glance he knew that Anna was unlike anyone he had ever met. There was a freshness about her that gave him a window into God-knows-what. All he knew was that it was quite foreign and about as far from the dusty libraries and stuffy chapels, where he had spent the bulk of his hours, as any place on earth. Albrecht tried several times to begin his interview with Anna, to raise the subject of his investigation with no gentle prologue. Each time he tried, a member of the household interrupted with a trivial nicety that could not be ignored.

After breakfast, Michel brought Anna and Albrecht into Anna's room. He instructed Anna to answer the priest's questions honestly, and told her, while staring at Albrecht, that he and her mother would be just beyond the door.

Once they sat alone together, Albrecht took a deep inhale, which he held unnaturally long before releasing it sharply, drawing a new breath, and speaking, "I have seen your friend Maria. She looks well."

It was a breakthrough for Albrecht, to approach the interview so gently, so personally. It backfired. Anna took what little he had said to that point and commandeered the conversation.

"Yes. She is so pretty. She is getting married. Did you know that? She is going to move far away. I will miss her terribly. I wonder if they have a fountain where she will live. Maybe she will meet a new friend and I won't have to worry about her. I should go back to the fountain. Maybe *I* will meet a new friend."

Albrecht felt the conversation being ripped from his hands. He did not know how to gently reclaim control. Finally, he blurted, "Maria asked for you when she was sick."

Anna simply nodded.

Convinced that he was back on track, he continued, "She must have thought you could do something for her."

Anna saw no question in the last statement, so she only looked at him.

He prodded, "Did you? Did you, Anna? Did you do something for her?"

Anna perked up and crossed her legs beneath her, then answered lightly, "Of course I did. How could I refuse to go to her? Of course, my father had to go with me. I'm so very glad he did. Mother came later, and my brothers. Did you know that? My mother came to Maria's house. We were all there. But Maria was already much better by then."

Albrecht tightened his grip on the reeling conversation, interjecting, "Why did you go to Maria? What did you hope to do?"

Anna grew serious and spoke with confusion over the question, "I *hoped* to see her... because she asked for me."

"And when you got to her, what happened?"

"She did not look well. Her mother was crying and I thought she was dead. Then I stepped closer and I could see that she was breathing. That was a relief. I thanked God."

"Then?"

"Then I took her cold hand and told her that I had come, just like she asked. She squeezed my hand. I could tell that she wanted to look at me and to talk to me, but she was too weak, so I climbed onto her bed and I sat beside her."

Feeling like he might finally get to his point, Albrecht spoke quickly, "Did you feel like anyone else was there with you? Did you feel another presence?"

"Well, yes. My father and the baron's servant were there."

"What about after they left, after you were alone with Maria?"

"No," she answered in confusion, "I was... alone with Maria."

Albrecht sighed deeply and rolled his head in every direction but Anna's. Not only had he never met anyone like Anna, but he had no experience with children. He was out of place among them since well before his own adulthood.

Albrecht refocused, looked Anna in the eyes, took her by the hand and asked, "When you touched Maria's hand, did you feel anything strange, any... power from your hand to hers?"

"Oh, I see," she answered, surprising Albrecht by taking his other hand, "you want to know if I healed Maria."

"I want to know how she recovered so quickly."

Anna was truly bewildered by the question, and she asked him, "Aren't you a priest?"

Anna did not mean her question as a rebuke of his faith. She was earnestly confused. But Albrecht took the question to heart and blushed with shame.

Anna withdrew her hands from his, not certain what to make of Father Albrecht and why a faithful Christian would ask such a question.

Anna continued, "I prayed for her. Lots of people prayed for her."

Albrecht argued, "I have seen many sick people for whom many great people have prayed. I have never heard of a recovery like Maria's."

Anna slouched back and crossed her arms at her chest, more doubtful now than confused, and asked, "Haven't you?"

She crawled from her bed and left the room without another word. Albrecht stared at the doorway for several seconds before standing to follow her. After he took one step toward the door, Anna reappeared, holding in her delicate hands a printed copy of the Bible. Printing had not long been available, and Michel spent more than he could afford for the copy. But it had become the centerpiece of the family.

Anna jumped back on the bed and thumbed through the pages saying, "I have heard of many people being healed. Here, let me show you."

Albrecht, half-giggling through his shame, placed his hand over hers and closed the book, saying, "I have read this already, all of it, many times."

Anna cocked her head to one side and questioned, "But you said—"

"I misspoke, little one. I have read about all of God's miracles."

Anna's eyes grew wide and she asked, "All of them? From all over the world?"

"Well," he instructed, "all of the ones acknowledged by the Church."

Anna blinked her eyes several times, as if her puzzlement irritated them, and she asked, "Acknowledged?"

Albrecht changed course. He asked her, "Do you believe that Maria was healed by God?"

"Of course she was. She was almost dead."

"And what did you do to help this miracle?"

"I just stayed with my friend. I talked to her. I prayed for her, and when she was strong enough, I prayed *with* her. You don't think I performed a miracle, like Christ and the Apostles?"

Albrecht's eyes drifted from her, and he answered more to himself than to her. "I'm not sure what to think."

His faith was drastically altered by this child. Her love of life was only matched by her faith in God. The simple but towering truth of her words and actions bubbled his earliest memories to the surface. Through the filter of those memories, the testimonies of Maria and Anna made sense to him. The image of Anna sitting on the bed and opening the Bible to show him examples of healing remained clearly in his inner eye.

He snapped himself back and addressed her directly, "I am sure of one thing, little Anna. You are a sweet child and a good friend. Thank you for talking with me."

The turnaround was sudden, and Anna was not sure if she could trust this apparent end of questioning. Albrecht bowed to Anna and left the room. He thanked Michel and Margarethe for their hospitality and congratulated them on their beautiful family and faithful household. He was so very congenial that Michel and Margarethe believed the matter to be put entirely to rest.

As far as Albrecht was concerned, it was at-rest. He wrote a report about the power of local prayers and the healing faith of the community. He wrote of Maria's future and the Will of God, all in the most appropriate terms as to please all concerned with the matter. He chose his words painstakingly to settle the mystery of the moment, with no notion that his report could play a part in the affairs of the distant future, an oversight he would much later regret.

He returned to his Jesuit House in Frankfurt and resumed his previous duties, but not as he had performed them before. Anna changed him. She made him question the power of his faith. Oh, he still studied his sciences and applied the Scientific Method to his studies, but always laid over a foundation of faith that, whenever weakened by skepticism, was always snapped back into form by the remembrance of little Anna's voice and the Schwarz family Bible on her lap.

Chapter Four:
Into the Books

FATHER ALBRECHT'S REPORT put an end to almost all thoughts of Maria Echter outside of Aschaffenburg County. Only a few zealots harbored suspicions. The Archbishop was so pleased to have a quiet end to the matter that even Albrecht's abbot spoke no more of it. Local rumors still abounded, but the event was so pleasing to all who still spoke of it that it could not be connected with any evil. Albrecht went back to preaching against Protestantism. So powerful was his encounter with Anna on his spirituality that he was unable to let her slip into his past. He wrote to her within a few weeks of his return. His was not a mind able to lower itself to the level of a child. In both language and content, the letter was mature, academic, and scholarly. He thanked her for her frankness and explained in detail how she had changed his life. He quoted the Scriptures, as well as the writings of Augustine and Aquinas.

Michel and Margarethe read it to her and explained those parts she could not grasp. They were honored to learn of their daughter's effect on a prominent theologian and man of God. It sparked many deepening conversations around the table, reaching depths well beyond the years of little Anna. Anna quickly rose to the conversations, displaying a mind rich and fertile. She surpassed her brothers in depth of understanding. She wrote back to Father Albrecht. She thanked him for his letter and described to him the new dinner table dynamics it spawned. She mentioned that she had never heard of the philosophers he had quoted but would be very interested to read more about them.

Mainz was the printing capital of Europe. Books, especially those of an ecclesiastical nature, were among the prime exports along the Main and Rhine rivers. Albrecht had access to a full library, with new material reaching him daily. He took it upon himself to send Anna a newly printed and bound version of *The Confessions of Saint Augustine*. It pleased him tremendously to think that he could elevate her spirituality as she had done his. The books arrived in Kleinostheim to grateful hands. It was a volume of thirteen individual books, beautifully bound with gilding on the spine and front cover. The books became a permanent centerpiece of the family table.

Anna did not wait for the evening family readings. She pored through the pages on her own, storing questions and comments in her head for safe keeping, until after dinner, and what had become an unyielding practice of evening family study. She found intriguing how normal, how human, and how troubled Augustine's early life had been. In the evenings, she provided insights into the writings that her opulent mind had stirred and agitated all day.

By the time Anna turned nine, she and her parents had read, dissected, and debated Augustine's writings — and they hungered for more. Michel and Margarethe enthusiastically encouraged her studies. She had been too carefree, with little seeming able to seize her attention, until that first letter from Father Albrecht arrived. It focused her and occupied those many hours she had previously spent roaming mindlessly through the village.

Michel and Margarethe delighted in their daughter's new drive. They wrote to Albrecht, asking for suggestions of other reading materials. Within a month, a long list arrived, covering three pages, written in his minutest penmanship. Books were expensive and they did not have much money. Michel started at the top and bought *Disputed Questions on Truth,* by Saint Thomas Aquinas.

They dove immediately into the book. But Aquinas did not capture Anna like Augustine did. She did not sit and read all morning. She waited until the evening study sessions to read and debate the Aquinas book with her parents. She spent her days much as she had, with light ramblings through the village and along the river, but with much more than a friendly good day to pass along. She readily shared what she had learned with anyone whose schedule permitted the breathless chatter of a nine-year-old girl who had too much time on her hands and too many thoughts in her head. Most nodded and smiled at her first utterances and moved quickly on their way. The topics were beyond most, and few took her words as more than the mumbling of an eccentric child. Anna blossomed under the eyes of the village, with few realizing what an exceptional child she was becoming.

The recovery of Maria Echter faded in the thoughts of the locals after Maria married and moved away. The Echter Family, though influential, kept mostly shut into their rustic home in the Spessart Forest. Some in the community recalled the event, especially when one of their own got sick. Believing Anna to be some sort of religious charm, able to channel prayers, families called upon Michel and Margarethe, imploring them for the services of the child. Anna's parents knew that their daughter had no magic powers, and they were reluctant to draw the attention brought on them by Maria's recovery, or worse yet, the ire that would result from a worse outcome. Anna was not allowed to visit the very ill, but she saw the friends and neighbors of her daily acquaintance when they were bothered by some minor affliction.

Nothing nearly as miraculous as Maria Echter occurred, but Anna sat beside sick and injured people and brightened their spirits as she had done before. This time, her playful and uplifting stories were accompanied by philosophy and the sort of high theology only held in the most elite minds of Europe. Few understood that her words came from the nightly readings at their table and came from no more mysterious sources than books. Among the superstitious, Anna's service to the Echter Family was purely mystical, and her conversations with the unlearned only bolstered the rumors.

No more rumors reached Michel and Margarethe. They continued to save their money and add to the growing family library. Anna read every word. By the time she was twelve, books and pamphlets cascaded from the shelves. Anna forbade her parents to part with a single page. Michel dissolved his business and began trading in books. Hundreds of books made their way through his hands and Anna got first crack at all of them. By the time she turned fourteen, she spoke Latin and Italian. They all did, for each word read by one was shared with all.

In the spring before she turned fifteen, Anna's character took a turn. Her brother Martin had followed Aulgoin and young Michel out of the house and into apprenticeships, leaving Anna as the only recipient of her parent's attention. She studied nature and resumed her old passion for the forest and the river. She studied at night, and in the morning she walked. Older and taller, she found herself more often in conversation with the people around her. The same notions, the same philosophies, were far less enigmatic coming from a full-grown girl, and the people of Kleinostheim came to delight in her ready quotations and philosophical quips. Light and spritely as ever, she made heavy topics frolicsome. The people engaged her, and light-hearted debate became her favorite pastime. She still took delight in the antics of the neighborhood animals, and wove seamlessly through topics mundane and infinitely lofty with an equal love of all.

In Anna's studies, she came across a manuscript of herbology and natural remedies. She was thought of and spoken of as a healer since she was eight. It was long a part of her identity. The medicinal nature of her herbology manuscript awakened a passion that had been waiting inside of her for her to come of age. Her walks through the forest became less drifty and more focused. She knew well of her lingering reputation as a healer and thought that a proficiency in herbal remedies might accompany her natural ability to lighten hearts.

Anna's walks through the forest took longer and longer to complete, as she stopped to stare at and admire the diversity of plant life flourishing beneath the forest canopy. She wondered how, for so many years, she passed right over the marvelous colors and shapes at her feet. Hundreds of varieties of plants and fungi declared themselves to her searching eyes. She found their sketches in her book and collected samples.

Michel moved his book trade to Aschaffenburg, liberating room in the house for Anna's new pursuit. She wasted no time sharing her concoctions with the village, but it was her company they desired. Her remedies were little more than a fun topic of conversation and a chance for people to bond with her. She started spending more time in the village than the forest, more time talking of the delightfully mundane than of the herbs in her jars or the theology in her library.

Father Albrecht fell mostly out of touch. He thought often of Anna, and she of him. Of all in her possession, her thirteen books of Augustine remained her most treasured. Many books saw the inner walls of her home, but *The Confessions of Augustine* belonged to her, gifted specifically to her by Father Albrecht. Her memories of their encounter during the investigation were faint and romanticized. He was a living statue in her memory, placed among other figures in stone and marble. She wrote to him once, when she was sixteen. He wrote back four months later. The letter was cordial but impersonal. Its sentiments did not take the passage of time into account. He wrote to an eight-year-old who had long gone out of existence. Anna never wrote to him again.

The space between Anna and Albrecht was not the only social chasm in her life. The village went about village business. They loved Anna. They delighted in her. But her mind spun above those concerns that even her parents found themselves adhered to. Despite almost constant company, she was lonely. Her evening conversations with her family were supplemented by passionate symposiums and fiery debates played out in her imagination during her long walks through the village, in the forest, and along the river. At seventeen, she was as lonely as she was lively, as melancholy as enchanted.

Anna's storage of herbs spoke to her with as much intellectual interaction as most of her fellow villagers. Her loneliness brewed discontent and she looked into every eye she encountered with a deep hope and half-expectation to see within it some spark that would speak to her in terms she longed to hear from another. She longed for love, but could not have placed her finger firmly upon her feelings.

Chapter Five:

Jodocus Koob

IN THE TOWN OF STOCKSTADT AM MAIN, across and down river from Kleinostheim, a family grew slowly from serfdom to affluence and prominence. By the middle of the sixteenth century, they owned more than sixty acres of land southwest of town, with livestock and a vineyard. They were the Koob family, the patriarch of which was an intensely proud man named Valentin. His eldest child was christened Jodocus, but the family and their friends called him Jost.

Valentin stood near enough to the family's obscure, impoverished past to fear falling backward and losing all that his father and grandfather had gained. The Koob family was situated just one step beneath the titled nobility of the region. They hobnobbed with the region's elite and hosted guests of the highest ranks. Jost grew up with daily retellings of a particularly honored visitor to their home, the Duke of Bavaria, Wilhelm IV.

Valentin was hard on Jost, pushing him forward toward what he believed should be the next step in the family's road to titled nobility.

"Land and marriage," Valentin preached to Jost, "that is your duty, to increase our holdings and marry above our station."

This mantra was repeated with the utmost sobriety into Jost's ears since well before he understood the words.

"A baron's daughter, at least. No less will do."

Poor Jost did not have the opportunity to develop his own personality, tastes, and ambitions. Those things were prescribed to him before his own name was given.

When Jost was twenty-two years old, in late spring of 1583, and already influential in managing his family's land, his father arranged an apprenticeship for him in Kleinostheim. There was little in the way of knowledge that Jost could gain from the arrangement, and he never quite understood why his father settled on it. His master was a landowner of slighter but sound repute. Valentin paid him well to teach Jost the precepts of business and estate development. With those skills and steady gains in the Koob estate, a match could be made with the daughter of Baron Someone-or-another, or even a less attractive daughter of a count. That was the script meticulously written for the play of Jost's life. And the notion was too rigidly ingrained into Jost's identity to be mourned or objected to.

Jost moved to Kleinostheim and lived in a small but sufficient room in the house of his master, Johann. Johann's family was neither on the rise nor decline. They worked hard and had minds for little else but business. Johann was a middle-aged man who appeared a good ten years older than he was. He wore an old suit that was quite fine in its youth, when his grandfather bought it. He did not wear it to save the money of a new suit. He wore it because he believed it was still fashionable. His tastes in clothing, like all of his opinions, were a full half-century behind. Despite his premature weathering and dated fashions, Johann could have been a handsome man, had he portioned an extra minute or two of his daily routine to taming his wild graying hair, or trimming his wiry, feral whiskers.

Jost adjusted well, and for the first couple of weeks wanted for nothing. He expected his schedule to loosen, allowing him time for pursuing his personal studies. He had an insatiable appetite for philosophy. He bought books and papers whenever they passed his eyes. There was no time for books and papers, no time for Aristotle, no Saint Augustine or Thomas Aquinas. He was on his feet early, surveying Johann's holdings, documenting needed improvements, crunching numbers, and carrying on his shoulders every concern of a middle-aged landowner.

Even this was tolerable until his common sense came into conflict with Johann's unyielding practices. Jost learned quickly why the status of Johann's family remained stagnant. He discovered that his young mind was already better suited to expansion and innovation than Johann's. His master's estate was not in neglect, but simple improvements and a little forward thinking could have drastically advanced the estate and further enriched Johann. Those steps had not been taken. Jost readily offered his opinions and suggestions, but he was the apprentice, and Johann the master. Johann made it clear quickly and unmistakably that, no matter how slight the suggestion or how gentle the tone, any further "suggestions" would be considered an intolerable impertinence. Jost was no apprentice. He was little more than a clerk, running errands and keeping books. He learned nothing about the innovative promotion of an estate, nothing that would help him advance his father's ambitions.

With each passed opportunity to improve the estate, each bite of his tongue, Jost grew to despise his position and his master, and none of his previous sources of repose and revival were at his disposal. Every hour was another link in a never-ending relentlessness of closed minds and unearned self-assuredness. One day, about six weeks after he joined Johann's household, Jost reached a saturation point. He could bear no more blind adherence to outdated ways. He spoke his mind. Johann yelled at him like an angry dog owner yells at a bad dog, spoken with language and vulgar contempt that was well beneath Jost's breeding and education. Other than in age, Johann was inferior to Jost in every conceivable fashion. Jost felt the insult keenly. He stormed from the village, into the woods to the north.

It was not a common practice of Jost to roam through nature and allow his senses their moments to stretch themselves, free of the incessant, miserly control of the mind. It was, however, very much a common practice of Anna. She was in the same woods that day, for a different reason and in a very different state of mind. She was seventeen years old.

Jost's long, daily walks through Kleinostheim on matters of business brought him into much company, drawn into conversations on whatever topic crossed the minds of Johann's tenants. Anna often crossed the minds of the inhabitants of Kleinostheim. She was a consistent subject of conversations. Jost had heard of Anna. He had seen her, and when he saw her in the woods that day, he recognized her at a glance. In the intimacy of their village, she was notorious in the extreme. She may have seen *him* a thousand times in passing and still could not have picked him out of a crowd of absolute strangers. This was no accident and no oversight on her part. His obscurity was his most cherished possession. Blending into the background was a skill both natural and well-practiced in him. But there, in the woods north of Kleinostheim, he was conspicuous among the trees and brush, and she fixed her eyes on him.

Jost froze and stared at her, then he turned awkward and shifted his focus to a twig at his feet. He held that defensive gaze until he heard her rambling toward him. They had never been face-to-face, never so near as to make a study of the other's features. When he looked up and saw her taking the last several steps toward him, he was captivated. She did not appear to him as a striking beauty. He had seen more delicate faces and more tempting figures. But there was an intense spirituality about her features that promised to provide him much, much more than his eyes could ever desire.

His attention was fully in her grasp. It was in his nature to shy away from intimate encounters, but he could not look away from her.

Anna strode to within an arm's reach of him and introduced herself as if they had met on a street, where such encounters are to be expected, "Hello, my name is Anna."

It was Jost's turn to speak. His failure to do so, and the long staring pause, brought a grin to her face.

He continued to stare. She giggled and asked, "Do you live near here?"

He explained that he came from Stockstadt, across the river, and that his father had arranged an apprenticeship in Kleinostheim. She pulled such pleasantries and minutia from him before he realized he was speaking. Her easy air loosened his jaw without his knowledge. They walked north together, deeper into the woods, and spoke of the casual details of their lives.

It did not take long for Anna to dip into much deeper and heavier topics. She astonished him by referencing some of his most beloved philosophers. Jost gleefully admitted his favorite pastime, but when given the opportunity by her skillfully placed pauses, he did not follow her in conversation, as his heart undoubtedly wished to. While their legs strode the same path, side by side, their minds diverged. Jost listened and grew nervous as Anna spoke of spiritual things, of faith, of hope, and of philosophies ancient and new. His fidgeting extremities displayed his increasing uneasiness. His studies had always been private and personal — never discussed, and certainly never debated. It did not take her long to realize that the conversation would not so easily take her desired course. In gracious frustration, she abandoned the attempt and contented herself with a silent walk at his side.

Her voice was in no way abrasive to him. It was simply the intimacy of honest expression that rattled him. She would have much preferred conversation to a silent walk. But she watched his posture relax, and even become comfortable and natural after all talking ceased. He gave no outward sign of the giddiness and invigoration he felt in her company. He thought his face was flush, but he appeared, even to her perceptive eyes, simply as a man going for a walk in the woods. A few times, his lips parted and he inhaled sharply. He wanted to speak, to quote Augustine and hear the quotations finished by her voice. He wanted it so badly, but feared her in a way he could not identify. He knew that she would haunt his thoughts for the foreseeable future, and she wished to peel back the protective layers over his deeper self. In his reticence, she saw something hidden, something worth hiding, and worth discovering, a smoldering passion that steamed and bubbled deep inside of his casual exterior.

Their walk took them in a loop and they found themselves at the threshold of the forest. He told her that he enjoyed their walk together, but stopped well short of expressing how much he wished to see her again.

In her flamboyance, she filled the empty spaces between his sparse words, telling him, "I walk this area of the woods every day. You can find me here whenever you want to walk with me."

The invitation was bold, and it drew Jost's blood to gather in his cheeks. He stumbled through an awkward explanation of how strangely coincidental he found it that they would happen upon each other as they did.

She smiled broadly, stared penetratingly into him and answered, "What is seen by most as chance has a deliberate intelligence behind it. It knows what it is doing."

He could no longer hide his glow. His smile grew wider than hers. He gave her a low bow and turned away from her.

Back in his humble room, his fine memory drew to the forefront every detail of his walk with Anna, every contour of her face and inflection of her voice, the crack of every twig she strode upon, each double-stitch on her hem, everything his eyes, ears, and nose encountered thrusted itself again on his consciousness without the efforts of his imagination. But it all began to melt away as he reclined in his bed, everything but her. The liveliness of her speech and the surprise revelation of her knowledge and wisdom electrified him. He went half-mad with joy.

He wrenched on his upper arms with his tightly wrapped fingers. He bit on his lower lip until he nearly drew blood. After an hour in bed in this manner, he fell asleep, but not in joy. He regretted his inaction. In hindsight, he saw clearly her attempts to draw him into a conversation that would surely have thrilled him beyond measure and established a mutual bond that he came quickly to desire deeply. Everything that Jost was, everything he and his family expected from his life, died as he fell asleep that night. What's more, Jost felt its death. He perceived it clearly and had no idea how to feel about it. He knew one thing for certain, that the village would look very differently in the morning. It would not be the home of Johann and his antiquated business practices. It would be the home of Anna; and every feminine figure to catch Jost's peripheral vision would spin his face in involuntary curiosity, searching for her and rendering impotent all of his other faculties.

Jost had always been intensely introspective, perhaps to a fault. He knew himself well. He was not surprised when his experience of the following morning was exactly as he imagined it. The lenses through which he viewed the village were precisely as he envisioned them. Prior to that fateful walk in the forest, he believed himself to be unfree. His body was not at liberty to do as he believed he should do, his mind without the time to think the things he wanted to think. After meeting Anna, he was infinitely less free. His thoughts of her were a covetous tyrant, unwilling to loosen the chain around its captive's neck.

During that next day, and the three that followed frustratingly behind, Jost meandered a loose imitation of his standard course, seeing to his duties, but in twice the time. He sought Anna, and portioned only five percent of his mental capacity to fulfilling Johann's orders. His skills and intelligence were more than able to take up the slack of his meaningless tasks. Johann was none the wiser. If Jost could have found a seven-year-old with a good head for numbers, he could have trained his replacement in a leisure hour and spent his days in the one pursuit that had the backing of his heart.

Each time he went to bed having not seen her all day, he replayed in his head the many things he wished he had said during their walk. He began to believe that his inaction squandered his only chance at greater intimacy. He slowly resigned himself to a life of being haunted by a beautiful specter, shrouded in a glowing dress of regret.

On the fifth morning after the forest walk, Jost's body and about one one-hundredth of his mind filed through Johann's door and into the streets of Kleinostheim. Anna was waiting for him. She had situated herself to be sure that he would see her as he entered the street. His senses communicated little with his mind that morning. They were in two very different places. He did not notice her. To her, he seemed to look directly at her and pay no mind. He simply walked the path of his duties as if she was any of a hundred people he had no reason to notice.

She walked beside him, silently, much like the second half of their walk in the forest, only without the mental tumult inside of him. She walked to his right — directly to his right. Suddenly, the congestion of his thoughts slowed his limbs and he fell one pace behind her, noting her in his peripheral vision. He jerked his head toward her and dropped his papers and ledgers on the ground.

"Anna!" he said loudly, for a moment believing that the vision beside him was a vivid manifestation of his imagination and not the quite tangible young woman he met in the forest.

It was only in his reaction that she realized she had been invisible to him until that moment. She laughed and bent down to pick up what he had dropped. She expected him, with all his social refinement, to bend down beside her and insist that he alone gather what was dropped. But he did not. He stood high above her and stared as she lifted and dusted his possessions. When she stood to hand him his papers, his expression was telling. Behind the thin layer of shock was delight and admiration. Delight and admiration were not new to Anna. She was universally adored. Jost's eyes spoke of something much deeper. Upon seeing her in the forest, among the free and wild things of nature, he thought of how suited she was for her habitat. There, on the street, with the measured constructs of mankind around her, she was equally in her element. In his eyes, she made congenial whatever happened to frame her image.

He took the papers from her and continued to stare, until she asked if she could accompany him. He blurted his acceptance before the proposal was finished. Johann's stagnant estate found no entrance into his thoughts for the rest of the day. They did not walk the paths mandated by his duties. They could not have told you at the end of the day, with any accuracy, where they had walked, but that they remained among the buildings of the village. No doubt

49

they passed many hellos and how-are-yous, but if pressed to recount just one other face or feature of their walk, neither could have.

Anna spoke of her mother and father, of Michel's collection of books and papers. She quoted her favorite theologians, and he mouthed the quotations silently with her. She did not overtly attempt to draw him out. That would have been frustrating to them both. She spoke and he listened, and with every syllable she uttered, his attachment to her rooted more deeply into his innermost self.

They eventually wandered by her home.

"This is where I live," she informed him with an uncharacteristic blush.

They stopped walking and looked at each other, each waiting for the other to do or say something to navigate their next actions.

Finally, she added, "I walk in the forest most mornings. Would you like to join me tomorrow?"

A thousand bold affirmatives blared through his head but made no outward sign to her. She shrugged her shoulders as if to say, "Well?"

Only then did he become aware of the awkward silence, and he answered, "Yes… that is, yes. I would enjoy that."

A delighted giggle escaped her, accidental and quite informative of her feelings. She instructed him to meet her at that very point where they stood. He turned quickly from her without another word, not at all by any desire to remove her from his senses, but from a desperation to put the day and all of its pleasures securely into his past without blunder, and welcome as quickly as possible the intimacy of the following morning.

Jost went to bed hopeful. He awoke with an unbroken line of thoughts from the night before. Moments before he stepped out of Johann's house, he flew into a panic.

"A gift!" he shouted aloud.

He had nothing to give and no time to peruse the shops. He cursed his thoughtlessness.

"Surely I will meet her parents. I have nothing for them."

He scanned his room. The only items of value that were his to give were his books and papers. His books were not peculiar, certainly nothing to present to a book merchant's family. Anna had spoken openly of her family during their two walks. He knew their business. He knew their interests. One item came to mind. He kept it pressed between boards. It was a magnificently scribed copy of a letter of Ignatius of Loyola. It was about the care one should take in letter writing to aim the words to a universal audience for the Glory of God. It was rare, indeed, and Jost knew that it would be a treasure to any book merchant. It was certainly a treasure to him, one he would have risked his life to save. Never would he have considered gifting it, until that very moment, when the decision to do so seemed perfectly right.

Chapter Six:
A Worn Oak

WITH HIS TREASURED LOYOLA LETTER IN HAND, Jost walked to Anna's house. His lingering delight in his perfect gift did much to dispel his nervousness, until he saw that nobody stood where she had ordered him to meet her. He stood on the spot for less than a minute. It felt too strange to hold one position in the street, staring at her door. He paced several laps in front of the house, barred from proceeding by that brand of hesitation that grabs and rattles the nerves of a man so newly and insecurely in love.

He gave the slightest of thoughts to leaving the house, going about his day, and excusing it later as a misunderstanding. The thought barely touched a toe onto his mind before flapping its wings and flying away. After what felt like ten minutes in front of her house, he conjured the courage to knock on her door. Michel answered and invited Jost in with a warm greeting.

Anna's descriptions of the house had been vivid. She had no shortage of words. It was exactly as Jost had pictured it. Stacks of books and papers hung precariously from every flat surface. The house was by no means messy, but a cozy clutter seemed to cradle the inhabitants. The two older boys, Michel and Aulgoin, were grown and out of the house. Martin too was an adult, but he remained at home as an intimate apprentice to his father's business. He was away from Kleinostheim that morning, procuring new inventory.

With thoughts of his gift, Jost's smile grew until it hurt. Margarethe and Anna joined them from another room. Jost wasted no time. In the middle of formal pleasantries, he presented his gift.

Jost extended the Loyola letter toward Michel, mumbling, "Anna has told me... that is to say... I have come to understand..."

Before he could finish his presentation, the letter was in Michel's hand. Michel studied it closely. Jost waited for a comment but his host kept his eyes down. With a point and a curl of his finger, he beckoned his wife to see. Margarethe stood beside him and they both read the letter in its entirety. Anna stood beside her mother and looked at the letter, but her angle was too sharp to read it with them. Jost was beginning to sweat. The silence and utter absence of motion was driving him mad.

Jost interrupted the reading, saying, "That is for you all. I thought you might like it."

At length, Michel raised his eyes to Jost and handed the letter to his wife, who showed it to Anna.

In a reverent whisper, Michel told Jost, "That is the most thoughtful gift I have ever been presented."

Margarethe added, "It is... a *very* thoughtful gift."

Anna looked to Jost with a blush and a forcefully subdued grin. Margarethe asked Jost if he had eaten. Anna was already well enough acquainted with Jost's shyness to fear bursting that delicate social bubble she shared with him. She would allow no opportunity for disastrous awkwardness so early in their relationship. She announced, with abrupt sharpness, that they were going for a walk. She took Jost by the hand and pulled him through the front door before another word could be spoken by her parents.

They did not stray from their plans. Anna led Jost through her forest walk. Generally, her mind took flight before she left the village and her paths varied. It was an altogether different experience that morning with Jost. She planned each step, careful to include those sacred spots where she did her best thinking, and those verdurous, unworn areas where she could show off her knowledge of the local flora. She hoped to see more in him. She hoped that the same mossy rocks and ancient oak trees that drew wondrous imaginings from her would expose his heart. She paused their walk at every spot where the scenery and some gentle prodding might shake loose what was bound so tightly and deeply within him.

He was fascinated by her *mind*, but in the forest, when she staged herself perfectly, with the morning sun filtered through the trees, she glowed rather angelically. Anna was never a particularly vain girl. She also never had to work for the affection of others. But she wanted his regard most eagerly. His social restraint caused uncertainty in her in a manner, and to a degree, entirely new to her. She was slow to engage in those topics that had drawn them to each other. The first twenty minutes of the walk featured conversation of the shallowest nature. With little risk, his contributions almost matched hers. Once she began to speak of those deeper parts of her heart, of her dreams, her fears and sorrows, and of the things most precious to her, his lips pushed together. Words on such topics were no more welcomed in his father's home than they were in Johann's, and he was unaccustomed to speaking them.

He was overtly reticent, both naturally and practiced. But his deepest feelings found their own medium of expression in his illustrative eyebrows, which demonstrated, without his knowledge, those sentiments he strictly forbade to mount his tongue. Even his most peripheral acquaintances learned to look there for an honest supplement to his meticulously chosen words. Anna was no peripheral acquaintance. She had, in only two encounters, become the one being with the strongest claim to his heart. She enlivened those expressive eyebrows much more than any other, and his deepest thoughts and feelings pronounced themselves to her with every rise and twitch.

He had no idea how easily she read him. She giggled inwardly at *how* unaware he was. He was so measured in every response and in every attempt to gain understanding of her. He placed each word like a master bricklayer, while his eyebrows sang like a drunken bard. It was enough to give Anna a teasing taste of what was in his mind and heart, but only made her crave more.

Despite his churning emotions and the wild effect they had on his eyebrows, he spoke in obvious tones of suppressed emotion. She paused their walk at a carefully chosen place in the forest, a spot that had hosted many a wild and free fantasy and more than one imaginary academic symposium, with phantom scholars passionately orating their heated opinions. In that spot they sat. They leaned against a giant oak, the unnaturally large base of which showed signs of smoothing from the many hours Anna had already spent leaning against it.

Anna placed pauses in her speaking, ones she hoped he would fill with his own thoughts. He simply nodded in agreement with her, offering nothing from within him. She stood sharply, stepped away from the tree and turned to face him. She encouraged him to express himself more liberally, pleading with him, using words that energized him, and with spritely vocal inflections that tantalized him in ways he did not understand. She liberated his caged feelings to fly wildly within him, but his tongue was so unaccustomed to free effusions of sentiment that it tripped on itself. The conversation grew awkward as his natural inclinations stood firm against his desires. It was frustrating for them both.

Anna began to walk away from Jost, following the path they had been on. He remained seated with his back against the giant oak until, after several steps , she turned to him, tilted her head adorably and looked at him with turned down eyebrows and a wrinkled nose that shouted silently to him, "Why aren't you walking beside me?"

It took a second for him to interpret the look. When he did, he jumped obediently to his feet. They walked as before. She spoke of books in her father's collection. He spoke of the books he had owned. She did not wish to spend their time together talking of the dry subjects of academia. However, she understood that he could quote the musings of others more easily than verbalizing his own. After countless silent steps, she halted her feet so abruptly that it drew his concern. She raised a subject that she knew he would engage.

"Thank you for your gift," she said, "It was thoughtful and shows an understanding of the recipients. I can't imagine what you could have given my parents that would have been better suited to them."

Jost began constructing a script in his head of the many things he wished to say in response. He wanted to tell her that attaching himself to her parents was important to him, but not nearly as important as securing *her* affections. He wanted to say that the gift was meant, above all else, to inflame her passions and inform her that he shares them. Awkward time elapsed while he placed his words in order. They never left his mouth. She did not expect them to. She read his eyebrows and saw the care he had for her. She spoke of Loyola and her other favorite philosophers and theologians. It worked. With *their* words to rely on, he joined the conversation as an equal member. He had a great many quotations set to memory and they came out of him with ease.

The rest of the walk was intensely engaging for both of them, but when she demanded a supplement to his knowledge, something personal, the discussion clogged, and she had to restart it gingerly. Restart it she did, several times before their walk concluded just before noon. They had mindlessly returned to where they had entered the forest. Anna stopped sharply, refusing to abandon her hope that the trees would somehow pull free-flowing professions from him.

They had returned to the subject of the Loyola letter, and Anna demanded something deeper than another quotation, asking him, "I have read Loyola. I know how we should pray. I'm asking what *you* pray for. When you are alone, with only you and God, how do you pray then? When you place yourself as a child in God's hands, what are your fears and hopes?"

Jost began to answer with another quotation. Anna's shoulders dropped in disappointment. She did not mean to display it, but she did not mean to hide it either. He read it clearly and stopped his quotation in the middle of a syllable. His eyebrows were acrobatic. But it was his *words* she wanted.

She told him, "Beside my bed at the end of my day, when I am vulnerable before God, I ask for two things… never to be the cause of pain in someone I love, and to know my path when it is laid before me."

He answered with surprising candor, "Then those are the two things you fear the most, to hurt the people you love and to walk blindly past opportunity."

She was delighted with his insights, but corrected him, "It has less to do with opportunity."

"What then?" he asked.

"Destiny, I suppose. I am afraid of being blind to my purpose."

Jost grinned and spoke quickly, without his usual pause for the meticulous choice and placement of his words, "I struggle to imagine you being blind to anything important. If there is one thing you have in abundance, it is vision."

Anna was greatly relieved by the compliment, but continued to prod him to respond in kind, "And you, Jodocus, when you are vulnerable before God, fearful like a child, what do you pray for?"

His honest answer was clear in his head, that his fear was to remain alone, as he had been at home and as he was in the home of Johann. He feared that he would never find someone who favored his pastimes and could ignite his mind as Anna did. The truth is, that prayer had been answered and replaced by a new fear — that he would be unable to secure Anna's affections through some fault of his own, and he would return to his loneliness, but with the added pain of regret. An open expression of those thoughts at that moment would have done much to ensure his success. Of course, he could not. He said something about his father and something about calculating the assets and liabilities of an estate. They were thoughts that were meant to lead him to an honest answer. They were the beginnings of a convoluted but genuine answer to her question. He never moved past them, but circled them with more framework and more setup.

She sighed heavily. He ended the conversation abruptly and excused himself from her company. She was frustrated with him, but she could see that his emotions were stirred. She just could not read them precisely. She rejoined her parents in their home and spent the rest of the day trying to put words to his every gesture and every dance of his eyebrows.

Jost hurried home, intent on giving his hand a chance to profess what his tongue would not. He turned directly to his writing desk. The sentiments that still buzzed inside of him required little coaxing to work their way to his fingers. The words were his, to be sure, but ablaze with an intensity of feeling that his hand was quite able to express, where his mouth would have stumbled. Sentiments Anna had looked for in him, ones which had remained securely within the rigid confines of his humble decorum, bounced from the scratchings of his pen and animated the words to fly freely from the pages to her eyes in a manner as much hers as his.

He wrote, "Your company is the first I ever recall to truly bring me pleasure."

He realized that she had quickly become the most intense facet of his life and filled the finest contemplations of his evenings.

He continued, "If I never saw your face again or heard your voice, just the memory of you would be the brightest thing in my life. You have already enlivened me and altered me."

As he wrote, his words confirmed to him what his heart had already known — that he could see nothing of his own future beyond being her husband and could desire nothing more from life than that she be his wife. He made no such proposal in his letter, but he answered her question.

He wrote, "I am alone now as a child in God's hands, and I pray that I do not misrepresent myself and turn you away from me. I know that what I feel is right. I pray that what I say and do reflects me clearly to you. I am not the bumbling fool I must seem to be. My sensibilities are in line with yours and I curse my inability to engage you in conversation as openly as you deserve. I, too, fear missing my destiny, but not due to blindness. I think it must be worse to witness your destiny abandon you because of your own blundering than to walk past it blindly. How self-fulfilling fears can be."

Having answered her last question to him, he ended the letter there. He folded it and paced his room. Every few steps, he determined to destroy the letter, and he poised his hands to tear it in half. Each time, he stopped himself and resolved to give it to her. This cycle repeated in intensifying waves until he slammed it onto his writing table and went to bed.

In the morning, he decided to go about the routine of his business with the letter in his possession. He would not seek her out, but should he happen to encounter her, he would decide then if the letter should be given. Fearing a decision that could steer the course of his life, he kept his eyes low and moved quickly about his business. Intense fear of the life he *wanted* made him very proficient at the one he did *not*. He concluded his business for Johann by early afternoon. He did not encounter Anna.

He walked to the door of Johann's house and reached to open it. In a swell of courage, the source of which he could never have speculated, he turned on his heels and walked at a determined pace to Anna's house. Michel was outside of the door bidding farewell to a visitor. Jost stood and waited. Michel, wanting to thank him again for the gift and to receive a report on the previous day's forest walk from Jost's perspective, rushed his farewell and invited Jost to join him.

A serious air surrounded Jost, one that savored heavily of fear. Michel did not want to interfere and only asked what he could do for him. Jost had the letter held out in front of him before he knew what he was doing. His heart leaped into his throat and he had to swallow it back down.

"I have written a letter to your daughter," he answered choppily, "It is filled with the things I wish I had said. I ask that you please give it to her."

That morning, Anna had been open with her parents. They knew of her conversations with Jost and all of the associated frustrations.

"You and your wife may read it, if you wish. Please, feel free to read it," Jost added defensively.

Michel put a hand firmly on Jost's shoulder, while taking the letter with his other hand and saying, "There is no need for that. I am sure I understand."

Michel took one step backward, away from Jost and toward his door, shook the letter at eye level, and repeated, "I am sure I understand. Anna will be happy to receive your letter, and I will be happy to deliver it."

Michel and Margarethe had their own set of fears regarding their daughter. They struggled to imagine any young man deserving her, but struggled much more to imagine one well-suited to her sensibilities — one that would liberate her to remain herself, allow her to grow as she traveled down her own path and not cram her into the mould of a provincial wife. They saw in Jost a man attracted to Anna by that one trait for which she was most peculiar, that one trait they prayed most that she would never lose — her liberty of mind.

The men smiled at each other. Jost nodded and turned away. He walked at a comfortably quick pace until he knew he was out of sight, at which point he slowed to a near crawl as his body felt like it too had to march through the mire of his thoughts. Michel watched as Jost disappeared behind a building. He had spoken honestly. He understood Jost, and he understood the effect Anna had on people. He understood that a young woman who is handled by the Angels, with one foot still in the Heavens, must be difficult to relate to. Anna connected easily with everyone, but no one connected with her. He did not know the depth of Jost's connection to Anna, but he was determined to facilitate any connection that could give as much to Anna as it received. And yes, he was happy to deliver the letter.

Chapter Seven:

Eloquent Ink

JOST FELT PRECARIOUSLY OUT ON A LIMB, having unmasked his heart as he did in the letter. Through the evening, he asked himself relentlessly, "Has she read it? What does she think?" He exhausted himself and fell asleep early with a headache from his clenched jaw and with weary legs from the evening's ceaseless pacing. He awoke with greater resolution, convinced that an honest heart has its own merits, regardless of Anna's reaction. He set about his day determined to keep an eye for her, hoping she would seek him out, but affixed to the decision that he would go to her at the end of the day if she did not come to him first.

The morning was young when Jost passed by the river. Four men were unloading merchandise from a boat. Anna was among them and they flirted with her shamelessly. Jost knew that she was much admired. It did not surprise him that other men would be drawn to her, or that she would receive the flirtations with the grace and compassion that was uniquely hers. There was nothing he desired more than to speak to her, to gauge her reaction to his letter in the subtleties of her first glance. Something in him forbade it. He remained at a distance and tormented himself by observing the flirtations.

The men poured many bold compliments onto her, which could not have been sincere, for they spoke of character traits the strangers could not have quickly learned, compliments that may have sent aflutter the hearts of other young women but were poorly placed on their current subject. They told her she was the prettiest girl on the river. She hardly raised an eye. They compared her to many pleasant things, from a sunset to fresh water. She paid little mind. The apparent leader, whose face and posture displayed finer breeding than the others, adjusted his compliments toward his target.

"You have a good eye for quality," he told her, "You are sharp of wit."

The leader commandeered the flirtations and the other three backed down. He was a tall man, broad of frame and bold of masculine features.

"You like an adventure," he presumed to declare, "You have that light in your eye. Your thoughts are beyond this village. With the cargo out of the way, there is room on our boat for you. Let us take you up the river a ways. There is much to see."

They laughed when she blushed and turned her eyes back to the ground in front of her. There was nothing authentic about their regard for her. Jost *had* learned her character, and it pained him that their compliments were accurate. It pained him with regret.

"He is right," Jost thought, "There is a light of understanding in her eyes. But they cannot see it as I do. I should have told her those things when I was the only one near her. I should have and I did not."

Anna saw clearly the nature of the flirtations. They meant little to her beyond the slight gratification of her scant vanity. She credited the leader with no clairvoyance into her character. The words were poetically delivered but smacked heavily of seduction and Anna was well beyond his reach. She was in no danger. As Jost watched from a distance, he did not fear her weakness. He feared that his own words, his earnest compliments, would be seen as theirs — shining words over feeble sentiments.

He wanted his letter back to amend it somehow, to add words that would bring to her eyes some undeniable distinction between his love and the frivolous flirtations of other men. He did not know if she had read it and feared both possibilities equally.

He thought scornfully to himself, "Had I only spoken when she begged me to speak."

The flirting tradesman was a handsome man, who had undoubtedly hosted many a young villager on a romantic river tour on his boat. It is unlikely he ever encountered the likes of Anna. While Jost's tongue was too tightly bound, this man's threw syllables into the air with too much ease, words not at all supported by weighty thought. It was all rather pathetic to Anna, and the more he pressed his proposal, the more distasteful the notion of it grew. As she explained years later, "It is better to work at a shell I cannot open but know contains delights than to open easily a shell that is empty."

She would have enjoyed a river tour, but not with such company. The sights would have spawned conversation that would have been out of this man's league. There was little inside of his eyes that demanded a deeper look. Although broad and beautiful in structure, his face and its expressions were only suggestive of what is sensual and not at all of what is spiritual or cerebral. Were it within her nature to indulge in passing fancies and the most immediate and temporary desires of the flesh, she may have followed him to his boat.

He did not disgust Anna. To her, his flirtations were as innocent as her own dear heart, and she knew nothing would come of them, so she allowed them to continue, mildly entertained by the diversion. Jost viewed the encounter through a man's eyes — and a man very much in love. The others rejoined the flirtations. Jost saw the nature and depth of their attraction to her. He watched her giggle as they pathetically and fruitlessly pressed their wishes. Her giggle was not one of an affected little girl, but one of a higher being looking down upon lower ones. Nevertheless, it was a giggle and Jost misinterpreted it. He knew the men to be beneath her. He also knew that one single, slight gesture of interference from him would insult her independence and implacable morality. He could only look on, while green-eyed jealousy gnawed ravenously at his heart like hyenas around living prey.

About the same time that the men realized their effort was not worth the prize, Anna, too, grew tired and unamused. The encounter broke by mutual motive. The tradesmen returned to their toils and Anna continued her museful walk, with no lingering effects of the incident. The experience remained with Jost. He had no desire to trade his character for that of the handsome tradesman. But he envied how easily he spoke and how quickly he grabbed Anna's attention. He left the riverbank that morning with a deeper determination to attach himself to Anna with rich expressions of all that was inside of him. She had shown her curiosity in him, begging him for his opinions. He abandoned his duties and took immediately to the pen. He thought back to every conversation, every question she asked of him, and he wrote his answers with stripped, naked, vulnerable disclosure, regardless of the fears that jumped up and down from the peripheral of his focused thoughts and waved their arms to get his attention.

His fingers gave voice to his opinions on many topics, each addressing the subjects of their conversations. His pen said everything she wished his mouth to say. It proved that he had listened closely to her and contemplated her words deeply. At the end of the very long letter, he addressed in cryptic elegance the incident with the flirtatious tradesmen. He wrote.

You know (a creature remarkable for so many enviable virtues, I am sure you must know) that any application for your affection comes to you from a position of debt. I pray nightly that you do not find the imbalance unforgivable in me. Yet you are a gracious creditor, kind and humble where others would be cruel.

As Saint Augustine wrote, "Humility is the foundation of all other virtues hence, in the soul in which this virtue does not exist, there cannot be any other virtue except in mere appearance."

You stand above me in all virtues, even in humility, the only virtue for which I should have a greater claim. One claim I make for myself above most others is the talent of vision. I see you, and I believe I know and understand you, much more than the men who might pass through our village and shower you with attention. They speak to a girl. They do not speak to Anna, for they do not know Anna. They speak to a pretty face. I write now to an opulent mind and a virtuous and open heart. I write to you, Anna, for I know you.

Jost concluded with the standard elegancies of a well-thought letter, claiming to be hers "In Admiration and Affection." He was content with the effort. In the early afternoon, he walked directly to her house. He gave the letter to Margarethe, who tried to engage him in conversation on topics she knew they shared. Anna had read his last letter and shared it with her parents. The sentiments within, and the words chosen for their expression, adhered Jost securely to the affections of Anna's parents. Michel and Margarethe were almost as interested in bringing Jost more intimately into their lives as Anna was. Despite Margarethe's overt attempts to draw him in, he answered with distant pleasantries and excused himself. This frustrated Margarethe but did not surprise her. Anna had shared everything with her — her growing admiration for Jost, and also her frustrations with his reticence.

By the evening, Jost had delivered two letters for Anna and was not sure if either had been read or how either was received. When he knelt for his prayers that night, he thanked God for the gift of his writing hand, and for the ink-and-paper lifeline that kept his hopes alive.

With both letters in hand, Anna sat in her bed that night with her own blossoming hope. She read both letters repeatedly, as if they were one long conversation, placing with some strain on her imagination Jost's voice over his written words. She had every reason to hope that their next encounter would be different. The letters displayed openness. She saw them as an invitation to walk her own private path into his heart. By the time she fell asleep, she had plotted, in detail, their next walk through the forest.

The following morning opened a perfect mid-August day. It was Maria Himmelfahrt, the Catholic feast of the Assumption of Mary. The day was for honoring the Mother of Christ and all mothers. Jost arose to the muffled sounds of conversation through his bedroom door. Michel was there speaking to Johann and Jost recognized his voice in an instant. He joined them to find Michel's elegance in action. The learned bookseller spoke with Johann on the menial topics within the simple man's grasp. He kept the conversation lively nevertheless and Johann was delighted by the company. He spoke of Johann's affairs with genuine interest. The old man felt like he had gained his first new friend in decades.

Michel's visit was not for Johann's sake, but for Jost's. He came to invite Jost to join them that afternoon for a picnic in the forest. Johann, who certainly would have reached beyond his rights as an apprentice's master and conjured some reason why Jost could not go, was so well-warmed by Michel that he encouraged, even prodded, Jost to attend. Jost's *own* family didn't recognize the day, relieving him of any obligation on that front. He gleefully accepted.

Margarethe packed a picnic box with bread, cheese, and wine. They found a scenic and secluded spot not very deeply into the forest, sparsely wooded enough to allow the sun to drench the small blanket Michel set out for them. The day was teeming with life. The bright grass was animated by the insects that hopped about or found some hidden game to play just beneath the blades. Birds performed feats of acrobatics to the lively songs of their brethren. Whether by the air of peace exuding from the picnickers, or by the holiness of the day, the usually shy rabbits of the forest threw off their inhibitions and reveled in the sun within arm's reach of the blanket. The breeze went by with a coy swinging step, flirting with the picnickers' cheeks and the fine hairs on their arms. The outing was a project tinglingly alive.

They were all relaxed, and found no immediate reason to speak. Nature around them gave much to admire, and the silence was not awkward. The food and drink remained packed and the four of them allowed their eyes, ears, and minds to wander the area freely. Jost's attention did not stray long.

Anna was fittingly within her element. Nature suited her perfectly. The direct sun gave intense depth to her hair.

Infinite variations of browns and golds seemed woven into her head, not as a portrait hardened in oils, but very much alive, rolling around each other with every slight tilt and turn.

Jost lost himself in her hair, and then in her forehead and her cheek. It may be safely asserted that no man had ever looked at a woman with such exquisite fascination. But Jost was seeing more than hair and skin. He saw Anna, and all that he knew that made her Anna. She turned to face him. He was dreamily engrossed in looking not only at her, but into her, and did not notice that their eyes were locked to each other's. He was deep in a glorious study of her, too deep to hide the adoring gaze that was so fixedly upon her. She was in full blush before he caught himself and forced his eyes to a blade of grass beside him.

Anna thought about the letters and connected the sentiments within them to those fiery eyes she caught staring at her. She assumed that raw, honest conversation must follow such letters and such a gaze, as surely as night follows day. It was not her place to unpack and serve the food. But she wanted to get him to herself. She was ravenous to hear him speak openly on the many topics she hoped to raise. There could be no walk until after food and drink, and no food and drink while it remained closed in a box. Anna rolled to her knees and raided her mother's picnic box. The impatience of her movements was grossly incongruent with the scene.

With the bread and cheese distributed and the wine poured, their crowded blanket began to resemble a dining table, a tiny, almost uncomfortably intimate dining table. Food and drink were never the order of the day. Conversation and the kindling of new relations was the outing's ultimate design. Michel wasted no time engaging Jost on his favorite academic subjects, not allowing minor impediments like a mouth full of bread to interfere. He spoke through rushed swallows, using the Loyola Letter as the ice-breaker.

The participants were in place for a lively theological symposium, the anticipation of which had the pulse of each unnaturally high. On that little blanket sat three radiant faces of desire and one wretched victim of anxiety.

Michel proposed, "Ignatius of Loyola writes that we should make ourselves indifferent to all creatures and in this way we do not prefer health to sickness, wealth to poverty, honor to dishonor, a long life to a short one. If he is right, and we are to be indifferent to temporal things, why did God place in us the instinct to live and to protect ourselves from harm? Can temporal misfortunes be a punishment from God if fortune is not a blessing to be relished?"

It was an excellent question, rich soil for the growth of lively debate. At the end of the question, Anna and Margarethe shifted their gaze in unison from Michel to Jost. A hot, punishing blush came over his face. The question aroused in him a hundred points and counterpoints, which flew around his head and crashed into the inside of his skull, but were afforded no passage into the forest air.

Mother, father, and daughter continued to wait for an eruption of Jost's thoughts on the question. It was clear that no other words would be spoken on that little blanket until Jost had his turn. He could not free his thoughts from their restraints.

The icy waters of rigid control quenched his fiery mind and coated his words. He answered with another quote, "Ignatius also writes that among the many signs of a lively faith and hope we have in eternal life, one of the surest is not being overly sad at the death of those whom we dearly love."

Michel probed, "So you agree that we should make no effort to extend life or soothe suffering, or to improve in any way the human condition on earth?"

That was not at all what Jost meant to say. The silence that followed was more prickly than the last. Jost begged his tongue to unbind itself, to do its job in reflecting to those around him what is truly in his heart and mind. He silently composed answers that he knew would never be heard.

He followed with another formal quotation, "He also writes that we should prefer the glory of God above everything else . . . Let your thoughts, words, and actions be in Him. . .and let God s commandments take first place over everything else that is good."

Jost was certainly quick with a quotation, and that one was fittingly placed. It placed firm punctuation on the matter and closed it well short of its intended glory.

Margarethe decided to take a different angle. Leaving the books entirely, she asked Jost about his family and his home, hoping that topics of a more personal nature might loosen the conversation. There was no deceit behind his answers. They were blunt, short, honest, and forbidding. That trail of discourse collapsed more quickly than the last.

Anna had been devouring her food at great haste. After all, the letters were written to her. The fiery gaze was at her. If she could only get him alone, he would open up his heart and reveal the truths within. When her last morsel was down, despite the fact that Jost had hardly begun, she took him by the hand and invited him on a walk.

"Yes, yes," Margarethe quickly interjected, "You two go ahead. There is a place I want to show my husband."

Michel and Margarethe waited for Anna and Jost to take their first few steps, then chose the opposite direction and walked away.

Anna and Jost were alone, and she yearned for a vocal recitation of the sentiments in his letters. She felt as if a proposal of marriage might come to her on that very walk. His letters felt strongly of eternal commitment. He walked beside her where there was room and followed behind her where the trees tightened. They walked and she waited. He did not speak. Frustrated and impatient, she sighed loudly and posted herself against a tree, facing him.

When he had written his letters to her, the only image of her was in his mind, not in his eyes as it was then, softly glowing from the late summer sun through the filter of oak leaves. She stood aglow, in perfect position and scenery to enhance her figure, and no portrait painter could have situated her more perfectly to attract. The object of his affection reflected in his eyes *and* in his mind and in his heart.

With every word of the letters zipping around her mind, Anna's desire to hear him speak grew urgent, and she raised the subject, "I have read your two letters—"

That was all that needed to be spoken. A squall of emotion overtook him. With his tongue still bound tightly, his feelings forced another outlet. He charged the three steps between them and kissed her. There was no clumsy bumping of noses or knocking of foreheads, no stepping on feet or poking of eyes. It was almost musical. It was certainly melodic. It was as if nature grew impatient with them both and seized control of them like a puppeteer. Their lips met with the soft silence of a leaf landing gently on the forest floor. Their arms remained at their sides, but their lips embraced like they had arms of their own. It was a soft but unrelenting embrace, as if their mouths forgot that they served any other natural purpose. It was in no uncertain terms a perfect kiss, both for how it happened and for the honesty of the sentiments it represented.

Chapter Eight:
United in All Matters

AFTER THE KISS, neither showed outward signs of awkwardness or regret. Jost pulled away from Anna and took one deep step backward, keeping his eyes on hers. He waited for any sign of response from her. The nature of the kiss gave him reason to hope. It would be inaccurate to say that she kissed him back. There was much greater unity than that phrase might suggest. The kiss was in flawless unison, mutual. They were perfectly together and united in the kiss, not a bit more of one than the other. Still, Jost studied her entire form waiting for a twitch or a grin, or any little symbol of her thoughts. He was terrified to speak, as he prayed that relief from his anxiety would come in some form from her.

Anna's mind was not much calmer than his in the wake of the kiss. But she did not give him the approving grin he sought. His lips spoke more to her than he realized. She had never been kissed and had nothing to compare it to, but the sincerity of his affections declared itself in the resolute tenderness of his kiss. Her life changed at that moment. She no longer saw herself as one, but half of two. No matter what would have come of the relationship and the future of these two people, Jost would be, from that point forward, her one and only true love.

As he pulled away from her, she was more desirous of his free and honest conversation than ever. Her heart thumped resoundingly in her chest as she watched his lips. She watched for them to part and make way for a proposal of marriage and his effusions of love. His lips twitched, but remained tightly together. Her frustration doubled, but so did her patience, for she now saw the development of their intimacy as a lifelong endeavor. Such is the power of a perfect kiss.

Had the change in her been displayed in any fashion recognizable by Jost, he would have been much relieved. The tumult in her mind churned beneath a placid surface as she stared back at him. After what felt like a full minute of silent staring, Jost could take no more. He half expected her to laugh and embrace him, and half expected her to scold him and run away to her parents, never to speak to him again. Worst of all, he could not force himself to ask her how she felt. The questions knocked silently and fruitlessly at the inside of his mouth, like a boneless beggar.

He turned away from her and took a few steps along the path they had been walking. He turned back to her with a face that begged her to follow. Of course, she did. She joined him by his side and they walked as if the previous moments had nothing extraordinary to boast. Anna was silent, strangely silent, with a trance-like expression of extreme introspection. She debated fiercely with herself about what the kiss meant to her, what it meant about him, and how their relationship might proceed. Oh, how differently the story of our species might read if we could know the silent thoughts of others. Jost did not interpret Anna's silence and alabaster expression the *wrong* way. He interpreted it in *every* way. Every possible thought he imagined she could have took its turn at the center of his heart.

Another twenty minutes of walking together may have loosened their tongues and allowed their crowded, clogged thoughts to reach the other. They did not have those twenty minutes. They came across Michel and Margarethe. Both Anna and Jost snapped from their contemplations and engaged Anna's parents with as much counterfeit normalcy as they could manage. The four of them returned to the place of their picnic. They packed their things with light and frivolous topics filling the air around them. Eventually, Anna and Jost's moods evolved to match them.

Jost walked them back to the Schwarz house. Margarethe and Michel went inside and Anna remained at the door. As she looked at him, she was not sure what she desired more, a fluid effusion of his feelings or another kiss. She received neither. They spoke at the same time, each trying to prompt the other with similar questions spoken over each other.

She asked, "Did you enjoy today?" while he said, "Did you enjoy our walk?"

The awkwardness was comical and both giggled. She said, "Yes," and he responded in kind. Jost turned from her and walked briskly around the nearest building, then very slowly until he reached Johann's home.

Through the night, Jost's poor dreams volleyed between torment and delight. He awoke resolved to finally end the awkwardness and secure his future by professing his love to Anna. He rehearsed many times in his head the things that he would say to her. Breakfast at Johann's table ended his rehearsals along with any hope of seeing Anna that day. Johann had important estate business for Jost to attend to. He had arranged Jost's travel to Frankfurt, not by boat, along the River Main, but by cart — by noisy, bumpy, rickety cart. Jost was well west of Kleinostheim by the time Anna left her bedroom.

The young romance was in no state to be left unattended for many weeks. But that is precisely where they stood. So many things needed saying and needed hearing. When the need was dearest and the prize nearest, Jost was pulled away. There was no chance to write while on the cart. There was hardly a chance to think.

Once she was up and the Schwarz household was in motion, Anna told her parents about the kiss. Margarethe advised Anna to wait at home until Jost came to her. Michel, in great animation, suggested that she go to him. She sided with her father. Anna walked to Johann's house with a pace that gradually increased so that nobody could tell exactly when the walk ended and the run began. In any case, she was at her full sprint before she stopped at Johann's door.

The news that Jost was gone for work was not disheartening. That he was gone for weeks — that tortured her. She knew just enough of him, and just little enough, to think that he escaped the village because of her. Not knowing better, she blamed the kiss for his sudden departure. She did not doubt his affections for her. The kiss had spoken clearly enough of that. But she did not know if his affections alone were enough to unite them for a lifetime. She imagined that he left to think, to decide if he wanted to commit his life to her. She felt as if her destiny were on a razor's edge and she had no power to urge it in the desired direction. She would have traveled to him by foot had Johann disclosed his location. He did not, and she had little to do but crawl to the comfort of her parents and pray with them.

Her walk back home was slow and lonely. The village bustle bloomed in its usual patterns. Those same neighbors who had mended her scrapes for years recognized her mood and offered the same services. She did not hear them. She did not acknowledge them. For the first time, like him, she wondered what she should have done differently.

It was a peculiar reversal. He was inclined to speak to her, and had no choice but to write. When he settled into his Frankfurt lodgings, he did not pull out his pen, but thought about the flirtatious traders. He was mortified to imagine that she would interpret the kiss wrongly, that she would see him as another flirt, with no respect for her virtue and no understanding of her character. After a tiring day of travel, he retired early, and snuggled tightly with that mortification through the night.

He awoke with one determination. Whether she would ever be his, the idea that she would think of him as she did the dockside flirts could not be borne. She would know the height of his admiration. Half-dressed and quite the portrait of absentmindedness, he sat and wrote her a letter.

> *I did not think seriously enough on the volatility of my passions to guard sufficiently against haste and to shield your honor against my own rising desire. I struggle to reconcile how fervently I covet your company with how very far above me I esteem your worth. I pray that you do not misinterpret my weakness against my impulses as a diminished regard for your virtue.*
>
> *I kissed you, and the memory of that moment is both my most wretched sense of mortification and my most powerful source of hope. I can't imagine you understand how I fear soiling something so beautiful with such unworthy hands as mine. Dare I continue — to stretch the length of my merits in order to touch heaven, or do I content myself to remain a distant admirer? I suppose I answered that question in the forest.*

Stefan Scheuermann

And now, like Icarus, I take my
makeshift wings and flap clumsily and
frantically toward the sun. If my
wings should melt, and I crash to the
earth, I can sink into the dirt knowing
I felt warmth as no man has. I have
been nearer to you than any man
deserves to be. My heart will stay
near you, as I intend to remain
always,

> *Yours in Respect,*
> *Admiration, and Affection,*
> *Jodocus Koob*

Jost folded the letter sloppily and unceremoniously, having written it more for the relief of his own anxieties and not at all certain it would ever reach Anna's eyes. He crammed it into his pocket and went about his day. The letter was addressed to nobody, which was no oversight. Jost could not bring himself to write, "Dear Anna" or "My Dear Friend" or anything of the sort. It was not from a lack of searching for the perfect beginning to the letter. Even as he went on with his day, with the paper in his pocket, a thousand variations ran through his head, but none captured what she meant to him. No endearment could encircle his feelings. All of them either smacked of presumption or fell too short of framing her as she deserved.

For two days he carried the letter with him, still unable to pen the perfect endearment. He was not at all satisfied with the letter, but his desire to get it into her hands grew as he imagined what might be going through her head in his absence. He sent the letter as it was, without addition or amendment. It took six days for the letter to find Anna. She was left alone in her room to read the letter in private. Through her door, her parents heard deep sighs, sobs, and

78

giggles, all blending into each other without borders. When she came out of her room, her tears had drenched a wide and glowing smile. The letter spoke everything she needed to hear. Still, she longed for what she had never had — the lovely eloquence of his professed love rolling in her ears, carried by his voice, not his pen. But the letter gave her patience.

Before the letter arrived, there was little talk of Jost Koob in the Schwarz house. He was an awkward subject that neither parents knew how to approach. After the letter, his name was constantly in the air. They spoke of him all day, and when Margarethe led the family in their evening prayers, she begged,

"Lord, bring him home safely. Bring him home quickly. And bring him home in love with Anna."

The time between Jost's departure and Anna's receipt of the letter had moved quickly but painfully for her. The time between the letter and his return moved much more slowly, but gracefully. The morning Jost left for Frankfurt, he had no time to see her and say good-bye. When he returned to Kleinostheim, nothing pressed on his time or forced his feet where they did not wish to go, except for the weariness of travel. Weariness was nothing to him. He dismounted the cart at the edge of the village and ran to Anna's house. It was very late in the afternoon. He had not eaten for hours. He had not slept, and he felt none of the effects. He was entirely singular of intention. He ran with freshness and knocked on her door. A high-pitched squeal from within the house followed the very first tap on the wood.

The squeal was not Anna's. It was not Margarethe's, but Michel's. He and his wife had fallen for Jost. His goodness may have hidden reasonably from those not inclined to look for it. But to those who sought it, and Anna's parents looked intently, it was as visible as the clothes he wore. During Jost's absence, Michel and

Margarethe watched their daughter pace the house and bite her nails, not answering questions that were asked of her, and answering questions that were not. She spoke in nonsense, and behaved in ways that were quirky even for her. The whole household longed for Jost's return, and Michel, more than anyone, prayed for Jost to return with a proposal of marriage.

Jost had that very intention, but not that day. His proposal needed to be scripted flawlessly. He did not feel that he could trust his tongue with such an important commission. He ran to her house to see her, to see them all, but his proposal of marriage to Anna would be composed by his hand, at his desk, alone, not by his lips with her before him.

Michel answered Jost's knock and invited him in with as much cordial control as he could muster. Inside the Schwarz home, the air was electric. Jost sat at the table and Margarethe served him dark bread and a light and sweet white wine. They tried to calm him with food, drink, and light conversation, hoping to loosen him enough for his professions of love to roll forth. But try as they did, the scene was awkward and the conversation was forced. It did not have the comfort of the picnic, and Jost could not account for the difference.

Anna, who stood in one place, behind and to the right of Jost, listened. Michel and Margarethe began to tug Jost along, asking him questions about his walks with Anna, their talks, and all the things they have in common. It was beginning to work. Jost agreed and began to speak of his admiration for Anna's mind. He wanted to erupt with emissions of sentiment, not just to Anna and her parents, but to the world. His heart shouted, "I love Anna Schwarz!" But his mouth was slow in catching up.

Knowing what her parents were doing, and anticipating where the talk might lead, Anna remained still. She did not notice how shallow her breaths were. She grew lightheaded until she collapsed and drew all attention away from the table. Margarethe tended to her daughter. Michel dampened a cloth and handed it to his wife. Jost remained seated. He turned around to look at Anna, still lying on the floor. Margarethe helped Anna sit up. In the seated position, Anna's face turned flush.

Amid the bustle, time stood still for Jost. To him, Anna had never looked so angelic. He did not see the daughter of Michel and Margarethe. He did not see the girl he walked with, or the girl he kissed. He saw his wife. He would have shooed the parents away and proposed on the spot, were it within him to do so. He wanted to embrace her and never let go. It was not the time to do such things, not while she was flush and faint and receiving the care of her parents. He stood abruptly, desperate to get his proposal on paper. He excused himself awkwardly and saw himself from the house.

Jost ran home, so much faster than he had ever run. Perhaps Johann tried to speak to him. Perhaps Johann was not even home. Jost could not have spoken either way. He went directly to his desk and scribbled, scratched, crumpled, tore, sighed, pounded his fist, and scribbled and scratched some more, well into the night, until his proposal of marriage was tolerable to his own sentiments. He resolved to go to Michel the next morning, show him the proposal, and walk with Anna into the woods for the most important moment of his life. The plan did not go exactly as he foresaw.

In the morning, Jost was dressed and pacing his room before Johann opened his eyes. In the silence of the still house, every terror and every delight that could possibly result from his proposal played through his mind in repeating patterns. He wanted to appear at the Schwarz home early enough to show his concern for Anna's condition, yet appropriately late to show his respect for their privacy. The wait was excruciating. The tension was broken slightly when Johann arose. Jost had never shared anything personal with his master. This day was different, this circumstance was so unlike anything his young heart had ever known. He showed Johann the letter. Johann had nothing intelligent to say on the matter, nothing worth relaying to you readers. It did not matter to Jost. He was relieved to have shown it.

There was not an hour to waste, hardly a moment, in Jost's mind. Having received no discouragement from his master, Jost left with a level of confidence one slight degree above shaky. He walked a steady pace to Anna's house. He trembled as he began, but as he drew nearer, and his memory replayed for him all of her encouragement and all the encouragement of her parents, he turned stable and increasingly confident.

Jost stood at the door and raised a hand to knock.

"Flowers!" he thought, "I should bring flowers."

He ran to the forest. An early frost had wilted most, but after some effort he was able to piece together a small bouquet — and a slightly smaller one for Margarethe. He arrived again at their door, ready this time. Margarethe opened the door before he could knock. He looked the part. Obvious care had gone into his presentation. He carried two bouquets of flowers. Margarethe had little doubt that this was the day. She invited him in and called for Anna before he had cleared the threshold.

Jost gave the smaller bouquet to Margarethe, whose emotions commandeered her arms. She wrapped Jost in a motherly embrace. Anna entered the room to that very sight. She saw the flowers and suspected a proposal might come. What she had little hope for — what she could not allow herself to hope for was that he would profess his affection in the only way she wished to receive it.

Margarethe rushed them out of the house before Michel could join the scene. To Anna's delight and surprise, Jost took her by the hand and led the way. He was not sure where he would present her with his letter of proposal, but he was sure he would know it when he saw it. They walked for about an hour, west along the edge of the forest, then turned south toward the river. Their talk was much as it had been, but with a conspicuous touch of anxiety from both of them.

Along the river, west of the village, the scenery, the natural sounds, the very air they inhaled seemed perfect. Jost stopped in mid-pace. He still held Anna's hand and yanked to a sharp and awkward stop. With no prelude, no romantic setup or long, deep, adoring gaze, Jost pulled from his pocket the proposal he so painstakingly wrote in a letter to her. He reached it toward her. Anna shook her head and pushed his hand away, forcing it to his side. All hope he had in life, everything lovely he expected from his years on Earth, left him in the next exhale. Of course he did not voice the crushing sensation, but his expressive eyebrows demonstrated more sorrow than the most masterful poet could capture in a hundred verses. He clutched the letter in his fist, distorting it into a disfigured wad of paper. His fingers lost the strength to hold that which had represented all of his hopes. He dropped the letter and it fell at his feet.

Anna took one half-step nearer to him, close enough to clearly hear his straining breaths, and she said to him, "No more letters. I want to *hear* you, to *see* your lips move as your words reach my heart, not to imagine what you might be doing or thinking as I read. You fuel my mind. You spark that fuel and set it ablaze, but leave me with no one to share its warmth. Then I must douse it alone and mourn the cold and darkness that follows."

After a long pause, where several times his lips parted slightly, raising her anticipation, only to close again without a whisper, she followed, "Please, Jost. Look me in the eyes and say to me what you wish to say."

83

It was more than enough encouragement to lift him from the darkness he had fallen into. He took a deep breath, took her hands, dropped to both knees and said, "I am living in the irresistible conviction that I exist for no other purpose than to be yours. I offer myself entirely to you, to benefit you and enrich you in any way I can. But any such rewards are surely insignificant when stood in comparison beside all that I seek to benefit from you. In your goodness, you incite me to virtue, well beyond my natural inclinations, convincing me that the only way to my best self and salvation is at your side. I know the generosity of your heart, so I ask you for my sake—"

His eyes watered and he fought back his shivers and a hysterical cry, but continued through a faltering voice, "—will you take me as your husband and grace me with a blessing greater than fate should grant any man?"

Anna's cheeks turned pink, and her watering eyes began to swell. She pulled at his hands until he stood. She pulled again until his face nearly touched hers. His breath was held and his face turned red.

She answered, "I will only take you as my husband if you consent to take me as your wife."

Jost released his held breath, squeezed her hands and giggled as he said, "I consent, my dear friend. I consent."

Somewhere deep inside of him, a voice demanded that he lift her up and spin her in circles. That notion never approached command of his actions. He only stared at the deep, rich, lush green forest of her eyes, and in them, realized a new definition of "Home". He lost himself in that stare, until she shut her eyes, tilted her head slightly, as if posed just so by a portrait painter, and leaned in and kissed him. She hung her hands on his waist and he held firmly to her shoulders.

If her eyes are to be compared to his home, in the blindness of his closed eyes, her lips were like a plush and comfortable chair within that home, richly upholstered, and more soothing than thrilling. The kiss was very different from their first. Through the silent embrace of their lips, they both imagined their lives together. There was a comfortable and unspeakable rightness to the engagement, and the kiss imitated that sensation. Through it, they expressed to each other their absolute unity in all matters of life.

As if controlled by the same master hand, they released the kiss together and pulled away, still holding to each other as they had. Anna looked down and saw the crumpled letter on the ground. She looked up to him and raised her eyebrows, as if to ask permission to read it. He smiled and nodded slightly. Anna bent down and picked up the letter. She unfolded its disfigured form carefully, handling it like it was as fragile as it was precious to her. She opened it fully and read the words. They were not at all the words Jost spoke on his knees. They were eloquent and heart-felt, but infinitely distant compared to his spoken proposal. They did not ride on a voice faltering by excessive emotion. They did not giggle or cry or pause to regain their composure. Jost's spoken proposal was honest and vulnerable, and expressive beyond anything the written word could ever reach.

Anna folded the letter and tucked it into her dress, regarding it as a relic of their old relationship. A new openness was born that day between them, and a new identity, one which made their spirits indistinguishable from one another. The letter had been written by a man who no longer existed. Anna took the new Jost by the hand and walked with him back to town. During the walk they both spoke freely, in a conversation that was charged with love and hope. Sentiments, much more real and raw than anything his hand had ever written, sprang forth from his tongue readily and without delay.

They walked through Kleinostheim on the return to her house, resplendently reflecting what was inside of them to each person they passed. They were the portrait of unity. It was not from their held hands, nor from how tightly their shoulders pressed against each other. It was not their pace of travel or their lightness of step that made passers-by congratulate them. It was the depth and fire of their conversation, focused entirely on each other, and the glow of two faces that would soon have the pleasure of the other's constant company.

Chapter Nine:
Anna Koob

IT WAS NOT A LONG ENGAGEMENT. Jost had nothing to prove and nothing he needed to gain before marrying. Although he was an apprentice with a miserly stipend, he was to inherit his father's estate and businesses. He was industrious and well-respected. Most importantly, Anna's parents already loved him. They knew that four, maybe five men in the world would be well-suited for their daughter, and they counted among their blessings the great fortune that one of them would come to Kleinostheim and fall in love with Anna.

There were no guests coming from outside of Aschaffenburg County, and therefore no reason to delay the wedding. Michel planned a wedding to take place in four weeks. Those four weeks were not spent as they were intended. Just four days into the engagement, Jost's father died. Jost had not yet told him of his bride-to-be, which was just as well. Anna was no baron's daughter, and would do nothing to elevate the family into the ranks of titled nobility. He would have seen it as a step backward, toward the impoverished and obscure roots of the family's distant past.

Jost's mother went to Grossostheim, a village south of Stockstadt, to live with her sister's family. Jost delivered invitations to his wedding there, just five days after his father was buried. To Jost, Kleinostheim was home. It was where the brightest moments of his life occurred, and where the brightest people lived. He extended his father's business to Kleinostheim and sold the family home in Stockstadt. A full week before the wedding, he broke his apprenticeship with Johann — that fruitless arrangement designed by the ambitions of a deceased father. He bought a nice but humble home on the outer edge of Kleinostheim. He maintained the sixty acres outside of Stockstadt, and was well-equipped, despite his exposure to Johann, to manage it with innovation and industry.

Anna hardly saw Jost during their engagement. He put eighteen hours a day into the transition of the estate and the purchase of their new home. Miraculously, he nearly accomplished it fully by the day of the wedding. During that time, Jost wrote to Anna twice a day, but he did not have the letters sent to her. In the few moments he had with her, he delivered them by hand and spoke their written sentiments in much more lengthy and exhilarated terms than what the paper held. Their separation had no power to revert him to his previous self and return to Anna the old frustration his proposal had finally shattered.

The wedding day could not have been better chosen. It was unseasonably warm and successful harvest celebrations were in full swing. Every villager whose day had ever been brightened by Anna's laughter was in attendance. There was little distant family and no peripheral acquaintances. The ceremony took place in Saint Lawrence's Church, not nearly large enough for the horde of attendees. The ceremony adhered strictly to the rules of the Church. It was stiff, awkward, and utterly unbefitting the couple involved.

Afterward, a reception took place north of the village, where all could join the celebration. A long table was set at the exact spot where Margarethe had set the picnic blanket on that August day, on the Feast of the Assumption of Mary. The scene was much like any outdoor festival. There was a delightful chaos about, with children playing unchecked by parental guidance, and the constant high clamor of happy people in spirited conversation. Anna and Jost remained tightly in each other's grip, with Michel and Margarethe attached closely to them like a dangling appendage. There was no organized band of musicians, but instruments were brought and instruments were played. It came together as if quite orchestrated.

Michel whistled loudly and drew the silent attention of all. Jost had prepared his own vows, outside of the rigid confines of Church proceedings. With the whistle, all eyes went to Michel, until he gestured to Jost. Jost turned square to Anna and held her hands in his palms. He cleared his throat loudly and spoke.

"The Lord has granted, in accordance with my liveliest desires and most passionately pleaded prayers, that for the rest of my life I may spend the bulk of my days and whole of my nights with his loveliest creation. Before you gifted me your affection, I crept feebly through life, with no idea of how weak and unstable I was, with nothing truly divine to hold in comparison against the condition of my life. With your hands in mine, I feel the full Host of Heaven's Angels at my back. I see the goodness of God in the bright green of your eyes and know that this is the closest I will come to the Lord until my body is at its final rest and my spirit stands in his hands."

Jost wanted to say more, but he began to cry, choking his words from his throat. A few more unintelligible syllables pushed from his seizing chest and burst through his quivering lips. Nothing more needed to be said. Anna engulfed him in her arms and a concert of sympathetic admiration erupted from the crowd of attendees.

They danced, and they spoke some more. They mingled freely through the crowd of friends and neighbors. Jost received many compliments for the sincerity and eloquence of his vows. Anna, too, spoke from the heart in terms no less romantically eloquent than Jost. But she had long been certain of gaining golden opinions from the faces at the wedding. Such attention, such authentic admiration, was a new sensation for Jost. He smiled, nodded, and bowed more times than he could count.

Not all opinions are held with equal weight. Near the end of the celebration, Margarethe and Michel faced the young couple with dewy eyes. Margarethe placed her palm on Jost's cheek, leaned into him, and lightly kissed his other cheek. She stepped aside and made room for her husband. Michel stared at Jost for a full minute before pulling him in for a strong embrace. It was Jost's words he thought of while holding his son-in-law. "I feel the full Host of Heaven's Angels at my back. I see the goodness of God in the bright green of your eyes." These were the words that echoed through Michel's head. He knew that Jost alone, among all of the people who knew and loved Anna, saw her as he and Margarethe did — handled by the Angels, with one foot still in the Heavens.

After all that was communicated through the tight embrace, Michel pulled away and flattered Jost with joyful compliments. No gift could have been more valuable to Jost than praise from one whose praise is such an honor to receive. Michel was no idle flatterer. Jost set to memory every word spoken to him by Michel that day. He wrote them down in his private journal and treasured them for the rest of his life.

The party at the forest's edge ended shortly before sundown. It had been the perfect representation of the couple it celebrated. It was not regal, certainly more rustic than Jost's father had planned for his son. There were no airs, but a quaint charm about the scene. Conversations were light and not entirely unlike those things Anna recited to Maria Echter many years earlier. Children played loud and raucous until they fell asleep in their parent's arms, where conversations flowed easily over their sleeping scalps.

It wound down naturally. The crowd escorted the newlyweds from the celebration to their new home, losing a family here and a couple there until only Michel and Margarethe remained with them as they arrived at the door of the home. It was a very nice home, grander than the Schwarz house.

After kisses and hugs were given, Margarethe told her daughter, "Good night, Anna Koob."

It was both torturous and delightful to say. Michel and Margarethe stood outside of Anna and Jost's closed door for a few minutes and held each other. They walked slowly back home, in the dark, laughing and crying, hardly able to tell one from the other.

Anna had long been a partner in the Schwarz household. Being the matriarch of her own household was not a strenuous transition. On the wedding night, she led Jost in their prayers, but to her delight, he led the discussion. They talked until dawn knocked on the underside of the horizon, then they went to bed.

She had no idea what was expected of her in her wedding bed. She was nervous. It showed through chills that waved across her body. Fear, anxiety, these were not the sensations Jost wanted dominating their new home on their wedding night. He kissed her on the cheek and asked if he could just hold her. She consented and *that* is how they spent their wedding night, in an embrace that was both tight and tender, loving and respectful, without fear and without expectations. In short, it was as a wedding night should be — prescriptive of the marriage that followed.

Chapter Ten:

An Exotic New Friend

JOST'S NEW BUSINESS VENTURES received little of their due attention for the first few weeks after the wedding. He and Anna did not travel. They did not dine in fancy restaurants or visit distant locations. They began their marriage as their relationship began, with long walks in the forest and along the river, with deep discussions on vast and varied topics, but most importantly, they began their marriage together, with each spending hardly a moment outside of the view of the other.

Jost wanted to give Anna the world, to supplement her extensive studies with some first-hand experiences. Travel beyond Aschaffenburg County was not feasible. So he provided her what he could. Jost used his business connections to order Anna some exotic goods. Four months after the wedding, the gifts began to arrive. Fabric from Hungary, spices from Spain, and trinkets from as far as Russia arrived at their new home. It was all much more than she needed, and she told him so. Still, she treasured the gifts, and they sent her eyes to the books and maps, and her imagination to the ends of the world.

Brighter than the Flames

The final gift came in the early summer of 1584. It was a selection of Turkish herbs and a book of recipes and remedies. It was delivered by a man traveling with his wife. Anna and Jost welcomed the travelers into their home. They were not deep into conversation when they realized that the wife, a woman named Miray, was the true expert in the field. She dominated the discussions, showing Anna the recipes and providing precise instructions on preparation and storage. Safet, her husband, seemed proud of his wife's knowledge and was pleased to rest back, sip the wine that was served, and allow Miray to instruct.

It all fascinated Anna. Included in the recipes were not only culinary uses for the herbs and spices, but medicinal uses. Miray turned to the last pages of the book and showed Anna recipes for tonics and elixirs against a number of common ailments, from headaches and nausea to anxiety. Anna found a friend in Miray. While Jost and Safet spoke lightly on those peripheral topics one uses to kill time with a distant acquaintance, Anna and Miray dove quickly into much more academic subjects and a much more intimate friendship. Miray was clearly well-read and had a sharper wit than her husband. Safet knew this and he contented himself comfortably with the fact. He clearly adored his wife and respected her vast knowledge, yielding to her on virtually all subjects.

Miray and Safet spent five days in Kleinostheim, staying with Jost and Anna. Safet was dark-complexioned. His German was rough. He had a thick accent. And he was familiar enough with local prejudices to avoid conspicuous appearances. Miray was a different specimen entirely. Her German was exquisite. She kept none of the remnants of her native tongue branded into her German that is seen in most foreigners. Aside from her complexion, which was much paler than Safet and not so very out of place, an inside knowledge of her history was all that would indicate to her company that she was not raised along the Main

River, and nobody within the sphere of this story had such knowledge, except for Anna, Jost, and Safet. Miray felt free to wander the village and countryside, and wander she did. She accompanied Anna on walks, drawing few second glances, and no more suspicion than would be turned toward any unfamiliar face.

After the five days, Miray and Safet were on their way. Jost paid Safet for the herbs. The book was Miray's to dispose of as she wished. She gifted it to Anna without charge. Miray had seen an uncommon portion of the world. But she had met no other woman quite like Anna, as filled with knowledge, and as free of tongue as she was of thought. Anna begged her to visit if they ever found themselves along the Main River. Miray said that it was unlikely they would be that way again soon. Safet gave Jost and Anna a blessing in his own language. Jost returned with a prayer of safe travels, and Miray and Safet were gone from their lives as quickly as they had entered.

Anna tinkered with the culinary recipes, but they were not what interested her. She had always been a healer. She had not forgotten Maria Echter and the service she provided to her "friend from the fountain", a service provided in similar fashion to many whom she knew. The medicinal recipes intrigued Anna in the extreme. During her walks with Miray, her exotic new friend hinted at a much deeper knowledge. Anna wished to have what Miray had, to know what she knew. Anna mixed the medicinal recipes and stored them until they might be needed. But her new knowledge alloyed with her intense compassion and her nurturing nature to spawn in her a strong desire to heal.

Anna's first opportunity to employ her new skills came just a few weeks after Miray and Safet left. A neighbor came down with a fever. It was not life-threatening, but the sick man's wife appealed to Anna to visit. Anna came with more than stories about neighborhood cats. There was nothing in her book for fevers, so she blended the recipes in a way she thought might calm them, intending it more for the nervous wife than the sick husband. She visited. She talked and laughed with them, bringing lightness to the household in her usual manner. She also served a tea from her foreign herbs.

Within a day, the man's fever had broken and his strength had returned. Anna did not know what, if any effect came from the tea. He hadn't been very sick and a rapid recovery was far from miraculous. Jost told Anna that it was most likely his lifted spirits that had improved the man. Still, the success only increased Anna's craving to expand her knowledge. She appealed to Michel to find her books of medicinal recipes. It was not exactly the sort of high-academia Michel was used to peddling. But he promised to look.

Anna regretted letting go of Miray so soon, and she regretted every moment of silence between them that could have been filled with information. That autumn and winter brought Jost much to occupy his days. The estate was expanding and business was good. He built more cottages on his land and tended responsibly to his tenants. He was much on the road and Anna supplemented her usual studies with experiments. She took every opportunity to buy more and different herbs and spices. She used the few recipes she had as a base of understanding to be expanded outward. Jost returned home each day to a new concoction for him to try. Some provided, in slight degree, the outcome Anna intended. Some were unpalatable, and some were nauseating. In each case, Jost was happy to partake. They debated the effects. They noted the successes, and they laughed at the failures.

Like everything else in their lives, Anna's new interest became a point of bonding between them. She began to cultivate some of the herbs herself, and although Jost embraced it and involved himself in her interests as much as he could, Anna never forgot how it began. She thought regularly of Miray and wondered where in the wide world her friend could be, who she had met, and how she and Safet fared in their travels. Those thoughts were happy and hopeful. Anna believed deeply that she and Miray had not taken their last long walk together.

Chapter Eleven:
The Happy Tonic

ANNA AND JOST SPOKE OCCASIONALLY about having children. They were both young and content to simply live and love and leave the rest in the hands of God. Anna's interest in herbology grew steadily. The Main River was a major trading route, and Anna went often into Aschaffenburg, where she lingered around the riverside tradesmen with an eye wide open for new ingredients for her herbal concoctions. As her knowledge grew, she took her search into the local forests, departing for her walks with an empty basket and returning with straining arms. By the time she was twenty years old, the majority of her recipes were written in her own handwriting.

It was not a business. It was never intended to be. Anna sold nothing she gathered, nothing she bought, and nothing she mixed. She shared freely, and used her remedies as a reason to gather with friends and family. It was not a vocation of hers. Although she believed in the effectiveness of her remedies, she knew they were not miraculous. The medicinal effects were minor. This was a hobby, a fascination that took its humble place among her many interests. That changed when Margarethe became ill.

Fear has a way of exaggerating our faith in things that our reason denies. Margarethe's illness began with physical weakness and the unpredictable loss of random memories. They believed that Anna's company and an occasional cup of one of her teas would set Margarethe right. Weakness became excessive sleep, and memory loss became general confusion. Margarethe lost sight in one eye, followed by total blindness the next day. When hope in her recovery went paper-thin, when loving talk fell on confused or unconscious ears, Anna's lightness of spirit had little to offer. She turned heavily to her recipes. The greater part of her knew the futility of her efforts, but it was shushed and humbled by swelling fear. Every moment Anna was not at her mother's side, she was mixing herbs and natural remedies that were fruitlessly administered to a dying woman.

Anna was not alone in her desperation. Michel, a man of liberal thought and high reason, turned to superstition. Margarethe had a day of gentler decline. For the next two days, Michel wore the same shirt he wore that day. When his wife took a bad turn, Michel avoided placing his feet exactly where he had walked or sitting exactly as he had sat when she suffered most. A part of him cursed himself for yielding to such feeble thoughts, but he could not help himself. Margarethe's sudden illness and rapid decline made no sense to him. He looked for something to blame, anything or anyone. His mind went so very far beyond his reason, and well past the boundaries of his faith. Hatred rose in him against many things and people, distant and near, to which no real fault could ever be attached. It is not from moments of despair that human opinions should carry weight — I will set that aside for now. Sadly, there will be occasion to write more of it before this story ends.

Margarethe's death brought despair to the family at a magnitude none of them could have imagined. Jost had mourned the loss of his father just a few years earlier. But

Margarethe's death struck him with a level of grief he had never known. Michel was broken. Anna and Jost tried to hold his pieces together while tending to their own shattered spirits. Anna turned more industriously to her hobby. She made an herbal drink she had been perfecting for many months. She called it the Happy Tonic. It could not save Margarethe or bring her back from the dead. But when served to Michel, Jost, and herself, it soothed the edge off of the emotional trauma and slowly transformed silent sobs into tender reminiscing. Biting internal guilt turned into sad but endearing storytelling, even laughter. It helped allow them to not only mourn Margarethe, but to honor her as she would wish her family to honor her.

At last Anna's skills could be bent toward her own healing, and not just that of others. In the wake of her mother's death, Anna committed what remained of her mental clarity to her recipes, foregoing all other study. She also committed more of herself to her neighbors. Having experienced true grief for the first time, her compassionate heart reached all the more sympathetically to those who grieved around her. Much like in her younger years, she was again beckoned to the homes of the sad and the ill, bringing more words and caresses than herbal concoctions — and reviving a reputation that had just gone dormant. She was extremely raw of spirit. Mundane emotions stung her excessively. She gained a great deal of practice in nurturing, as she adopted her kind mother as her unofficial patron saint, and assumed Margarethe's position as the keeper of the family faith. In the following weeks, she made the full transition from the naivety of her youth to a woman of strong maternal instincts.

As the weeks rolled on, in tending to her father's and husband's needs, and those of every aching soul she encountered, Anna experienced an expansion of character like very few in her species are capable of. Her spirit and her mind grew hand-in-hand. Her spiritual deepening coincided with industrious study. Michel was lonely and Anna whiled away his hours in *his* world, in the world of books and academia. During the day, she studied with her father. In the evening, she taught her husband all that she had learned. She set many new quotations to memory, particularly those that reminded her of her mother, those that could be dropped into casual talk and bolster the faith of her loved ones. She brought many books home to Jost, so many that he built her a massive set of shelves. On it she kept her books, her recipes, and her entire store of ingredients.

Over the course of the year, Anna's collection grew. She experimented with the medicinal effects of her herbs, with many successes. But still, the administering of her craft remained a centerpiece for conversation and for the real medicine she had to offer — her light and loving company. But her lightness had a new depth that gave it a potency never experienced by Maria Echter.

Anna reached the shallow limits of herbal usefulness and mixed her tonics more for flavor than for any narcotic effect. Even the Happy Tonic recipe found a steady home at the bottom of seldom touched books and papers.

Anna prayed often to her mother. She prayed for a family of her own, and for a chance to be that which she thought most noble in the world — a mother.

In June of 1586, Anna was pregnant. The news came as Michel, Jost, and Anna were still struggling to walk through the mire of loss after Margarethe's death. They all believed the baby to be an answer to Margarethe's heavenly whispers in God's ear. It lifted them from depression and gave their thoughts of Margarethe a brighter hue. Four months into the pregnancy, Anna began to cramp and bleed. One week later, the baby was lost. They mourned for the baby. Of course they did. But they mourned for Margarethe all over again. Anna felt that the child was as much her mother's as hers. The pregnancy kept Margarethe alive in her heart and in her belly. The loss of the baby tore her mother from her a second time.

In September, Anna was pregnant again. Her joy in the pregnancy, her ambitions for the child and for herself as a mother, were muted by her experience in the summer. In early November, she began to cramp and bleed again, just as before. Jost tried to calm her, to convince her that this time was different and the baby would be born to them. His fears were as deep as hers and he did not hide them well. Anna slept little, waiting. expecting to lose the child at every hour.

It was an uncommonly warm autumn, with an abundant yield of local crops. The festivals were boisterous and trade along the river was active. The nights felt like late summer nights and the mornings warmed quickly. Just after dawn, following a fretful night for Anna and Jost, a visitor knocked on the door. It was Miray. It was only Miray. Safet was not with her. Jost welcomed her into the house, where a pall of fret and anxiety hung with undeniable weight. Miray seemed like a different woman entirely from the one who had walked away from them with her husband two years earlier.

The concerns of the Koob household paused, stopped in their tracks by anguish in the face of their guest. Miray hurried through the opened door and cut quickly around the corner where she could not be seen from the outside. Jost shut the door quickly in subconscious cooperation.

"Is Anna home?" she demanded of Jost.

Jost was underslept. In a fog he stuttered in response, "She…, she is still in bed."

Miray tore her attention from Jost and went directly to the bedroom. Anna had hardly changed positions since early the previous morning. But she startled quickly to attention when Miray entered the room.

Contemplating no reason to avoid the question, Anna asked quickly, "Where is Safet?"

Anna sat at the end of her bed and Miray's knees buckled beneath her. She dropped to Anna's feet, held to both of her ankles, and cried.

"For heaven's sake, my friend," Anna pleaded, "what has happened? Where is your husband?"

Miray did not answer directly, but she gathered herself enough to straighten erectly on her knees and speak, "I was once a woman of consequence in my native land, with friends and fortune. Then I was in exile, but exile in the company of my true love was no punishment. Now he is gone and no place in the world feels like home."

The speech was far from a vivid account of her circumstances. It gave Anna, and Jost who stood silently in the bedroom doorway, just enough information to send their imagination into a frenzy. The back of Anna's throat filled with an abundance of questions more bountiful than the autumn harvest. But her tongue held still, not sure how to balance her curiosity with the needs of her guest.

She snapped her thoughts from the enigmatic and answered, "You have friends *here*."

Miray sat back on her heels, leaning slightly from Anna as she asked, "Do I? I have seen the faces of your neighbors."

Anna's expression went stern and she leaned toward Miray to make up the lost space between them, as she answered, "You have friends within *these* walls, and while you are in my house, mine is the only opinion that matters..., mine and Jost's."

Anna gestured to Jost in the doorway. Miray followed with her eyes. Jost nodded in agreement with his wife. He spoke nothing. He didn't need to. His smile was broad and warm, and abounding with authentic friendship. Jost's validation of Anna's profession drew all of Miray's strength with her next exhale. She turned toward Jost and sank at his feet. Her features, which in their previous encounter had been so bold, so strong and confident, lay delicate and fragile at his feet. They expressed her despair clearly, inflaming the compassion of Jost and Anna.

Each tremble of this previously free and stout woman spurred their interests more warmly in her favor. Anna bounced from the bed with more energy than had pulsed through her body in a week. She and Jost hunched over their friend like two parts of a single turtle shell. Miray was covered. She was warm and protected, and she let loose an untethered cry that appeared to have spent a long time waiting to be set free.

When Miray's sobbing subsided, Anna and Jost helped her to her feet. They did not pry for answers. She was too fragile for such a brutish approach. They assisted her to the table, where she sat opposite of Jost, while Anna pulled from the depths of her papers the recipe for her Happy Tonic. The primary ingredient was an herbal liquor, an elixir distilled at a nearby monastery, with some local and some foreign additions of her own that Anna had on her shelves. She had barely enough of the liquor remaining to make three servings. She mixed it all as quickly and accurately as possible. Within a few minutes, she was seated beside her husband, putting back into employment her favorite recipe.

Jost broke bread to accompany the drink. They ate, drank, and talked. Miray told them that she and Safet had been as far as the North Sea, happy, free, and most importantly, together. They had a large store of spices they were selling to a small community. One customer was dissatisfied, either with the price or the product, or the foreign voice and foreign face of the salesman. Safet was accused of something unholy. Miray never understood the charges. She understood what mattered. Safet was taken from her and put on trial. She never learned the outcome of the trial. She had no chance to. She was escorted out of town and told never to return.

She had no product to sell. She had very little money. She had no husband. She thought immediately of her only friends on the continent. She made her way to Kleinostheim, having never before been on her own. She feared for her husband's life. She feared for her own life. For the first time, she saw suspicion behind every pair of eyes that beheld her, as she worked her way from town to town. But there, at the Koob table, there was no suspicion. There was only rich compassion, pouring upon her in excess. By the time the bread was fully consumed, and the Happy Tonic well into their blood, the three of them were discussing Miray's circumstances calmly.

Anna did as she had always done. She spoke of lighter things, and of hope. She drew from Miray's lips hopeful, encouraging thoughts that had been locked in a dungeon of fear and hopelessness until set free by Anna. Miray was calmed enough to inquire about the lives of her hosts. Jost dropped his head, unsure of how to speak of their misfortunes in light of Miray's circumstances. He looked to Anna, hoping she would have the strength to tell their friend about what they had lost and what they feared to lose again.

When he caught Anna's face, it bore none of his darkness. Anna's face was bright, even delighted. A tear came to her eye as she rubbed her belly.

"I feel no cramping!" she exclaimed too loudly for the proximity of her audience, "In fact, I feel good. I feel that the baby is good."

At the mention of the baby, Miray stood and walked around the table to embrace Anna and place her palm on Anna's belly. The Happy Tonic may have softened the sharpened edge of anguish, but it was the company of friendship that raised hope, and it was raised hope that further tightened the friendship. The conversation turned entirely around the affairs of Anna and Jost. It was good for Miray to focus on the good fortune of her friends for a while. Anna and Jost told her of their lost pregnancy and of the repeating symptoms that had them in such fear until that morning.

"You have been cramping constantly for a full week?" Miray asked Anna.

"Yes, until just now, until Jost looked at me and I thought about my belly."

Miray looked at her empty glass and asked, "What is in this tonic of yours?"

"It is not the tonic," Jost returned quickly to Anna, "It is your healing compassion, my love. You turned your thoughts to the welfare of another, as you always have. And in healing Miray…"

Jost was not sure how to finish the sentence, how to explain the phenomenon of his wife's healing spirit. He had no need to elaborate. His point was made, and both women agreed with him.

Miray remained with them, never leaving the house, never nearing the door or windows. Anna remained attached to her, so Anna, too, remained indoors. Jost used his business connections to inquire about Safet, but no word on the trial or outcome reached them. On the sixth day, Anna invited Miray for a walk through the forest. She insisted upon it. The two women snuck into the forest before the village awoke.

Chapter Twelve:
Miray and Safet

ANNA KNEW THE PATHS OF THE FOREST and could have walked them blindfolded. She had no problem navigating through the dimness of the infant day. She led her friend deep into the woods, into a section of the forest that had known few human feet other than hers. To that point, their relationship saw newness and excitement, absence and intrigue, fear and protection. It had not known intimate honesty. Anna and Jost never asked of Miray and Safet's background, or why they traveled the Main River, so far from their home. Previous circumstances had not demanded such intimacy. Now, Anna found herself harboring a woman who had been banished from another town, a woman whose husband was accused and arrested.

She trusted in the goodness of her friend, which she saw plainly from first glance. But to protect her, to defend her, and to keep her in her home, she must know the whole story. Under the seclusion of dense forest, they settled to sit against the trees. They stared at each other quietly as even the noises of nature seemed hesitant to speak. They each had so much to say to the other, and so much to ask.

Their words hid at the base of their throats. Miray knew that an honest recital of her history was due.

When Anna finally opened her mouth and a partial syllable broke the air, Miray shouted in interruption, "I know! You have questions and I owe you answers. Prepare yourself my friend. Mine is a story of great elation and of deep and sticky sorrow. What I tell you has been shared with none but my husband. But you are all the family I have now, you and your dear Jost."

Anna shifted from a position suitable for a quick rest during a walk to one that awaited the telling of a long story, signifying to Miray that her mind and heart were open. Anna was ready to hear whatever Miray wished to share. Despite knowing that she would not be judged or ridiculed by her intimate company, Miray began to shake. She shook in apprehension, but she also shook in remembrance, as she licked her lips damp and prepared them to share a hundred stories of the sweetest and most rancid moments of her young life.

Miray was born to a respectable Turkish merchant family. Her ancestors raised themselves by buying and selling goods that traveled the Silk Road. They dealt in silks and perfumes, cinnamon and ginger, and exotic teas from India and the Far East, selling to Europeans who were willing to pay a middle-man rather than traveling beyond Turkey. Their ancestral town became a hub of international trade, and like many families, they took advantage.

When the land routes dried up and tradesmen took to the seas, Miray's family led the way. Over the generations they developed a merchant fleet that grew to eight ships by the time Miray's father controlled the family. In his younger years, her father was adventurous, preferring to travel with his ships. Miray was his last child, with a space of eleven years between her and her nearest sibling. With the father so often away, Miray's mother ran the household and all local and immediate affairs of business.

As soon as Baby Miray left her mother's breast, she joined her father on the seas. She was more often on board than at home and her father was the only family she knew well. Her only friends were salty sailors and red-blooded dock workers. It was the only way she knew and the only way she would have it. By the time she was ten years old, she captained alongside her father. She knew the maps. She knew the shipping lanes. She knew the ports and she knew who could be trusted. Her father was her entire life, and his entire life was her.

One summer when Miray was thirteen, the ships docked at a different port, one unknown to her. They were on an island southeast of Thailand. She had seen countless dozens of ports, but this one was different, not for the docks themselves or the dockworkers, not for the shops, the cuisine, or the accommodations. The difference was in her father's mood. He was excited but apprehensive. Among it all, Miray sensed her father's fear most profoundly. In the middle of their first night on the island, her father grabbed her from bed and carried her in frantic haste to the ships, though he was not a large man. They left behind all that they had brought ashore.

There was terror in her father's eyes. As Miray told this part of the story to Anna, she unknowingly mimicked that vivid memory, striking her father's expression identically. Her cheeks shook and sweat appeared on her brow. Anna moved to her, sat beside her, placed an arm around her and calmed her. After regaining her normal rate of breath, Miray continued her story.

The ships left the dock without the necessary provisions for the journey. Rations were paltry while they sailed and supplies were entirely exhausted by the time they returned to Turkey. There were many ports on the journey home that could have suited them up well. But Miray's father would not stop. The brave adventurer was struck to the bone with terror by something that occurred the night they left so suddenly. He never spoke of it, not to Miray, not to his wife, not to anyone. From that moment onward, he was a broken man. Nothing of the father she loved and depended on existed inside of the shell left behind. He gave up his business, sold his ships, yielded his place at the markets, and contented himself with the wealth he and his ancestors had already amassed.

Miray's father was opposed to any and all adventure. His older children were all well beyond his control by the time the mystery terror transformed him. But Miray was not. She had grown up on ships. All she knew was travel. But after returning home at thirteen years old, she became a prisoner in her bedroom. Her father was paranoid and forbade his daughter to walk beyond the gardens of their home. It was in that condition that she remained until she was seventeen. She missed the ships. She missed the waves and the crusty sailors, the exotic docks, different foreign accents at every stop, strange and delightful cuisine. She missed the life that was contentedly hers until ripped away from her with such violent and abrupt force.

When Miray was seventeen, her father arranged her marriage to a neighboring family. The family did not have their wealth or connections. Her arranged husband had no prospects for advancement. He was the curator of a library, a man with a decent reputation, known to be kind and honest. But he was no adventurer. He had never left the region, and at forty-seven years old, likely never would. Miray was in the house, but she was not home, and her prescribed future boasted no large, sparkling white sails. She saw that everything her father did since that fateful night was done out of fear — some fear he would not share. The arranged marriage certainly had the same motivations.

One month before the wedding, Miray ran from her home to the docks. It was the first time in four years she had seen the water. It called to her. It was there, on that day, that she met Safet. He, too, was a tradesman, but a low-level, second-rate catchpenny with less than scrupulous business practices. Ah, but she was drawn to him. His eyes shone with an impetuous fire of adventure. His smile melted her heart. In his eyes, she saw her father, before he was broken. In his voice and manner she saw the many sailors she had grown to adore. In every facet, he reminded her of her best years.

Safet regaled her with tales of his time at sea. She astonished him with vivid stories that made his sound like schoolboy anecdotes in comparison. She maintained all of her knowledge of shipping and trade. She knew the names of important people in dozens of port cities across Africa and Asia. He was impressed and enthralled, and she was enlivened by their conversation in ways she had not felt in years. When evening began to fall, she found it difficult to peel herself from him and return to her house, where a heavy blanket of suspicion and dread pushed down against any and all brighter thoughts.

Her future was sealed the following morning. She knew that one more visit to the docks to see Safet would destroy her ability to swallow the future fed to her by her father. Despite the previous night's scolding, she ran from her house again and sought the young man with the adventurous eyes.

"I knew more than Safet," Miray explained to Anna, "I knew more than any of them, and I knew I could succeed, as my father had. But I was a woman, a young woman, and my knowledge and skills could not outweigh that one nullifying factor."

Anna pretended to understand. But the truth is, she did not. If anything, Anna was given more liberties than her brothers, and an equal portion of her own household control with a fair, adoring, and liberal-minded husband.

Miray put her head on Anna's shoulder and asked, "What was I to do?" When no answer came she continued,

"He fell in love with me, Safet, in that first encounter, he fell in love with me."

Miray went back to the docks that next morning. Safet was there, looking, darting his eyes in every direction like a lost child. With a glance, she knew what he sought. He seemed to glow when his eyes caught her. She accompanied him as he dealt in his business of the day. She did not simply hang from his pocket like a pretty accessory. She spoke when her words could benefit him. Her scrutiny proved prudent, and prudence was not his strongest attribute. She was also more scrupulous and steered him away from unsavory deals.

At the end of the day, Safet had acquired a commodity in bulk that he wished to sell overseas. He was already very attached to her and saw plainly how her skills could benefit his business. He invited her to travel with him. Miray broke down and sobbed at his feet. As he tried to comfort her, she told him her story. He learned of her adventurous childhood, of the mysterious night that changed her life so drastically, and of her arranged marriage. He asked her if she wanted to marry the curator.

Miray cried as she relayed this part of the story to Anna, "I told him, 'What do you think? From what you know of me, what do you think?', and he…"

"*What* did he do?" Anna prodded.

"He said that my betrothed did not know me as he did, and that my father knew me even less."

In two days together, Safet understood her better than anyone else in her life. He saw the capabilities of her mind and the spirited nature of her heart, and he knew as well as she did that her arranged life would bring a final death to the girl who traveled with her father. In a moment of strength, the free strength that had been choked from her by degrees since she was not yet fourteen, she agreed to travel with him. But she warned him that by sailing away with him, she would never again be able to return to her hometown.

There was one thing in her favor. She knew that her father was too frightened to seek after her. He would never board another ship. Once water flowed between her and her family, the connection would be severed forever. They could never go back there, and she made Safet promise that he would never take her back. He was hesitant to make the promise. Although it was not his home, he had business connections there that he was loath to dissolve. He proclaimed that there was no reason to address the issue then, that many miles of ocean sat between them and that decision.

It took eight days for Safet to arrange transport of his goods and passage for two. In that time, Miray told more lies to her family than she had in the seventeen years prior. She went to the docks every day. At home, she showed no signs of schemes or plans beyond her wedding. On the day of departure, Safet was unlike himself. He was nervous, edgy, and abrasive in conversation. She demanded an explanation. He told her that he was being pursued by a previous business acquaintance. He was no longer safe in the city, and he hoped they could lay low and undiscovered until their ship sailed that afternoon.

Safet feared her reaction. He expected her to call it off, return to her father, and marry the curator.

"What did you do?" Anna asked, very thrilled by the exciting turn in the story.

"I smiled at him. You see, neither of us could return. It was a sure sign to me that I was on my right path, that I was supposed to leave with him, or that he was supposed to leave with me."

The smile soothed Safet and he fell more deeply in love. He was not found by those who sought him. The ship departed with Miray, Safet, and a haul of goods that set them on a prosperous path of trade. One month later, they married in Italy. It was only a week after she was set to marry the curator. They owned no ships, no land, no property. They had his excitement and charisma, and her knowledge and shrewdness. And they had a large world to discover together. They sold to buy more, and bought only to sell. They stayed light of possessions, but neither would have had it any other way.

Miray learned languages at an extraordinary rate. Within days she conversed with the locals, mimicking the local accents and dialects. It was her favorite part of her job and it proved priceless to Safet and his dealings. Miray was home again, home among strangers in foreign lands, and alongside sailors on ships she had never boarded. She was home in the arms of a man she had not known long, but one she knew well, sharing an intimacy she had had with nobody since her early years with her father.

Miray cried heavily as she recounted her adventures. Anna cried along with her. Her friend's story struck her as familiar. Although her and Jost's courtship was drawn out and slow with its steps forward, and Miray's was quick and filled with exciting intrigue, there were uncanny similarities between the two romances. Anna listened intently to Miray, but thought heavily of Jost.

Miray continued her story, with many adventures and very few moments of mundane existence. She told of many towns and many salty sailors and unsavory merchants. She told her story to the point when she and Safet fulfilled an order for a wedding present in tiny Kleinostheim, on the Main River.

"That was a wonderful time for us, meeting you and Jost," she reminded Anna, "It was the height of my existence. Safet and I were closer than ever, and we had just met two new friends, two wonderful friends who showed us another way to live. After dining with you," she added with tenderness, "Safet and I began to speak of settling down. You seemed so happy, so in love, and all the adventure you needed was within your own walls."

Anna was honored beyond speech. She and Jost had no idea they had so impacted their new, traveling friends. The tender moment did not last. Miray began to shiver. She continued her story, beginning with the plans she and Safet made to settle in Germany, within easy reach of Anna and Jost.

They continued to trade, and even made trips to Africa. But they focused their attention on Germany, on establishing business ties in a place and in a manner that would facilitate their new domestic plans. It did not go at all as they had planned. As traders, in and out and not long on the eye, they were tolerated. As they slowed down and their faces lingered long enough to be studied and recognized, the troubles for them began. If there was something to be blamed, they were blamed. Where there was something suspicious, they were suspected. Instead of spending hours in a location, they spent weeks, trying to find a place to call home, a place like Kleinostheim, a home like Anna and Jost's. They settled in northern Germany where they made a few friends but many more enemies. They caused no harm to anyone, other than spoiling their neighborhoods with different sounding voices and different looking skin and hair.

One night, soldiers seized Safet from their bed. He was pulled from Miray's arms as she screamed in her native Turkish. They struck her across her face, harder and many more times than was needed to end her protestations. They held her against her own bed until long after Safet had been taken away. They took her to a building where she was eyed suspiciously until dragged to the edge of town and told never to return.

As Miray relayed her tragedy to Anna, she had little breath left to give her words. She sobbed profusely and gasped like a fish out of water. Anna kissed her head and rubbed her shoulders and tried everything within her deep well of talents to soothe her friend. When nothing worked, she wrapped her arms around Miray and squeezed as tightly as she could. Miray's frantic sobs turned slowly to a low, vocalized hum.

"You are with *me* now," Anna reminded her, "You will stay with us until we can figure out what to do next."

In a half-hum, barely parting her lips, Miray turned her face to Anna, nearly touching their noses, and said, "Anna, tell me that I will see my husband again, that we will travel roads and rivers again, that I have not slept my last night in his arms."

Anna dropped her head. She would not lie to her friend.

The morbid truth was evident in the silent dropping of Anna's head, but Miray went on, "I know. You don't need to tell me the truth. I will not make you say it. I know it well already. It haunts my every moment. But Anna, if you tell me I will see him again, I will believe you, and that will add a spark to my dark life."

Anna responded in full sincerity, "You will. You will be with Safet again."

She spoke a spiritual truth, not a temporal lie, and her calm honesty came through in her voice. Miray was satisfied. Her breaths regained normalcy and she stiffened inside of Anna's embrace. In that moment, she loved Anna above all else in her life. She loved her, and she feared for her.

Miray pulled herself from Anna as if frightened of her and said, "I was with Safet and now he is likely dead. Now I am with you and Jost. What will happen to you? When will they take you away, pull you from your bed in the middle of the night? I loved my father. It destroyed him. I loved my husband. It destroyed him. I love you, Anna. I can't...."

Miray continued to speak, but the words were swallowed by gurgling sobs in broken German. In her distress, her flawless local accent failed her and she reverted to her native voice. Anna could make no sense of it. She encased Miray in the same constricting embrace as before, as if trying to embed the overflowing emotions in a glacier deep within her heaving chest. Slowly, it worked, as Anna sang to her in a whisper. When Miray was recovered enough to stand by her own strength, they made directly for the house and closed the shutters. Only when shut up tightly, with no light from the outside, did Miray feel calm enough to sit and properly receive the nurturing attention of her only worldly friends.

Chapter Thirteen:

Incriminating Friendship

ANNA AND JOST QUICKLY REALIZED that Miray was like an infant in their arms. She was completely dependent on them. As intelligent and capable as she was, she could not work the trade circuits as a single woman of foreign background, and she could find no local employment. She had a keen eye and was always alert. She had been more perceptive than her hosts. Anna and Jost began to recognize the suspicious gazes cast upon their home, exactly as Miray told them. Friends and neighbors, business associates, and even Anna's own cousins saw something ungodly in Miray's presence in Kleinostheim. She could not be sent out. She had nowhere to go. She could not go home. She could not even walk the markets of their own county. Jost still went about his business, but with much less frequency. Anna hardly left the house. She remained locked in with her friend, which only served to heighten suspicions.

Anna and Jost were shocked by the sudden turnaround in their neighbors. None of them spoke directly against Miray, at least not to Anna or Jost, and it is possible most of them bore no negative feelings. But Miray was terrified, and Anna encrusted her reclusively. Jost avoided unnecessary contact with friends and clients. There *was* a sudden change in them that was initiated by Miray's arrival. Even their most liberal-minded friends could not deny it. It is natural that rumors, from the most benign to the wretchedly vile, would begin to circulate. It did not rise to general hysteria, but horrible things were spoken and believed.

The pregnancy progressed healthily, but even that joyous news could not be a shared point of celebration with their neighbors. Rumors spread that the baby was placed in Anna with witchcraft — placed there by Miray. Perhaps Anna and Jost took the wrong approach. Perhaps, if they had gone about their lives as before, addressing contention and rumors as they arose, the following pages would have been written very differently. But they remained locked away, and the expectation of many was that the baby, once born, would bring great destruction with it.

Some said that Safet was dead and that Miray resurrected his spirit in the body of the baby, that revenge against the people who killed him, against the people of Germany, was the purpose of the pregnancy. The child inside of Anna was the product of the purest love to grace the region in a hundred years, and of the most devout and faithful prayers to God. That an innocent child brought into being under such righteous circumstances would be viewed with such blind disdain and anticipated with such hateful fear is one of the darkest tragedies of this story. Despite the madness brewing outside of their door, within the Koob home love abounded. It did not matter to any of them that Miray had a different name for God. They prayed together, and the parallels between their religions were illuminated resplendently under the light of their love for one another and their shared faith in God.

The three of them hunkered down for months. As Anna was nearing full term, she grew fatigued. Her complexion went pale, and Jost became concerned for both his wife and his child. She spent too many hours indoors.

She needed air and exercise. Miray demanded that she walk. The necessity of it was agreed upon by Jost and Anna. But with the local hostility toward them, Jost could neither send his pregnant wife from the house alone nor leave Miray alone in the house. Much selfless debate went into the matter. It was decided that Anna must walk and that Jost must walk with her. They left the house as the faintest light of dawn cast almost invisible shadows.

They feared going into the woods, where isolation could present fanatics with a perfect opportunity to act upon their fears. They walked through the village, where there would always be some friend willing to defend them. The walk went calmly. It was a slow walk. Anna carried a large, healthy baby in her belly, and though she felt her strength return in slight degrees with every step, she was still weak and sickly. They encountered a few harsh and suspicious glares, and a few heart-felt greetings. They began to believe that the hysteria would pass and that the baby would be born into the same congenial village that welcomed Anna into the world. That hope was dashed as they returned to the house.

The sun had just barely brought clarity to the scenes surrounding the house, but already there was a crowd of eighteen people surrounding the door and yelling for Miray to come outside. They knew that Anna and Jost were out of the house, and they took their first opportunity to confront Miray and drive her from the village. Anna and Jost approached the crowd from behind.

They were not noticed until Jost yelled, "What are you doing there? Get away from our door!"

His voice cut easily through the clamor, and most of the crowd turned to face them. It was obvious at a glance. These people were not going to be reasoned with, nor would they lean upon old friendships. They had been whipped into a frenzy. Jost was prepared to confront them directly, to match his wits and morality against theirs, using all of the relevant quotations stored in his head. Anna saw the fury in their eyes and knew better. She grabbed Jost tightly by the hand and pulled him through the crowd as quickly as possible, nudging and pushing some aside to make their way. No courtesy was given to Anna for her swollen belly. She was knocked and bumped, and the baby took an elbow from one side and a hip from another before they reached their door. They entered their home with some of the vilest words thrown at them, but little physical resistance.

Miray was not immediately visible. Anna's heart leaped into her throat with the thought that her friend had left. Then they heard a whimper from their bedroom. Miray was seated on the floor against their bed, with both arms wrapped around her head and humming her childlike whimper to drown out the noises from outside. She did not hear Anna and Jost come home. Anna ran to her and took her sharply by the shoulders. Miray kicked at her and screamed something in her native tongue. It took a full ten seconds for her to realize that she was in the company of friends and in no immediate danger.

Once Miray recognized her hosts and friends, she calmed quickly, despite the noise of the lingering ruckus outside. Her fears shifted from her own welfare to that of her anxious and pregnant friend. While Anna calmed and comforted Miray, she wrapped her arms around her belly, as if still protecting the baby from the flailing limbs of the mob. Her distress was obvious and Miray turned readily from victim to comforter. Once Miray was back on her feet, Anna stood tall. Her knees went lame beneath her. Miray supported her under one arm while Jost took the other. They helped Anna to her bed.

Jost remained with Anna, but Miray left in a hurry to the kitchen. Jost and Anna fell asleep to the sounds of rapid and industrious efforts, dishes being moved, spices being ground, and all sorts of kitchen clamor. Jost awoke several hours later, and Miray could still be heard toiling away in the kitchen. He woke Anna and the two of them investigated. They found Miray elbow deep in her efforts.

"Sit, sit, I made something for you, for the baby," Miray instructed.

Anna obeyed and took a seat at the table. The kitchen was a mess. It was not the mess itself but the hours-long effort in creating it that stirred Anna's emotions.

Anna's concern for Miray came out in a scolding tone, as she said, "You had a trying morning, but you haven't rested all day. You've gone through all of my ingredients."

Anna did not care about the ingredients. That is not what she meant, but Miray addressed the charge anyway.

"Yes, well, I am sorry about *that,* but not about spending my hours as I have."

Jost understood what Anna meant and he amended his wife's comment, "We don't care about the spices. You were shaken and you must rest."

Miray paused her frantic preparations and answered, "Rest now, and not give you what I worked so hard to give you?"

With a much calmer air, Miray added the final touches to a tonic and a balm. She shook the tonic in the bottle and handed it to Jost along with a mug. While Jost poured his wife's medicine, Miray coated her hands in the balm, knelt in front of Anna, reached under Anna's dress, and rubbed the balm on her belly. The lingering aches from pushing through the mob melted away. The baby rolled toward the nurturing hands, then settled into stillness. When the tonic was drunk and the belly was tingling from the spicy balm, Miray rubbed the last of the balm into Jost's temples. She wiped her hands, kissed her friends, and went to bed happier and more satisfied than Anna and Jost had seen her since she returned to their lives. She slept through the afternoon, evening, and night.

Stefan Scheuermann

The next morning seemed better somehow — more hopeful, and it was felt by all three of them. The mob outside had long gone back to the details of their individual lives. Anna and Miray remained locked indoors. Jost felt confident enough to leave the house early and tend to some of his neglected business. He returned home very late in the evening, and in a visual state that betrayed something too horrid, too terrifying, to be uttered coherently through his quivering lips.

Jost sat on the floor in a panting panic, while Anna knelt in front of him, grabbed him by the knees, and demanded, "For Heaven's sake, Jost, what has happened?"

He did not immediately reply, but looked to Miray, who stood behind Anna. His eyes locked on her with a frightening mix of pity, fear, and anger. He paid no attention to Anna in front of him until she repeated, "What has happened?"

Jost rubbed his eyes, vigorously at first, but gradually slowing along with his breath. His hands stopped and his breath held for what seemed to Anna and Miray to be too long for a mortal man. Jost drew breath as he uncovered his eyes to lock them on Anna.

He answered their impatience with alarming calmness, "Two young children have grown ill today, one in Mainaschaff and one here in Kleinostheim. Two very different illnesses, two different families, in two different villages. But in their minds, they have connected the two. They watched us all day yesterday. They heard the efforts in the kitchen. And now two children grow ill at the same time. The people have drawn connections where there are none. They think that Miray has made the children ill, an act of revenge for the loss of her husband."

Anna and Miray remained as they were, captivated by horror. They both felt pity for the children and for their families, but fear overwhelmed their pity, and they began to sweat.

Jost added, "It won't be long. They will come for us in an attempt to save the children."

"There is no us," Miray snapped, "They will come for me."

Anna tried to assure her friend that they will face whatever comes together.

Miray wanted no such assurance, and she followed, "You have a baby, an estate and a history here. I have nothing, not here or anywhere. If you stand by me, they will burn us all. I will not repay your friendship in that way. I will leave. Without me, they will have nothing to suspect you of."

Of course, Jost and Anna protested forcefully, but Miray held her ground, declaring, "I have already lost everything. I have nothing left to lose but you. You have everything to lose. The most innocent of lives, your unborn child, will suffer no more from the trouble I have brought into your home."

Jost uttered a few syllables in rebuttal, but the truth was before them. The innocent child within Anna was a consideration not to be taken lightly. And the whole situation had heated so rapidly and furiously that it was bound to consume them all. Despite these blazing truths, Anna and Jost loved Miray. She connected with them both on a level they shared with very few. They had seen her smile and they had seen her suffer. Sending her from their home into an unforgiving world where no place imaginable could truly be called Home was a duty they were unable to perform.

Anna tried to delay, begging her friend, "Just stay with us a few more days, until you have a plan and a place to go."

The sick children were not so very ill. But if they turned for the worse. If the worst would happen, and Miray was still with them when the children died, the retribution on their household would be severe. Miray made that point, and Jost, having witnessed the frenzy first-hand, agreed. Miray had to leave. But the nature of her departure was still in question.

They all slept on the matter that night. In the morning, Jost awoke to an empty space on the bed beside him. Miray awoke to a panicked Jost. Anna had risen early and decided to confront the issue head-on.

"I have ill neighbors," she thought to herself, "I will tend to them as I always have."

Anna did not know the family in Mainaschaff, but she knew the family of the sick child in Kleinostheim. They were Karl and Katherina Horning, and their sick son Peter. She took a vial of a mild mixture, nothing of real medicinal value, but a recipe she had shared with many people over the years. She took it to the Horning house. Karl was not in the home, but Katherina was seated beside the bed of the child when Anna knocked on the door.

Katherina answered the door and Anna could see that she was not in distress. Anna was welcomed into the home by a woman who bore no ill will against her or Miray. The two women talked for a while, then Katherina invited Anna to Peter's room. She had grown up with Anna. She had seen what Anna had been and done for her village. And she welcomed any help Anna could give. Anna was relieved to see that the child was not very ill. She gave the boy a sip from the vial. It tasted good and Anna followed it with a few funny stories that lifted the boy's spirits. She remained in the home for less than an hour and was seen to the door with gratitude and well-wishes.

Anna returned to her home to a worried friend and a missing husband. Jost had gone looking for his wife. When he came home, Anna assured him that all would soon be better. She described her visit to the family and the condition of the child. For the rest of that morning and afternoon, the air of the Koob home was lighter than it had been. Miray spoke of her future with hints of hope behind her words. As the afternoon aged, a knock came to their door. It was an old family friend come to warn them. Peter's illness took a sudden and fatal turn. He died that afternoon, as did the child in Mainaschaff.

There was no more debate. Anna, Jost, and Miray began immediately planning Miray's escape from the region. Jost suggested that he and Anna walk her to the river and secure her travel with some merchant or another, someone not tied intimately to the affairs of Kleinostheim. He insisted that compassion for the unborn baby would keep them from violence until Miray was long from the area and all undue suspicion with her. Anna recounted the mindless shoves and knocks against her belly that she and the baby suffered as they pushed through the mob at their door. She suggested that they wait until the safety of darkness and sneak Miray away while the village slept. No determination was made, but planning and preparations for the departure continued.

Miray went into her room and began to pack up what little belonged to her. Anna and Jost packed food and money, and little valuables that could be easily carried and sold. They were far from content with their care package, but it was all they had to give on such short notice. They packed it all in a sack and took it to Miray's room. Miray was gone. In the bustle of the evening, she had slipped away. The cost of goodbyes would have been debate and delay. The cost of delay could have been the lives of her friends. So, with no care package and nothing of tradable value, Miray snuck away from their lives in an act of self-sacrifice that struck deeply at Anna and Jost's hearts.

There was one quick and fleeting thought of pursuing her, which they abandoned before it took breath. They sat on Miray's bed, held each other, and cried for the dismal fortunes of their only intimate friend. Naively assuming that the danger snuck from their lives with Miray, they went to bed. Exhaustion outweighed despair and they both fell quickly to sleep.

They awoke in the morning to a strange and disdainful atmosphere about their house. A pinch of residual fear from the night before was stirred into melancholy, giving the eerily still home a rancid air for them to breathe. Still, neither spoke a word of Miray or the troubles they had faced. To a fly on the wall, the morning appeared as a lethargic version of any normal day's beginning, the same words and gestures, but with a slowed pace and a weary tone.

Were Jost's wits about him, he would have never considered leaving Anna alone in the house. But he was in a fog, and he went through the preparation for a normal day of business. He walked only fifty paces from his door when he was met with angry zealots. He turned on his heels and walked briskly back to the house. The mob seemed to grow behind him with every stride. They were shouting about dead children and witchcraft, about Miray, and vile, demonic rituals.

Jost did not respond. He only increased his pace as the threats turned mindlessly violent. He made it home and secured himself indoors. The mob began chanting in unison, demanding that they hand Miray over for judgment. Much terrified debate went into the next decision, but Jost met the mob outside of the front door.

They screamed at him, accusing him of no crime beyond allowing his household to be seduced by the Devil. Peter's father, Karl, a tall and portly man, stood first among them. The depth of his despair was authentic and on bold display. His face shook red as he screamed, and more spit than syllables flew from his mouth. Jost screamed several times into the crowd that Miray was no longer with them, that she had left in the night and was long gone from the area. With each repeat, a few more heard and understood, and the mob slowly quieted until all could hear him.

"She is gone!" he repeated, "All that is left in this house is us... Anna, whom you have known since she was born, and the innocent child within her."

Some of the crowd looked around for Miray. Many shouted, demanding to know where she had gone. Some did not believe Jost, and they pushed past him and into the house. They stormed through every room, with no mind for what they broke and displaced. But when they were done, they had to admit the fact that Jost had spoken honestly. Miray was not with them. Had the sick children still lived, the zealous mob may have walked away in hope that Miray's departure might bring them better fortunes. The children did not live. Both had died within an hour of each other the day before, solidifying in their superstitious hearts their theories of diabolically supernatural retribution.

With no Miray to take away, attention turned to Anna. Wild accusations were attached thinly to truths of Anna's distant childhood, and of her more recent fascinations. Karl told the mob that his son was not so ill, and he and his wife were confident in his recovery, until Anna gave the boy a potion. Jost feared the worst and prepared himself to defend his wife to his death. Many in the crowd, who had been just as eager to get their hands on Miray, still held tender sentiments for Anna. They began to speak up in her defense. The posture of the mob softened when the most angry of them realized they were outnumbered, and Anna Koob would not be hauled from her home that day. Disagreements among them grew heated, and fists were thrown in defense of Anna and Jost.

The violence settled and the mob dispersed. As they scattered, some spoke of the wedding and the many other fine memories they shared of Anna. Others spoke of Satanic rituals and the brewing of cursed concoctions in the Koob kitchen. In both cases, the comments were made in retreat. The immediate crisis had been averted, and Anna and Jost shook and cried for hours to come. Other than their faith in God, only one thing could serve to supplement each other's arms in their recovery. Using the very last of the ingredients, Anna mixed a slightly altered and diluted version of her Happy Tonic. They sipped it from the same bowl, and they did not part by more than an arm's length for the rest of the day and following night.

Chapter Fourteen:

Fickle Fortune

JOST AWOKE IN THE NIGHT TO ANNA'S SCREAM. In his sleepy stupor, his mind recalled images of angry mobs. His fists were ready to fly. But the house was still and only his wife shared his roof. Anna screamed again and rolled to her side. The truth struck the expectant father. Anna was in labor. The baby was coming, about to join them in a world that had just become treacherous to them. Jost gave no thought to taking Anna from the house or bringing anyone else in. He cleared away their blankets and prepared to deliver his child from Anna's womb.

Jost was a gifted man, an intelligent man, with knowledge and skills far beyond most people he knew. But he was a stranger in a strange land. He knew nothing of delivering a baby. Panic stirred his thoughts forcefully in his head, preventing him from focusing. Each scream of his darling wife shook him and set him to tremble. Whether Jost was ready, the baby was bursting into their world that night. That was not the thought that pulled Jost together and brought calm attention to his mind. It was Anna who did that. She seized his hand, freezing him in place with a fierce grip. Her hand relaxed when he stopped shaking, but she held to him still, gently, with a soft caress of her thumb.

He looked to her eyes, which seemed deeper than the forest, and she whispered, "I love you."

The moments that followed heard no screams and saw no shaking panic, only the soft and synchronized breathing of a wife and husband who were still united in every facet of their being. Jost leaned to Anna and gave her a tender kiss. He pulled away from her to see a broad smile, which he returned in abundance. The next wave of pains came and Anna screamed again. The scream did not rattle Jost as before, but focused him. His calm instincts instructed him admirably. Within a few more minutes, he held their son in his hands. He severed the cord, wiped clean the baby's head, and set Anna's son to her breast. Jost sat beside them and ran his fingers through Anna's hair.

"Christoph," Anna whispered, staring at the baby.

"Christoph," Jost repeated, still gazing adoringly at his wife.

"Yes," Anna continued, "after our Lord, who has always heard our prayers."

Jost drifted his focus to their son, leaned to him, and kissed his head. He pulled his lips away just enough to repeat, "Christoph," then returned to kissing the baby's head, never withdrawing his fingers from Anna's hair.

Christoph had no horns or tail, no magical powers. He was as fragile and dependent as any newborn. His addition to the household did not return to life the young children who had died. His birth did not bring instant comfort to Karl or the other family members of the lost children. Christoph did not settle the paranoid anger brewing to a boil in Kleinostheim or dispel the danger that faced the Koob household. But he swelled a young couple with an intensity of love and gratitude that pushed their troubles to the background of their thoughts. Fear held there. It was real. It was immediate, and it stuck to them. But it was diminished in proportion. It sat in the shadow of one of history's most dynamic romances, now aggrandized by the addition of their child.

Anna remained in bed until the following evening. Jost stayed beside her when he was not fetching her something she desired. Christoph slept and Christoph cried. He ate and slept some more. That was their first day as a family. Occasionally, people gathered outside of the house. Murmurs were heard, but no shouting. Nobody knocked on the door. The screaming during delivery was undoubtedly heard by neighbors. It was assumed by many that the child was born, yet nobody dared to touch their front door. Whatever congratulations and whatever contention awaited them held its place through the day. But they could not remain locked away forever. The world awaited them with its uncertainty and its contradictions. Hatred and love in both extremes buzzed around the village.

Jost padded an old chest with blankets and dragged it beside their bed. He placed Christoph inside of it with all tenderness befitting his value, and he took his place in bed beside his wife. Anna performed for him that service she had provided to so many others over her few years. She lightened his spirits. Well after Jost slept, Anna remained awake, alternating her attention between the breaths of her husband and her child. They were both precious to her beyond expression. With her eyes fixed to the ceiling above her, she pondered in torment every decision she had made that brought the present peril into their lives. She knew what awaited them outside of their walls, and it haunted her to a level of mortification and melancholy that forbade rest. Yet through her troubled thoughts, she sang. She sang a calm and dulcet lullaby to her husband and her son.

Their troubles were daunting enough before a helpless infant slept beside them. Anna had always been optimistic. It was always *her* spirit that lifted others. But there was no *Anna* for her. Her mother was dead. Her father, still in deep mourning, was kept as distant from their problems as possible, and Jost, dear as he was, did not have Anna's gifts. He was ready to suffer any laceration of body or spirit for Anna and Christoph, and his love and devotion to them both was unquestionable. But he was not a natural bringer of hope. Anna despaired through a long night, at the end of an exhausting day. She prayed and tried to brace herself for struggles, the extremities of which she could not imagine.

In the morning, Anna's long night of dark contemplations tainted the air of the house. It filled Jost's nose the moment he awoke. The heaviness sobered his proud and joyous heart. Even Christoph seemed to perceive what his parents felt. He embraced his second day tentatively. His vivacious cry from the day before was a muffled whimper, as if little Christoph was afraid of stirring the air of Kleinostheim and bringing upon his parents the wrath that still slept that morning. Their faith may have been weak that morning, but their love was as strong as ever and their determination to serve each other was at its height.

Jost waited until the buzz of the village morning settled before venturing out. He went to Michel's house to tell him of the birth of his grandson. Anna wanted to see her father, but she knew that the baby in her arms would be little deterrent against the violence aimed at her. She remained at home with Christoph, but sent Jost with a letter, an effusion of tender sentiments from an adoring daughter.

Jost knocked several times on the door before letting himself in. He found Michel on the floor beside the table. He was breathing but unconscious. Jost lifted him and carried him to his bed. He knew nothing of medical matters. As difficult as it was for him to lay another burden on Anna, he had no choice. He ran home and told her what he knew. Jost took Christoph while Anna gathered any and all ingredients she thought she might need. Anna was still recovering from giving birth, but she ran, with her arms full of bottles and herbs. Jost squeezed Christoph against his chest and kept pace.

The nearest medical doctor was in Aschaffenburg. Jost pounded on the door of Michel's neighbor and begged him to ride as fast as possible for help. The neighbor had no horse, so Jost sent him away on Michel's horse. Inside, Anna tended frantically to her father, mixing herbs at his bedside with one hand while rubbing Michel with the other and begging him to wake up.

Michel awoke, muttered something calmly but unintelligible, and slipped back into unconsciousness. Anna presumed that her father had suffered a heart attack. She mixed a concoction she hoped would help, but had little reason to believe it would. She dripped it onto Michel's lips and rubbed it onto his gums. Michel swallowed, awakened slightly, lifted a half smile, and drifted out again.

About four hours later, the doctor arrived from Aschaffenburg. He was Ludwig Eisert, an old friend of Michel's. Eisert went to work like a man who had much to lose. Jost left the room with Christoph, and Anna remained to assist. By the time the sun was low in the sky, Michel was awake. He was weak and would never regain his strength, but he lived. He wanted to hold his grandson, which he did to wonderful medicinal effect. Christoph cooed to his grandfather and giggled when Michel spoke.

Eisert remained at Michel's house through the night. Anna and Jost went home. Before they did, Michel called Jost into his room. He cleared the room of all but Jost and asked his son-in-law to take over his business.

"I know it is much to ask," Michel told him, "You have so many of your own concerns. But the book business always meant much to Anna. When I am gone, it will be a part of me and of her mother she may hold on to."

Jost knew that the book business could not thrive under his care as it had under Michel. But Eisert made it clear. Michel was lucky to be alive and would never again be healthy enough to travel. Jost accepted. The business was his, come what would of it.

Michel was in capable and friendly hands. Anna gathered what remained of her bottles and herbs. Jost placed Christoph in Michel's arms for a goodnight kiss. They both promised to visit first thing the following morning, and they walked toward home with their newborn son.

They were less than halfway home when they realized they were being followed. They quickened their pace but did not run. Anna stared fixedly ahead of them, but Jost glanced behind them every few steps. As the pursuers drew nearer, Jost recognized them. Karl led four men in the uniforms of Aschaffenburg soldiers. Other members of his family, and the family of the other dead child, followed behind. Jost's heart sank. There was only one reason soldiers would be with them. They came to arrest Anna, to take her away from him as Safet was taken from Miray.

Jost handed Christoph to Anna and told her to run home. Anna dropped her bottles and herbs, took her child, and obeyed her husband. Jost turned to face the angry families.

He tried to speak to Karl, "I am a new father. I understand the pain you must feel, but—"

Karl said nothing. One of the soldiers interrupted Jost, "Move out of the way. We have come for Anna Koob."

"On what charge?" Jost demanded.

"She is accused of murdering two children. She must face the court in Aschaffenburg."

There was nothing Jost could do that would not worsen the situation. But he would not get out of their way. He assured the soldiers that their weapons were not needed. He begged them to follow him calmly to his home where the matter could be discussed properly. They seemed relieved by the chance to perform their duties peacefully, and their rigid postures relaxed. They did as Jost asked. They all followed Jost home. Jost opened the door and invited the soldiers into his home. They entered.

Karl and the others tried to follow. Jost stopped them in their tracks and asked the soldiers, "There is no need for an angry mob in this business. What use are these people to you?"

The soldiers gave the question little thought. They agreed that the business of the law had no need for the angry families. They would have their day in court. The soldiers sent Karl and the others away.

As he was crossing the threshold, Karl turned back to face the interior of the house. Anna was not in his view. He shouted, addressing the soldiers, but speaking loudly for Anna to hear, "Take that baby, too. It is not a natural child but a creation of witchcraft and the Devil."

Karl gave a gloating smirk to Jost, a nod of affirmation to the soldiers, and he stomped out of the house. When he and the others were gone and the house was calm, the soldiers explained the charges against Anna. Anna cried, but Jost assured her that superstition had no place in the secular courts of Aschaffenburg. Any accusations against her would require evidence, and there was none. Anna was innocent and Jost promised her that the court would come to the same conclusion.

The soldiers were not inclined to superstition, or at least they separated their beliefs from their duties. There was a professional composure in their deportment. They made no gesture toward Christoph. They allowed Anna to hand the baby to Jost. Anna had been accused of murdering the two children. She had to face the charges. The soldiers did not seize her with emotional zeal, but simply commanded her calmly to go with them.

Anna kissed her husband and she kissed her son, then went silently and peacefully with the soldiers. A carriage awaited them on the outskirts of the village. Anna entered calmly but fearfully. The carriage rolled away toward Aschaffenburg, a short trip that seemed to last for days.

Chapter Fifteen:

Accused

JOST WAS AT HIS WIT'S END. Although he was in his own home, with his child in his arms, he spent a night no more comfortable than Anna. He tried to imagine her, what sort of room she was kept in. He prayed for her calmness, that she would not, in her fear and nervousness, say something that could jeopardize her defense. He had faith in the court, and he had faith in Anna, but the stakes were high, with everything to lose. His chest tightened. He felt as if the air of his own home turned thick as tar. It filled his nose heavily and clogged his throat.

The soldiers brought Anna to a room, a normal room with a row of chairs against a wall. They told her to remain there until called before the court. The night was still young, with many hours before the court would convene. She was offered no bed and no food. But the room was clean and safe, and she occupied it alone. The soldiers left her there and locked the door behind them, leaving a single lantern lighting the dim room.

Anna sat stiff and still until she began to ache. She heard nothing from the other side of the door, nothing from any direction. She curled up and laid herself across three of the chairs. With a clear and blissful mind, she could not have slept as she lay. Her mind was crowded with thoughts that were far from blissful. She strained her mind for anything that could connect her to the children's death. The vial she gave to the child contained nothing more than a sweetened bark tea with mint and spices. The ingredients were sound. The case against her was weak, but accusations were made, and the grieving families had their right to be heard.

Jost did not close his eyes all night. Well before the sunrise, he took Christoph and paid a carriage for passage to Aschaffenburg. When the court convened, Jost was the first to enter the room. The judges followed behind him, as did the families of the dead children. Once all of them were settled, a soldier fetched Anna from the room where she had spent the night.

The courtroom was not large. It was used most days for private business meetings and clearly not intended for large gatherings. It was square, with a large, bulky, ornately carved desk at one end. Three chairs sat behind it, upon which three lay judges sat. These were ordinary citizens, land owners and businessmen taking time from their lives to act as judges in the case. Directly in front of the desk, there was a single chair surrounded by a circular banister rail with a small gate on the side. The soldier led Anna to it, and she sat facing the judges.

The rest of the room was not at all as Jost had expected. There were small tables with chairs around them, not spread in any uniform way but haphazardly scattered around the room, like tables in a cabaret. Jost did not know where he was allowed to sit, so he took a chair at the table nearest Anna. The accusing families took two tables to the right of the defendant's chair, all but Karl, who stood behind a chair he claimed as his own.

A clerk stepped between Anna and the judges. He faced the judges and read the accusations against Anna. There was nothing in the read charges about witchcraft or satanic rituals, nothing about demonic inseminations. The accusation stated plainly that Anna was accused of poisoning two children she had visited. The clerk stated that the result of the poisoning was death, making the charge against Anna two counts of murder.

The clerk stepped aside, and the center judge asked the accuser to step forward. Karl stepped sharply to the judges, with a stomp in his determined paces. Katherina and the other family sat still, clearly content to leave the matter in Karl's hands. Karl turned to face Anna. He stepped menacingly to her and leaned against the banister rail that surrounded her, towering over her.

He shouted, "This witch killed my son. She cursed him to death with a potion she made alongside her witch friend!"

Karl was interrupted by the hand of a soldier on his shoulder. He turned to the soldier, who pointed with his other hand to the panel of judges.

"The court asked you a question," the center judge reminded, "and you will address the court, not the defendant."

It was a small victory. But Anna and Jost were both relieved to see that Karl would not have his way in the courtroom. Karl faced the judges and told his story. He said that Anna's friend, Miray, was a witch from a foreign land, who taught Anna the ways of witchcraft. He accused them of conspiring to kill the two sick children.

"This is not an ecclesiastical court," the center judge reminded him, "the accusation is murder, not witchcraft. Please speak to that charge only."

Karl explained that Anna had been with his son shortly before both children died.

"Why was she with them?" the judge asked.

"She was there to poison them," he answered.

"But why was she permitted in the home?" the judge prodded.

"My wife invited her in, believing the witch would help our son."

The judge grew angry at another mention of witchcraft, and yelled at Karl, "We are not here to try a case of witchcraft. We leave that to the Church's courts. We are here to view the evidence of murder against Anna Koob. Do not mention witchcraft to this court again."

Karl huffed, then growled, then nodded his head in compliance.

The judge on the left asked Karl, "And the other child, why was she with the other child?"

Karl saw his case grow weaker, but the judge asked him a question, so he answered, "I don't know that she was with the other victim. I don't think that she saw her. She must have cursed her from a distance."

The center judge stood sharply from his chair and shouted, "Do not make me tell you again!"

Karl apologized and continued, "Anna Koob mixed something from strange ingredients and gave it to my son, Peter. Peter was getting better, but that afternoon he grew suddenly sicker. My son, my only son, died that very day."

Karl's words choked with bitter mourning. He was not only an angry man, but a deeply affected father, suffering an immense personal tragedy. Despite their opposition in the courtroom, Anna shed a tear from her compassionate heart. The judges, too, were moved. They gave Karl a few moments to compose himself before continuing.

The judge on the right asked, "You say that your wife thought that Anna Koob could help your son. What was wrong with him?"

Karl's face turned red. He turned to Anna and walked beside her chair. He turned to face the judges and answered, "He was not feeling well."

"He was already sick?" the judge on the right asked.

"He was feeling a little unwell. But he was not dying, not until Anna Koob mixed her potion and gave it to my son."

The center judge asked Karl, "Do you know what was ailing your son? If he was only slightly unwell, why did your wife seek the help of Anna Koob?"

Karl had no answer that would strengthen his chances at a conviction. He raised his raspy voice, "My son was not dying until she came into our home and poisoned him."

The judge on the left asked, "Can you think of any motive, of anything Anna Koob would have to gain by the death of your son?"

The center judge stood slowly, knowing that accusations of witchcraft, of working for the devil, swam inside of Karl's closed mouth. Karl stared at the judges, looking as if he might explode. He growled again, apparently in frustration for not being able to spin his superstitious accusations as he had planned. He did not answer, not with word nor gesture.

The center judge sat down and waved a hand at the soldier, who escorted Karl to his seat. He asked Anna directly, "What was in the drink you made?"

The court seemed bent in her favor, and she answered with confidence, listing the exact bark she ground for the tea, and which herbs and spices were used and what each provided. She informed the judges that a similar recipe had been given to Karl's wife a few months earlier, and Karl's mother about a year before that.

"The herbs have certain medicinal properties," she explained, "They are used by apothecaries all over the world."

"Where did you get them?" the judge on the right asked.

"I gathered some of it from the forest north of here. I bought some and traded for others. Some were given to me."

"Given by whom?"

"By my friend, Miray."

"And the recipe?" the same judge asked, "Where did you get the recipe?"

"That was also given to me by Miray."

The center judge seemed very interested in Miray. He asked, "Where is she now?"

Tears poured freely from Anna's eyes, but she kept her sobbing inside of her. She answered in a faltering voice, "I do not know, but I fear she has come to a terrible end."

Anna went on to speak of Miray, of the troubles she and her husband had faced, and of the bigotry she faced right there in Aschaffenburg County. The judges, particularly the center judge, who appeared to lead the panel, displayed faces of troubled contemplation as they listened. Anna was not sure if they felt compassion or suspicion for Miray. Their following questions indicated the presence of both.

They asked Anna how she met Miray, and how long they had known each other. They were very curious about Safet and his demise. Miray had shared very little with Anna about the accusations against Safet. Anna's inability to answer questions on that incident savored strongly of deceit. The body language of the judges seemed to turn in Karl's favor.

The judges had made it clear that they would hear and consider only what evidence pertained to the death of the two children. The many questions they asked Anna about Miray and Safet indicated that they believed Miray connected to the case at hand. They were clearly suspicious, and Anna felt herself more tightly entangled with every one of her awkward, choppy, incomplete answers. She turned her head behind her and saw Jost with his face buried in his palms. His hair shook atop his trembling head, while Christoph hung awkwardly from the nook of one elbow.

The judges' questions turned again toward the tonic Anna had mixed for Karl's son. They made her repeat each ingredient and specify exactly where she had acquired each. They pressed her to say how well she knew each ingredient and how easily she recognized them. Her knowledge was vast and comprehensive, and pronounced itself clearly in her detailed answers. They returned their questions to Miray, asking why a foreign stranger would bring such things to their little village.

Anna replied with a newly defensive tone, "She and her husband were traders, making a living like any trader. They had an exotic commodity to sell. They traded successfully with people all along our river."

The left judge leaned forward in his chair and asked in a lower, menacing tone, "What makes them exotic?"

Anna sighed heavily. She was clearly frustrated and fearful at the frightening turn in the proceedings, and she answered with exasperation, "Only that they cannot be easily found here." She continued in a scolding tone which she immediately regretted, "That desk you sit at is not from local lumber. It is an exotic wood I do not recognize, yet I do not view it with suspicion. I look at your coat. I think those textiles are not from this region. Some trader brought them here. Yet I do not believe you responsible for every death that happens near you."

The judge sat back in his chair with his eyes turned downward. Anna and Jost, in fact everyone in the room, wished to know how to interpret the gesture. The judges put their heads together and whispered among themselves, at points in apparent agreement, and at points in obvious contention. They broke from their huddle and assumed their rigid postures. Anna and Jost were not familiar with the proceedings in such cases, so they were both surprised when the clerk invited Karl to confront Anna directly.

Anna still saw clearly the broken, hurting man behind Karl's angry face. Her compassion battled fiercely with her fear. Karl looked at Anna very differently than Anna looked at him. He held no compassion for the pain and fear she suffered. He thought he faced pure evil. He saw nothing of humanity, nothing of righteousness inside of Anna. He did not see a doting daughter, a loving wife, nor a tender mother and kindhearted neighbor. He saw a witch, a tool of Satan and an evil blight upon their village, brought into their lives by the sinister witch named Miray.

The liberties of confrontation not permitted Karl at the opening of the trial were suddenly his in abundance. Anna had to sit on her little chair inside of the constricting banisters, while Karl was able to thunder around her as he pleased. He was not addressing the judges. He was allowed a much longer leash to raise subjects of a more mystical nature. And he did. He let all of his suspicions mount his tongue and spring with vehemence into the air of the courtroom. The judges sat still and listened. Anna looked regularly to them while she was berated more than questioned by Karl. Her face pleaded with them to stop Karl and return the courtroom to the sort of order that began the day. They did not interfere. This was Karl's opportunity to confront her, as afforded him by law

Karl barely drew breath, not allowing the slightest moment for Anna to respond to his accusations. She would have her time to confront her accuser, as allowed to *her* by law. Until then, she was in Karl's hands. Jost listened helplessly, with his arms folded and wrenching tightly with his hands on his opposite upper arms, while he held Christoph in a forced seated position between his tightly squeezed knees. The grinding of his teeth was seen clearly in the flexing of his jaw. Karl looked occasionally to Jost, but only when he confronted Anna about bringing evil into a good man's home.

Finally, Karl allowed a moment for response, after he squeezed the banister rail and leaned over Anna, asking, "How did Miray seduce you? How is it that a traveling trader came to share your home after such a short acquaintance? Did she seduce you into bed?"

Anna stood in aggressive defiance. She came barely to Karl's collarbones, but she stood with such fierceness that Karl stepped three full strides backward, almost to the judges' desk. He turned to the judges as if to say, "See? She is a witch." He gestured a hand toward Anna, expecting the judges to reprimand her. They did no such thing. Anna was allowed to stand or sit as it pleased her, as long as she remained within the banisters. Seeing that his silent appeal would bear no fruit with the judges, he turned again to face Anna, shortening the distance between them with one small and tentative step.

Anna waited for Karl's eyes to meet hers before she spoke, "I was seduced by nobody. I found friendship in a like-minded person, the sort of friendship that does not take long to develop. When Miray returned to our lives, she had just suffered a terrible tragedy. Our compassion reached out to her, and she grew closer to us as we nursed her broken heart."

As Anna spoke of broken hearts, she saw deeply into Karl's. Her shoulders dropped and she tilted her head to one side, feeling keenly for Karl and his family. She continued in a much softer tone, "I am so sorry for your loss, Karl. You and your wife are friends and neighbors. I had no idea your son was fatally ill. Had I known, I would not have tried to improve him with my subtle recipes. I would have called for a doctor from Aschaffenburg. Believe me that I weep. I weep heavily for you and for your family."

She turned her head around to glance for a moment at the grieving family from Mainaschaff, turned back to Karl, and added, "And for the other family as well, though I do not know them. I wish I knew them better, so I could comfort them as a friend in their loss."

Karl seemed to soften. Anna's pure compassion was on bold display, and it began to affect him. But he caught himself. He turned to the judges, pointing at Anna, and said to them, "Do you see what she is doing? A witch's deceit is on exhibition in this room. You must not be seduced by it."

Anna sat down and responded, "What I have said to you is true. I weep bitterly for your loss."

Karl shook his head and growled, to which Anna calmly added, "I have suffered my own misfortunes of late, but I tell you honestly, my neighbor, I feel far worse for your misfortunes than for my own. Yours are infinitely worse, and again, I tell you…, I weep for you and Katherina."

Karl stomped to Anna and resumed his previous posture, gripping the banister rail and leaning over her. He spoke coarsely, with saliva spraying in abundance onto Anna's head, "You are only trying not to follow your Turkish friend to hell. She died in pain, screaming your name. I witnessed it myself. Can you explain that?"

Anna stood sharply. She had no thoughts of a response. She thought only of Miray. The thin thread of faith she held for her friend's welfare snapped, dropping hope to the floor of the room to shatter in a thousand pieces. Her imagination could not help itself. It ran every possible horrid image of Miray's final moments through her mind's eye. She could hear Miray's scream in her head. It drowned out all sounds of the physical world around her.

Anna's eyes swelled red and coated with a thick layer of tears that refused to let go and run down her cheek. Her jaw quivered as a violent sob demanded release. She held it. She swallowed it. But it found relief in bursts of breath that popped from her nose as she bit hard on her lips. Miray was dead — tortured and cruelly slaughtered at the violent hands of people Anna once loved, people she had comforted with her stories, people who laughed with her at her wedding.

The revelation of Miray's demise had a very different effect on Jost. It was then that his wife's true peril became clear.

In a desperate attempt to relieve the fear that waved outward from his marrow and crashed against the inside of his skin, he mouthed silently to himself, "This is no mob. This is no mob. This is a court. They will want evidence of guilt."

Precisely as Jost calmed himself, Anna's mind shifted from mournful and sympathetic thoughts of Miray to her own perilous circumstances. Her shoulders dropped sharply as she considered her own execution. She lost the ability to draw breath. To her watery eyes, every figure in the room seemed to descend upon her. Her legs went limp, and she fell to the floor in front of her chair, flailing her arms in all directions.

Jost witnessed the transition and collapse, and he knew exactly what went through her head. Since their first walk in the forest together, he had held back many urges to take her in his arms. He had no strength to do so while he watched her writhing on the floor. He lunged to her but was held back by the many hands around him.

It was a fair court, a civil court, that still saw Anna as accused, not as guilty. The proceedings were adjourned and Anna was tended to with compassion. She was returned to the room where she had waited all night. The trial was set to resume the following day and the building was cleared. Jost rode home with Christoph. He fed neither the baby nor himself, but set his son gently on Anna's side of the bed. He curled up around Christoph and cried himself to sleep.

Jost awoke to Christoph cooing and patting him on the forehead. When he rose, he saw the blood his mouth left behind. In his tortured sleep, he had chewed on his inner cheeks. His chin was caked in dried blood while fresh blood continued to slowly fill his mouth.

Chapter Sixteen:
Uncaged

THE FRANCONIAN SKY WAS SLIGHTLY BRUSHED with the dark orange of an infant sunrise. Jost mashed some beans for Christoph and took a single bite of bread for himself, and again was on the road to Aschaffenburg. Christoph was silent in the carriage, offering no distractions from Jost's toxic thoughts. His imagination painted a far worse condition for his wife than what she actually suffered. His pity for her was extreme and pinched and pecked at his heart with relentless violence.

Anna's first few hours after the adjournment of the hearing were brutally painful. She bounced tumultuously between sweating fears of her own demise and weeping grief for her dear friend's miserable end. But a long night of restlessness, alternating between sprawling over chairs, sitting up rigidly, and pacing the floor, brought her surprising calmness. By the time Jost was on the road, Anna's faith returned to her — her faith in the court, in her husband, her faith in herself, and in God. A few times that early morning, she caught herself smiling widely. She thought of Jost and Christoph. Those thoughts held images of togetherness, not mourning, not separation. She envisioned a successful day and a celebratory evening.

Jost's mouth donned no smiles that morning. Less than one mile from the courtroom in Aschaffenburg, the wheel of the carriage sank into a muddy rut and could not be pulled out by the single old horse that tugged fruitlessly at it. The rented driver had not the knowledge or passion to work it free with expedience. Jost felt the entire physical world falling down upon him. He thought of leaving the carriage behind and running with his baby in hand. After rejecting the notion several times, he saw no other choice. Without a word to the lethargic driver, he tucked Christoph under one arm and ran down the road. In seven minutes, he was at the courthouse without enough breath to expel a single syllable.

The sprint was unnecessary. With Christoph crying from being so shaken during the run, Jost clambered into the courtroom a full hour before Anna was brought in. Business was being conducted in the room, business unrelated to the plot of this story. The comings and goings of the new day's business flowed around Jost like an underground river, beneath him, beneath his sour musings. And this frenzied little river was not redirected in the least by the stone-still presence of a father and husband or the squirming whimper of a baby boy.

All business left as the room prepared for the second day of the trial. The defendant's chair and banister rails were brought in by custodians of the building. The sight took Jost's breath. He did not see a chair and polished wooden banisters and rail. He saw a cage, inside of which his wife would soon be locked. The free and light woman, this winged spirit, this creature who always appeared to him as larger than life itself, would be crammed inside of the railed circle of banisters. Anna's little frame sat well and comfortable within the rail, but to Jost's amorous eyes, she would need to be broken in half to fit.

Jost sat alone staring at his wife's "cage" for a stretch of time he could not have determined, until the familiar thundering of Karl's barbaric boots shook his attention to the public entrance. He was followed, of course, by the quiet and subservient trail of family members that dragged in his demonstrative wake. Like the business transactions earlier, Karl and his clan did not notice Jost and Christoph, even as they took the same seats as the day before, mere feet from the room's only other occupants.

The judges came in next, entering the room in mid-sentence on some unrelated case. Jost strained to determine Anna's fate by their moods, by their gestures and the tone of their voices. They gave no such hints while they settled behind the bulky desk. A soldier entered the room and the judges wasted no time ordering the entrance of the defendant. The soldier fetched Anna from her room.

It is hard to say what Jost expected to see when his eyes beheld his only lover. He knew she was treated fairly by the secular court of Aschaffenburg. Yet he half-expected Anna to enter the room bleeding from being whipped, thin and gaunt as if deprived of nourishment for weeks. Anna had a familiar glow about her and a slight grin to see her husband and child. Jost looked at her like he was beholding an angel. This broadened Anna's smile further. Anna took her seat in a prim and professional manner, thanking the soldier for escorting her in.

Jost was lost in a euphoric trance, taken away from the tragedy of the moment by his wife's inner-beauty, until snapped back to the moment by the voice of the center judge, reminding him of the previous day, with all of its horrors. The judges drew the attention of all with a slap on the desk and a united rise to their feet.

"This trial adjourned under frightful circumstances," the center judge announced, "But we see that the room is calm, and we demand that it remain so as we bring this case to its conclusion."

Still standing behind the desk, the left judge addressed Karl, asking him if any further evidence of Anna's guilt could be brought forward. Karl's eyes darted side to side as he strained for one last argument to hand him his revenge and the closure he hoped it would deliver.

After an excruciatingly long pause, Karl stood and answered, "The Turkish *woman* escaped her husband's fate and brought her retribution to Kleinostheim, where she seduced this woman into an unholy life. Now Anna Koob is lost to goodness. She killed my son for her wicked friend and now this court must do what is just."

Karl sat down with a scowl of self-satisfaction, which was wiped quickly away when the left judge remarked, "So your answer is no. You have no evidence connecting Anna Koob with the sickness and death of your child or any other child."

Jost sat up firmly, and drew a sharp and loud inhale of excitement, which drew the glances of all in the room.

The judges remained standing, and the center judge gave their ruling, "If the residue of a poison had been found and presented to this court, if the children had not been already ill before Anna Koob visited the home, if Anna Koob had had any contact with the other child, this court would have much to consider. But what has been presented in the case leaves us nothing to consider. There is no evidence to continue the case of murder against Anna Koob. This court releases her with the hope that the families involved can find some peace with themselves and some reconciliation with each other. In the meantime, we urge the stricken families to turn inwardly in your mourning and restrain from unnecessary contact with the Koob family. We have recommended an investigation into the fate of Miray."

The two outer judges stepped from behind the desk to stand on either side. The center judge announced with much more formality in his voice, "Mister Hornung, you leave with the compassion and prayers of this court." He turned to Anna and continued, "Anna Koob, you are free to join your husband and newborn child. Good luck and Godspeed."

The soldier opened the banister gate, took Anna by the hand, and escorted her from her seat. Jost wasted no time. He ran to Anna, pressing Christoph between them for a quick embrace, and ran his wife from the building. The sun was higher, and it set a gentle warmth kindly upon them. Though carriages were aplenty, they walked home. They walked slowly, taking the length of the day, but it was a day of new hope and new beginnings, one that allowed the unsullied celebration of their newly expanded family.

Home alone and safe, Jost prepared them a small meal. The blessing of the meal took longer than the time they spent eating it. There was much gratitude under their roof, but also much to be mourned. Their hearts were simultaneously light with relief and heavy with burden. The meal was brief and a soft bed and loving, protective arms beckoned Anna into the deepest of sleeps. Long after he knew she slept, Jost continued caressing her and placing tender kisses on her head.

The morning came late. Christoph was hungry and dirty. He cried like any uncomfortable newborn. But her son's cry in the open chest beside them only served to serenade Anna with a grateful lullaby. Jost had fallen asleep hours after Anna. Yet they awoke together just before noon. They tended to the comforts of the baby and to their own needs and they set out for the home of Michel.

News of Anna's arrest and trial never reached Michel. Anna and Jost began telling the story, but seeing that the account was causing Michel distress, they tried to minimize it. Michel was far too sharp of wit and keen of compassion to not see the truth behind their words. He urged them to leave Kleinostheim, to take some time away while the grief and anger of the stricken families subsided.

Jost was receptive to the idea, but Anna would not discuss it. She feared that her flight from the region would appear as evidence of guilt, and she insisted that the reparation of her reputation required her presence. Her point was sound, and the notion of departure was tabled.

The day passed pleasantly. Any nosy neighbor who peeked in on them would have seen quite a scene of familial pleasantness. The truth stung them from beneath the facade. The kinship and admiration in which Anna had spent her youth was soiled indefinitely. So much bitterness and suspicion swirled around the Koob home. It filled Kleinostheim with a putrid air and settled on everything around them with a sticky film that could only be washed off with time. Anna and Jost left Michel that evening in full awareness of the challenges that faced them.

Knowing of something and being able to live with it are often two very different things. Jost conducted his business as he always had, never relying particularly on the warmth of relations. Anna, on the other hand, was so ready to put the entire affair behind her, even so much as to forgive anyone involved in Miray's death, that she addressed her neighbors with the familiar tenderness and good-humor that had endeared her to her fellow villagers since she was a toddler.

Anna passed the same smiles and greeted others with the same authentic sympathy. She assumed that her ability to mend hearts would power them all through the pain of the moment. It did not happen. Her voice was not a comfort to those who shared her circle. Her smile melted no coldness. When her warmth and genuine goodwill was not returned, it stung her sharply, and she quickly fell into a deep, cold, and salty melancholy. She cried through the night, until she didn't anymore, then nothing could make her cry. Nothing could stir her to any feeling.

Jost had no childish notion that Anna would spring back to her younger self the day after the trial, but weeks later, she continued to grow darker. She lost interest in all of the mundane delights in life that Anna, above everyone he had ever known, savored to the fullest. Anna's attachment to Jost callused over and her words turned sharp. It hurt him deeply, yet he continued to defer to her — until she began to neglect Christoph.

In the middle of the trial, when Anna's very life was held in the balance, she was still Anna, as compassionate and as in love as ever. In the weeks and months that followed, his concern for her welfare was deeper than during the trial. He was not witnessing the *potential* of losing her. He *was* losing her. Something had to be done, something desperate, something bold. In his private and desperate musings, he revisited Michel's request to remove from the region while the village recovered from the traumatic events. But each time he brought it up, she scolded him ruthlessly.

One afternoon, about nine weeks after the trial, the desperation of their circumstances hit its zenith. Anna curled in bed, late into the day, which had become her daily practice. Christoph was in the bed beside her. The baby screamed shrilly. Anna stared blankly at the wall beside the bed. She seemed to hear nothing and see nothing. Jost stood at the threshold of the bedroom and watched the crusty, lifeless shell of the once vibrant woman he loved, as she was clearly deaf and blind to her own child.

Jost had never traveled far, but he had an old travel case given to him by Johann, his old master. With a fury nobody had ever seen in him, he began packing clothes and trinkets, dishes, and even fresh flowers from a vase, into the case. As he stomped from room to room, shoving random items in the case, Anna followed him with her eyes but did not move. When he could fit nothing else in the case, he sat on the floor and wept. He sat beside their bed. Christoph revived his shrill cry with a vengeance. Jost stood and took his son from the bed. As he did, he noticed the tears that flowed in abundance from Anna's eyes. He bounced Christoph gently in his arms until the house was silent, then carried his son from the room.

Before he left the room, he turned to Anna, stepped back to the bed, hovered over her for a few seconds, kissed her head, and said, "We are going away together, as your father suggested, and we are leaving in the morning. We will sit together for dinner tonight and plan our travels."

Jost shivered violently as he walked from the room. He feared what cruel and uncharacteristic confrontation would result from his proclamation. But he was prepared to bear it, and he set immediately to composing his thoughts and arguments.

He stopped in mid-stride and marched back to Anna with his first argument growing too big on his tongue to remain in his mouth. He poked his head into the room and spoke, while his expressive eyebrows danced above his eyes, "Remember the words of Saint Benedict, 'Run while you have the light of life, that the darkness of death may not overtake you.' Let us run, my Love, and see what we may, while we have life."

Jost had two businesses under his name — the management of his own properties, and the book trade bequeathed to him by his father-in-law. His absence from the area would hurt his business, but the book trade had much to gain from travel. Jost was out of the house for the rest of the day. He shared his intentions with Anna's father. He solicited Michel for any advice, any guidance in the traveling trade of exotic literature. He placed Christoph in Michel's care and spent the rest of the day securing a manager for his properties. The foundation was laid for their departure from Kleinostheim and nothing, not the fear of Hell itself, would persuade him to abandon his scheme to revive his wife.

When he returned home, he found Anna out of bed. She had set the table and poured the wine. Paper and ink sat ready to receive their plans. She thought deeply after Jost left the house that day, and mortification in her own behavior sobered her from her depressed stupor. She stared at him with bedewed, apologetic eyes. She did not *say* she was sorry, but she declared it plainly enough in the loving anguish displayed in her face. He read it well and accepted her apology with an embrace that was both firm and delicate.

They sat. They ate. They planned. Fear and disappointment still left its stench in Anna's thoughts, and revealed itself in her words. But when Jost laid a map on the table, one marked by Michel with his suggested destinations, excitement evicted fear. Anna pulled her feet underneath her, so that she squatted on the chair. She bounced giddily as she perused the map, like a little girl awaiting dessert. Jost had not seen the slow transformation of Anna's inner thoughts, the battles that took place in her mind while he was out of the house. He saw an instant and comprehensive alteration in her behavior, but he did not question it. Across the table from him was the woman he loved, with all the liveliness of spirit that made her unique among every creature he had ever known. He stared at the glow in her eyes and he praised God.

Michel had circled on the map the Mediterranean city of Nice, in the Duchy of Savoy, on the coast of modern France. Nice was a powerhouse of Mediterranean trade, enjoying a revival in the wake of the plague of 1580. The Dukes of Savoy were notoriously well-read and hosted in their palaces more intellectuals than royalty, and Nice was the port of entry into their court. Scholars from three continents gathered there, and the printed word was a growing and lucrative enterprise. Anna and Jost spoke of the possibilities, while the passions of their younger selves bubbled to the surface in a rolling boil. The arguments Jost had silently composed earlier in the day were of no use and they were dropped and forgotten entirely. They were going to Nice, and from there — God knows where.

Logistics were a concern for another day, for another conversation. That evening was for dreaming, sipping from a shared bowl of imagination, and enjoying their mutual intoxication. They spoke of Miray and Safet, not in mourning terms of loss, but in speculation over the lives they lived traveling the routes of trade. It was not the terrified Miray they saw in their minds, not at all the image their eyes last beheld of her. They imagined her in the ports of the Mediterranean, laughing, dancing, and loving.

Their planning did not feel like an escape from something terrible, rather a charge toward something good. They slept that night in an embrace, as tightly intertwined physically as they were spiritually. The sunrise splashed the house with color, inviting them not only into a new day, but into a new life, one of faith in each other and in God, where trepidation could find no footing. They ate breakfast with Michel, absorbed every drop of advice he could give about the trade, loaded a cart with books and ledgers and a beautiful baby boy, and they drove southwest. Anna left her troubled home behind, but her *life* was packed snuggly in the cart with her. She felt encased in a bubble of well-being, into which no trouble and no danger could seep.

Chapter Seventeen:
Gypsy Scholars

ANNA, JOST, AND CHRISTOPH ROLLED SLOWLY down the roads of Southwestern Germany. Jost had traveled. The experience was not altogether new for him. He had never gone so far as Nice, nor had he ever traveled in such a state of mind. The conversations were endless and seamless. The crisp spring air was fresh with hope. They slept most nights in the cart and drove far longer without rest or food than most would find tolerable. They often forgot to eat, and were only reminded of the mandates of nature when the growling of their stomachs spoke more loudly than their voices.

In their second week of travel, they stopped in Reutlingen. Only a few years earlier, the city council signed the Augsburg Confession, a Lutheran document of faith. Protestantism and Catholicism rubbed elbows in Reutlingen, and did so with friendly, congenial banter, not at all like the religious contention of Lower Franconia. Our travelers had not intended to remain at any stop between Kleinostheim and Nice, but the academic air of Reutlingen was electric and intoxicating.

As they rode the primary thoroughfare, they beheld a sight that halted them in amazement. It was late in the morning and a tall, four-story half-timbered building rose above a bustling patio. It was a popular bistro that overflowed into the street, where a variety of foods and drinks crowded small, circular tables, and sent a tantalizing aroma into the air. There were plenty of chairs around the tables, but not one was occupied. Circles of men aged from seventeen to seventy clustered in groups, too full of intellectual energy to take a seat. They seemed to hang from the patio like bunches of grapes, leaning over the tables, propping a foot on the unoccupied chairs, and waving their arms about in impassioned conversations. It was a sight entirely foreign to Anna, unlike anything she encountered in Kleinostheim, or even in Aschaffenburg.

They stopped the cart and walked along the edge of the patio with Christoph in arm, straining to pick up individual lines of conversations among the many voices talking over each other. A dozen topics were being debated in that cloud of succulent aroma. Quotations flew freely, and Anna recognized many and mouthed them silently in unison with the speakers. Nobody seemed to notice the strangers in their company. Anna froze amid a group of five men, entranced by the liberty with which religious debate swam from mouth to ear among them. Jost, holding Christoph, continued to meander until he found himself at the entrance of the building.

Anna had no idea that Jost was not still beside her. She was entirely engrossed in the conversation she voyeuristically observed. The group was speaking of religion in politics, a topic that had fascinated Anna since her earliest discussions at her parents' table.

One of the men, a boyish-faced fellow whose graying temples beneath a head of thick red hair contradicted the fairness of his skin, began a quotation that Anna knew well, saying with conviction and a strong breath of beer, "A tyrant must put on the appearance of uncommon devotion to religion."

Prompted by instinct alone, Anna continued his quotation, speaking loudly enough for the men in her circle and a bit beyond, "Subjects are less apprehensive of illegal treatment from a ruler whom they consider god-fearing and pious. They less easily move against him, believing that he has the gods on his side."

Their small portion of the bustling patio froze in silence as the faces of that conversation all turned to the only woman among them. It was only when she saw the amazement in their eyes that Anna realized she had butted into their discussion. In a slow wave outward from Anna, the other conversations hushed, until every eye in the patio was upon her. Jost, intrigued by the aroma of a hot drink he did not recognize, had entered the building to purchase samples for him and Anna. He walked from the building and onto the patio to the surprising silence and saw the many men around him staring at his wife. Chills rolled across him as he was unaware of the nature of the strange moment.

Without moving her head, Anna scanned her eyes back and forth several times across the patio. She locked her eyes on the red-haired gentleman and said in an instructive tone, "Aristotle."

Some heads tilted. Some jaws hung open. All eyes widened, all but the man she addressed directly. He simply smiled and asked her, "Do you believe Lutheranism to be as tyrannical as Catholicism?"

Anna did not notice that Jost had reentered the patio, awkwardly juggling a baby and two mugs of the hot beverage, yet she spread her widening smile in perfect synchronization with his.

She answered quietly, speaking intimately to her fair-faced questioner, forcing all others to lean in or cup their hands at their ears, "I find it tyrannical in a different way, a *younger* tyrant with fewer faculties but greater zeal."

Some hummed softly in concurrence. Others turned to those around them and nodded. Some scratched their heads, puzzled by her response, and obviously considering it deeply.

Anna continued, "Luther intended to open doors, which he did. But his followers built walls around those doors, walls that look much like Catholic walls and are no easier to walk through."

Such sentiments from his wife's lips were not strange to Jost, and he bloated with pride as he watched the crowded patio respond to her with so many nods of approval. Others leaned their bodies toward her with the faces of eager students, waiting for the next morsel of sustenance to fall from her intellectual table.

The redhead asked her, "Are you a woman of faith?"

"I am," she calmly answered.

"Are you Catholic or Lutheran?"

A voice from outside of their tight circle of six interjected lightheartedly, with a giggle in his voice, "That is a dangerous question."

Anna's face turned intensely sober. Blood rushed to her cheeks as she recalled her recent trial, and she answered solemnly, "I foresee a great deal of spilled blood in the coming years, as Europe tries to decide *whose* walls will enclose them. It will all be for nothing."

The very air seemed to hold still in consideration, and Anna continued with the intense focus of the entire patio upon her, "Stone is stone. Bricks are bricks. God will remain unchanged. It will all be for nothing."

Jost moved quickly to Anna, fearful of the reactions to her comments. There was nothing to fear among those people. Opinions among them were strong and freely expressed, but also pliable and desirous of outside influence. One of the men nearest Anna pulled a patio chair from the table and offered Anna a seat. She took it. Jost sat beside her and gave Anna her drink. She set it on the table and took Christoph from him.

The patio returned to its previous form, with smaller groups breaking back into their clusters and continuing those topics that Anna's voice had interrupted. Those nearest Anna, plus a few more who had broken from their groups and pulled chairs near her table, continued *their* debate, but with eyes and ears turning to Anna between each ventured opinion. They sat and slouched so as not to raise a single head above hers. Oh, she was a strange sight indeed, entirely new to their eyes. She held her infant son with the soft arms of a mother, and kissed his head with loving, maternal lips. Then those same lips parted and released more quotations and more insightful interpretations.

The points made by the men were well thought out and came from a rich source of education within their heads. But they were heavy with rigid masculinity. With ease and grace, Anna took their words and ran them through her feminine sensibilities, awakening them to a new, light, and refreshing perspective. Jost, being a man of great insight but few words, dropped abbreviated opinions sporadically into the debate, but savored the atmosphere no less than his wife. Mostly, he delighted in Anna's contribution to the lives and opinions of the strangers around them. He watched them being altered to the core by his wife. It was a portrait of humanity like Reutlingen had never seen. A woman, a mother, as womanly and motherly as could be found, and a scholar whose literary background displayed its vast depths with the turn of every phrase from her delicate lips.

The evening aged in untimely fashion. It was the nip of the spring night, not the loss of the sunlight, that alerted them all to the lateness of day. They had all been blind to their surroundings and focused absorbently on the topics they discussed. Jost excused them from the group, noting the lateness and the squirming baby in Anna's arms. Their new friends begged them to stay longer. When Jost refused, their redheaded colleague paid for their stay in a room above the bistro house then begged them to reconvene their little symposium the following night. Everyone on the patio added his own plea. Anna declined. She wanted a day, evening, and night with her family. Each in the party praised Anna extravagantly and excused himself from the group, until Anna, Jost, and Christoph remained alone. They took their room with hearts full of thought, faith, and gratitude. Neither Anna nor Jost had ever spent such a day.

Before adjourning to bed, Jost unpacked his books and ledgers, determined to give Reutlingen a few days of his attention before continuing to Nice. They were no longer rooted to Kleinostheim, nor were they so deeply rooted to their plans. They were gypsies — gypsy scholars, bound only to each other, in subordination only to each other, and in need of only each other.

The following morning, our heroes walked by Reutlingen's academic center. It would much later become a university, but when Anna and Jost were there, it was nothing more than a small cluster of buildings committed to scholarship. Together they researched the books, sold a few from their collection, and bought a few to replace them. There was nothing exotic in their purchases, nothing to bend their way of thought, but Anna had not yet read them and she looked forward to passing their traveling hours with her nose deeply buried in something new.

In the afternoon, they walked along the Echaz River southeast of town, and passed a day not unlike many they had known together, with the addition, of course, of a baby boy who seemed hypnotized by the babble of the water, the steady vibrations of his mother's footsteps, and the nurturing safety of her muffled voice as she held him against her chest.

As promised, their new friends met them the next morning on the patio. There would be no leaving their apartment without first passing some hours in debate. There were several new faces among them. From the extravagant praise that had reached them, they expected a goddess to descend from the rooms above, like Venus radiating from an opening seashell. Instead, they found Anna, a young woman not at all uncommon to the eye, with a baby in her arms and a subtle, understated husband at her hip. They knew it was Anna when the red-headed scholar jolted to embrace them. He had many books in his hands and he dropped a few clumsily as he stumbled through his greeting. He knew what had been done to him when they last spoke, how authors he had long read shone differently under the light of Anna's feminine morality. He wanted to run all of his favorite philosophers through that same filter, and he wanted all of his friends to witness it.

The patio was no fuller than on their first night in Reutlingen, but this time, they were all together, and all there with a singular purpose. They wasted no time securing Anna and Jost some food and drink and a seat at their crowded tables. There was no time spent warming slowly to the topics. The books were opened. The pamphlets were unfolded, and quotations from various philosophers and theologians were hurled at Anna, so much faster than she could consider a response. Eventually, things settled down and debate arose at a more natural pace. Jost enjoyed it as much as Anna, and he contributed beyond what was common for him.

Such was their time in Reutlingen. The Koobs spent ten days there. They had plenty more symposiums, pickled in the thick aroma from the bistro kitchen. They also took solitary days in the blossoming fields and forests outside of the city. They shared meals in the homes of new friends (who quickly came to feel as old friends), were introduced to students, scholars, and clerics, and traded liberally in books and opinions.

At the end of ten days, the city that hosted them was reluctant to let them go. Anna and Jost felt no such attachment. They treasured their new acquaintances, and tucked their images of Reutlingen safely into the deep pockets of their memories. But they packed and mounted their cart without care or regret. Their redheaded friend made gifts of many books and papers. He was clearly a man of some means who was as liberal of pocket as he was of mind.

They rolled out of Reutlingen, toward Nice. As they did, as the hard streets of the city gave way to the softer roads beyond, Jost turned to Anna. She stared ahead, lost deep in thought, with Christoph at her breast. To Jost, she seemed twice her size. She had grown in Reutlingen — spiritual and intellectual growth. She swam freely in the waters of scholarly conversation, and those waters were good for her skin. She glowed in the sun as he stared at her. He thought also of the growth of the many men she influenced on that bistro patio.

"What an extraordinary woman I have married," he thought to himself, floating high on a self-congratulatory cloud. His humility brought that cloud to ground level, as he felt the full weight of the debt he owed to God and fate.

His suckling son, his singular wife, a cart full of books — Jost strained to consider one single thing the world could offer that would possibly supplement the great gifts he already had. He squinted his eyes and smiled to the sky, thanking God for his life.

Chapter Eighteen:
The African Manuscript

OUR TRAVELERS PASSED QUICKLY THROUGH ZÜRICH. The air of its local academia was stuffy and not inviting to the opinions of others. But there were manuscripts of a much greater variety than they found in Reutlingen. A college of theology opened in 1525, the atmosphere of which was far better suited to Jost than to Anna. They spent half of a day there together. Anna felt out of place and thoroughly unwelcome. She was viewed by the scholars there as little more than an appendage growing off of Jost's hip.

Jost spent the second day at the college alone. They had a handsome collection of newly printed volumes and Jost bought several books. He knew they would sell in Nice, where European thought departed for ports across the globe. Their stay in Zürich was not spiritually or intellectually enriching, but it promised to be good for business.

After two long days, filled with bloated, languid hours, they left Zürich. They continued south and traveled a difficult pass through the Alps as an unremarkable part of a caravan. They met up with the Rhone River and followed it southwest along a much easier path. Those were wonderful days for Anna. She read their new acquisitions and debated the finer points with her husband. Along the Rhone, the road was easy, the skies fair, and those traveling beside them kept to themselves. They remained with their caravan until stopping in Martigny. The town had a surprising collection of Roman literature. They sold a few books. They bought a new German translation of Horace and a full set of Juvenal's Satires in Latin. Once those resources were consumed, Martigny had nothing to offer. They rested. They ate. And they turned south toward Nice.

Their passage through the mountains west of the Matterhorn peak was treacherous and uncomfortable. The weather was foul and the road was rough. There were no moments for study or conversation. Uneasiness and displeasure defined those days. Once clear of the mountains, the low valley beyond did not much improve their conditions. It rained until it snowed. The snow was welcomed. It was cold, but did not soak them through and through. The books and the stores of food and personal items were all that made it to Turin in comfort and dryness. Just as they entered Turin, their cart lost an axel. Fortunately, there was plenty of traffic and our travelers found friendly transportation into Turin, for themselves and their cargo. They abandoned their cart where it broke.

Turin was a logistical nightmare for Jost. He could not find a suitable cart for a price he was willing to pay. They would have liked to have stayed in Turin for weeks, had it been feasible. There was much there to tempt the minds of our heroes, but there was no place for them to stay. Jost found a caravan to Nice and arranged for their rented passage the very next day. They were exhausted, and found themselves unrecovered on a stranger's cart, on the road again. The weather remained bad until they were again in the rolling foothills with mountains ahead of them.

The sky cleared and calmed, and the mountains seemed less daunting. The improved conditions lightened the hearts of their fellow travelers. Light pleasantries grew into conversations. It was nothing like their patio symposiums in Reutlingen. These were businessmen, traders, whose minds never drifted beyond the operations of their trade. Although talk was shallow, Anna bloomed in the congenial company of good people, under a warm sun, the effect of which was apparent on every face in the caravan.

Anna entertained a light company for another eleven days of travel. The caravan moved quickly, and the pace should have exhausted them all. But it did not. The time passed well, with enough restful stops and meals that were shared liberally among the many strangers in the caravan. Many years later, in trying to tell Christoph of those days, Anna had warm memories, but little to tell. She recalled none of the conversations and very few of the faces. Those who rode and broke bread with them from Turin to Nice were pleasantly mundane people. Anna always spoke well of those days, but never passed much detail, as very little stuck to her memory.

Nice introduced itself gently to their senses. At its outskirts, the farms and houses were not at all unlike what they saw as they left Aschaffenburg County. As they rode nearer the coast, the sights turned foreign, strange even to Jost's eyes. The city center had tight rows of tall, colorful buildings, placed one upon the next. The streets were narrow and the alleys even narrower. Nice was much more than either Anna or Jost had imagined. Neither had been to a coastal city, a Mediterranean city, and a confluence of cultures from the three continents that shared the sea.

One of the first things they noticed, when the caravan dropped them in the heart of the city, was that one could hear a dozen different languages being spoken in only a few blocks of walking. Two different hearts would have been quite daunted at their prospects. They were left on the side of the street with five crates of books and two large chests filled with everything else they brought with them out of Kleinostheim. There is one thing both of them shared without a word passed between them on the subject — they both wanted to remain in Nice for a while. They were done with traveling and wanted a few shallow roots to grow from their feet into the streets where they stood.

How language dictates perception. They were dirty. They were smelly. But their clothes were of quality. They had money in their hands. They carried themselves with dignified deportment, and most importantly, they spoke as finely as anyone in any court or college in Europe. They quickly found residence in the city center and set themselves without rest to settling their belongings for an extended stay. It was an apartment on the third floor of a bright yellow building. The day was late when they moved their things into their new rooms, but they stayed up until sunrise, outfitting it to their desires and taste. They spent the next few days procuring comforts, not selling books or meeting academics. They wanted something to resemble a home, at least until they got their feet beneath them.

They were careful with their money, not knowing how well they would do in Nice and having no way to quickly tap the resources from the estate in Kleinostheim. At the end of the first three days, their apartments were comfortably their own, but with much more creativity than finance invested in the effort. They had one central living room. It had a high ceiling, one orange wall, and four dingy brown walls that had once been white. There was no room for stately furniture, nor could they have afforded it. Jost bought an oversized, well-worn Persian pillow and laid it on the floor against the wall, and three smaller pillows to act as the back of a couch. One colorful rug was the only other thing they purchased to adorn the living room. It would have been gaudy in most settings, but it suited that room perfectly and added an exotic richness to the space. Jost piled his crates of books against the wall, opposite of the Persian pillow, making the narrow room even narrower.

They had two other rooms. One had a metal-framed bed that looked dangerous to approach. Anna leaned her weight into it with a rag until she brought it to an admirable polish. There were no shelves or closets. They pushed the chests against the wall, and those were all the needed storage. Few clothing items traveled with them and the chests contained them with room to spare. The third room was little larger than a closet. It was the only room that had no window to the street. They bought a fifth pillow to serve as Christoph's bed and nestled it in the corner of the third room.

By the fourth day in Nice, Jost was eager to see the main seaport, with its tall ships and blue waters beyond. Anna was tired, as was Christoph, whose patience during travel was near saintly for a child his age. Now that they were settled, a long day of stillness was in order for the mother and baby. They stayed behind when Jost left to explore the trade center of Nice.

The coast bustled. A narrow thoroughfare separated the docks from a long, tall crescent of offices and warehouses. There was little to be gained on that day. Jost's head spun and he struggled to get his bearings. It was a splendid scene of ordered chaos. Finely attired gentlemen rubbed elbows with salty sailors. Friars from the nearby monastery bargained for supplies with coarse and vulgar locals. It was thrilling, but all a bit much for Jost. He returned to the apartments after an educational but exhausting hour.

He told Anna all that he had seen, heard, and smelled. She revived with curiosity, and the two of them sat on the Persian pillow, pressed against each other, and planned their next steps while Christoph napped. Early the next morning, Christoph seemed recovered from travel and as eager as his parents to experience his new city. Jost led them to the docks. It was everything Jost had described and so much more. They allowed themselves about an hour of discovery before advocating their business. They inquired of everybody who understood them where books could be bought and sold. They had no luck that day. The only things they purchased were a few Spanish trinkets from a street vendor and a loaf of spicy bread.

It would be inaccurate to say that their circumstances were dire, but the realities of their fantasized relocation fell upon them. They needed to establish their business, make connections, find sources and customers, and they needed to do so in a foreign city. German speakers were not hard to come by. But in the city center, most business was conducted in French or Italian, and on the docks, conversations seemed to be stitched loosely together in a quilt of many languages. Jost knew some French and a phrase or two in Italian. Anna was well versed in Italian and Latin and could produce many quotations in Greek. She was unable to splice those quotations and reorder them into conversation. They both silently missed Reutlingen, and the friends and comforts that came so instantly and easily to them there.

Back in their rooms that evening, Anna pored over their store of books and began an industrious study of the languages represented. While Anna was in intense study, Jost returned daily to the docks. He was driven to improve their circumstances. He spoke and he listened. On the fourth day at the docks, he caught wind of a collection of foreign literature recently unloaded from a ship out of Palermo, a Spanish city on the island of Sicily.

Jost broke himself free of all shyness and trepidation. He asked around and was led to a merchant warehouse west of the main docks, overlooking the water. The merchant was not in the city, but the merchant's clerk met Jost at the door of the warehouse and invited him in. The clerk brought Jost to the back of an upper room. Large windows faced the sea and allowed equal portions of light and salty air into the room. In a dark corner, where dust sat thick and only disturbed by a single set of footprints, wedged in against the walls with little care or order, were dozens of unopened cases of books and papers. At the front of them were three newer crates, undusty and with brighter planks.

The clerk opened the new crates for Jost. The first was filled with dozens of printed copies of the Greek Bible. They were beautifully bound, handsome books. The other two crates had nothing of either interest or significant trade value. Jost was interested in the Greek Bibles. The price was high and the clerk was unmovable. Jost determined to return when the merchant was back in hopes of finding more pliable negotiations with the proprietor. He bought ten copies of the overpriced Bibles. He knew he could not sell them at a profit. He did not intend to sell them, but to hold them to be gifted at some later time, as a gesture of good will to some later acquaintance.

The clerk knew the trade well enough to know that Jost was new to the business. He recommended that Jost spend less time roaming the docks and seek business acquaintances in the academic circles on the north side of the city. He directed him specifically to the Monastery of Cimiez, a Franciscan Monastery of notoriously liberal sensibilities. Jost thanked the clerk and earnestly promised to follow the advice.

Jost asked about the other crates, the older and long-neglected collection piled in the corner. The clerk tried to deny him access to them, insisting that nothing within them would interest him. He explained that they had sat there, unsellable for many months. The denial only made them more tempting. Jost insisted strenuously and was allowed to look inside of them. For the most part, the clerk was correct. The books were in poor condition. They were not handsome to behold nor interesting to read. There were ledgers of some old Tunisian warehouse, a collection of half-decayed legal papers from Corsica, and many dozens of other books that were as filthy as they were unimpressive.

One book stood out among it all. It was African, hand-copied in Arabic with exquisite script and colorful illustrations by a master's hand. For its beauty alone, Jost offered a fair price. The clerk offered it complementary with the purchase of the Greek Bibles. There was nothing acquired that morning that promised a handsome return, but Jost left pleased. The Bibles would serve to charm new acquaintances. The African book he intended to be a present for his wife.

It appeared that a sound partnership formed that day with a good and accommodating merchant. Not only did the clerk gift the African manuscript, but he ordered a servant to carry the books into the city center and deliver them to Jost's apartment. Jost waited to accompany the servant, not out of mistrust, not from any fear for his modest investment. He wanted the company. The servant was Tunisian. His French was clearly influenced by his employer and resembled the French of Paris more than of Tunis. As they walked together, Jost delightfully stumbled through the rough beginnings of many would-be conversations, each of which ended when the topics grew beyond his vocabulary.

The servant carried the Bibles up to the rooms, where Jost introduced him to Anna. He was surprised to be spoken to at all, let alone with the casual respect he received from Anna. It made him nervous at first, and he glanced with obvious agitation to the door. But he calmed when she placed a hand on his shoulder in sisterly fashion. The truth is, she longed for company, much more than Jost did. She threw some French at him, and filled the gaps in her knowledge with Latin. He seemed to understand her perfectly. She praised the loveliness of the Bibles as if the servant printed them himself. He smiled, nodded, and answered her comments cordially. He was relieved of his awkwardness when Christoph began to scream from another room. The servant excused himself and left them.

Jost bragged about the new connection, presenting as evidence the complementary African manuscript. Anna marveled at the workmanship. It was indeed a marvel. As a work of visual art it was pleasing, and neither of them could comprehend its being considered so valueless. Anna studied every pen stroke and grew intensely curious about its content. The next day, when Jost set out to find the Franciscan monastery, Anna sought a translator of Arabic. The Port of Nice hosted ships from across the North African Coast. Translators of Arabic were in high demand. After only a few inquiries, she found one just a few buildings away. He was a short, gray-haired old port official named Cadieux, with one foot in retirement, who spent many more hours in the taverns of the city center than on the docks.

Anna met Cadieux at the street tables of a restaurant not far from their rooms. He was intrigued, not for having his services solicited. That was common. He was captivated by Anna, by her giddy eagerness to unlock the secrets of the book in her hand. He was also entertained by Christoph, who bounced on Anna's lap with a mumbling giggle and a flirtatious grin.

Cadieux was curious about the book's origins and he made many repeated inquiries on the subject, despite the fact that Anna could give him no answers. He asked if he could hold on to the book while he worked out the translation. There was honesty in his eyes and she consented without a thought of caution. He promised to give the commission his full attention and he excused himself from her company. Anna and Christoph returned to their rooms and awaited Jost's return.

Jost found the monastery precisely where the clerk directed him. They boasted of a substantial library and sought to expand it. Jost gave a brief description of the books in his possession. They showed interest, but the curator of their library was in Spain and was not due to return for two weeks. Jost made an appointment to return in two weeks and he walked back to his wife and son. As he described his experience to Anna that night, he glowed with hope. Their prospects in Nice were improving and his brief visit to the Monastery of Cimiez left him with a strong sense of well-being.

The air of central Nice seemed particularly sweet that night. It felt almost alive, like a spirit that invaded their bodies through their nostrils so it could luxuriate in the sensual pleasures of its native city. Someone in a neighboring room was playing some exotic stringed instrument, the sound of which was new and enticing. It was a haunting melody, played at a moderate tempo that started their toes tapping. The sound dulled through the walls, which gave a soulful richness to the melody. It serenaded Christoph to sleep on the colorful rug.

The music had a different effect on Anna. It lifted her to her feet. She walked to the window and opened it in a trance, her every twitch synchronized to the rhythm of the music. With the window open, the sound came to them more crisply and seemed to accompany the sounds coming through the walls, though they came from the same instrument. The two sounds mimicked our two young heroes as they listened. One came spritely and directly, the other came through heavy filters, quieter and subtler, but with an equally powerful effect on the soul.

Anna turned from the window and stared at her sleeping son, then drifted her head slowly to her husband. She raised a hand in invitation and Jost joined her at the window. He took her in his arms and began to sway to the melancholy tune. The musician was tireless and the song rolled on while Anna and Jost danced at the window. The light from their room cast their united shadow on the wall of the building across the narrow street from them. They both noticed the shadow at the same time. They stopped their dance and stared at it, allowing it to remind them of that truth that held them steady through many joys and terrors during their young marriage — that they were united in all things, the edges of each of their spirits indistinguishable from the other's. They held that pose and gazed at the profound truth being cast in metaphor across from them, until the musician retired his fingers for the night.

The next morning had a buzz of excitement about it. They left their rooms pressed against each other's side. Jost had spent his entire adult life in the management of landed estates. His business was always fixed implacably to property, always stable and immeasurably slow in its evolution. His objective was always the maintenance of the old, never the discovery of the new, and he did so with cold distance. It would have been in his previous form to sit for two weeks and wait for the Franciscan curator to return to Nice. Prompted by much more than their financial circumstances, he ventured out early the next morning, and early every morning that followed, meeting people, endearing himself to strangers, and doing so in a manner that would have been unrecognizable by his earlier acquaintances.

He adjusted surprisingly well to the life of a traveling salesman. He sought any nook in the streets of Nice where a book could be bought or sold. He spoke with ease to tradesmen, innkeepers, politicians, sailors, and professors, to any and all people they encountered. No matter with whom they found themselves in company, Jost played the part, saying the right things and doing the right things. Anna fell more deeply in love than ever, for a depth of spirit and intellect that had shyly hidden inside of him found wings in Nice.

After the night in the window, it was rare that they would spend five minutes out of each other's company in the length of an entire day. What needed to be done by one, was experienced by both, and by Christoph, whose little feet rarely met the floor, for he was almost always in somebody's arms. They were all together when Cadieux called on them and informed Anna that he had finished the translation of the African manuscript.

The old man was as giddy as a child. He set the manuscript in the center of the rug and plopped to a seat in front of it. Anna and Jost joined him, one on either side.

After a deep inhale that was held beyond its natural life, Cadieux released his breath with the words, "You were right to bring this to me."

Anna and Jost both turned their attention from the manuscript to the translator, and they stared at a man whose old face turned radiant with passion for the subject before him.

After another deeply held breath, Cadieux continued while pointing to the book as he spoke, "You were right. This writing here is Arabic, but these markings beside and above are in a language called Chinyanja, from the Kingdom of Maravi, in Southeastern Africa."

Cadieux slid back so he could look at his hosts together. He put a hand on the shoulder of each and said in a tone of profound gravity, "This is a book of ancient proverbs, a philosophy they call uMunthu."

Cadieux delighted to see Anna's face illuminate to match his own. What ancient truths were secured inside of that book? Anna could not wait to see.

Cadieux told with great energy, like a rambling child, his efforts to unlock the secrets of the book, "The Arabic was easy to translate. The other writing was a mystery to me. I know a man, a captain of a merchant vessel. He lives here in Nice. He would know. I thought for certain that he would know. He is more often ashore these days. He is old, you see. I brought him your book and he knew it at a glance. He lived many years in Maravi, and he knew it at a glance."

Cadieux was too excited for his own good and he rambled like a fool. Jost paused the story to serve them all wine. After a few sips and expressions of gratitude, Cadieux continued calmly, and more like his sober, adult self, "The Arabic is a translation of the Chinyanja. We sat for hours and discussed the translation. He said that it did not translate well into Arabic. We debated it line by line, and now I think I can give you not only a translation of the Arabic, but an accurate understanding of the uMunthu Proverbs. He wanted your book badly. He offered me a fortune for it. I told him it did not belong to me. He would have to discuss the terms with you. Would you like me to arrange it? I am sure you will be happy with his price."

Anna looked to Jost. Jost returned with a look as if to say, "It is *your* book, my Love."

"I would like to keep it!" Anna blurted with much more force than was necessary.

The money would have served them well, but Jost shrugged his shoulders and replied, "Then you keep it."

Cadieux translated the proverbs into German, which proved frustrating. The meaning in Arabic came as distorted into German as it had from Chinyanja to Arabic. The topic ignited an impassioned debate on the ability of cultural concepts to be accurately translated out of their indigenous languages. Cadieux taught Anna to speak the lines in Chinyanja, as he had learned from his friend. And so they passed their evening, Anna, Jost, and Cadieux, sipping wine, alternating between lounging comfortably and pacing the floor, from slow and soft voices to loud and fiery, reciting and debating with various intensity until they could not expel another word. The wine, the budding friendship, and the subjects of discussion cooperated in producing a narcotic effect that can only be felt in good company. Anna and Jost walked Cadieux to the door. He sternly demanded to enjoy their company again very soon. They embraced and saw their new friend from their rooms.

They could have collapsed on the spot and slept quite comfortably piled upon each other in the doorway. Such was the sort of day they had. But they did not sleep, not immediately. They sat against a wall and talked about the book, not about the accuracy of translations, but about the proverbs themselves. The uMunthu Philosophy spoke loudly to them. As they ran their fingers over the scribblings, they thought about the scribe who penned it, and about the ancient uMunthu philosophers who originally spoke the proverbs. As the book sat straddling their two laps, it shone in their eyes as their dearest earthly treasure. They needed no adhesive to bind their spirits, but had they needed one, the African manuscript would have served the purpose.

Chapter Nineteen:
Young Franciscans

WHEN THE TIME CAME TO MEET with the curator of the monastery library, they went together, Anna, Jost, and Christoph. Not many young children had been brought into the monastery, and Christoph's laughter echoed awkwardly from the walls. They were shown into the impressive library. There must have been at least 250,000 volumes. Perhaps they waited there for five minutes, perhaps an hour. They could not have said. Time had no relevance while they scanned their eyes across the many shelves. Eventually, the curator greeted them. They were surprised to behold a much younger man than they expected. He was a tall, Italian man named Marcello, maybe a year or two older than Jost.

Jost came with a Greek Bible to present as a gift. Marcello accepted it with delight, less for its value to his library, for the library had beautiful Bibles in a vast multitude of shapes, sizes, and languages. Marcello delighted at the grace and humility with which it was presented by his guests. He led his visitors to a large unoccupied room. It had one long, broad table surrounded by at least twenty chairs. At the head of the table was one chair that stood out from the rest. It was obviously intended for the master of whatever assembly gathered there. Assuming a modest chair at the side of the table, Jost plopped a ledger down in front of him. Within it was a list and categorization of all of the books he owned in Nice, including the German translation of Horace and the full set of Juvenal's Satires in Latin, which he acquired in Martigny. Anna brought the African manuscript with her, hoping it might spark a discussion. To Anna and Jost's surprise, rather than taking up a chair and reviewing the ledger, or commenting on the exotic manuscript, Marcello excused himself from the room and left Anna, Jost, and Christoph alone.

He returned twenty minutes later with something that, between them, only Jost had heard of. Marcello came back with a tray and three mugs of coffee. Coffee had been introduced to the city of Nice by a ship from Malta. The beans had come from Turkey and did not sell in Malta. The captain took the entire shipment to Nice and refused to disembark until his cargo holds were empty. Eventually, just to remove the ship from their docks, the city purchased the coffee and promoted its consumption. It became a craze, and demand for more shipments kept the port busy with beans. A single roaster roasted all the coffee in Nice. It never closed its doors. As he gave them their coffee, Marcello told them about a new coffee house in the southeast part of town.

"It sells nothing but coffee?" Jost asked, "and it keeps its doors open?"

"It is the busiest building in all of Savoy," Marcello answered.

Anna lifted her mug to her lips, but was startled out of her progress when Marcello belted, "Go easy! It is hot and very strong. Sip it slowly."

It was bitter, but it found Anna's palate at the right time. The book of African proverbs had her starving to experience and understand the exotic. Her tongue anatomized every particular of the coffee, the bitterness, the smokiness, the viscosity. Even the uncomfortable heat heightened the excitement. Marcello took frenzied elation in introducing it. He had clearly developed a passion for it and was thrilled to share that passion with others. They sat together and sipped their coffee, talking about Malta and obstinate ship captains, about roasters and coffee houses, and not at all about books or libraries. Not yet aware of the effect of the caffeine, Jost dipped his finger into his mug and allowed Christoph to suck the coffee off of his finger. It took little time to saturate his blood, and little Christoph, who had grown much in the months since they left Kleinostheim, wiggled and squirmed, and proved quite the distraction to conversation.

No servants came to clear the tray of mugs. Marcello did that himself and disappeared from the room as before. He came back within a few minutes and sat at the side of the table, putting Anna and Christoph between the men. He inquired about Jost's collection. Jost began with an abbreviated version of their travels to that point. He slid the ledger in front of Anna, and Marcello leaned against her to see it. The four of them (counting Christoph) huddled in front of it. Marcello was as liberal of finance as he was of taste. Jost described each volume represented in his ledger and, one at a time, Marcello agreed to buy most of them. Anna had already read most of their collection, including the new German translation of Horace, but she had not finished Juvenal's Satires, and she tried to diminish their value in description.

Marcello saw right through her and played no word games with her. He told her plainly, "I would love them for our library. You finish them. Take as long as you need. I will pay you for it up front, along with the rest, and you can deliver them as you finish them."

Marcello was astonished that she would covet Latin versions of Juvenal and would not dare to do anything to discourage her. He dropped a few quotes from the early Satires, to which Anna answered with flawless quotations of her own.

All business being concluded, Jost sat back as a proud spectator. Quotations from Juvenal moved on to Virgil, then Cicero and Seneca, then opened into free conversations in Latin. Jost caught the occasional word or phrase. The conversation could have been in German and he would have been just as deaf to it. His amorous eyes fixed on his wife and relished the graceful ease with which she conversed with the friar. Anna pointed a few times to the African manuscript, having been successful in pulling the book into the conversation.

Their voices carried loudly through the open door and into the hallway, attracting curious monks. One, then three, then another two, followed later by several others, entered the room. Some were monks, some friars, some guests, and some lay employees of the monastery. All were young and they filed in to fill every one of the chairs around the table. This woman with the tongue of a Roman senator's wife enamored them all with her Latin, and much more with the content within.

Others joined in the conversation, all in Latin, until Anna stopped in mid-phrase. They all stared at her during the long pause that followed, and after some wrinkled-eye contemplation, she explained in German, "There is no way to say that in Latin. It does not translate."

One of the monks asked her, "What do you mean?"

She explained that the proverb she was referencing in the African manuscript could not be spoken in Latin.

He corrected her, saying, "All things translate. The human experience is universal."

Anna had no chance to respond. The monk's statement fired off a barrage of simultaneous opinions across the table. The noise caught the attention of a few older monks, who stepped a few paces into the room and stood silently against the wall.

The arguments consumed the attention of everyone at the table except Anna and Jost. They were the only two who remembered that it was Anna who sparked the debate. Nobody else seemed to notice the visitors at the table, sitting awkwardly and holding a caffeinated child.

Jost leaned in near Anna's ear and said, "We have conducted our business here. Let's go."

Jost stood first and nobody noticed. They just carried on arguing. Anna stood next, which despite her being of smaller frame, drew their attention. In a wave from Anna's position outward, silence swept the table.

One young friar, realizing their rudeness but unwilling yet to release the topic, drew Anna in, saying, "You say that your thought could not be translated into Latin. But fundamental truth transcends language."

She stared across the table at him and looked gently into his eyes, with the confidence of wisdom behind her, and told him, "Nothing transcends language when it is passed only *through* language. All philosophy is either spoken or written, heard or read. The truth within is not just carried *on* language or delivered *by* language, where it can be separated on its arrival. It is sewn comprehensively into the language. The uMunthu philosophy written here has no Latin equivalent."

Marcello, in the tone of a student, not an opponent, asked, "Are you saying that truth does not exist without language?"

"Of course it exists without language," she responded, sliding her chin smoothly to face him, "but we are not talking about truth *existing*. We are talking about it being taught, about its meaning being passed from one person to another, from one culture to another, and culture lives strictly within the confines of its language."

A voice from the far foot of the table sprang loudly, "I do not believe that it does."

He made this remark in a questioning tone, with more uncertainty than stout belligerence. Anna turned to him and saw a face that eagerly invited her response. He clearly wanted to understand the matter as she did, but had not yet wrapped his fingers around it. The following pause was easily read by all in the room. Anna was to elaborate. They looked to her to clear the fog from the matter. She was an enigma, sitting beside her husband with a child in her arms, like any wife, but springing Classical quotations into the air in flawless Latin, and challenging their long-held notions. So strange a figure did she appear in their eyes, that she could have grown a horn from her forehead, right in front of them, and they would have accepted it with the rest.

At first, she was frustrated by the following silence, misinterpreting its cause, and she snapped impatiently, "You cannot simply shove your thoughts into their words, or theirs into yours. If you are to truly translate a text, I'm afraid you must meet them halfway and study not only the words of their language. You must search vigorously for their meaning. Word-for-word translations are a cheap, thin copy, not a true representative of the original text."

Among them, the men in the room had scribed many translations. They were proud of what they knew and of what they had accomplished. Anna's argument shook them to their bones.

One of the older monks standing against the wall near the entrance spun the heads of the room when he asked, "How do I do that if I cannot uproot and live among them?"

Anna turned slowly and was taken aback by the wrinkled face that housed such a youthful voice. She realized at that moment that she was in a monastery, addressing a man whose experience and wisdom was written plainly on his face. She was intimidated, but she answered nevertheless, "You will find all you need within their writings, but dig. Dig deeply. Find the many ways the words are used. The context of many samples should reveal the cultural meanings of the words. But even with such efforts, an indigenous truth might have no body in a foreign language."

All eyes fixed on her, and their lips showed no sign that they intended to part. The moment Anna realized nobody in the room would either speak or move until she answered, she continued, "Has French or German, Latin or Greek developed in a way that can envelope African philosophical thought? There are many cultures in sole possession of indigenous thought, so that no other language has *needed* the words to describe it. For such words, there are no translations. For such thoughts, there are no foreign equivalents. In passing those philosophies through your language, you are passing more of your own thoughts than theirs."

After moments of deep contemplation among them, and many subconscious sighs, Anna added, "Charlemagne said that to have another language is to possess a second soul."

Those words spoke clearly to Anna and Jost, and to a few among them, but the rest needed clarification, so she explained, "The human experience is diverse. Human thought is diverse. Since there is no way to fully envelope a culture outside of its own language, learning another language opens the eyes, mind, and heart to another existence. With a second language, when that language is read and spoken, and used to truly understand its people, you can double yourself, especially if the new culture is very different from your own."

The minds of the room swam, and rolled the eyes within their heads. Comments in support of Anna's assertions flew across the table, as did arguments to the contrary, all in good-hearted, but passionate debate. Jost and Anna went to the Monastery of Cimiez to buy and sell books, not to engage in debate with young Franciscan theologians. Yet there they were. The walls of the monastery had not heard such fiery voices since the Siege of Nice by the Turks. They drew more and more opinions into the room. There must have been quite a crowd in the hallway outside of the door, beyond the notice of Anna and Jost.

One new attendant to their gathering could not be unnoticed if he tried. His appearance through the doorway was conspicuous in the extreme and drew the attention of the Franciscans. It was their abbot, the head of their cloister. He had listened in the hallway to all that Anna had spoken. Marcello introduced his guests to the abbot, who welcomed them warmly. After the initial greetings, there was silence. The abbot eyed Anna scalp to toe while the monks and friars waited for one of them to speak.

A surge of uneasiness waved across Jost. He had his finger on the pulse of the times. It was not an age of liberal religious tolerance. They were not so very far removed from the trial, from accusations of witchcraft, which, although ultimately fruitless, turned cherished neighbors into ravenous beasts, and put Anna's life in jeopardy. In the silence of the room, Jost's hairs stood erect, as if each was ready to defend Anna.

Finally, the abbot broke the tense air, saying in a hoarse whisper, "There is much truth in the things you say. You display understanding beyond your years, yet there is so much more to the matter than you can see. Despite its shortcomings, I find your insights refreshing in someone so young, and I encourage you to explore these subjects further."

He said nothing else to her. He nodded his head deferentially and walked slowly from the room, drawing all eyes in his wake. Anna was honored by the compliments, and she took the challenges to heart. He spoke of her being young, not of her being a woman. He suggested that it was her age and experience, not her sex that held her from the grander truths that eluded her. There was little else to be said. The monks left the room with the remnants of a spirited debate still lingering subtly on their lips. Anna was thrilled that her words sparked such exquisitely fervent thought. Jost's admiration for his wife swelled exponentially.

When only Anna, Jost, Christoph, and Marcello remained in the room, the business of the visit was given its due. Final arrangements were made for the sale of the books. Marcello offered a gift, but would not say what it was. He asked if he could visit them the following day, show them the coffee house he mentioned earlier, and present the gift then. They gleefully accepted. Christoph turned restless, reminding Anna of how neglectful they had been of his needs. Marcello escorted them from the monastery and saw them off like an old friend, with kisses and embraces.

The motion of the walk and the quiet of the streets soothed Christoph from his uneasiness. Anna was not soothed. As she and Jost walked and talked about what had just occurred, she became vivacious to an extraordinary degree, stirred to delight and antsy within her own skin. She hardly drew breath during the entire walk back to the city center. To Jost, it seemed as if she expelled one long exhale, filled to brim with African philosophy, linguistic theory, cultural sociology, and love for the new life they were building together, so far from what had once been their only home.

Chapter Twenty:
Aromatic Jealousy

ALTHOUGH ANNA WAS BEGINNING TO THRIVE in the halls of academic debate, and she left gatherings like the one at the monastery with more spiritual energy than she entered them, she too needed recovery. The young woman from the quiet village of Kleinostheim still needed the secluded company of her own household, little as it was. She needed to still her tongue and soak in the bliss of quiet intimacy. Jost left the monastery exhausted and only returned to form once his wife and son were locked securely within their rooms.

For a few moments, the domestic bliss they both sought was theirs in abundance. They sat on the floor a few feet from each other and taught Christoph to toddle between them. He stumbled and giggled. They laughed heartily in response. The world seemed to melt away, leaving the three of them as God's only remaining creations. It was far and away Jost's happiest moments. But Christoph grew tired and fell asleep, and the intimacy of their own company turned awkward.

Anna became intensely thoughtful. There was a great deal for her to ponder, and her thoughts were not tolerant of interruption. Jost had shared Anna like he never had to before. He was so proud of her, but he was also jealous. Anna bonded tightly with Cadieux as they went through his translation of the African manuscript. She bonded with their red-headed bistro companion in Reutlingen. She bonded instantaneously with Marcello and the other young Franciscans. Even the abbot, in his brief appearance, formed a bond with her. Now that they were in their own rooms, with Christoph peacefully asleep, Jost still could not have Anna to himself. He tried to engage her in discussion on topics he knew she would enjoy. She was unable.

She thought about the things that were said at the monastery, and the things that should have been said. She scraped her memory for applicable quotes, and was quite ensconced in her private musings. She did not mean to appear annoyed when Jost tried to connect with her as deeply as strangers had. She did not know that she did. Her gestures shunned him without consulting her consciousness. Poor Jost! Although the circumstances of the moment were infinitely preferable to the courtroom in Aschaffenburg, to Jost, the sensation was similar. He felt just as restricted from reaching her. With a heavy heart, entirely out of sync with the lightness of hers, he kissed her on the head and laid down with Christoph.

Anna stayed up for two more hours in hypnotic contemplation, unable to say afterward if she had stared out the window or at a blank wall. When she returned to the physical world around her, she was surprised to find that Jost was not at her side. Jost awoke refreshed, with the confidence to try again. The opportunity did not present itself. Just as the buzz of the household morning calmed, and they all had eaten, a visitor called on them.

Marcello appeared at their door with an exquisite bouquet of silk flowers for Anna. At the end of the sixteenth century, the presentation of flowers did not carry the same symbolism it does today. It was right and appropriate for him to bring her flowers when he visits. The Franciscans took a vow of poverty, and Marcello could boast of no earthly possessions, but the monastery had money, and Marcello considered the visit to be monastery business. He invited Anna and Jost to accompany him to the coffeehouse.

Although the flowers spoke nothing of Marcello's feelings, his eyes were emphatically boisterous. Still dripping with the prior evening's jealousy, Jost saw it plainly. Marcello was enamored with Anna. It was a cerebral attraction, carrying an infant enchantment of the heart. It was not a physical attraction. Anna enamored nobody at a glance. Hers was not that sort of beauty. She and Jost had worked their way through crowded streets and squares without drawing an eye or passing a word. But those who shared their company for more than a few passing seconds, those who passed more than fleeting pleasantries, were lit ablaze by the fire of her spirit and dumbfounded by her wit.

Marcello was a young man and a passionate philosopher. He had never met anyone like her. The pull at his head and heart would not have been much lessened were she a man. But she was a woman, one who presented to his ears, for the very first time, the authority of feminine strength. Anna and Jost could not have understood how he felt, because *he* could not have understood.

Anna suggested leaving Christoph with Cadieux. He had offered the service. Jost rejected the notion emphatically. He wanted nothing more than the isolation and tightness of his wife and child. He could not have the one. To compensate with the other, he took Christoph tightly to his chest and followed reluctantly.

The coffeehouse was near the sea and already abuzz with the full variety of Nice's inhabitants. None of the restrictive walls that keep humans from one another were erected there. The tones of skin were as varied as the fashions and the languages being spoken. Unlike Reutlingen, Nice was comprehensively a Catholic city, though it was tolerant of the various influences that flowed lucratively through its port. The air did not carry a whiff of the tensions of the Counter-Reformation that were so pungent in central Germany.

It was all the same to Anna. Catholic, Protestant, or otherwise, she saw little difference between them. She had as her teachers Aquinas *and* Luther, Mohammed, Virgil, Seneca, and Horace, and philosophers well beyond the common readership of Christendom. She saw the beauties and the absurdities in all of them. Inside of her head, they maintained their clear distinctions while blending into a colorful hue of universal truths and falsehoods. And she brought them all with her to the coffeehouse.

Marcello knew the coffeehouse well. He knew its regular customers and had engaged in many fine debates with his nostrils flaring above the steam of his coffee. He planned this particular visit meticulously. It had to be *that* morning. It had to be *that* early. He knew which coffeehouse regulars would be present, and he had fantasized during the previous evening about initiating a debate with his coffeehouse friends like the one that arose impromptu at the monastery. He escorted his new friends to a seat then purchased them coffee and rolls. When he sat at the table with them, his excited spirit poured forth in an unhuman glow.

Marcello wasted no time sparking conversation. He reintroduced the debate from the previous day, asking Anna if she, being German and raised speaking German, could truly connect her thoughts to him, who was raised Italian and speaking Italian.

She looked at him puzzled, tilting her head like a puppy hearing a strange sound, before she answered, "That is why we learn other languages, other cultures, why we expose ourselves to other influences."

He did not ask the question with genuine curiosity. They already felt the same. He poked her with the question like poking a dwindling fire, giving it air and hoping it roars back into flame.

He kept poking, adding thoughts he had often heard but did not share, "Shouldn't you be careful not to allow so many influences to sink you into degeneracy?"

Believing his question to be in earnest, she asked in confusion, "What sort of degeneracy?"

"Degeneracy of faith and of truth."

Anna had been sitting forward in her chair and leaning into the table. She dropped to the back of her chair, took a slow sip of her coffee and shook from the surprising bitterness. She glared into the mug as if expecting the coffee to apologize for offending her. Jost smiled for the first time that day. He knew what sort of answer his wife would give, what sort of truth-lashing Marcello was about to receive across his brow. They both mistook Marcello. He would have taken any chastisement to spur debate in the coffeehouse. He was, as they say, playing the devil's advocate.

Anna's sudden fascination with the strange drink in her hand obliterated Marcello's design for the moment. He attended to her immediate needs, asking, "Did you burn yourself? Is it the taste? Do you not like it?"

Although Anna had an entire untouched roll in front of her, Marcello tore a piece from his roll and offered it to her.

She turned her eyes from her coffee back to Marcello, leaned forward again, and resumed the topic, just as Jost knew she would, saying in raised volume, "Truth can only degenerate when it is unyielding, and is your faith so fragile? I suspect that I view truth more fluidly. But if truth is as stalwart, as implacable as you suggest, what reason would you have to fear any influence hitting its shore, whether in gentle waves or in terrible storms?"

Jost could not help himself. Giggles shook his throat and his attempt to hide his smirk created a contorted grimace that looked hardly like himself. Marcello betrayed his intentions when he scanned his eyes right then left, while curious strangers scooted their chairs closer and fixed their eyes on Anna. He grinned with self-congratulations and gestured an invitation for all to join. Some knew Marcello well and were introduced to Anna and Jost. Some skirted the perimeter of the circle but were no less engaged. There was plenty at the coffeehouse to settle thirst and hunger. But the patrons that morning starved for something else. They swarmed around the conversation like gaunt vultures, ready to pick an intellectual morsel from their abundant table.

Marcello had worked the situation masterfully to his desires. Friends of his began to ask Anna questions. Jost sighed in perplexed delight. He was not immune to her charms, to the magic of the Mediterranean air, or to the exotic atmosphere of the coffeehouse. He was more inebriated by Anna than any of them, and fully as enthralled academically. But the experience was different for him than for the other men in the coffeehouse. It was much more complex. He had simultaneous and conflicting desires. He wanted to raise her high for the world to see, and he wanted to shove her into his pocket, run to the heart of a forgotten forest and hoard her for himself. That conflict raged violently inside of him as the questions firing across the table were followed by stares of anticipation.

Christoph sat still, while his senses darted greedily around the room. He was not difficult in Jost's arms. Still, Jost handed him to Anna, hoping that her son would keep her grounded to those two people with the truest claim on her, while strangers basked in her light.

By her manners and address, Anna drew up the set of rules that governed the conversation. Those engaged with her followed her unwritten rules to the letter. Anna's supremacy in this free symposium was in part due to her vast knowledge of the printed word, and in part due to her sex. Women in such a setting were far more commonly in mindless service to the desires of the men. The masculine eyes in Anna's company did not look to her for a refilled mug or to savor the thrills of a feminine figure. They turned to her for accurate quotations and a wise and refreshing, distinctly feminine interpretation of each.

She did not just echo the points of the philosophers she quoted, simply speaking their masculine points in a higher, softer voice. She soaked their arguments in feminine sensibilities, hydrating them, giving them wholeness and balance, and making them succulent on the tongue and savory in the ear. Those in attendance were besotted — spun dizzy, no less by the rich and tender wisdom carried to their ears by her feminine voice than by the narcotic effect of the coffee.

Marcello was in ecstasy. The debates raged on for hours, with Anna maintaining the chair. Jost was drawn in. How could he not be? He devoured such topics, albeit in a subtler manner than those around him. His understanding was second only to Anna's. Were Anna not there, Jost could have ruled the tables. But Anna was so far above and beyond them all, and Jost found himself once again like an unwilling host, sharing reluctantly from his own bounty, sharing his wife with a world that could not seem to get enough of her.

The air of the coffeehouse bore an intellectual sumptuousness, which was as sweet as Franconian wine to those inclined toward the scholarly, and equally repugnant to the brutish little minds that skirted by mostly unnoticed by Anna and Jost. They were not unnoticed by Christoph. His little ears compared the conversations of his parent's table with those words he heard being exchanged around them.

He was just over a year old. Still, the contrast could not have declared itself more boldly to his supple little mind. This would be the defining theme of his earliest years. But he did not judge. Already he saw the beauty and necessity of all, for primary among his parents' philosophical discussions was the topic of human equality, a moral precept that was stitched to his innermost being since he was old enough to comprehend language. At any given point, when the three of them were home alone, at least one of his parents was reading aloud. Christoph took it all in and had a vast understanding well before he could respond in kind. There will be occasion to write more on that later.

The talk in the coffeehouse did not wind down to a natural end. The morning grew late and Anna and Jost's bodies demanded a change of scene. Their stomachs grumbled for more than the breads and pastries of the coffeehouse, and their heads spun from far more coffee than was good for them. They wanted to stand and walk, for they were given no opportunity during discussion. Another mug of coffee and another roll appeared in front of them magically throughout the morning, delivered to them by hands that did not seem attached to larger parts. They ate and drank and did not divert their busy minds from conversation to consider the source of the food and drink.

The morning was not entirely social. It was lucrative. This was a highly literate crowd, and Jost secured the purchase and sale of many books. Over one shoulder, he made a sale, then turned immediately over the other to engage in the conversations. The morning went well for him. In far subtler ways, he contributed to discussions as much as Anna.

Surprisingly, it was Anna, not Jost, and certainly not Marcello, that broke the gathering and excused herself and her family to a quieter setting. Their ears were in shock from the constant clamor. They did not realize how much so until they walked to the eastern edge of the city's shoreline, where traffic was minimal and more birds than people could be heard. They set Christoph to his feet and each took a hand, slowing them to the pace of a toddling child who had barely learned to walk.

Despite his nagging jealousy, Jost enjoyed their time in the coffeehouse. His mind was electric with thought. But once outside of the scene, the intimacy of the afternoon gave the chaos of the coffeehouse a bitter taste, as bitter as that first sip of coffee. The quiet closeness of the afternoon was like a sweet and juicy bite of fruit, purging the bitterness. Jost covetously embraced the sensation and was loath to discharge that feeling. He determined to hoard his wife and son to himself and to allow their recent experiences to simmer in a safe and constant setting.

Once in the stillness of their own rooms, Jost replayed in his head the events of the day. The coffeehouse was an experience that tantalized him. But as the images from the morning clarified in his memory, his previous jealousy began to simmer deep within him. Jost's passion for Anna blazed intensely, and like any fire, it can warm and comfort, but can also burn and blister. In Kleinostheim, he almost lost her to the passions of another. In that case, it was the passionate vengeance of a grieving father. In Nice, the circumstances were entirely different, but the sensations were similar, and from that simmering jealousy, blistering fear steamed upward.

In Anna's company, a mystical light shone from Marcello's eyes that was not there when they first met him at the monastery. She affected him intensely. The friar was a moral man, a pious man, but Anna was an extraordinary woman, superior in so many ways to any man or woman he had ever encountered. Nobody knew that better than Jost. Her superior spirit possessed him and navigated his every thought since the first time he laid his eyes on her in the forest. The light in Marcello's eyes was all too familiar to him — and it frightened him. His fear proved well-warranted. Marcello appeared at their door just before sunset with another invitation for the following day.

The invitation was not to another coffeehouse or monastery. It was to a different scene with a very different crowd, but for the same purpose. Marcello kept a diverse circle of friends and was eager to show Anna to them all, or show them all to Anna. Jost allowed no time for Anna to reply, or even for her thoughts on the matter to be determined by a look. He declined the invitation abruptly and forcefully. Marcello acquiesced gracefully, but his disappointment could not hide behind his Franciscan robe, nor was he able to subdue the obvious signs of his addiction. He was addicted to Anna. It was a quickly formed and tyrannical addiction to the entirely unique feelings she brought into his life.

Despite his reserve, Jost's jealousy pronounced itself within his refusal. It embarrassed Marcello, who only at that moment began to deeply evaluate the nature of his feelings for Anna. They heard nothing from Marcello for the next six weeks. It was time spent in quiet walks, time spent as parents and as lovers. Jost visited his clients and he established new ones, but always with his wife and son at his side. Anna, too, saw the jealousy behind Jost's last encounter with Marcello. She too was embarrassed, not for anything she had done, but for what she had been unable to see. She still burned with passion for the subjects she read, but for several consecutive weeks, that burning lit only the faces of her husband and son.

Marcello made no overt attempts to throw himself in Anna's path, nor did he try to avoid her. His circle intersected naturally with hers, and he made a conscious effort to keep their encounters as appropriately distant as possible.

Chapter Twenty-One:
The Scribbler

JOST'S BOOK TRADE DID NOT ALWAYS BRING into their possession literature of his tastes. His personal inclinations had *some* influence on his dealings, but the majority of the volumes piled against their wall was of little interest to him. On the subjects of his liking, he could soundly debate anyone in the field. On the other subjects, he was perfectly content with his shallow, layman's knowledge. Anna was altogether different. She, too, had her preferred subjects, but each printed or scribbled word to cross her threshold enticed her, and she consumed them omnivorously. For each subject ever written about, Nice had a circle of impassioned devotees. Anna loved fiery deliberation and knew that excited minds in any field were never more than a short walk away. When Jost failed to engage her with frenzied affection on subjects that were outside of his tastes, she began to itch. It was an itch that could not be relieved in the intimate company of her family.

She remained sensitive to Jost's jealousy. It pained her to see it stirred in him. So she took to writing all of the things she would have spoken. Jost often caught her mumbling to herself, as she engaged in imaginary debates with the poets, painters, priests, and professors she conjured in her mind. Jost was Anna's one and only lover, but not her only love. She never gave him a reason to doubt her fidelity or her commitment to her family. Still, he knew he was not her intellectual equal, and as much as it pained him to admit, he could not alone satisfy her needs. In response, he determined to take her where she could be fulfilled.

He took her quietly to the libraries and colleges, often planning excursions to neighboring cities when the academic wells of Nice ran dry. They found secluded corners of dusty rooms where Anna could devour literature at her own pace. Jost took great care to arrange these outings at the time of day and in the manner that would not make his wife a phenomenon to attract. He tried to engage with her as she needed to be engaged. Where he failed, he encouraged her to write. Anna took liberally to the pen and wrote during those sleepless hours, when her mind flew too frantically for rest.

Jost read all that Anna wrote. After a good deal of encouragement, he convinced her to let him take her papers along with their books to be viewed and considered by their customers. Anna believed them valuable only as they served her need to express her thoughts. Jost knew well otherwise. Anna's penmanship was exquisite, a rather uncommon trait among thinkers. There was a delicate flow to her scribblings, which suited her chosen words and the philosophies behind them.

Anna wrote on all themes to cross her mind. She wrote in response to every book she came across. In general, her words were soft and her content encouraging. But when a scathing remonstrance was fitting, she gave it. For this reason, she and Jost agreed that her writings should remain anonymous. As soon as the ink dried, they placed her papers among the many others stacked against their wall, to be sold as any other acquired literature.

Jost read each scratch of Anna's pen. He read them with delight. He read them with astonishment and wonder. And he read them with trepidation. Anna took no sides on the Reformation, but she wrote things that would upset both sides. She blended the truths of distant religions with the truths of Christianity. She lent as much credit to Plato as to Saint Paul. Her musings were brilliant, and would have perfectly suited a readership four centuries younger. But amid the boiling tensions of the Counter-Reformation, before the morning rays of the Enlightenment washed Europe, they were dangerous, especially from the hand of a woman.

As her writing became more critical, Anna and Jost argued on that point. Less than two years removed from accusations of witchcraft, Anna was fearless. The truth was obvious to her and she believed that her words would speak well enough in their own defense. Jost had vivid flashbacks of mobs following them down the street and surrounding their front door. The fates of Miray and Safet rang as loud warnings in his ears and one night he passionately made that point.

Anna stared at him as she never had before. Tears welled in her eyes and she spoke with a faltering voice, "Do you think I have forgotten our friends?"

Jost had caused her pain. He was mortified by guilt. He shook his head, but did so subtly, unrecognized by Anna.

Anna waited for an answer that he was unable to give, so she continued, "I loved Miray very much. She connected with me in ways that only she and I shared. I mourn her every day."

She paused and stared at Jost's lips, waiting for a response. He shook violently inwardly but made no motion that she could see, so she added, "Ignorance killed her. Hiding the truth now, after all we have seen, would be like handing her over to an angry mob to be executed again."

Jost's still lips were relieved of their duty. His eyebrows and his teary eyes spoke clearly enough for them. With her penetrating vision, Anna saw through him — to his fear for her safety, to his mortification at causing her pain, and to the full depth of love his watery eyes held for her. Anna being Anna, she set immediately to comforting him, wrapping him in a tight and tender embrace.

Placing his feelings into words would have been a futile effort, yet he tried, able only to stutter, "I... I..."

"Ssshhhh," she hushed him before calming his lips with a kiss.

They understood each other, but they had much to sleep on. They had grown accustomed to sleeping with Christoph between them. But the boy slept soundly in his own room that night. Anna and Jost laid so tightly intertwined that they could not have said where their own body ended and the other's began. They had critical disagreements. Nevertheless, what they would decide would be decided together, with love and faith in each other. A strange energy flowed between them that night, an energetic alloy of fear and gratitude, sorrowful memories and blinding hope, and searing passion that welded their spirits together more tightly than ever.

The city center was not the place for the morning's conversation. They packed a picnic. They left Christoph with Cadieux, who could not wait to bond with the boy, and promised to entertain him thoroughly. Anna and Jost booked a ride to the hilly forest east of town. It was a four hour ride from their rooms, but they found a spot handcrafted by God for the eyes of poets and painters. It was on the south side of a hill, with an opening in the tall trees that framed the blue Mediterranean. By this point, they had both seen the sea many times, but never just so, never presented in a way that pushed their minds to the ancient past and made them feel as one with the sea's legendary history. Before addressing any of their immediate concerns, they recited what stories they could recall from the many cultures that had shared those waters.

Their recitations and musings primed their courage for a very different sort of conversation than they would have had in their own rooms, or even at the aromatic tables of the coffeehouse. By the time they were rolling back to Nice, they had determined to uproot themselves and see more of the Mediterranean Coast, trading in books and papers, finding new friars, new port officials, new translators of exotic texts, new sights and new cuisine to tantalize their senses. Christoph was not out of their minds, rather an intimate part of their deliberations. They plotted an upbringing for their son that would place him hundreds of years ahead of his time and entirely misfitted for his ancestral home. Kleinostheim and all thoughts of it were immeasurably distant.

While Anna and Jost picnicked and pondered, Cadieux and Christoph acted more as two old friends than as one old port official and one little toddler. Christoph was still not speaking, but that did little to deter the delights they shared together. Cadieux taught Christoph an ancient game of marbles. They visited the market together and shared exotic foods. Although the child did not respond, Cadieux asked him questions and told him stories and regaled the curious child with many a humorous and enlightening anecdote. He saw Anna's light shining from Christoph and loved the boy even more for it. It was the most joyful day Cadieux could ever remember spending. It is good that he did not know that Christoph's parents were plotting their departure from Nice.

Anna was more attached to the people and places in and around Nice than Jost was. He was more eager to uproot than she, but not from some sudden wanderlust. He foresaw safety in anonymity and in being away from anybody who knew them. Nice was large and the Koobs were mere drops in its pool of faces. But within certain circles, Anna was notorious. Jost thought to himself, not daring to mention it to Anna, that Miray and Safet were happy and trouble-free as long as they were in motion. It is only when they settled that their existence became dangerous. So Jost tempted Anna with visions of new places and new faces, new cuisine, new neighbors to meet, and many other allurements for an adventurous spirit like hers.

They stopped at the monastery before returning to their rooms. They called on Marcello. It would have been ungracious and ungrateful to leave Nice without speaking to him first. It was early evening and Marcello was not at the monastery. They went to the coffeehouse, but their friend was not there. They went back to the city center, to Cadieux's apartment, and there, with Cadieux and Christoph, was Marcello. It was Providential, having in one place the only people they needed to speak to before leaving Nice. Cadieux poured wine and Anna and Jost shared all that they discussed and all that they planned that day.

It is so rare that good people realize how they affect the people in their lives. Marcello was a passionate and expressive man. His reaction to the news of their departure was as Anna and Jost expected. He praised them both and promised to keep them in his prayers. Cadieux, who had probably not shown a powerful emotion in decades, cried aloud and unencumbered by shame. He offered to pay for their travels. He offered to arrange lodgings in any city between Spain and Croatia. His years as a port official afforded him many connections.

They would not take his money, and they wanted the adventure of making their own way, without fixed schedules or destinations. But the truth was, they did not have much money at their disposal. Income from the estate in Kleinostheim trickled in from the property manager, but that was not a resource that could fuel them while they were unsettled. Cadieux reminded Anna of his friend, the one who offered a fortune for the African manuscript. Anna agreed to sell it and the deal was made. Cadieux gave them the money for the book. He gave much more than his friend offered. It was his way of paying their way without them knowing. At any rate, it was more than enough money to set them comfortably on their way.

Anna and Jost suspected that Cadieux gave more than he would get in return for the book. In exchange for his goodness, they gave him several of Anna's own writings. They knew his tastes well and flattered him with everything she had written about their discussions together. Of course, Cadieux made an instant treasure of them. They kept Anna vividly alive in his life whenever he sat and pored over them. Anna and Jost would never see him again after leaving Nice. But the old man read the papers daily and could hear Anna's voice behind each curve of the ink, and he remembered their conversations together. He died several years later, having prayed for the Koobs daily, having thought of Anna almost hourly, and having thanked God countless times for the young woman who brightened the twilight of his life.

Cadieux's warm reception of her writing emboldened Anna to write more. They bought their own horse and cart and provisions for travel. They left only three days after their fateful picnic. Anna wrote whenever their road was smooth enough to write, and read when it was not. When they stopped, she belonged to Jost and Christoph.

They traveled east along the sea, into Italy. Along the way, they stopped in some towns for a few days, others for a few weeks, some for months, if the weather and the company suited them. They lingered in those areas near enough to the ports to be lively with interesting faces and exotic accents, yet far enough away to expose them to the local artisans and fiery young orators in their local haunts.

Stefan Scheuermann

Anna thought often of Miray and easily pictured her in the same streets, laughing and loving with Safet at her side.

They were unsettled, but that is not to say that they were alone. They had money. They did not need to force themselves into the company of business, allowing them to choose with great leisure the sort of halls and tables they occupied. They sold their books and they bought new ones. They sold Anna's papers, which drew excited interest amid their chosen crowds. Every philosopher and progressive theologian seemed to fall into their path and find their company. Anna's papers remained anonymous, but her debates did not. Somehow they floated from one enlightened audience to another. Well before any trouble could brew or Jost's jealousy had any reason to swell, they were on the road again.

The coast gave them little to discern the turning of seasons. Their best sign of the passage of time was the size and weight of the boy on their laps. Christoph was always a talking point with new friends and neighbors. Anna and Jost kept strange hours, and little Christoph's year was spent being carried night and day from libraries to docks to the homes of strangers, from wharfs and warehouses to churches and libraries, to monasteries and coffee houses. Well after he turned three, adorable sounds came from his mouth. They were expressions of love, joy, and comfort but never put in the form of recognizable words. Anna and Jost tried to get him to speak, but he only giggled at their prompts and made more unintelligible noises. Jost worried that there was something wrong with him, that the instability of their lives was somehow stunting him, damaging him. He would have been well relieved had he only understood what a rare and beautiful education his son was getting.

They crossed the Italian peninsula and settled into an apartment in the city of Trieste. Christoph turned four years old helping his parents carry books from the cart to their rooms. His young eyes had seen more late evenings than mid-mornings. His mind was filled with echoes of great debates, in the voices of his parents, and in voices whose faces had long vanished from his memory.

Trieste was a powerful seaport and had belonged to Venice during the heyday of Venetian naval dominance. In 1509, it was yielded to the Habsburgs and was, by the time Anna and Jost landed there, very much an Austrian city. Its tastes in all things aesthetic were still Italian, with hints of the Slavic influence from the east. But the centers of study and the religious sensibilities wore a distinctly Germanic cloak.

Anna came to Trieste with a mind overflowing with diverse languages, cultures, and religions — overflowing onto her papers, and also onto the ears of whatever company found them. There was a much more rigid Germanic orthodoxy filling the academic halls of Trieste. But the international influences of a bustling seaport demanded tolerance. Trieste was Austrian, and yet not so Austrian. It was as if Austrian orthodoxy grew old and lost the energy to fight for its way. It remained itself, but the outside world grew comfortably around it.

One late evening, a little over a month after they arrived in Trieste. Anna, Jost, and Christoph found themselves at a Turkish coffeehouse in a well-lit piazza, just a few blocks from the wharfs. This was not a common haunt of the Austrian elite. A group of young Austrian university students were traveling from Athens back to Salzburg. They too found the little Turkish coffeehouse. The proprietor of the establishment usually closed the doors before sunset. But the students were a paying crowd, who attracted others to their fine clothes and fancy words. It should be no surprise to you, my readers, that Anna and Jost found themselves centered among the young students.

The students were proud to flaunt their new cosmopolitan ideas, and they could not wait to take

Salzburg by storm. They were the perfect company for Anna. They were slow to embrace the words of a woman, particularly a German woman, when they were in full rejection of all things German. But she wooed them in time, with her casual injection of comments and criticisms. Before the night grew too old, once again, Anna presided over the tables.

The students were bold. They were young and self-assured, but they were still students, and when Anna's knowledge proved itself beyond theirs, they quickly fell into the role of disciples. They probed her for any personal opinions that could accompany her quotations. She provided them liberally. In earnest curiosity, she probed them in return. Some of their answers pleased her and some did not.

They were a fraternity, each from an established Austrian family. Although they were young and full of new ideas for the world, those ideas were still rooted deeply in a privileged upbringing. One of them spoke of the natural rights given to all men by God, and of the sacrifices a man must be willing to make to secure those rights.

Jost interrupted, "And women? How much should a woman sacrifice in finding her place in your new world?"

Thinking he would impress with a Classical reference, the young man's face lit up and he answered, "She should follow her father's example, or suffer the fate of Icarus."

Anna looked at him through a cocked eyebrow, so he elaborated, "He did not follow his father and was drawn to what was not his to have. The result of his failure is well known."

Anna relaxed her harsh gaze and asked him, "Are you saying that we should all follow directly in our parents' footsteps? You seem to be charging back to Austria with very different notions. So I ask, as my husband asked. How much is a woman to risk in finding her own way?"

The young man turned red in embarrassment. He had simply repeated a notion he had spoken many times, before his travels, before his education. Anna and Jost made him look at the matter differently. The encounter changed him.

"You are right," he responded after clearing his throat several times, "Icarus is the wrong analogy. Surely the wisdom of the Ancients has a better one for us."

This began a debate among them all. Icarus *was* a poor analogy for the rights of women in a changing world. But what was the right one? Many quotes and half-quotes, misquotes and paraphrased parables were put forward. Christoph had dozed and reawakened many times on Anna's lap during the evening. None had realized that he was alert and drumming on the table with his hand while they searched for the perfect Classical reference. When Anna finally noticed him, his drumming turned to knocking, followed by banging and squirming.

"What is it, my treasure?" Anna asked him nurturingly, "Are you hungry?"

Christoph answered, not in grunts or giggles but in his first words, "What about Plato's cave?"

Anna and Jost were in shock at hearing their son's voice finally put to words. They were unable to connect what he said to the debate at hand.

One of the students drew the line accurately and spoke, "Yes, yes, of course, Plato's Cave, from *The Republic*. He's talking about the Allegory of the Cave."

Most of the students had read it. Some had not. They all turned their eyes to Anna, who was speechless as she stared at the top of Christoph's head.

Jost released a breath he had not realized he was holding. He smiled, kissed Christoph's head, kissed his wife, and explained the allegory to them all.

"There are people who have lived in a cave since childhood, shackled so that they cannot move and can only look ahead, only able to see what is in front of them. A fire burns behind the people, casting its light to their backs and onto the wall in front of them. There is a walkway between the fire and the shackled people, and a low wall in front of the walkway. People pass behind the wall, but sometimes they carry things like statues and other carvings above the level of the wall, so that the shadows of these things are cast onto the cave wall in front of the shackled people."

One of the students who knew the passage well quoted the next line with a smirk, "This is an unusual picture you are presenting here, and these are unusual prisoners."

Those who recognized the quotation chuckled, and Jost continued.

"These prisoners had never seen anything but the shadows that are cast in front of them by the fire and the passers-by. Some of the passers-by would be talking to each other, and those sounds would be echoing off of the wall in front of the prisoners. Wouldn't it be natural for the prisoners to believe that the shadows from the statues and other figures were in fact beings before them, and that the echoed conversations were being spoken by those beings?"

Most of the students began to see the connection between Plato's allegory and Anna's question about the place of women in a new world, albeit thinly. They all stared at Christoph, amazed that the child would recall the passage and recognize its place in their conversation. They half-expected him to take over for his father.

Anna broke the awkward moment, saying, "I read it to him last week."

One of the students, wanting desperately to make the wise connection for himself, asked, "So, the prisoners in the cave are the women?"

"No," Anna answered, snapped suddenly from her shock at Christoph's words, "Plato tells us that the fire is social doctrine. For the purpose of our analogy, women are the statues and figures whose images are cast thin and distorted onto the wall by the fire. The voices of the passers-by are the words of men, speaking for the voiceless statues. The wall in front of the prisoners is the social standards of today."

A quiet student, one who had not yet spoken, chimed up, "Who are the prisoners in *our* analogy?"

Anna smiled at his eagerness to learn and answered his question, "The prisoners are the men and women of the past, and of today. Until they are unshackled and can investigate the phenomenon, they will have a false understanding of what they see and hear in front of them. And they will think that the words of men are the thoughts of women. They will be wrong."

The wisdom of Christoph's analogy came clear to them. The students were spellbound, by the little boy who proposed the topic, by the bookseller who rambled off Plato without a wince of concentration, and by the woman who tied the lesson to them in a way that even Plato would have admired.

The proud parents swelled. Jost ran his hand ruggedly through Christoph's hair and said, "Well played, my boy."

The coffeehouse closed and the students went on their way. Before they parted, they cheered Christoph like he was part of their fraternity. They shook Jost's hand heartily. To Anna's surprise and delight, they shook her hand just as rigorously, treating her not as some delicate flower or some other creature entirely, but as a teacher-comrade, with no regard for her sex. It seems that the lesson of the evening was learned, or at least healthy seeds were planted in fertile minds, to be taken back to Austria to bloom where most needed. Anna and Jost congratulated each other on that point, and they praised their son.

By the time they returned to their rooms, they were less surprised that philosophical thoughts had been waiting in Christoph's head for the perfect time to spring forth than they were excited that their conversations with him would now flow in both directions. Christoph read. He had been reading, but now he read aloud and spoke openly on what he read.

Anna wrote. The evening with the students at the coffeehouse enlivened in her musings on a primary topic — the place of women in a changing world. Her pen danced with great ease on the subject, and her papers piled high in the corner. It was a dangerous topic. But it was an important topic to Jost. His wife addressed it as only Anna could, and Jost felt safe to continue selling her papers anonymously.

It is hard to guess the scope of their distribution, or if any of those papers survived the centuries since. Perhaps Anna's words found their way into the hands and hearts of later writers. She produced a great deal of work in the months that followed. They did not continue to travel as they had planned. Anna seized the pen early in the morning and often scratched away late into the night. Trieste hosted delightful firsts for them and it burrowed its way into their affections.

When Anna's pen was still and there were no sales or purchases to be made, they went on excursions to neighboring towns. They went on walks in the forest. They rode on boats along the coast. Christoph continued to display a profound grasp of complex philosophy. He seemed to maintain every word read to him since he was two years old. He read his mother's writing, along with much that passed through his parents' hands. By the time he turned five, he was translating simple Latin and beginning to handle the fundamentals of Greek. It was, in short, a happy and fulfilling time for them all, much more than they would have presumed to pray for.

Chapter Twenty-Two:
Homesick

THE KOOBS LEFT NICE CONTENT to be untethered, but with Trieste tempting them into a longer stay, they secured their lodgings for the long term and established communication with their estate in Kleinostheim. After four months in Trieste, word came that the estate was not faring well. The manager had sold off some of the properties. He had no money to show for it. He claimed that the proceeds from the sales were needed in immediate investments in the remaining estate. Jost was enjoying a period of bliss, with little affection for past people or places, otherwise he would have traveled back to Kleinostheim at full speed and set his affairs back to order. He had no trust in his manager, but he had little care for anything outside of his immediate household.

Once the dam of Christoph's speech had broken, the flood rushed in with force. He was unlike any child in Europe. His uncommon natural intelligence was supplemented by an education that only his unique upbringing could offer. During all of those bistro, monastery, and coffeehouse debates, where he sat on his father's lap or in his mother's arms, he had engaged his surroundings in silence. The quotations, the arguments, the

213

philosophies debated, they all soaked into him, and his active little mind pondered the experience in the quiet, domestic moments in between.

Christoph was entirely out of place with other children. That was all well and good. He spent very little time with other children. He fit like matching china with the small circles of thinkers and scholars that daily shared one table or another with his parents. At home, his newfound voice rang constantly though their rooms. Like any child his age, he asked "what" and he asked "why", but he also contributed to conversations in ways that were beyond much of Anna and Jost's adult company.

One afternoon, Jost received another letter from his manager. As usual, the news was bleak. Jost read it aloud and both he and Anna chuckled at the apocalyptic tone taken by the writer. Christoph understood the words used, and he had a pretty good grasp of the concepts. He was confused that his parents would laugh so lightly at the condition of their own estate. He asked them about it, which spawned an overdue conversation about the boy's hometown, why they traveled selling books, and why the state of their own affairs affected them so slightly.

Anna and Jost took their turns telling their son the stories of their life together. Anna spoke with great fervor of her childhood, of her parents and neighbors. She told Christoph the story of Maria Echter and of Father Albrecht. Once revived from their long hibernation, a torrent of vivacious memories swelled from deep within her, bringing fresh color to her skin, smiles so broad that they hurt her face, and tears that fell to her lap before she knew they had left her eyes.

Anna had grown wise since leaving her childhood home. She had studied like no scholar in Europe had studied. But sleeping within her all the time was the vibrant little girl with the electric personality. That child assumed full control of her as she told her stories to her son. The nostalgic air of their small apartment in Trieste almost began to smell of the Spessart Forest and of the muddy, narrow streets between the house of Johann, Jost's old master, and the home of Michel and Margarethe. Christoph's mouth had run like a wild horse since he spoke at the coffeehouse. But he sat in silent bewilderment while Anna told her stories.

Jost stared with fixed and enamored eyes at the woman before him. What he saw was every bit the passionate girl he knew from years ago, but enhanced and enriched by knowledge and experience to become the most magnificent specimen of a human being he could imagine. Without moving his head or scanning his eyes from side to side, he saw, in a single intimate frame of vision, his wife and his son. His sense of Divine Blessing was so overwhelming that it nearly buckled his knees. He would have engulfed them both in a shared embrace, but would not interrupt the scene before his senses. So he just consumed it decadently, and considered himself, not for the last time, the happiest creature alive.

It would be fair to say that Anna and Jost's flight from Kleinostheim was every bit as much an escape from the dreadful as a lunge for the delightful. They did not make a particular effort to forget their home county, but the rush of exotic experiences that bombarded them as soon as they passed the Alps buried their thoughts of home beneath more immediate and more appealing contemplations. Their talks with Christoph raised to the surface musings both tender and atrocious. In both of them, but more so in Anna, their quiet times of independent thought began to feature scenes of the past.

Even if thoughts of Aschaffenburg County had not risen from its hibernation inside of them to dance hand-in-hand with their every movement, Christoph developed a fascination with his infancy and with the stories of his parents' youth. He begged hourly for anecdotes and prodded Anna for every detail. She was a fantastic storyteller, and the images of Kleinostheim in Christoph's head varied in few details from those in Anna's.

The more they thought and spoke of Kleinostheim, the less Trieste felt like home. Their previous few years felt like a long vacation, and vacations, no matter how pleasant or exciting, eventually grow tiresome, and one wishes to cuddle again beneath soft familiarity. These feelings may have passed or been buried again beneath all that the Mediterranean Coast had to offer, if not for a tragic letter from home. Along with another bleak report of estate affairs from Jost's manager was a pack of letters from Anna's brother, Aulgoin, with the news that their father had died.

The report came with several letters from his neighbors, each assuring Anna that her father died peacefully and painlessly. The letter from Aulgoin weighted Anna's heart. It was filled with brotherly affection, but laden heavy with despair. The letters from the neighbors bore a different tone. These were not people angry with Anna over the death of sick children. Their words spoke nothing of suspicion, of witchcraft, or of foreign visitors with strange herbal brews. They spoke only of fond memories of Michel, Margarethe, and of Anna and her brothers. The letters, coupled with Anna's loss of her father, made her very homesick.

Homesick or not, they needed to return to Kleinostheim to see Anna's brothers and say goodbye to Michel. They spent the following morning discussing the details. Neither was sure if the other wanted to quit Trieste altogether or maintain their apartment for an eventual return. It was a Friday early in the season of Lent. They all walked together in silence to the Cathedral of Saint Justus to pray over the matter. During the walk to the cathedral, Anna and Jost quietly came to the same conclusion. The scenes around them, exciting as they had been, had gone stale to their senses. They felt like they were walking through their past.

They prayed at the cathedral. Although the chants that resounded through the chamber were unlike anything to be heard in Kleinostheim, they still seemed to command each of them, separately but identically, to snuff the candle of their wanderlust and return to a family and an estate in need of their attention. After the service, they spoke with the priests and arranged the sale of much of their collection of books. Anna felt a strong urge to travel light. In truth, they were both ready to put the life they had been living behind them, including the book trade. They found homes for the remainder of their collection, some sold and some given away, including all of Anna's writings.

They had a nice cart of their own with little left to fill it but the wife, husband, and son. Within six days of receiving the news of Michel's death, they closed the door to their rooms for the last time. They rode to the markets near the wharf to purchase provisions for travel. It was a cool spring morning. There was a calm bustle in the air. The voices around them were pleasant and the fragrances were fine accompaniment. In those last hours on the Mediterranean Coast, Anna and Jost truly savored an atmosphere that they never, until that morning, fully delighted in.

Christoph had known many apartments and many towns. His every memory was among the commotion of seaports and in the exotic atmosphere of foreign influence. He had no memories of a quiet German county on the River Main. His adieu to the city of Trieste was different. But the magnetism of his images of Kleinostheim, painted vividly in his mind by his mother, took all sting from their departure. After a calm and casual morning at the markets, the Koobs rolled out of Trieste with hearts too full to speak. The only sound that accompanied the clop of horse hooves and the roll of cart wheels was Jost's subconscious humming of the chants they heard at the cathedral.

The days on the cart were long. The spring was warm in the valleys and cold in the high passes of the Alps. They had no need to suffer. They had money and no particular timetable, so they traveled only during daylight hours and stopped at almost every inn along the way. Their leisure pace presented them with many hours of conversation. Rolling slowly in the cart under a warm sun, Christoph pressed his parents for more details of his past. He asked about his birth, a period of tremendous turmoil for Anna and Jost.

There was no way to tell of the pregnancy and birth without speaking of Miray. When Christoph demanded to know more about her, they paused their narrative and told the story from the beginning, from their first introduction to Miray and Safet. They told him about Miray coming back into their lives, distraught and uncertain about the fate of her husband.

Christoph asked, "What did Safet do wrong?"

"I doubt he did anything wrong," Jost answered, "He was a good man, but he was different from the people around him."

"How was he different?"

"He looked different. He sounded different. He wore different kinds of clothes and called God by a different name."

Jost attempted to explain the fury of human prejudices and the violence it can lead people to commit. He had no need to. Christoph had long been exposed to vast literature and conversations on the subject.

The boy surprised his parents with a quotation from the Roman poet Juvenal that had been waiting in a quiet corner of his young memory, "You may look for the same themes from the greatest poet and the least."

"Yes you may," Jost replied, "You may look for it anywhere and be sure to find it."

It was a heavy topic for a child so young, but Christoph seemed to have a grip on it.

Jost continued the story of Miray's return to Kleinostheim, which led him to the death of the two children and the accusations against Miray and Anna. He stopped mid-syllable when his emotions rose too sharply. Anna took over until she needed to pause to recover. They took turns in this way as they re-lived every moment, from the mobs outside of the house, to Michel's illness, Anna's arrest, the trial, and of course, Miray's death. Christoph encouraged his parents and tried to soothe their tattered emotions. But his own fears began to creep into him through the stories.

While Jost spoke of the acquittal, Christoph tugged on Anna's dress. When she turned to him, he asked in clear agitation, "Will you be safe in Kleinostheim?"

She assured him that she had nothing to fear from the law. She had been cleared of the charges against her.

"That was years ago," she comforted him, "and the people of Kleinostheim are good people. They are our friends and neighbors. We have no reason to think that trouble awaits us there."

Anna looked to Jost as if to beg him to agree. He turned his eyes downward for a few seconds of contemplation, regained eye contact with Anna, grinned naturally and complied, "Yes, no reason."

They spoke no more of Miray while they traveled, no more of accusations of witchcraft, and no more of angry mobs. Anna chose quiet, pleasant stories to read to Christoph. When they spoke of home, it was in the recollection of their brighter moments. They told and retold the many details of their comically awkward courtship. Christoph giggled at them all and their hearts lightened. They took a full seven weeks to travel from Trieste into

Aschaffenburg County. And they primed their hearts well for the familiar sights of home.

In abuse of a worn and tired cliché, absence makes the heart grow fonder. From their great distance on the Mediterranean Coast, that was true for Anna and Jost. The horrid images from their last months in Kleinostheim receded beneath the swell of fond memories they chose to focus upon. They had also, in many ways, absorbed the Mediterranean culture, so that they viewed their past through altered eyes. They had been well removed from the abrasive tensions of the Reformation and the Catholic Church's medieval approach to counter it. Even their thoughts of Miray and Safet did not sting the tongue so bitterly when they spoke of them. Had their hearts been truly rushed with vivid and accurate recollections of what they had suffered, they would have foregone their reunions and turned on the spot for Trieste.

The heart might be fonder, but the eyes are wider, with the power to penetrate what was once opaque. Kleinostheim did not change in their absence, but what a rustic, provincial scene it appeared as they rolled through it to Michel's home. They went there first, eager to see Anna's brothers. Their own home and the affairs of their estate could wait another day or two for their attention. They arrived late, and it is a very good thing that they did. The neighbors were mostly shut up indoors for the night. The alterations in our heroes' perspective of their home village was enough to chew and digest, without taking in the neighbors in the same glance.

Aulgoin answered the knock at their father's door. He was alone. He had left his wife and children at their home, and returned to Kleinostheim alone to tend to Michel's funeral and settle the estate. Michel was long laid to rest beside Margarethe, and Anna's other two brothers, Michel and Martin returned to their lives. Aulgoin had already dissolved all of what had remained of the bookseller business in Kleinostheim. He did not know that Michel had passed the business to Jost.

Anna missed everything — the funeral, the reunions, the settlement of the estate, everything. But there was no blame from her brother. It was, despite the circumstances, a joyful reunion. The house was barren, with few material items to spur nostalgia. Even the family Bible that Anna had thrown on her bed in front of Father Albrecht was gone. Anna wondered about it but dared not ask. She felt that she didn't have the right to. They didn't need material items. Childhood memories radiated from them so concretely that the house appeared to them in full, lively function.

Aulgoin met his nephew with familial affection, and Christoph embraced his Uncle Aulgoin as if reuniting with a long-lost love one. They spent three days together in the home of their parents. Then the house was sold and Aulgoin returned to his family in Frankfurt. For Anna and Jost, the short trip to their own home, to the building where Christoph was born, was harder than passing the Alps. It was only then that the full rush of memories crashed upon them. Their pulses raced and Jost looked with startled suspicion at every neighbor they encountered. They secured themselves inside of their own walls to find the incompetence of their estate manager on bold display.

Chapter Twenty-Three:
Recovery and Reconciliation

THE FOLLOWING WEEKS WERE A PERIOD of recovery, recovery from travel, mourning, and emotional reunion, and recovery of the estate from years of neglectful management. Jost met with the manager and received the bleak report of affairs. He did nothing immediately. Their home reminded them of wonderful times of love and family, of friends and laughter. It also reminded them of wounds that never healed but were simply scabbed over. The sights, sounds, and smells of their native home and house tore the scabs from their spirits. Blended in equal proportion with the many feelings stirring wildly inside of them was a haunting sense of dread. Whether it was a reminder of past fears spurred in them by walls, roads, trees, and people they had last seen under malignant stress, or it was a premonition of some future misery, they could not tell, but it made both Anna and Jost reclusive and defensive.

The return to Kleinostheim was an entirely different experience for Christoph. He had no memories of the place, and the quiet village was unlike anything familiar to him. He wanted to explore, to meet the neighbors and engage in the sort of conversations he grew up with in Savoy and

Italy. There was nothing of the sort to be found in Kleinostheim. He wanted to see the forest where his parents fell in love, but Anna and Jost were wearily reluctant to go beyond their own front door. Christoph was curious about the many jars and bottles of long-stale ingredients still stored on dusty shelves in the kitchen. He was more than curious, he was obsessed. But Anna refused to look at them, let alone touch them or speak of them.

During the many idle hours they spent in that house, Christoph discovered the sensation of boredom for the very first time. He took to investigating all there was to study within their walls. He found some of Anna's old recipes. When he found one labeled *The Happy Tonic,* his obsession with his mother's abandoned hobby took him by the throat. He would have attempted the recipe himself if he could have reached the upper shelves or identified the unmarked jars on his own. So with great trepidation, he approached the subject with his father.

He was remarkably aware for a child his age. He knew that these secrets of their past were more repugnant to his mother. They were *her* past, and she had changed much in the years abroad. One day, while Anna was reading in the living room, Jost was in Christoph's room repairing a shelf. Christoph brought the recipe to Jost and asked him to help him make it.

He presented his argument with authentic concern, saying, "I think it would be good for mother."

He handed the page to his father. Jost took it and stared at it in silence for what was an awkwardly long time to Christoph. He sat on the floor in the corner of the room and continued to stare at the recipe. It reminded him of a deeply hidden part of his dear wife. Like *The Sleeping Beauty,* it was a lovely part of a lovely woman, lying dormant and awaiting the kiss of a prince. The prince in the metaphor was not her lover, but her son.

223

Still sitting in the corner, resting his forearms on his knees and holding the recipe in front of his face, Jost let out a long sigh. That wheezing release of air spoke more to Christoph than fifty pages of succinct writing. It spoke of love and worry, but also of determination. Jost put the sheet down between his feet and covered his face with both hands. He closed his palms together to clasp his nose tightly, then lifted his face from his hands. He looked like a man in devoted prayer.

He abruptly took the paper at his feet, stood, and said, "I think you are right, son. It will do her good. It will do us all good."

Jost took Christoph by the hand and led him to the kitchen. He began pulling jars and bottles from the shelves and handing them to Christoph, who tried his best to organize them on the counter. Jost tried to be quiet, not to alert Anna to their design. But Christoph was a comical blend of excitement and clumsiness. I'm certain the clanging of jars could have been heard from outside. It was most definitely heard by Anna. She assumed that her boys were merely cleaning and discarding, and she was quite content to let them do it.

The dried ingredients were still usable, as was a liquor that had been well sealed. It was not the same herbal liquor from the recipe, but for the moment, it would have to do. Jost pulled out a bowl and he and his son started their attempt to make the Happy Tonic. Some of the herbs were unmarked and only recognizable by Anna. This fact would not dampen their enthusiasm. Father and son threw into the bowl whatever they thought was right. Jost knew well that they were blundering the recipe atrociously. Christoph had a pretty good idea it was not right. Together, they laughed at their own ineptness as they continued to mix old, stale ingredients.

The clanging of bottles did not draw Anna's curiosity, but the laughter did. It was the sort of laughter that has a powerful gravitational pull on anyone with love in her heart. It lifted Anna to her feet and dragged her into the kitchen. She stood at the threshold of the kitchen, peeking in at her family. Her smile was involuntary and almost painfully wide. She recognized the paper on the counter. She knew what they were trying to make, and she knew how terribly they botched it. Still, she watched, secretly and silently peering in on them.

Finally, she watched Christoph toss into the bowl an ingredient that was as unusable as it was incorrect. She stepped firmly and demonstratively into the kitchen, still wearing her enormous smile, and said, "For Heaven's sake, what sort of wretched poison are you trying to make in here?"

Very honestly, innocently, and lovingly, Christoph answered his mother, "We are making the Happy Tonic for you, to make you... to make you happy again."

"Well," Anna responded, "if it is going to be made in this kitchen, it is going to be made right."

Anna took a strong step toward the counter, examined the jars and bottles, glanced at the recipe, scratched the side of her head, and walked out of the kitchen. She took a few coins, a pair of gloves, and a small sack, and walked through the front door with lightness in her step.

Christoph began to follow her, but Jost took him by the shoulder and said, "She needs to do this on her own."

Christoph had heard the stories of the trial, and of Miray's murder. He asked his father, "Is she safe by herself?"

Jost patted him a few times, and with a slight crack of his voice, he answered, "She is as capable of escorting herself as any man I know. Besides, there are no charges against her. She will be safe."

Despite what he told his son, an itching fear tempted Jost, and it was all he could do not to scratch it. But he knew, if Anna wanted his help, she would have asked for it. The fact that she left the house so determinedly on her own spoke loudly to him that she wanted to do this on her own. To occupy themselves in her absence, Jost and Christoph began deconstructing the abomination they had begun in the kitchen. They cleaned the mess and they prepared the kitchen for Anna's arrival. Anna returned three hours later with everything she needed to make the Happy Tonic.

It had been several years since it had been mixed and served in their house, but the Happy Tonic tasted just as it always had. The paper holding the recipe may have gone faint and yellow, but the recipe itself lost none of its potency. Christoph laughed that evening like a young child should, and Anna and Jost laughed like children even younger. They awoke the next morning revived and inspirited. Jost dressed early, took his dusty ledgers, and embarked on an inspection of his properties. Anna pored through her stores of herbs with Christoph's assistance, discarding what was useless and relabeling empty containers that awaited fresh contents.

While Jost was out on the long day's work, Anna took Christoph into the forest north of the village. She showed him where they celebrated their wedding, the paths where she and Jost walked and talked and fell in love, and the worn oak tree where they sat together. Along the way, Christoph helped his mother gather what the forest had to offer their cupboard. They giggled and played like any mother and son, and they debated scholarly topics like no other mother and son.

Jost found the state of his properties much as he expected — neglected and in an embarrassing state of disrepair. The value of his estate plummeted in his long absence, and many of his properties were empty and contributing nothing. Jost searched all of Kleinostheim for his manager. The man was nowhere to be found. Jost left word with each of his tenants that the landlord sought the manager's attention as soon as possible. He scribbled feverishly in his ledgers and compiled an ambitious and expensive agenda to bring the estate back in order. The tenants were pleased to see their landlord. They had suffered much under the neglect of the manager. Even those who were not particularly fond of Jost before he left the region, even those who had bought into the charges against Anna, welcomed Jost with warmth and smiles. They knew that their conditions would improve under his personal eye.

It took several days for Jost to complete his evaluation, and several days more for him and Anna to decide on a course of action. During this time, his negligent manager was conspicuously absent. It was a full three weeks after Jost had seized his affairs with his own two hands that the manager finally knocked on their door. By that point, Anna had brought the house back to its previous glory. When the manager entered the house and saw the difference, he knew that his time in their employment was over. The man had no good explanation for the decline and no well-ordered books that explained where the money had gone. It was clearly not invested into the properties. It was not sent in substance to Anna and Jost while they were away.

Regardless of the terrible disservice the manager provided, and what was certainly a criminal misappropriation of estate funds, Jost thanked him graciously for his service, shook his hand, wished him well, and dismissed him from service. The man left Kleinostheim and was never seen again by anyone associated with this story.

The Happy Tonic was not the only thing that kept their spirits high. Jost set immediately to his planned improvements. This elevated the lifestyle of many people, and the friends and associates of many people. The village's regard for Jost rose above its previous heights. This approbation spread to Anna and Christoph. The old good-humor that had been Anna's since she could toddle the streets of Kleinostheim bringing joy to her neighbors was hers again. None of the fears that nagged at them as they rolled back into Aschaffenburg County proved merited.

In a stroke of poetic timing, Anna and Christoph were mixing spices and filling jars in the kitchen when a knock came to their door. It was Karl, the distraught father who accused Anna of devilry. Karl appeared many years younger than when Anna last saw him. He had lost weight. His lightness of *spirit* was even more obvious. He was nervous to speak to Anna and Jost, even more so to see Christoph, whose gypsy childhood was a direct result of Karl's accusations. He stood at the doorway, wringing his hands. His rough hands made quite the sound as they rubbed restlessly against each other.

Anna was surprised to see Karl, but she was not disturbed by the visit. Karl wore his lightened disposition plainly. Anna invited him in, and in a move of defiance, invited him to join her and Christoph in the kitchen where she continued to prepare ingredients for her tonics and elixirs.

Large beads of sweat formed on Karl's brow as he stuttered, "Is your... is... is Jodocus home?"

"No," she answered in a calm, soft, melodic half-whisper, "only me and our son."

Karl continued to stumble over his words, "Thank you..., that is..., thank you for letting me in, letting me see you- speak to you. I understand if you..., I would understand if you did not..."

The poor man was slogging so fruitlessly toward his point. He stood and sat again several times. Anna's compassion jolted her into action.

He had one hand resting on the table. Anna lunged to him, placed her palm over his hand, and said in a soothing, maternal, almost angelic tone, "Karl, I am so sorry you lost your son. I always have been, and I have prayed for him and for you every day since he died, even as I stood in that courtroom."

An uncontainable wave of long-harbored emotions rushed from Karl. His eyes turned red and puffy until his tears finally broke through. He tried to speak, but he sobbed heavily, and only disjointed and unintelligible syllables came through. Anna wrapped both arms around him and held him like a baby. She rubbed and kissed his head. Compassion, forgiveness, reconciliation, and authentic neighborly love declared itself resoundingly through her touch and her kiss. Christoph had never met Karl, not since his earliest infancy. But he knew the story and his sharp mind quickly put the pieces together. He joined in his mother's effort, resting his head on Karl's lap and reaching his arms as far around the man as they could go.

Karl ran his rough fingers through Christoph's hair and he managed to calm himself enough to say, "My poor boy. I ran you from a home that should have loved you. I ran you from your grandfather's arms. I pray I have not caused you to suffer terribly."

"Ssshhh," Anna shushed him, "My old friend, I can settle your heart on that affair. I could not have planned a better beginning to my son's life."

Karl pulled away from them and asked, "You did not suffer?"

"Of course we suffered," she answered quickly with a slight edge of scolding in her voice, "We fled our home in terror, and we tended those wounds for years. But we found our way. We saw new and beautiful things. We met remarkable people, and we learned so very much. Didn't we, Christoph?"

"We learned many things and met many people," Christoph answered. He spoke not in a mindless recitation of his mother's words, but with an obvious collection of vivid thoughts associated with his response.

Karl apologized profusely for the harm he caused in his grief. Anna forgave him and reworded her forgiveness with each new apology. By the time Jost came home in the afternoon, the conversation in the kitchen had grown almost comfortable. Anna and Christoph both regaled Karl with details of the places they had been, the people they had met, the things they had tasted, and the many things they had read and debated. At first sight of Karl, Jost's heart skipped a beat. But the scene before him was tranquil, and warm with neighborly affection. He joined the storytelling with perspectives and descriptions that were uniquely his.

As Karl left their house that evening, the final remnants of lingering leeriness flew out the door with him, leaving behind it three villagers quite at home with their surroundings. It was not as though they had never left, like they had never traveled. How could it be? The Mediterranean and all that it placed inside of them was still there, slumbering restlessly and dreaming actively. There was no book business, but there were books to be had.

They lived in Kleinostheim, but went often to Aschaffenburg and beyond. Anna mixed and brewed her recipes, but continued to write. Her counters were active, but so was her desk. Christoph turned six, then seven, then eight, making the rounds with Jost on one day, learning to manage the estate, and walking the forest with his mother the next day, gathering wild herbs and berries, reading in the afternoons, expanding his knowledge, and stretching the limits of understanding in the evenings, debating academic topics with his parents like he was a young Franciscan in a monastery or a traveling student at a Mediterranean coffeehouse.

Chapter Twenty-Four:
Parts United

ERAS OF HISTORY DO NOT HAVE THE CLEAN LINES of distinction that are drawn for them in history books. They creep onto the scene and ease their way gradually into social sensibilities. Such was the case with the Enlightenment. There was no switch flicked by some godly scholar. Aschaffenburg, like most European cities of its kind, saw a steady influx of new ideas and new writings, challenging the assumptions of the past. They poured over the city limits to the surrounding communities, including Kleinostheim. For those who sought it, fascinating new ideas were there for consumption. For those not inclined in that direction, Kleinostheim was as quiet a little pocket of the world as anyone could seek. As the sixteenth century entered its final decade, Anna, Jost, and Christoph had friends and neighbors of each sort.

Their circles were nothing like what they shared in Nice and Trieste, but there were those with whom they freely debated theology, and those with whom they shared a more rustic bond. They lived a village life much as they had before meeting Miray and Safet, and they lived a scholar's life, with exciting things to read and enlightened friends to debate them with. Each year laid another layer of sediment over the terrors of their past. They found an electric calmness, an excited placidity. Their lives were a contradiction, but it was a contradiction that suited them well. Sandwiched between their polar acquaintances was their household of three, bound more tightly together by their uniqueness in the community.

As the tensions of the Counter-Reformation raged on, Kleinostheim and her neighboring villages felt little of it, like different games being played on the same field. For the rustics, it was a whisper, a rumor meant to scare, like the Boogeyman. For the scholarly, it was real but more theoretical than concrete. In truth, the Peace of Augsburg was two generations behind them, and the empire was on the brink of Europe's bloodiest war. While secular forces walked gingerly on a fragile peace, ecclesiastical forces were already in the throes of a cold war that would soon turn very hot.

Anna and Jost seemed the only two of all their acquaintances with an admirable degree of caution. Their travels, their studies, and their natural intelligence gave them a perspective none around them had. They knew the strategic value of Aschaffenburg to both the Lutherans and the Catholics. They foresaw the blood that would run through their county. Scrupulously avoiding any offense against either side, they declared as neither. Oh, they were devoutly Christian. Whether they celebrated that fact in a Catholic or Lutheran church, or in the forest north of their home, mattered little to them. They learned to graciously acknowledge the truth in the opinions of whomever shared their company. It was a skill that Christoph was slow to grasp.

On 18 January, 1597, Anna celebrated her thirty-first birthday, Christoph was almost twelve years old. There was no party with invited guests, but friends and neighbors from their various circles stopped by to wish her well. Anna and Jost had managed to keep those separate circles from intersecting. But the house was abuzz with comings and goings, and conversations were not yet concluded when the next ones began.

Jost was out and about on business, leaving Anna and Christoph to host the flow of guests throughout the afternoon. Anna put on a display of social mastery that would have humbled any politician. She spoke of pigs and harvests with one guest, only to turn on the spot and discuss Christian doctrine with another. Christoph was used to engaging in his parents' discussions. He had been doing it since the coffeehouse in Trieste. But he lacked his mother's diplomacy. He carried one conversation into the next, where it seldom fit well. Anna would not shush her son and discourage the open expression of his thoughts. So she danced a cunning waltz, rewording and explaining her son's contributions in a way that left each guest feeling assured in their mutual admiration and sustaining friendship. It was a powerful lesson for the boy.

When Jost returned and the house settled into quiet intimacy, Anna explained to Christoph why they could not approach each of their acquaintances identically. She used as an example one particular guest. He was truly an odious, little-minded man, and one with firm opinions and an easily ignitable heart. His name was Gregor. She pointed out Gregor's admirable traits and explained why he is a blessing to their lives, despite the constant spray of annoyances that came from him like a natural spring. As evidence, she presented the gift Gregor had given her that day.

Gregor knew that Anna read. He found a book from God-knows-where and bought it for her. It was the sort of book you only read during the day, because it is not worth the candle required to read it at night.

"Nevertheless," she instructed Christoph, "there was a moment of this man's life dedicated entirely to me, and that is no small gift. He sought a book, found this one, bought it, and presented it to me. I will read the book. If I gain nothing from it but the warmth of the gift, it has served me well and I am grateful for it. And since I am grateful for the gift, I must show gratitude to the giver."

Christoph's eyes widened with the revelation. His quick mind reviewed all he had witnessed that day, all of the authentic but creative compliments his mother gave, all of the smiles, all of the hugs, and all of the heartfelt friendship. He knew that his family was unlike any of the guests he had seen that day, yet they all adored his mother. She made them feel good. She made them feel righteous and admired.

Jost interrupted Christoph's private internal lesson to comment, "If the leaders of the empire could learn from your mother, there would never be another war."

"These things are not particular to me," she corrected him, "They may be taught by any woman who has loved a husband and raised children."

Innocently and sincerely, Christoph asked, "So why aren't the mothers in charge?"

Not for the first or last time, Jost swelled with pride in his wife and son, and answered, "Why indeed, my son!?"

From that point, Christoph challenged his parents daily about the socio-political order of their staunchly patriarchal society. They had few answers that satisfied him. He saw such value in that which was maternal, nurturing, and feminine, and imagined those traits — his mother's traits — sprinkled in fair proportion among all that he witnessed and all that he studied. He saw clearly the fallibility of such a patriarchal society and the solution was plain to him. He took a keen interest in the writings of women, including his mother's. There was little to be found, but what he read, he compared to the writings of men and saw the truth and beauty in each.

An idealist was born that 18th of January. He envisioned a world where the masculine shared influence with the feminine. It was a notion that itched him his entire life, and inflamed into an open wound many times, when he witnessed tragedies that just a touch of maternal sense would have prevented. Gender dynamics in his community became a fascination of his. He had few friends his age. The ones he bonded most tightly with were girls, and he prodded them for their opinions and feelings on many things.

When Christoph was fourteen years old, he met a girl named Anna Marie Notintz. Anna Marie was one year younger and from a family that had lived in Würzburg for generations before moving to Kleinostheim a year earlier. Unlike most of Christoph's young friends, Anna Marie answered his questions honestly. She opened herself freely to him. Like so many girls her age, she had many thoughts and opinions but was not welcome to express them. In Christoph, she not only found a friend she could run and play with, but who she could talk to, and one authentically interested in her words.

Anna Marie's parents were not of Anna and Jost's type. They knew each other. They respected each other. But they were not close nor would they easily become so. Christoph spent much time at the Notintz house, and Anna Marie spent much time with the Koobs. Both children were able to compare the two households. At the Koob table, Anna Marie learned to open up as widely as she did when she was alone with Christoph. At the Notintz table, Christoph learned quickly to keep his thoughts to himself.

As the children reached higher into their teen years, they grew even closer. Anna Marie came to admire Christoph's mother more than any person she knew. She saw the equality of the Koob home, and it soured the scent of her own household air. What a strange place Christoph's home appeared to her at first. Jost deferred to his wife on many subjects, and sought her advice openly and without embarrassment. Those experiences were quite foreign to the girl at first, but as she came to know Christoph's family, she saw their dynamic as the only proper way to conduct a household. The century turned, and Anna Marie felt a turn of her life coinciding.

Anna Marie often came to visit Anna when Christoph was out with his father. She knew she had much to learn from the Koob matriarch, much about many topics, and much about being a woman. Anna had been the only girl among brothers. She had no daughters of her own. She relished Anna Marie's presence in the house and her heart adopted the child as its own.

By the time Christoph and Anna Marie knocked on the door of adulthood, Anna and Jost discussed how flawlessly the two of them fit together. Of all the children growing up beside them in Kleinostheim, Christoph and Anna Marie were the only ones the other had truly bonded with. As they came of age, discussions of their possible marriage were difficult to hold back. Christoph and Anna Marie certainly seemed to be heading in that direction. Jost began to treat Anna Marie as his wife did — as an inevitable member of the family.

Anna had never been happier. Her son was much like her, and Anna Marie was much like Jost. Anna saw in the young couple a mirrored reflection of her own blessed marriage. For herself, she had finally brought together all parts of herself. She was again the spritely villager who delighted in muddy wagon tracks and dewy roses. She was again the friend of Miray, acquiring herbs and spices, and mixing them with great interest into tonics to share with friends and family. She was again the avid scholar, studying devoutly and writing her thoughts on many subjects. In short, she was the whole Anna Koob, finally united into one magnificent woman.

Chapter Twenty-Five:
Exhuming the Past

THE WANING YEARS OF THE CENTURY were like a fuse, burning nearer an explosion with each tick of the clock. In the period between the Peace of Augsburg in 1555 and the Thirty Years War in 1618, both the Catholics and the Lutherans attempted to build and secure their faith across the Holy Roman Empire. As the century turned, those efforts reached their zenith. Counter-Reformation extremists, who had been exiled from influence after 1555, found themselves again with power over people. Aschaffenburg County was still under the control of the Archbishop of Mainz. In May of 1601, Johann Adam von Bicken was elected as the new archbishop and confirmed by Pope Clement XIII.

Johann von Bicken zealously desired to keep his Catholic communities Catholic and bring the Protestant areas back under his control. He did not want to be personally associated with the terror required to do so, so he appointed men who did not mind getting their hands bloody. One of these men was a Benedictine monk named Balthasar von Dernbach. Dernbach was a member of the Fulda Monastery, about fifty-three miles north of

Kleinostheim. The citizens of Fulda had turned mostly Lutheran.

When Dernbach became the Prince-Abbot in 1570, he took his counter-reformation efforts to the extreme, evicting non-Catholics from the area. The Benedictine chapter and the local magistrates took exception and exiled Dernbach from Fulda. In 1602, von Bicken reinstated Dernbach as prince-abbot in Fulda. Dernbach's extremism had long simmered and concentrated. Back in a position of power, he let loose all of his vengeance on the people of Fulda. His goal was the complete restoration of Catholicism in Fulda, no matter the means.

By 1602, Christoph was almost seventeen. He was bright and learned, and preparing to travel back to Italy for his education. He was such an admirable blend of his parents' finest qualities. He had his mother's faith, charisma, and absorbent mind. Like his father, he was rational, prudent, but all too apt to fall in love. He remained very close to Anna Marie, but he fell wildly for many of the girls he encountered. With his mother and Anna Marie as a measuring stick, infatuations faded quickly. Italy was certain to expose him to someone better suited to his romantic needs, so Anna Marie arranged to travel with him, encouraged by Jost and Anna. This could not happen if they were not married. The quiet talk between Christoph's parents opened up to the general air. Christoph and Anna Marie began to speak openly about it to themselves.

Christoph's affection and attention mostly remained ensconced within the intimate circle of his immediate family. Since she fit so well with them, Anna Marie felt more like a sister than a lover to Christoph. Their love was deep, but lacked the pulse-rising excitement he felt around other young women.

Since he was a small child, Christoph held a place of equality in family discussions. Anna and Jost brought into the house every paper and pamphlet that interested them.

They had their fingers keenly on the pulse of the time and region. Dernbach's cruel zeal was infamous. It was written about copiously, both by those who favored him and by those who did not. Anna, Jost, and Christoph were well aware of what was happening in Fulda, and they watched Dernbach's influence work its way south toward their village. Traveling to the coast became more obligatory than optional for both Christoph and Anna Marie.

Kleinostheim and its neighboring villages were tolerant of religious diversity, much due to Anna's contagious compassion. The Koobs had been Catholic, but many of their friends and neighbors were Lutheran, as were some of the tenants on their estate. They took moral offense to what was happening in Fulda, but they also feared the disruption to their lives if the Fulda measures came to Kleinostheim. Fear became panic when Dernbach's campaign took a violent turn. He started using accusations of witchcraft to expand his control.

Local magistrates were still uneasy with his methods. They, too, had friends and neighbors affected. The witchcraft accusations served one purpose. It took proceedings out of the local courts and placed them in ecclesiastical courts, where local sympathies and unprejudiced law carried no weight. He hired Balthasar Nuss, a witch hunter of scathing renown, and gave him the title "Malefizmeister", Master of Evil. His title and presence alone were enough to draw lines of suspicion between friends where none had previously existed.

Anna and Jost knew all too well how quickly affectionate neighbors could turn violently against one another when accusations of witchcraft are thrown through the air of a small community. The poor citizens of Fulda did not have what Anna had all those years ago — a secular court with a high burden of prosecutorial proof. The abbot stirred suspicions, and neighbors turned, predictably, on neighbors. Nuss launched his investigations, and arrests followed shortly after. Ever at his hip was the *Malleus Maleficarum,* "Hammer of Witches", the "Witch Hunter's Bible", written in 1484 by Heinrich Kramer, a Catholic Priest. It was a favorite of *all* witch hunters. Not only did it give them carte blanche in the hunting, trying, and execution of accused witches, it established its own authority by declaring any opposition to its precepts to be heresy.

It was a terrifying time for the entire region. The Koobs feared little for themselves. They were Catholic and could foresee no reason they would incur the wrath of Nuss. They were terribly anxious for their friends and tenants and debated over many meals to what extent they would defend them. Protestants were not the only people caught in Nuss' net in Fulda. Anyone who spoke in defense of an accused witch, or God forbid, in defiance against the very proceedings, found themselves shackled beside the accused. In Fulda, they had lost their minds. Friends raced to raise accusations just to place themselves on the safer side of Nuss' war. Kleinostheim began to take measure of its own fragility. What seemed a stable foundation of loyalty and affection appeared precarious under the light shining from Fulda.

Christoph had turned seventeen and was to have gone to Italy. He would not dare leave his parents and his village under such perilous apprehension. Against the protests of Anna and Jost, he postponed his schooling indefinitely. Anna Marie was relieved. No proposal of marriage had come, and she feared his departure for the coast. Anna did what Anna always did. She floated within her circles, bringing hope and comfort to terrified friends. She kept them calm, kept them from turning on each other with preemptive accusations. Nuss reached as far south as the Main River, but Kleinostheim did not crumble as easily as Fulda. The Koobs were the adhesive that held it together.

Jost forgave the outstanding debts of his tenants and clients. He lowered rents and even presented his poorer tenants with necessities to lower their tension and reduce the likelihood they would panic and fall into Nuss' trap. It was a very good thing that Christoph stayed. It took every bit of all three of them to hold their village together. Anna and Jost were proud of their son. He calmed and delighted like Anna, while supplementing the spiritual with more temporal contributions, much like his father. Without him, Kleinostheim would likely have crumbled as Fulda did. Ever at his side during his efforts was his childhood friend, Anna Marie. During those compassionate outings, the girl shone more and more like Anna Koob, and Christoph began to realize what his parents had long known — that Anna Marie Notintz was the only young woman in his life that would ever fit him as a spouse should fit.

To Dernbach and Nuss, Fulda was not just about the people of Fulda. Their actions there were meant to be seen by the entire region, to frighten them into turning each other in. It was less about a witch hunt and more about creating a witch craze, where paranoia played righteous people right into their hands. Things in Fulda were taken to an intentional and horrifying extreme.

Nuss did not seek men. He wanted victims whose lives were not so intimately entangled in the affairs of business. He sought women, and he hated women. The *Malleus Maleficarum* was, first and foremost, a misogynist's book. It was little more than a list of excuses to brutalize women. In his first few months in Fulda, Nuss accused dozens of women of witchcraft, and he had the testimony of frightened, manipulated friends and relatives to hammer his convictions home. Once in his net, the accused did not escape. Every woman he accused was convicted, and every one of them put to death. It worked as designed. Husbands, fathers, sons, and brothers from cities, towns, and villages across the region rushed to accuse a neighbor if only to shine a light of innocence on themselves and their families.

The Koobs worked tirelessly to keep Kleinostheim together, often forsaking their own wealth and welfare. The moment things began to unravel, there was Anna and Jost, or Christoph and Anna Marie, offering a kind word, some provision, or simply a gesture of affection to stitch them tightly together again.

Dernbach was ambitious. Despite his atrocious success, he was discontent. Many communities like Kleinostheim were not falling into his hands like Fulda. He began poring through old legal records, searching for accusations of witchcraft that had failed in the local courts. He found an old case out of Aschaffenburg, where a young woman had been accused of murdering two little children with a poisoned brew, a young woman acquitted for a lack of evidence. He found Anna.

The entire county had held defiantly together in affection and tolerance. Aschaffenburg, Kleinostheim, Mainaschaff, Stockstadt, they all resisted and the abbot was desperate to crack them. He believed this one case to be his best tool. One arrest, one noisy trial, one blazing execution, and hysteria would sweep the people of Aschaffenburg County. That was his plan and he set Nuss on the case of Anna Koob.

Nuss reviewed the case. There was little for him to go on. The local courts did well to keep the proceedings on track and focus the trial on the accusations of murder. Nuss could not conduct this affair from miles away. He went to Aschaffenburg and spoke with the judges of Anna's case. Dissatisfied there, he went to Kleinostheim and interrogated Anna's neighbors. All of this was done in a day and Anna, Jost, and Christoph knew nothing of it until Nuss and his men knocked on their door.

Jost and Christoph were delivering gifts and Anna was home alone. Believing their village well galvanized against the hysteria, and having no reason to suspect that Balthasar Nuss was south of Fulda. Anna answered the door with a warm smile. It fell from her with a thud on the floor when the men seized her ferociously by the upper arms and Nuss announced her arrest loudly to the empty house, as if proclaiming it in a large and crowded town square. Anna was in shock and had no idea what to think, how to feel, or even how to pray for her own safety.

She simply repeated in a voice almost too quiet for Nuss and his men to hear, "Jost…, Jost…, Jost," as her wrists were bound and she was dragged from her home.

Her neighbors saw her pulled to a carriage and thrown inside. They were not ready to betray her with false testimony, no matter how much pressure was applied, nor were they ready to leap to her defense. They simply watched and whispered with sickened stomachs as their friend and neighbor, Anna Koob, was carried away toward Aschaffenburg.

Chapter Twenty-Six:
Miscalculated Witnesses

JOST AND CHRISTOPH RETURNED HOME with light and jovial hearts. Their work in the village was fulfilling and enlivening. Their hearty laughs alerted the neighbors to their return and they were met at the door. Word of Anna's arrest made it as far as Karl, who rushed to Anna's house in time to join the neighbors. Four in total stood between Jost and his own front door. They stood with somber faces that dripped with compassion and concern.

"What?" Jost shouted to them, accurately reading their expressions, "What has happened? Where is Anna?"

Karl, unable to control himself, lunged forward and wrapped Jost in an embrace of his mighty arms. With his head pressed against Jost's, he whispered, "They took her. The witch hunter of Fulda took her away."

Jost meant no harm to the bearer of the horrific news, but he pushed himself free of Karl then struck the much larger man in the chest. Jost's knees buckled beneath him and he collapsed.

Christoph, now a full inch taller than his father and more muscular, grabbed Jost from behind and hoisted him to his feet. Jost stood firmly under his own waning strength and thanked his son. Karl kept a respectful distance with tears rolling down his substantial cheeks.

"What do we do, father? What do we do?" Christoph begged with bouncing energy.

Jost did not answer immediately. Christoph looked to his neighbors, who all stood stone-still and silent. He turned to stand directly facing his father, and he repeated, while shaking Jost's shoulders, "What do we do?"

With battered resignation, Jost answered firmly, "We go inside and we plan your mother's defense."

They did just that, Jost and Christoph alone, leaving the neighbors standing at their door. Karl looked to the others and ordered, "We must do the same. They will question us, and we must know our answers beforehand. Return to your homes and prepare your families to defend Anna."

Karl was correct. Nuss wasted no time. The very next day, he canvassed the village, beginning with the homes nearest Anna's, like a slithering snake slinking from door to door, manipulating words and flicking venom from his forked tongue. Try as he may, and he most certainly tried, Nuss could find no testimony against Anna. He thought surely that Karl would be eagerly waiting to exact revenge on her. When he spoke with Karl, he found only a simple and adoring neighbor who regretted any and all suffering he brought upon Anna Koob and her family. He spoke of her as a devout mother, wife, and Christian, whose Christian charity saw their village through its toughest days. This description did not at all match the devilish depiction of a witch in his trusty copy of the *Malleus Maleficarum.*

Nuss widened his circle, but Kleinostheim held with Anna. Yielding defeat here would be devastating to the archbishop's and the abbot's crusade. So the investigation pushed on. Nuss reviewed all that the Church knew of Anna Koob. There it was, well beneath the papers on her murder trial, the case of a little girl, Anna Schwarz, whose seemingly mystical abilities healed the daughter of a local baron. The mysterious case of Maria Echter was before Nuss' eyes. Maria lived in Bohemia. Besides, documentation of her testimony did not make her an ideal witness against Anna. Maria's mother was dead. Her father was rumored to have lost his wits. None of the servants who witnessed Maria's recovery were still employed by the household. A few distant relatives and others connected in some peripheral way to the Echter family spoke with Nuss and described a teenage girl as near to death as a living creature could be, and a lively, skipping maiden shortly after she was visited by Anna. There was only one intimate witness to be drawn from the case — the Jesuit priest who initially investigated the incident and reported his findings to the bishop.

There was nothing in Father Albrecht's report that hinted at his tender affinity for the little girl who altered him so cheerfully and deepened him so profoundly. Nuss believed him to be just the weapon to sink Anna Koob and send the area into hysteria. Albrecht was in Austria and Nuss summoned him with the authority of the Archbishop of Mainz. Albrecht answered and reported again to Aschaffenburg on account of Anna. This time he came with a steadfast affection and long-held sense of debt. Had Nuss any notion of the witness he summoned, of his lingering love and gratitude for Anna, he would have had Albrecht sent to the farthest corner of the Earth.

Albrecht knew well of Balthasar Nuss, and when a summons came from him to testify against Anna Koob, he knew exactly what to prepare for. Albrecht, as sly as he was righteous and brilliant, set immediately to defend Anna while still appearing useful to Nuss. A straight-forward defense of the accused would get him dismissed from the proceedings, leaving him unable to help. So he calculated his testimony painstakingly to serve Anna while still seeming relevant to the case against her.

Jost and Christoph spoke and planned with the village. Nuss left every home in Kleinostheim grinding his teeth in seething frustration. The friends and neighbors of Anna Koob were well-organized and prepared for questioning. They held firmly together. Their coordination was obvious to Nuss, but there was nothing he could do to break their solidarity. There was one neighbor, a simple man named Jacob, whose job it was to organize the sanitation of the village. Jacob was not stupid, but his grasp of language was tenuous at best. Nuss mistook the bumbling words as imbecility and nervousness. He believed Jacob was just the sort of witness he could manipulate to his own ends. From all of Kleinostheim, Jacob was the only witness retained by Nuss in his case against Anna.

Nuss had two witnesses — one bumbling but loyal friend of the accused and one Jesuit scholar of the highest wit and affixed devotion. Nuss awaited only Albrecht's arrival to begin a case, the strength of which was based entirely on two witnesses who were not what he assumed them to be. Nuss knew that his case was weak. Even under the loose prosecutorial standards of an ecclesiastical court, with its broad burden of proof, Nuss saw little chance of success on his current path. He reached out to his mentor, his employer, to a man whose authority might tilt the case in his favor. He turned to the Benedictine, Prince-Abbot Balthasar von Dernbach. The abbot was waist deep in the Fulda trials. Nevertheless, he responded with haste to Aschaffenburg and assumed control of the case against Anna.

Dernbach arrived one day before Father Albrecht. He was already well situated with an office in the bishop's palace that he commandeered for his own purposes. He elevated his desk and situated it to command the utmost obedience from all who entered the office. And that is how

Albrecht met him, stepping gingerly before the stately desk and looking upward to a much shorter man. Albrecht felt, at his first glance upward to Dernbach, that he was the one on trial.

Dernbach had no malicious intentions toward his Jesuit guest. He believed that Albrecht would be his star witness, that behind his obscure report of a rural incident many years ago, some small detail was hiding and could be pried from his memory and from his lips by the cunning of the Prince-Abbot. He reviewed the notes on the case of Maria Echter's recovery and thoroughly perused Albrecht's report.

He sensed that Father Albrecht had more to write on the topic but held back his pen. This was keenly perceived. Albrecht did not include all that he thought and all that he believed in his report. But the abbot read inaccurately into Albrecht's restraint. Albrecht had been hesitant to report the honest beauty of the incident, and he did not write at all about what he had learned from Anna. His primary intention when he wrote his report was to put the matter to rest as quietly as possible and return the Schwarz family to their lives. Dernbach sought something sinister, so that is exactly what he read between Albrecht's lines. From the report before him, he assumed that Maria Echter had died, and through necromancy, was brought back to life by Anna, and with no explanation for Maria's sudden illness, he contrived another charge. He composed an argument that Anna poisoned Maria that day they met at the fountain in Aschaffenburg.

Albrecht's head was filled with the teachings of others, but he was often mindless of the teachings of experience. Ideals carried more weight than common sense. His faith in Anna and her brightness of spirit was stronger than his understanding of the abbot, regardless of the reputation of bloodshed that preceded him to Aschaffenburg. Despite Dernbach's notorious reputation,

Albrecht thought that Anna would lighten the abbot's heart and her innocence would proclaim itself so boldly that the matter would be settled as quickly as the matter of Maria Echter.

Nevertheless, Albrecht thought it wise to address Dernbach before he could confront Anna. Afterall, Albrecht had already interviewed Anna, years ago, and he thought that a presentation of his findings in that case could prime the abbot for a more favorable encounter. Albrecht spoke first, in well-placed words, but his affection for Anna hid poorly behind them. He advised the abbot on how he should approach Anna. Dernbach was impatient of any advice. He heard, but did not listen. His angry, zealous spirit writhed beneath his stone-still exterior. When Albrecht concluded, Dernbach scolded him like a master scolds a dog. He was intoxicated with pride and addressed Albrecht in a manner the Pope himself would not have dared.

From his high desk at the end of the room, Dernbach began questioning Albrecht about his report. There was a distinct high-handedness in the way he asked his questions. It did not sound at all like a man looking for answers, rather like a man implanting them. He slyly introduced his theories in a way that would have made a stranger in the room believe that they were written into the report by the hand of Albrecht. But Albrecht was no stranger in the room. He knew what was in his report. He had chosen his words meticulously after hours of deliberation. He also knew what Dernbach was doing. He did not want to encourage the blood-thirsty zealot, nor did he wish to alienate himself. He believed that his best position to help Anna in the coming trial was as a credible witness called by the Church.

Dernbach *was* the Church. In the eyes of those who witnessed him thundering around in his robes and belting scripture from his thick throat, he was the Church. To the layfolk of the county, if Dernbach said it, the Church said it. He was confident he could make the simple Jacob tremble before the court and say all he desired him to say. Nuss was certainly out of his depth with the people of Kleinostheim before Dernbach joined him. But he and Dernbach both were well-assured that Anna would burn before the eyes of her neighbors, who would burst into the same hysteria that took Fulda, and Aschaffenburg County would come trembling back to the fold.

He tried his powers of persuasion on Father Albrecht, railing as he had in many a witch trial. But Albrecht was more formidable of mind than the abbot's usual audience. He was far too astute not to see directly through the dark-aged rhetoric. He also knew that his own mind was painfully beyond most. He knew how quickly fear rallies mobs and mobs spill blood. He knew it well enough to begin to fear strongly for Anna's safety. Albrecht left his encounter in Dernbach's office with a growing ache in his stomach.

Albrecht left Dernbach's intimidating office and turned his eyes to Jost. The afternoon was late and he rode as quickly as he could to Kleinostheim. He found the Koob house but nobody was home. Jost, Christoph, and Anna Marie were about the charitable needs of the village, serving but also rallying. A great deal was owed by many to Anna, Jost, and Christoph. In Anna's absence, Anna Marie filled in admirably, and Jost and Christoph worked twice as hard to adhere those bonds of loyalty more tightly and unify the community behind Anna.

Christoph came home first and found Albrecht at his door. No immediate introduction was needed. Albrecht recognized much of the girl he knew in the young man before him. Christoph saw the compassion in the scholar's eyes. That look and his distinctly Jesuit robe revealed the identity of a figure long-glorified in his mother's tales of her childhood.

Christoph stepped nearer to clarify Albrecht's image in the dimming daylight, and whispered questioningly, "Father Albrecht?"

"You know me by sight, my son?" Albrecht responded, "And I know you. You are Anna's son. Of that there can be no doubt."

They greeted with the embrace of intimates and Christoph brought Albrecht into his home. Many times between the door and the table, Christoph thanked God aloud for sending Albrecht to his mother's defense. In the briefest of introductions, Albrecht could see that the boy in front of him had vision, knowledge, and wisdom well beyond his years. Still, he awaited Jost's return to speak openly of Dernbach's case against Anna, and of his own fear of its success.

Jost rode a wave of support and devotion down the paths that led back to his home and son. He prayed to Saint Michael to take up his wife's cause and fight in her defense. Crossing his threshold to find his son sharing their table with the Jesuit seemed like an immediate and pronounced answer to that prayer. Albrecht had no wings, no armor, no spear, no foot on the head of the serpent. He had books before him, a commanding voice, and a sharp intelligence in his eyes. Jost had his Saint Michael under his own roof, and his fear for Anna's life withdrew its fangs from his heart.

They spoke deep into the night, the three of them. Albrecht was frank and spoke with an often-faltering voice about Dernbach's case and his determination to prevail. But Albrecht's appearance in their home timed so flawlessly with his prayers that Jost did not see it as a case of Dernbach and Nuss against Anna Koob, or even the full force of the Church against Anna. He saw it as God against the untruthful, and he believed his family was on the winning side.

When he saw Albrecht to the door in the wee hours of the morning, Jost's heart was relieved of the pains it had been suffering. He went to bed lighter of spirits and fuller of confidence than he had since Anna's arrest. The trial was set to begin in three days. Jost did not dread it as Albrecht did. He wished for it, faithful that he would walk hand-in-hand back home with his wife after their quick and decisive triumph.

By the time Albrecht settled into bed, the desperation of the situation fully sobered the priest's thoughts to Anna's peril. He did not sleep, but laid in frenzied deliberation, darting from one hopeless scheme to another, doubtful but determined to interfere on behalf of an innocent woman, one who had been the innocent child that altered his faith years ago and raised him nearer to God.

Chapter Twenty-Seven:
The Armed Zealot

ANNA DID NOT SPEND HER INCARCERATION in an open room of a business building. She spent it in a cell. The dungeon of the archbishop's palace in Aschaffenburg was not large. It was not some dirty, mossy, blood-stained crypt for the walking dead. It was clean and well kept, with large windows that let in a healthy amount of light. But it was undoubtedly a dungeon. She ate a brothy stew with little substance, and drank sips of water from a cracked wooden bowl, all behind the thick bars of a cell that was not much longer or wider than her own dining table. She had no complaints of mistreatment. She had no claims of treatment of any kind. Nobody spoke to her. Nobody asked questions. The only person she saw was the servant who brought her food and replaced her waste bucket. It was not her conditions at all that drew such a torrent of tears from her eyes, nor was it her fear of the coming trial. She missed her husband and she missed her son, and she pitied them severely for what she knew they were suffering.

"At least I am in the good cell," she repeated regularly to herself, for the cell beside was much larger, larger and holding wooden contraptions that she assumed to be made for torture. There was an inclined table with straps at the

253

ends for the binding of hands and feet, and a thick, stately, oak chair that would have seemed regal, the sort that would denote a place of honor at a count's table, if not for the straps attached to it. At no point in her earlier trial did Anna feel like a prisoner, certainly not in comparison to her current condition. She was undoubtedly a prisoner this time, but one that was not detained indignantly, and not bound to the devices in the neighboring cell. For that, she was grateful.

Anna was on good terms with her neighbors. She could not imagine that one of them was bearing false witness against her. She was perceptive of the world around her and well-read on the atrocities occurring in Fulda. She knew why she was caged, but like Jost, she had faith that she would escape the fate of the women of Fulda. She was Anna Koob of Kleinostheim. There was no hysteria in her village, and she was a threat to nobody.

Seventeen days after her arrest, Anna was marched from the dungeon to a large hall on the main floor of the archbishop's palace. The room had a familiar chair with a familiar banister rail around it. Other than that, the scene was strange to her — strange and terrifying. The floor was ornate with marble inlays depicting biblical scenes. The walls were equally splendid, wainscoted with stately wooden panels beneath and bright paintings on a dark wall above. The railed chair sat distinctly inferior beneath a grand and elevated court bench. Behind the bench was a row of nine chairs.

Anna was seated at the intimidated little railed chair, and she crooked her neck awkwardly upward to see the top of the bench. She only had a minute to get her bearings before a panel of robed clerics filed into the chairs behind the bench. They spoke to each other as if Anna was not yet in the room. A couple of them glanced quickly at her but turned their eyes and their full attention to the petty talk that occupied the panel.

Anna felt beneath them in every possible way. This was not a room set up for an honest flow of information from her seat to the grand bench, but for heavy-handed dictates to flow steeply downward. Her heart jolted with the realization, and a wave of sharp, stabbing chills traveled from her chest to her extremities. She feared for her life, and for the first time, flashes of bonfires slapped at her imagination with open-handed violence. Sweat rushed to her skin and she went cold and clammy.

A clamor came through the doors behind her. The room was filling, but Anna could not turn her head from the despotic authority of the robed men on the high bench in front of her. The familiar voice of Balthasar Nuss rang directly beside her as he passed the banistered chair to greet the panel of judges. They spoke of light topics with carefree voices that seemed to bounce above her like sunlit bubbles on the ocean surface, above a dark, cold, battered shipwreck beneath.

A thin ray of that light reached her when another voice spoke beside her. This one accompanied a slight touch on her shoulder that spoke a thousand reassuring words in the briefest of moments. The voice attached to those fingertips was rich with purity and dripping with goodness. It was strange yet familiar, like hearing a song sung to you when you were a child. This second voice also greeted the judges. The formal respect shown to this man by the judges gave a slight sense of relief to poor Anna. When he turned to face her, and revealed an older, greyer, weathered version of the Jesuit priest she knew as a child, Anna felt as if she sat on the shoulders of an Angel.

Father Albrecht did not greet her familiarly, as both of them were tempted to do. He simply grinned at her. That subtle gesture did not relay unbridled confidence, but it spoke plainly enough of support, gratitude, and affection. That was enough for Anna until she perceived in his eyes a hint of pity. Her poor heart suffered through dueling cycles of hope and dread. Her body felt the full force of the whipping turmoil within her, and she caught herself holding a deep inhale well past its natural life. When she released it, it took her strength with it. Anna swooned. Her head rolled and her eyes turned back within their sockets.

Albrecht witnessed the transformation and called the room's attention to Anna. The judges did not show the concern for her that the lay judges of her first trial showed. Nobody responded until Albrecht demanded a glass of water. He shouted with such gripping authority that Anna could hear a dozen feet scrambling behind her. A pair of those feet were attached to a hand that appeared quickly beside her with the demanded water. Anna took it with two hands, scared of spilling it, as if such an infraction would be held against her in the coming proceedings. She thanked the faceless hand that delivered the water and held the glass tightly to her lips without sipping until her hands calmed enough to steadily tilt the glass.

Albrecht stood leaning against the rail in front of Anna. She looked directly at the rail, never lifting her eyes to his. But she heard his breathing. He drew and released intentionally audible breaths, prompting Anna to follow in kind. She matched her breathing to his, and in that peripheral unity, she took some of his calmness.

Anna handed the glass to Albrecht without lifting her eyes. He made sure that his fingers rested on hers for one quick and firm squeeze before pulling the glass from her. He understood what she did not — that nervous, erratic behavior would paint a hideous image of her in that little chair. The truth came to her, bringing a fresh rush of terror when a voice behind her said in an exaggerated whisper, "That is how a guilty woman acts."

Anna's attention, and that of the entire room, was drawn instantly from the comment by the entrance of the Prince-Abbot. It was not another voice speaking beside her that alerted her to Dernbach's presence in the room. It was the sudden silence and the captured stares of the panel of judges. The judges were men of prominence, men of consequence, yet their attention was deferentially obedient to the silent figure looming behind Anna. She heard the creak of the banisters as Dernbach's hands wrapped around the rail, mere inches from Anna's head, and he leaned his weight into it. No doubt it was all in a theatrical play to intimidate her. It worked. He loomed like death itself behind her, quiet, unseen, but casting a shadow that lowered the temperature of everything beneath it.

After what he deemed a reasonable amount of intimidation behind her, Dernbach approached the bench. He was in his formal clerical robes and held a book in his hands. He came armed with the only weapon he thought he needed, the *Malleus Maleficarum,* the Hammer of Witches. Anna could not see the title of the book while Dernbach greeted the judges. But when he turned to stare her down, he angled the front cover intentionally to expose it to her view. She knew it. Of course, she knew well of it. But it did not strike her with terror.

The book told her what sort of attacks she would face, and she closed her eyes and prepared her defense against it. Her eyes darted in frenzied thought behind their closed lids, as Anna drew from her substantial memory quotations from varied sources to battle the medieval rhetoric of the *Malleus Maleficarum.* Rational reason of the highest order shoved her fear to the depths of her being. Flashes of memories from late-night coffeehouse symposiums and monastery debates each deposited an argument at the front of her consciousness. Anna knew she was extraordinary among the women of the region. She was extraordinary among the men.

Anna's greatest ally was Dernbach's ignorance about her. He prepared well to stare down the rural child from Albrecht's report. He was entirely ill-equipped to face the likes of Anna Koob. She grew confident in her ability to reduce the mighty man before her in debate. But she was neither blind nor foolish. She knew that she was not seated at a monastery table in Nice or a coffeehouse patio in Trieste. Her tiny, shadowed chair and the grand bench that cast that shadow were steady reminders.

Custodians entered the room with small chairs in each hand. They lined the wall to Anna's left. No sooner did each chair settle into place than a body sat upon it. The gallery behind Anna was full. For the first time since being seated, she turned to look behind her, wondering who would have come to fill so many seats. There were many familiar faces, friendly faces intimidatingly surrounding the voice that said earlier that she looked guilty. And still standing among the seated gallery were Jost and Christoph.

Jost looked as firm and stalwart as ever, and Christoph appeared tall and muscular, like a statue of some pristine Greek god. When Anna turned back around, Dernbach seemed diminished in size. He looked puny and insignificant to her, and the high bench seemed to drop several feet and cast only a hazy, impotent shadow. Dernbach was most certainly outnumbered. He was intellectually overpowered. Anna drew another inhale and held it long. This time it savored of confidence and it was under Anna's control. She released it with a focused stare at Dernbach. He did not crumble at the stare, but held his own and returned it with one of equal determination. The pieces were set, and the contest for Anna's life began.

Chapter Twenty-Eight:
The Advocate's Ambush

THERE WERE FOUR PARTS TO DERNBACH'S CASE. He had Nuss and the little information he gathered during his extensive interviews. Of those, only Jacob was to testify, and little was expected from him. He had the case of Maria Echter and the reports and rumors that came from it. Those were decades old and no witnesses to them were called to testify. He had the testimony of Father Albrecht, whose position on the front lines of the Counter-Reformation suggested a holy warrior ready to do the Church's bidding. Dernbach had no idea what a miscalculation that would be. The cornerstone of the case against Anna was the record of her previous trial. In Dernbach's mind, the case had plenty to convict Anna of witchcraft, and only failed to do so because it was a lay court, trying her only for the death of the children, for which there was no evidence.

Dernbach started with his weaker evidence and called Jacob to testify. Jacob stood before the court and introduced himself. Dernbach took a seat and allowed Nuss to question Jacob. Jacob's simple mind was easy for Nuss to manipulate. The village sanitation coordinator was like a ship with massive sails and no navigation, ready to be pushed at great speeds wherever the wind wished to push him. He was incapable of using the wind to find his own destination. Dernbach counted on that, and Nuss began blowing his wind.

Nuss set traps that poor Jacob walked into. He asked about the tonics and elixirs that Anna notoriously served to the people of Kleinostheim.

"Did Anna Koob ever bring one of these potions into your household?" Nuss prodded.

Were Jacob a man of quick wits, he would have objected to the word *potions*. He stumbled with the question, darting his eyes from Nuss to Anna and back again several times before answering, "Yes. She gave something to my mother."

"And how is your mother now?" Nuss snidely asked, knowing well the answer.

Jacob tripped through another answer, "My mother is dead now. That is... she died. She is with God."

"How long after Anna Koob gave her the potion did your mother perish?"

It was a full seven months after Anna had made a tonic for Jacob's mother before the woman passed away, before she grew ill. But Jacob had no head for the calendar and he mumbled nervously, "My mother died after Anna gave her the—"

Jacob paused and Nuss took a broad, stomping stride toward him, thundering at him, "Gave her what?"

Jacob had no gift for language and could not think of a more appropriate word. He had no time. Nuss leaned toward him until he blurted forth the only word to come to mind, the word planted there by Nuss.

"The p...p...potion."

Nuss turned to the court and summed up Jacob's testimony with rhetorical mastery, "Anna Koob gave his mother a potion and then she died."

Jacob knew he was manipulated, and he knew his testimony sounded little like the truth. With a panic in his voice he said, "That's not why my mother died."

"How did your mother die, Jacob? How?" Nuss pressed impatiently.

"I don't know… she was not young."

Nuss turned quickly in a different direction, asking Jacob, "How much did your mother pay Anna Koob for the potion?"

"Nothing. Anna doesn't ask for money."

"Ever? She skulks around the village passing potions to people and charging nothing for it? Tell me Jacob, what does she get out of it? Why would she do such a thing?"

For the briefest moment, Nuss succeeded. Jacob considered the question. His mother had been dead for less than a year and he still mourned her. Distraught as he was, and as firmly under Nuss' masterful hand, he could not divest himself of his decades of neighborly affection. He and Anna had known each other since childhood. Anna used to visit his mother, and read and sing to her for years before she died. Jacob's mother loved Anna and spoke of her in the tenderest terms. In stirring Jacob's feelings for his mother, Nuss only managed to revive the gratitude and adoration for Anna that were held so close to his mother's heart.

Jacob answered Nuss' last question, "She had always done things like that. She cares. She cares about…"

Jacob turned emotional, as expressed clearly in his reddened face and cracking voice. Dernbach knew that the sentiments struggling to break through were not suspicion or anger, but friendship and loyalty for Anna, and they would not help his case. So, he interrupted before anything else could be said.

He stood abruptly and addressed the court, "This poor Christian man is suffering from his loss. Let us remove him from this setting and let him mourn in peace."

The court agreed and Jacob was quickly escorted from the room. Had the case rested entirely on Jacob's testimony, Anna would have been home by dinner. But Jacob was only the beginning, and Nuss played him exactly as planned. The next event for the court to consider was the strange case of Maria Echter. Dernbach patted Nuss on the shoulder and directed him to sit down. Before calling Father Albrecht, he addressed Anna directly.

Dernbach introduced the matter to the court, reading the introduction from Albrecht's report. He followed it with the statements of the witnesses who spoke to Nuss. By their descriptions, through the hazy memory of decades past, it sounded like Maria had all but died, only to rise in an instant to full recovery after only a few moments with Anna.

Anna corrected him, "That is not how it happened. Maria's recovery was much—"

Dernbach interrupted, "Are you saying that all of these people coordinated a lie against you. Does that sound likely to you?"

Without a breath of pause, Anna responded, "That was a long time ago." She followed with an instantly recalled and flawlessly recited quotation from *The Confessions of Saint Augustine*, "Times lose no time; nor do they roll idly by; through our senses they work strange operations on the mind."

Anna could not see Albrecht, but he grinned, having recognized the quotation from its first four words, and knowing that it came to her by his hand. He also grinned because he knew how unprepared the Prince-Abbot was to face Anna. Beneath the grin, however, a simmering fear rose in temperature within him. He understood Dernbach well enough to know that he would not idly suffer frustration at the hands of a lay person, and certainly not a woman. Dernbach also knew the source of the quotation, and he had a few of his own. But he pocketed them for the moment, to be drawn when they would be sharpest and most cutting.

Words from dusty memories were of little more use to Dernbach. Anna muted their voices with her masterful wielding of the quotation. He was not ready to invite another answer from her lips. He called Albrecht to the bench, knowing there was more to Albrecht's experience than was reflected in his report and believing he could cage Albrecht's responses and rearrange them to his benefit, the way Nuss did with poor Jacob.

Albrecht's report of the Maria Echter incident included the expressed opinions of the people he interviewed in Aschaffenburg. Many of them suspected unnatural interference. Of those, some gave the credit to God, others to the devil. Some believed it was witchcraft. It is safe to say that substantial fear surrounded Maria's recovery. It was that portion of the report that Dernbach brought up first. He asked Albrecht to detail the most fearful statements and the most damning accusations documented in his report. To assist, he had commissioned a copy of the report and handed it to Albrecht to read.

Albrecht did exactly as he was asked. He read the uninformed ramblings of those too distant from the heart of the matter to have any claim at truth, and he regretted including them in his report. But he surprised Dernbach when he concluded.

He turned to Anna and asked her, "You were much nearer to the heart of the matter. You spent time with Maria's parents and with Maria Echter herself. Did any of them fear you? At any point did they ask you to leave their home, or did they beg you to stay longer?"

Albrecht presented his questions in a way that appeared as if he truly sought answers from Anna, rather than posing rhetorical questions in her defense.

Dernbach turned him back on track by asking him, "Would you expect anything different from the father and mother of the girl? Have the faithful never turned in their grief to a necromancer. Have the fearful and mourning never shunned Christ? The more reliable sources are those who are at a greater distance, those whose fears are so well documented in your report."

Albrecht again surprised Dernbach by turning to Anna and asking, "You were a young girl when I last spoke to you. You are a woman now, so can you tell us plainly, what caused Maria Echter's recovery?"

The question had been posed and the court looked to Anna for an answer. There was nothing Dernbach could do to interfere.

Anna locked her eyes tightly to Albrecht's and answered, much as she did when she was eight years old, "Love healed Maria, and love is Divine. Surely this is not the first example you have heard of the healing power of God."

Albrecht nodded, rolled his eyes upward, and pretended to be thoughtful in the moment. He turned his eyes back to Anna and asked, "Can *you* explain the fear and opinions of people who were not with Maria and her family when she… got better?"

Anna closed her eyes, inhaled deeply, opened her eyes and released her breath as she spoke calmly, "Psalm 53… There they are, overwhelmed with dread, where there was nothing to fear."

Dernbach felt himself losing grip of the proceedings. He lost his head in anger and yelled at Anna, "Do not quote Scripture to me, girl. Do you say they have nothing to fear? What about evil? Should righteous people not fear evil?"

Anna was shaken by the outburst. She trembled and was unable to hide it. Albrecht's first instinct was to calm her, but he knew better. He knew that her trembling would make Dernbach look cruel, and that would play in Anna's favor.

Anna did not need Albrecht to ease her. She did that herself with a few deep breaths. She turned to Dernbach with calmness that contrasted greatly against his fury, and she answered, "Saint Gregory wrote that the Divine does not admit of an opposite."

Dernbach was boiling with anger, but he knew what Albrecht knew — that another rageful outburst would turn the court against him. He looked to Albrecht, who stood with folded arms looking at Anna. It was satisfaction on display in Albrecht, but Dernbach misinterpreted it and believed the priest to be just as insulted by Anna's flinging of scripture and theological writings. He hoped that members of the court felt the same. Those things were, afterall, theirs by right, not hers. They were the clergy, and they were men.

He looked at Albrecht like a comrade and asked, "What do you make of this woman, throwing Saint Gregory in our faces?"

He had already forgotten his lesson, not to ask Albrecht such open questions. There was no recalling the question. The room went silent in anticipation of a response.

Albrecht folded his hands and held them under his chin, looking downward over his knuckles to Anna's feet. Without changing his position, not turning to Dernbach or the bench or raising his eyes to Anna, he spoke, "I notice a very widespread tendency…" He paused, still staring at Anna's feet, composed his next words meticulously to turn Dernbach's behavior against him, and continued, "to react with suspicion, even with rage, to a comment made by a woman, when the very same words would be admired when spoken by a man, particularly a clergyman."

He unfolded his hands, turned his head and raised his eyes to view the clergymen behind the bench. "Truth and righteousness… do these things really change their natures when ringing out in a feminine voice?"

This was an unmistakable challenge to Dernbach, and the whole room viewed it that way. They all looked to him. Dernbach walked to the table where Nuss sat. Nuss began to stand and parted his lips slightly as if beginning to speak. Dernbach waved him back to his seat. He took from the table his copy of the *Malleus Maleficarum*, not to read from it or reference it at all, but to place the weight of its authority behind his own words.

He waved the book in the air as he addressed Albrecht, "We have seen countless examples of evil speaking with feminine voices, seducing and defiling, corrupting and misleading."

Albrecht cocked one eyebrow up and asked, "Have we?"

A new avenue of attack entered Dernbach's head. He walked to Anna with his book in hand. He tapped it on the rail in front of her and argued, "Without pause, without thought, she threw forth quotations from Saint Augustine and Saint Gregory. Are you suggesting that she had that knowledge, by her own genius and industry, in her little head, and that *God* granted this woman the ability to produce those quotations on the spot? Of all the great and learned men, do you believe that God chose her to speak for him? I suspect her inspiration comes from a darker place. Satan knows those verses too."

Albrecht had tried to that point not to openly argue in Anna's defense. But he could see where Dernbach was going, suggesting that the knowledge in Anna's head was placed there by Satan.

He could not allow Dernbach that path without resistance, and he asked, "Is it so hard to imagine that the daughter of a book merchant might be well-read?"

Dernbach exploded, "In the Scriptures, sure. Many girls are versed in the Psalms, but in Saint Gregory? In Augustine's Confessions? How could she get her hands on such a collection?"

"From me," Albrecht answered without thought, "I gave her the full collection of Augustine's Confessions when she was only a child, and I know for a fact that she read them and discussed them with her parents, even as a child. She—"

Albrecht paused. He was going to confess that his own faith and understanding were deepened by Anna's childhood wisdom. But he knew that would diminish him in the eyes of those who mattered, and their high opinions of *him* were the best thing going for Anna. The revelation of the gift of books to the child Anna was a strong argument in her favor, but it also revealed the depth of their association and of his bias in the case. He had already made himself an adversary of Dernbach. He could not afford to also alienate himself from the court.

Albrecht had to choose his next words wisely. He was, afterall, Dernbach's witness and could be dismissed by Dernbach at any time. The Prince-Abbot also had to tread carefully. Albrecht had the respect of the court, and dismissing him abruptly or railing wildly against him could paint the case against Anna as blindly fanatical.

The speech that was to follow Albrecht's revelation would have been impassioned and filled to its limits with truth. It never came. He ended his protest there, afraid to say more, not at all sure what would help Anna and what would stoke the flames against her. The court dismissed for the day. Anna was brought back to her cell.

Jost and Christoph took a room with a business associate in Aschaffenburg. They shared a small bed. Jost held his taller son like he did years earlier, falling asleep with his nose planted to Christoph's head, allowing the smell of his son's hair to bring his imagination to happier times. Albrecht returned to his room. Of them all, it was Albrecht whose rest was most ravaged by the circumstances. In bed that night, knowing the very different sort of conditions Anna suffered at the same time, he worded and reworded again and again all that he had said and all that he wished he had said, all that he wrote in his report years ago, and all that he wished he had not. He second and third-guessed his every move from the day, and the guilt and uncertainty were crippling.

Chapter Twenty-Nine:
A Crack in the Cornerstone

THE FIRST DAY OF THE TRIAL did not go as Dernbach had imagined. He was not discouraged. From the beginning, he leaned his case most heavily on the details of Anna's first trial. In an atmosphere of strong religious bigotry, her association with Miray looked promising, and he bent his efforts toward it. He read about Miray's death at the hands of the Kleinostheim villagers. He was not going to be ambushed again by clever quotations from honored theologians. He spent that night at his desk, setting to memory quotations for his own wielding. To that point, Anna and Albrecht appeared to be the authorities in the room, and Dernbach came across as weak and unprepared. He was determined not to let that happen again.

Anna had already spent so many nights in her cell, she was accustomed to the conditions. She slept better than the night before, having had a few triumphs in court to rest her head upon. She was cautiously confident that, like before, her innocence and goodness would shine through hysterical accusations.

Anna was still sleeping soundly and dreaming pleasantly in the early morning when she was roused and brought back to her little chair behind the rail. She was given nothing to eat or drink and no time to prepare herself. She was hungry and her hair looked wild. She looked disheveled, hardly the pristine scholar that appeared before the court on the previous day. This was Dernbach's doing, in part from spiteful vengeance for the victories she had over him, and in part to gain an advantage. She looked much less like the refined scholar and more like the wild pagan witch he was trying to prove she was. When he began his efforts against Anna, it was not personal. It had nothing to do with Anna Koob. She could have been any woman. After the first day of the trial. Dernbach wanted to destroy Anna. She had embarrassed him. The subject of his ire was no longer faceless.

With Anna facing the bench looking as she did, it was time to bring up Miray, and tie Anna intimately to the "Turkish Witch". Nuss was sternly instructed to remain silently in his seat until ordered otherwise. He was a witch hunter, and a successful one. Sitting silently on a chair against the wall was not easy for him. But it was Dernbach, not Nuss, who had combed through the details of Anna's first trial. He had the minutes of all that was said, of all that was accused and refuted. More importantly, he memorized the *Malleus Maleficarum.* Since there was nothing in secular law that would put Anna to the flames, the medieval precepts of the witch hunter's bible had to take its lofty place in the proceedings.

Anna looked more of the street than the monastery, and Dernbach wasted no more time with the faded memories of rustics or the reports of biased Jesuits. He set immediately to holding Anna within the frame of the *Malleus Maleficarum* to present a portrait of a witch to the court.

"Anna Koob," he began, "let us talk about your pagan friend, Miray."

He walked behind Anna and leaned against the rail, facing the bench. He lowered his head to within a few inches of Anna's raggedy hair, and he belted as if speaking to her from across the room, "After her husband was captured and brought to justice, Miray stayed with you in your home."

No question was asked, so Anna waited for one before answering. Dernbach walked around to the front of Anna and looked at her inquisitively. When Anna did not speak, he turned to the judges, tilted his head, and raised an eyebrow. He did not understand women, but he understood men. He understood *these* men perfectly well. He knew that if he presented to their imaginations erotic images of Anna and Miray, it would stain their thoughts permanently, and everything they heard and everything they saw for the rest of the trial would be seen through those stains. They would either be aroused by it, or repulsed. In either case, they would be affected and their sound judgment impaired.

Dernbach continued, "Was she ever upon your bed?"

Anna's throat was parched, and she answered with a crack in her voice that sounded hideous, even sinister, "Not in the way that you imply."

"Was she ever on your bed with you?"

Anna repeated, "Not in the way that you imply."

Out came the *Malleus Maleficarum*. Dernbach waved it over his head and recited it to the rafters, "All witchcraft comes from carnal lust, which is in women insatiable... Is that how she claimed you?"

His question was not prompted by evidence. Nobody had accused Anna of infidelity in her marriage. The interrogation smacked heavily of the arbitrary. The *Malleus Maleficarum* provided him a wide net to cast. He blindly threw it out, and to him, everything caught in it was a fish. With enough accusations, each member of the court would have his sensibilities offended by one of them and turn against Anna. That was Dernbach's plan — to taint them all against her in whichever way worked.

Anna tried to answer his last question, cracking with her hoarse voice, "Miray did have a claim on me, but not as you think. I have never known a *woman* as lustful as your book describes."

Dernbach rallied on, hurling more passages from his favorite book, "A greater number of witches is found in the fragile feminine sex than among men."

Albrecht, who had been seated silently in the gallery, stood and walked forward. Dernbach held his hand out, denying him another step. The prosecutor was overruled. One from the panel of clerics asked from behind the bench, "Father Albrecht, do you have something to add?"

Albrecht answered, "Not a statement to add, but a question to ask the Prince-Abbot."

The same judge gestured toward Dernbach and Albrecht asked, "Why do you speak singularly of women? Surely carnal lust grips both sexes equally."

Dernbach was prepared for the question, and with a demonstrative tone of self-congratulations, he answered, "These are not *my* words. The *Malleus Maleficarum* states that a greater number of witches is found in the fragile feminine sex than among men."

Albrecht turned to the bench and commented, "I do not understand why we are discussing Anna Koob's bed. If any sin has occurred there, surely it is between her, her husband, and God, and not a matter of discussion here. Is she being tried for witchcraft or adultery?"

Well-rehearsed and well-armed, Dernbach flared back, flipping the pages in his hand, "The *Malleus Maleficarum* states that demons practice the most revolting sexual acts, not for the sake of pleasure but in order to taint the soul and body of those under or on whom they lie."

Albrecht spoke over the final words, interrupting rather indignantly, "Shouldn't we ask ourselves if the Malleus Maleficarum is to be obeyed unquestioningly? I have read it, and it seems to me, first and foremost, a book of excuses for the hatred of women, by those already inclined to do so."

Dernbach could not sit back and allow the reputation of the Malleus Maleficarum to be soiled in that room. It was all he had left. He responded threateningly, quoting the book in its own defense, "Be careful Father Albrecht, careful of what you accept, and careful of what you deny. This book also tells us that belief that there are such beings as witches is so essential a part of the Catholic Faith that obstinacy to maintain the opposite opinion manifestly savors of heresy."

The threat wore no veil. Albrecht softened his tone but continued, "I am not saying there are no such things as witches. I only question the use of the Malleus Maleficarum as your only source for identifying them. The book is so sweeping in its scope as to require close scrutiny."

Dernbach strode an awkwardly quick circle in front of the bench, holding the book above his head, as he declared, "The Malleus Maleficarum is the foremost resource on the topic of witches."

"Yes. It is," Albrecht yielded, "But it is not Scripture. We may benefit from it only when we acknowledge its fallibility. Yet, you seem to be following it like it is the Word of God. I believe we should rely also on other standards, on secular standards of justice."

"You and your Jesuits are too much in the secular world, Father Albrecht, too much in your books. This is an ecclesiastical court, not a secular one."

Albrecht recognized the futility of pursuing the same line. He backed down, fearing that aggravating Dernbach while he had such command of the room would do no service to Anna.

He felt that the wind was beginning to blow in the wrong direction, so he moved to stifle Dernbach's momentum, "We have set an abundant table of food for thought. We should slow down, give ourselves time to consume and digest it before making another statement on the matter. Let us pause these proceedings until we have calmly considered all that has been said."

A few of the judges nodded in agreement, until stilled by Dernbach's waving hand as he spoke, "Those are wise words... being used for deceptive means. There will be no pause in these proceedings."

It was clear to Albrecht that Dernbach wanted Anna in the flames as soon as possible. This was no trial, no search for truth and justice. It was beginning to feel like a required formality, and Albrecht grew increasingly desperate to find some way out for his innocent friend while tending to his own safety.

Dernbach felt momentum swing in his favor. He was not going to let a moment of pause inhibit it. All arguments and evidence that remotely resembled a legal proceeding had failed abominably. What he presented from this point had to come from the pulpit. He drew a loud inhale, which turned all heads in his direction, and he conjured his most pontificating voice and posture.

He took all authority from the bench when he threw his arms widely to his sides and preached from Scripture, "Truth shall spring from the earth and justice shall look down from heaven!"

One lone judge at the far end of the bench took exception and spoke up, but only loudly enough for Dernbach to hear, rendering the Biblical response impotent, "The Lord himself gives his benefits."

When that whisper went mute, the room belonged comprehensively to Dernbach, and every semblance of judicial procedure evaporated. Nuss watched in admiration as his mentor appeared to double in size and put off his own glow. Every breath in the room seemed to await his permission to release. Albrecht could not understand how the day so suddenly belonged to his opponent. Anna, too, felt the change in the air. It sent a bitter chill to her core. She shivered violently and let out a quiet whimper. Jost felt encased in ice, wanting to stand and shout but finding himself strangely incapable.

With the obedient attention of all, Dernbach walked one slow lap around Anna. When he came around again to face her. He locked his eyes onto her and stared intimidatingly, hoping to frighten her into a slip of the tongue.

He kept that stare at Anna while yelling to the back of the room, "Miray was a witch. Of that, I have no doubt. Everything I have seen and everything I have studied declares it. She came into the Koob household, shared a bed with Anna Koob, soiled this Christian girl and turned her to Satan."

Dernbach paused to read the room. Nobody moved. Nobody protested. They hardly breathed.

He continued, "Anna Koob began mixing potions, just as Miray taught her. She poisoned two children... both of whom died. And when Miray was brought to justice and removed from this Christian community, Anna Koob took her place. She completed her transition from a child of Kleinostheim to a child of Hell. She was found out by her neighbors and she fled the area."

He exhaled fully, drew another deep breath and held it, only to build anticipation for his following quotation from Saint Augustine. He looked to the gallery and said, "Let the restless, the godless, depart and flee from Thee. How have they injured Thee? For whither fled they, when they fled from Thy presence? or where dost not Thou find them?"

He turned sharply to Anna and added, "We know where you fled. You fled to Savoy until driven from that sacred place and those holy people. Then you fled to Italy before being driven back here."

Dernbach stood glaring at Anna. He hoped that he could stare her silent and proclaim her silence to be a confession of truth.

Anna was not captured by the Prince-Abbot's imposing presence, and she answered, "I am Anna, not Miray. I have been altered by my experiences, as I pray we all have. I did not transition into anything. I am still my parent's child, my brothers' sister, my husband's wife, and my son's mother. I have traveled, as I believe, Prince-Abbot, you have."

Dernbach rocked backward onto his heels, folded his arms, and asked, "Are you claiming that in all the time she was with you, Miray did not influence you?"

"I am making no such claim," she replied calmly, in a voice incongruent with her appearance, "I cannot and would never wish to. I honor her contribution to my life. She was distinguished in her goodness. She was righteous, and Saint Gregory wrote, 'Anyone distinguished in life would be enough to fill our need for a beacon light and to show us how we can bring our soul to the sheltered harbor of virtue.' In fact, it is only through my thoughts of her and of her permanent mark on me that I was able to forgive my neighbors for what they did to her, what they took from me. It is her Christ-like example that guides me to calmness and forgiveness, for the damage they did to me that night was severe and has stained my life every day since."

Albrecht knew the quotation Anna recited. He also suspected that Dernbach did not. His eyes went quickly to the prosecutor's when Anna finished speaking. Dernbach's eyes darted side to side as he strained his mind for his next move, his next quotation. Nuss was picking at his nose. The words of Saint Gregory had not seeped into the outermost layers of *his* thoughts. Dernbach was reeling. He turned to Albrecht, hoping to trap them both by cornering him into an answer that would diminish him and Anna simultaneously.

He looked to Albrecht and asked, "She turned away from her own faith to find in that foreign woman a 'harbor of virtue'. Father Albrecht, would you say that she has turned toward God's light or away from it?"

Albrecht *had* an appropriate quotation, and with a grin of accomplishment, he mounted his surprise defense, walking forward from the gallery, and answering, "Saint Gregory also told us... 'Darkness has no substance. It is only the absence of light. Likewise, evil has no substance but is simply the absence of virtue. Light and dark cannot exist in the same place, just as virtue and evil cannot exist in the same place."

He glared at Dernbach like he was a teacher ready to scold a child, with one arm wrapped around himself and the other hand holding his chin. He drifted his eyes upward to the bench and spoke directly to the judges, "Saint Gregory also wrote that the perfection of human nature consists in its growth in goodness, not in the destruction of evil. Does this trial pursue the growth of goodness, or the destruction of an imagined evil?"

He allowed a few seconds for the meaning to sink into the minds of the room, then tied it to the case before them, saying, "Miray seems to have been troubled. But with all prejudice aside, I see no evidence of darkness. When Anna Koob speaks of her, I see love in her eyes and hear it in her voice. I know of no greater *harbor of virtue* than love."

The judges behind the bench all nodded subconsciously, clearly moved by Anna's words and Albrecht's validation of them. Dernbach's jaw hung open. The cornerstone of his case was cracked down the center and the whole thing seemed ready to fall apart. He took a deep breath and nodded his head like the judges, hoping to appear reasonable in their eyes, to lend a rational credibility to his accusations, and make the proceedings smell less of hysteria. Rather than following his instinct to lash out against Albrecht, he thanked the scholar for his quotation, and resolved to dismiss Albrecht that evening and be rid of him for the rest of the trial.

Dernbach thought it best to leave the subject of Miray behind them. Albrecht's words closed that avenue of aspersion. Nuss, an infinitely dimmer man, was not ready to let it go. Suddenly animating from boredom, he stomped forward and rallied the subject just as Dernbach was laying it to rest.

Nuss spoke snidely, "Your Turkish mentor was a traveler, dealing in spices. Is that correct?"

"Yes," Anna answered.

"She traveled the coast of the sea?"

"From what I understand, yes."

"And when she died, you traveled just as she did?"

"I traveled. I traveled with my family, in our own way, doing very different things with very different people than the stories Miray told me."

"You just decided to travel? A girl from Kleinostheim, who had never left her home village, suddenly decided to travel? Miray died and you assumed her wicked life right where she left it!"

Anna stiffened her back and spoke with commanding dignity, "I was no *girl*. I was a woman, a wife, and a mother. We took over my father's business, which required us to travel. We established connections in Savoy and Italy and we remained there to foster them. We spent those years like book merchants, not like dealers of exotic spices. So the answer is no. I did not assume anything that resembled her life. I pursued my own life."

Dernbach stepped to Nuss and gripped his shoulder. He squeezed tightly and pulled him backward. Nuss had improvised, and that was not in line with the calculating style of Dernbach. Anna handled him with ease and composure, leaning the court even more heavily in her favor. Dernbach growled his displeasure into Nuss' ear. Nuss withered backward and took a seat.

Dernbach was ready to retreat to his office when a courier came into the room with a package for him from the archbishop. The room sat in silence and watched Dernbach as he opened and read the papers within. A wide smile came across his face. He lowered the letter, looked at Anna, and shook his head at her with a fiendish grin.

Dernbach held a paper over his head and marched it in a grand circle around Anna, while announcing, "Archbishop Elector of Mainz, Johann Adam von Bicken has discovered evidence in this case, and he has presented it to me."

After completing the circle, he walked to face Anna directly. He signaled to Nuss, directing him to come forward with a piece of blank paper and a pen. Nuss scrambled obediently and handed it to Dernbach.

Dernbach held the paper he had paraded around, so that the writing faced Anna. He thrusted it to her face and declared, "You wrote this Devilish heresy."

He handed the blank paper and pen to Anna and directed her to write her full name. Anna took the paper and immediately handed it back.

"You will have no need to compare my writing to what is on that paper," she spoke plainly, "I recognize the writing and it is mine."

Dernbach's eyes widened as he asked, "Do you admit it, that you authored this paper?"

"I do, and I did," she answered without hesitation.

Anna recognized it with the very first line. It was one of the papers she wrote in Trieste. Jost had sold it to God-knows-whom, and somehow it made its way to the Archbishop of Mainz, along with the name of the woman who penned it. Jost's fears of many years past revived with a vengeance.

Dernbach turned to the judges and handed the paper to them. They glanced at it but did not read it. They waited for Dernbach to present its relevance.

"You will all see," Dernbach rallied on, "how the witch plants the Devil's seeds for him. She chastises the Church and condemns the holy men who run it."

Rather than reviewing the paper before them, the judges looked to Anna to speak in defense of her writing, and she answered, "You seem to have mistaken that paper for some other. In it, I write nothing of the holy men of the Church, nor do I denounce the Church's ways. I simply challenge Christian women to speak with their own voices and contribute to the Church as much as their fathers and husbands."

Anna knew that the pious judges before her were members of a staunchly patriarchal church and society, and would not be welcoming of such sentiments. She turned her defense of the paper to a tender matter of faith that was sure to strike the judges' hearts.

"We have every reason to believe," Anna continued, "that the Holy Mother of Christ, the Blessed Mary, had a strong maternal influence on her home. If she did not, if she was quiet and obedient, and remained in the shadows, why would we honor her as we do? In that paper, I challenge the women of Christendom to follow the example of Mary, step out of the shadows, and bring their maternal influence to the Church in a way that honors Mary's example."

Well, that had done it. By invoking the example of Mary, Anna galvanized herself and her paper against Dernbach's line of attack.

"Please," Anna pressed the judges, "read the paper and you will see for yourselves."

The judges each took their turn with the paper. The truth is, it was exactly as Anna described it. The paper contained no scathing rebuke of Church practices. It challenged Christian women to find their voices and make those voices heard within their homes, their communities, and within the Church, for the benefit of all. Only the most unmitigated sexists could view it as Dernbach did. Dernbach folded his arms in satisfaction as the judges perused the paper, believing them all to feel as he did. When they had all taken their turns and declared that there was nothing heretical or in any way sinister within the writing on the paper, Dernbach's brain scrambled for some other angle, some other way the paper could be used against Anna. He had banked so heavily on its effectiveness that its sudden loss gave him a sensation of falling.

He stuttered a few times before asking Anna timidly, "Have you penned other papers?"

"Yes I have," was her simple answer.

"And did you sew discord against the Catholic Church in those papers?"

"I did not and I never would. I shared my papers with many holy men of the Church, and discussed them openly."

"If you are so open with your opinions, why is your name not on your paper?"

"I did not sign my name upon any of my writings."

Dernbach looked over Anna's head to the gallery of attendees and announced, "Because you were afraid that your heresy would be tied back to you, and you would be held accountable for it!"

"No sir," Anna answered as if speaking to a child, "I did not attach my name to them because I am not a vain woman."

Chuckles came clearly from the gallery and the bench, and turned Dernbach's face crimson.

He leaned in toward Anna and warned her, "There is a search for your other papers. They will be found."

Anna responded, "If you find them, please bring them to me. I would like very much to see them again, and if you like, I will sign them in front of you."

Dernbach growled at her, then paced silently in front of the bench, trying to decide from which angle to attack

Anna next. He could think of nothing. The day was lost for the prosecution of Anna Koob, and the prosecutor did not know how to proceed. He recommended to the court that they dismiss for the day so he and Nuss could plan their strategy moving forward. The judges agreed and Anna was escorted back to her cell.

When she stood from her chair, Anna turned to look at Jost and Christoph. They smiled confidently at her, not the forced smiles of people trying to make her feel better, rather the beaming, uncontrollable smiles of a husband and son who could almost feel Anna in their arms again. The day had gone their way. Albrecht, Jost, and Christoph walked out of the palace together. Their conversation was as light as their hearts. They believed that Anna was a few formalities away from returning to her home.

Chapter Thirty:
One Cell Over

WHEN ANNA WAS LOCKED INTO HER CELL, she had no reason to expect a horrific night. Her prudent mind still whispered wise caution to her heart, to a heart that was lighter and more hopeful than it had been. She even began envisioning Christoph's wedding and Anna Marie glowing in her dress. Her imagination was brought back to the moment. The echo of the slamming door and the footsteps of the retreating guard preceded a silence that made Anna's breaths seem to her like the only sounds on Earth. She took notice of them and she treasured them. She thanked God for them.

Just one floor above her, Dernbach called Nuss to his office. The Prince-Abbot did not sit behind his stately desk and glare downward to Nuss. They stood side by side, and Dernbach put a hand on Nuss' waist.

"We have no case, my friend," Dernbach said while looking downward to their nearly touching feet. In the following pause, he pulled his eyes slowly to meet Nuss' and continued, "...not without a confession."

"Then we must get a confession," Nuss answered readily and undaunted.

283

"She is a pretty, local woman with a son and a prominent husband. She is popular among her neighbors."

"I see what you are saying," said Nuss, "but it is not as dangerous as you think."

Dernbach pulled his hand away and turned to face the wall. He grunted in uncertainty.

"This is *my* area of expertise," Nuss pushed on, "I will see to this and all risk will be mine."

"Like Hell it will! It is my name that will be spoken, my face that will be envisioned when they see what was done to her."

"Then it is your name they will praise when you rid their village of evil."

Dernbach grunted again and Nuss added with a cautious step forward and a deeply subordinate tone, "This is happening all over Europe. Witches are discovered. Witches are tortured. Witches confess. Witches are burned. And when they confess, nobody cares how the confessions are obtained."

Dernbach turned from the wall to face Nuss, and he said with uncharacteristic, fragile uncertainty in his voice, "If we present to the court and the gallery a woman broken by our hands, with only our word of her confession, the price we pay might be heavy."

Dernbach had a moment of rare introspection. He considered much in a few seconds of pause. He considered the women of Fulda, their fear, their pain, their families, and the possibility of their innocence. His thoughts must have painted themselves clearly on his face.

Nuss read them accurately and eased him, saying, "Then we will not present a broken woman to the court. I have done this before. Let us start slowly and see how it goes. She will not only confess to us. She will confess to us and she will confess to the court. Once that happens, and they all hear it from her own lips, she will not be broken enough for them. They will demand the flames and they will thank you for delivering her."

Dernbach was allowing himself to slowly be convinced. He rubbed his chin, scratched his head, and asked, "How can you be sure that she will confess before the court?"

Nuss folded his arm and answered smugly, "She is a woman. The same natural weakness that made Anna Koob susceptible to the Devil and the Devil's servants will make her equally susceptible to God, and to the servants of God."

Nuss brilliantly played to a prejudice that did not hide itself well behind Dernbach's mannerisms. Dernbach was nobler than Nuss. His life was elevated above his comrade's in every way but one. Nuss was superior in treachery, and it was Nuss' superiority that was needed in the demise of Anna Koob. He could not have told his boss how he would get Anna to the flames. He had not planned so far. He trusted in his talent, his ruthless talent, and his gifts in that area were abundant.

Anna was a full three hours alone in her cell, and she expected to remain so until the sun rose. She was startled to hear someone enter the dungeon. It was dark and the single candle held by the man revealed few features. He went into the cell next to Anna's. Anna had given no thought to that cell all night, no thought to the chair with the binding straps. It had nothing to do with her. This dark stranger entered the torture cell and lit several candles mounted on brass sconces. The swelling light revealed a simple man with coarse, ungraceful movements. He was middle-aged, plainly dressed, with a rustic simplicity about him. But he was clean shaven and steady about his business.

He was obviously preparing the chamber for its designed purpose. He checked the condition of the buckles of the straps, tending to the wrist and ankle straps of the chair and not at all to the straps of the table next to it. Anna felt compassion for the poor soul whose limbs would be bound to the chair. She stood and watched the man with morbid curiosity. She prayed she would not still be in her cell to witness it. It did not occur to her at first that the room was being prepared for her. When the notion fell upon her, it did so with force, instantly draining her of her energy and sending her to the floor shaking.

The man paid no mind to Anna. He continued about his duties. Once everything appeared satisfactory to him, he left the dungeon and returned a few minutes later with a metal contraption and some rope. Such a frenzied volley of thoughts and emotions bounced from the opposite walls of Anna's head. She assured herself that the preparations had nothing to do with her, only to picture herself strapped to the chair seconds later.

The man set the rope beside the contraption and stepped out of the torture cell. He leaned against the wall and waited as still and as silent as the items he prepared. He did not wait long. Nuss and Dernbach entered the dungeon and dispelled all doubt. Those men were only in Aschaffenburg for one reason, to prosecute Anna. Nuss unlocked Anna's cell and gestured toward the other cell. A deep, seizing ache took her by the chest, and what little strength remained left her, but she would not be dragged. She was an innocent woman, and she would always appear as such. She gathered herself and obeyed. She walked from her cell with graceful steps and head held high.

It would be untrue to say that her heart did not pound against her ribs as if trying to escape her heaving chest. She was terrified. She did not know what the metal contraption was. She had no idea why a rope was needed. But she was certain that horrors awaited her. Nevertheless, she entered the torture cell with the splendid heroism of a woman fully certain of who she was and what she believed. She maintained faith in her acquittal and release, and she prayed, not for an escape from the coming pain, only for the strength to endure it without confessing a falsehood.

Dernbach kept a distance from the cells, trying to shrink into the shadows near the entrance to the dungeon. It was only the abundance of his unmistakable figure that identified him to Anna. Nuss, on the other hand, was brimming with eager determination. His gestures were sharp and he bounced on the fronts of his feet. A snide smirk snuck its way from the depths of his dark heart and took a place of prominence on his face. Still, there was something eerily gentle, an unsettling calmness in the way he directed her to the chair.

Anna sat and Nuss took a step away from her. The man who prepared the room leaned forward away from the wall, entered the cell, and bound Anna's wrists and ankles with the straps. It is unlikely this man, this torturer, knew much of the world around him, but he knew his job. The straps were implacably but not uncomfortably tight. Anna made no attempt to pull against them. She knew the futility of any such effort and did not want to appear wild. She closed her eyes and slowed her breath, thinking of any and all pleasures that awaited her after her release.

Nuss called the torturer "Bubi", some crude and probably demeaning mutilation of his given name. He ordered Bubi aside and walked as close to Anna as possible, nearly touching his knees to hers. He leaned forward to look almost directly downward to her. Anna felt his presence. She heard his breathing. She raised her head and opened her eyes to look at his.

Nuss spoke calmly, "Surely you must know that you will suffer great pain tonight. It does not have to be. You can sleep tonight without pain and appear before the court tomorrow healthy and rested. This man will not touch you if you tell me now all that I need to know."

A thousand witty answers took their turns tickling her tongue. She dared not speak them. Insulting Nuss would only raise his ire and her pain in equal proportion. There was nothing she could utter that would not make her look more like a witch in his eyes.

She only responded quietly, "If you have questions for me, ask them."

Nuss smiled triumphantly, believing he had already frightened her into any confession he wished to plant in her mouth. He demanded in a raised voice, "Tell me how Miray seduced you!"

Anna answered, "She did not."

Nuss huffed in frustration, folded his arms and asked, "Did she leave a mark on you when you shared a bed? Did she bite you or make you bleed?"

Anna only shook her head. Her lips began to part as she considered describing the only moments Miray sat on Anna's bed, when Anna held her and comforted her. She sealed her lips quickly, unable to place the words in a way that could not be twisted and manipulated.

Nuss thundered on, "Tell me about your witch's potions. Where did you learn them? What was in them? How did you enchant them?... Who did you use them on?"

Anna tilted her head to one side and shook it slowly as she answered, "My kitchen had the same sort of remedies found in many households. I picked up my recipes here and there and I mixed them with love."

"With love of Miray? With love of the Devil?"

She drew a deep breath and let it out with a sighing, "No."

Nuss took one step backward, shook his head, scoffed, and spoke in a taunting tone, "You remember, Anna Koob, that I gave you the chance. When you are suffering tonight, you remember that. All I asked for is the truth."

Anna answered in a higher, louder voice, forced out of its nature by her rising fear, "Truth is all I have given to you."

With no Father Albrecht in the room and no gallery full of affectionate neighbors, with only Nuss and a torturer in the cell and Dernbach still hiding in the shadows, it was not a place to engage in debate. In Anna's mind, she had one choice. She had to survive the coming torture without saying a word, without giving Nuss anything he could twist into a confession. The trial had gone Anna's way and she was one long, painful, but silent night away from her freedom and her family.

Nuss gestured to the metal contraption and Bubi stepped toward it. Anna closed her eyes, not knowing what it was or what it would do to her. She repeated prayers in her head until she heard Dernbach from his distance, "Search her. Search her for the marks."

"You are right, Prince-Abbot. We might need nothing but that," Nuss said in a softened and subordinate voice.

Bubi unbuckled Anna's wrists and lifted her to her feet by her upper arms. There was no anger in his touch, no ambition, no agenda, nothing. He felt like a fleshy tool in Nuss' hand. Nuss waved his hand around, gesturing to Anna's dress. He flicked his wrist and indicated his directive. Bubi untied Anna's dress and pulled it from her in an instant. He stripped her completely, tearing from her what could not be pulled over her head. She stood naked with her ankles still strapped beneath her.

Nuss stepped aside and revealed Dernbach walking slowly into the cell. He examined her closely, instructing her very coldly and methodically what to raise and what to turn until he had seen every inch of her body. When he was done, he rubbed his eyes and let out a frustrated exhale. He opened his eyes and looked at her as he had never looked at her before. He bore an expression of doubt with a few distinct elements of concern.

Anna read him well. The room was cold, and Anna shivered in her nakedness. She folded her arms in front of her and begged, "Please. I am innocent. I have harmed nobody."

Nuss was very excited by the scene. He was not aroused sexually. His debauchery was of a different nature. This proud woman, who had thrown elegant quotations with pride, was standing exposed with bound ankles. She shivered. It was in diminishing her to that state that he found his excitement. It was his absolute dominance over her.

Nuss saw that the pathetic image of this shivering, naked, frightened woman was affecting Dernbach, and he could not afford to lose his mentor to compassion and doubt. He threw Anna's dress over her. Anna struggled to get her arms in correctly, she finally succeeded and she thanked Nuss for clothing her.

Anna looked at Dernbach and mouthed, "Thank you."

Dernbach turned his dewing eyes to Nuss and said, "She has no marks."

"That means nothing," Nuss yelled in response, "You know that. Look. Look how she is manipulating you. Could a normal woman, a righteous woman, turn you so quickly in her favor? Of course not. She is a witch, and we are in great peril if we do not succeed."

The thought snapped Dernbach quickly from his doubt and his compassion. He shook his head as if trying to wake himself fully from a half-dream.

"Thank God," he said quietly as he felt himself narrowly escaping some perceived evil, "Please, my friend, proceed."

Nuss pushed on Anna's shoulders and forced her back to the chair. Anna slowly and reluctantly placed her arms on the rests and allowed Bubi to buckle the straps. Nuss gestured again to the metal contraption and Anna again closed her eyes in prayer. It was not the voice of Dernbach that opened her eyes again, but the unstrapping of her left ankle. She looked down to see Bubi push her left foot into this thing he had brought into the room.

Anna's bare foot slid between two metal plates with a crank, one plate under her foot and the other on top. Its mechanics were simple to figure out. When the crank is turned, the plates close together and crush the foot. Anna whimpered uncontrollably until she rolled her lips into her mouth and bit down on them.

Bubi remained kneeling at Anna's feet with his hand on the crank. He looked up at Nuss and awaited his orders.

Nuss gave Anna one more reminder, "I gave you a chance to speak without suffering. Now pain will open your heart and we will see the truth laid bare before us."

He broke eye contact with Anna only long enough to nod to Bubi and return his hungry eyes to Anna. The crank was turned once. Anna felt immediate pressure, but it was not painful. It felt rather good, and she closed her eyes and braced for worse. She heard the squeak of the crank again. This time it pushed uncomfortably on the top of her foot. She felt hard pressure on a single bone. She thought that it could be relieved if she could only twist slightly within the device. She twitched at the ankle just as the crank turned again, and immediately again.

The device broke the bones in her foot, and she screamed one long, loud, shrill, cry and stopped, holding her breath and clenching every muscle in her body. She let her breath out in the form of a high-pitched hum. It was quiet enough for her to hear the creak of another crank and the crack of her crushed bones. She let out another scream, but this one rolled gradually into a steady whimper. She felt the pain shoot through her knee. She looked down to her lap and saw blood dripping onto her from her mouth. She had bit the inside of her cheek and drawn a steady flow of blood. She felt no pain in her mouth. Her left foot had every bit of her attention.

Bubi gave the crank one more turn. The crack of her broken bones was clear, as if dried twigs were being snapped right in front of her face. This last crushing crank sent pain from her foot to her throat. The metal plates of the device pushed deeply into Anna's foot and broke the skin. She shook violently from the pain, tearing it more severely. Blood poured from her foot, over the top of the metal plate and pooled under the chair. Anna did not know her foot was bleeding. She had no sensitivity to such a subtle sensation. She continued to shake while grunting a vocalized and rhythmic hyperventilation.

"Take it off," Nuss instructed.

The first crank of release seemed to add pressure. The broken bones of Anna's foot shifted and grinded against each other. But each releasing crank after relieved her of pain. When the device was loosened enough to remove entirely, Bubi pulled it from her, wiggling it free and tearing more skin. Once it was off, the foot throbbed. It was a very different kind of pain than the tightening of the plates, but one equally and uniquely miserable.

Anna's attention was so comprehensively on her pain that she did not notice that the strap around her other foot was being removed. She felt the strap being reapplied to her left ankle but could not spare it a thought. She ground her teeth together and released a slow, wheezing, whining exhale. The wretched sound was stopped short when Bubi forced Anna's other foot into the bloody device.

Anna turned her head sharply to Bubi and begged with the little breath left in her, "No, no, no, no, wait."

Nuss turned behind him and grinned at Dernbach, turned back to Anna and asked, "Do you have something to tell me?"

Anna looked him squarely in the eyes, inhaled, held it, exhaled, and answered with a level of strength and determination that disconcerted him, "I am ready now. Proceed."

Nuss stood in shock for a moment. For the first time, he was afraid of Anna. He truly believed her to be wickedly powerful. How else could she take such torture and order him so serenely to give her more? It took almost a minute for his chills to fully run across his skin. Once it did, and he regained himself, he ordered the torturer with ravenous bloodlust, "Do it. Turn it. Turn it. Crush her foot."

Six quick turns of the crank came without a pause between them. Anna's right foot buckled as violently as her left. The bones broke and folded in on themselves. The skin tore, and the pool of blood beneath the chair doubled. Anna screamed again, but less shrilly than before. In the doubling of her pain, it was somehow muted. It was less shocking. It hurt. But she found the ability to turn inward as her right foot was being crushed. Her cry echoed in *that* room, but her imagination was in a different room, in her apartment in Nice. Her scream was hollow. It was a physical reaction only. Her spirit did not contribute. It did not hear the turn of the crank or the crack of her bones. It smelled the coastal breeze and felt the moist Mediterranean air on the skin.

Nuss had presided over many more than one man's share of tortures. He recognized what he witnessed. He knew that while he mutilated Anna's body, he had lost his grip on her spirit. The screaming voice in front of him was not going to confess under the crushing pressure of the device. The longer it pressed on, the farther Anna's spirit was from the pain. He ordered Bubi to remove the metal boot.

With the removal of the device, Anna's mind returned to her physical surroundings. The pain, brutal as it was, was something she knew she could withstand. Nuss had administered his torture and Anna confessed to nothing. Her senses perceived two things upon opening her eyes. She could clearly see that Nuss was frustrated. He paced three or four steps, turned on his heel, and paced the same steps in return. She also saw Dernbach. His hands were on his chin and his elbows pulled in tightly against him. His was a look less of frustration and more of concern, perhaps even guilt and mortification.

Dernbach expected his captured "witch" to confess with the first broken foot bone. He believed that women were weak, weak to the temptations of the flesh and weak to the torture of the flesh. Anna's silence under torture gave him piercing doubt, something he was unaccustomed to feeling. Nuss' concerns had less to do with Anna than with Dernbach. He was afraid that if the torture dragged on without a confession, the abbot's compassion and doubt would be pushed to their limits and the whole effort would be brought to a halt. He had no patience and turned directly to the next phase of torture.

Chapter Thirty-One:
The Devilish Incantation

JOST AND CHRISTOPH SPENT A NIGHT FULL OF HOPE, as Anna was being tortured beneath the palace. Christoph took the trip back to Kleinostheim so he could see Anna Marie in the morning and share with her the news of the encouraging events of the previous day and prepare his mother's household for her return. Father Albrecht prepared a few statements, just some lines of Scripture to put the final nails in Dernbach's case against Anna. He did not stay up late, and he rested with gratitude and satisfaction for the part he had played so far.

Anna did not rest, nor did Dernbach, Nuss, and Bubi. Nuss allowed no time between the removal of the metal boot and the next phase of torture. While Anna remained strapped to the chair, she heard the action behind her. Bubi ran a rope through a pulley on the ceiling. Anna was torn between morbid, fretful curiosity in the commotion behind her and spiritual preparations to withstand what was sure to be worse than what had been done to her so far.

When the rope was ready, Anna was unstrapped. She could not stand on her broken feet. Nuss assisted Bubi in sliding the chair backward so it sat directly under the pulley. With the cold hands of business, Bubi pushed Anna forward by the back of her neck so that she buckled over her lap. She remained in that position when he let go of her. He took her by both elbows and pulled her hands behind her back. He bound her wrists together with metal shackles and tied the rope to them.

Anna heard the squeak of the pulley before feeling herself being pulled upward by her bound wrists behind her back. She was lifted off of the chair, forcing her weight onto her broken feet. Nuss kicked the chair away and Anna stood hunched over. Her arms were being lifted behind her, putting tremendous pressure on her shoulders. Every bit of pain from the boot returned to her in force as she tried to relieve the pressure on her shoulders by pushing against her broken feet. Her legs reacted instinctively and recoiled, trying to drop her to her knees. But her knees did not touch the floor. Bubi pulled the rope again, lifting Anna's hands closer to the ceiling. She dangled in excruciating contortion as her shoulders tore and snapped.

The pain was worse than everything she endured in the chair. Her shoulders felt on fire and the pain stabbed through her rib cage and around her neck. Her scream resembled nothing that had ever come from her mouth. It was shrill and piercing, but lined with a deep, hollow, and soulful cry that spoke of much more than the pain in her shoulders. Anna was broken. She could not stand. The pain in her feet was simply physical pain. As her shoulders snapped farther and farther out of their natural position, Anna's agony bore with it the understanding that her contorted arms would never again be capable of holding her husband as they had before, never again able to wrap and squeeze her son.

She was suffering acute and comprehensive torment to a degree she could not have imagined before that night. Her mind leaped at an escape. It flew again to the south, to the Mediterranean. She saw the face of her neighbor in Nice, the friendly old Cadieux. She saw him clearly, vividly, as if his smile were only inches from her eyes. She heard his voice translating the African manuscript.

Anna's cry stopped abruptly, which startled Bubi and forced an unintentional tug on the rope. Anna did not respond. She breathlessly mouthed those parts of the manuscript she had set to memory. Nuss thought he was finally getting the confession he prayed for. No confession came from Anna's lips. What came shocked the room. Anna's next exhale carried off her tongue beautiful, deep sentiments of Maravian philosophy, in its native language. Anna's voice, Anna's *true* voice haunted the walls around her. She sounded peaceful. She sounded calm, unlike anything they had heard from her in the cell or the courtroom.

The lovely sound of the Maravian language was foreign and peculiar to the men in the room. Its delivery to their ears through Anna's pure, low, calm voice disturbed them all deeply. Dernbach leaned toward the torture room but did not step. Nuss took a strong stride backward and his eyes widened. Bubi was affected most severely. He shook and dropped the rope, plummeting Anna onto her broken feet. Her legs did not take her weight. She fell to her side and smashed her ripped shoulder against the floor. She did not notice, but continued to recite the manuscript with Cadieux's friendly face in her eyes and his voice in her ears.

Bubi mumbled his prayers and only paused them to apologize to Nuss for dropping Anna to the floor. He reached for the end of the rope.

"No!" Nuss ordered with a quick raise of his hand, "There is no reason to put you at further risk."

Bubi's reaction to Anna's recitation set Nuss' thought in motion. The simple-minded torturer was still deeply disturbed. With every glance at Anna, who was still lying on the floor speaking in an exotic language, Bubi's skin crawled furiously. Bubi was scared. At Nuss' command, he backed away from the rope and away from Anna, whose dulcet voice continued to flow from her in a tone entirely incongruent with the broken body that pushed it forward.

"Go," Nuss commanded Bubi, "Go to the main chamber and wait for me there. We will deal with the witch."

Bubi scurried out of the dungeon with a fleetness of foot not seen in him for decades.

Nuss signaled to Dernbach, asking for help moving Anna. With a puzzled look on his face, Dernbach complied. They moved Anna to the chair. She descended from her foreign fantasy and looked around her. It took her a moment to remember where she was and what she was suffering. They unshackled her wrists and moved her arms from her back, setting her hands on her lap. The recollection of her reality and the pain of her shattered body all surged onto her at once. She moaned a dry, cracking, rusty cry that contrasted severely with her dulcet recitation of African philosophy, as if she transformed from an entirely different creature, back to the woman they had broken.

Nuss bound Anna's bloody, broken feet with strips of fabric. He bound them tightly, pushing the sharp ends of the bones stabbing into the surrounding tissue. Once tightly bound, her feet throbbed and begged for breath. They did not speak as loudly as her shoulders. The weight of her arms was all it took to wrench her mangled shoulders miserably. The pain spread to her back and down to her hips.

In a turn of authority, Nuss ordered Dernbach, "Help me move her to the other cell."

"Now?" Dernbach asked, "Do you mean to end the torture? She was just beginning to make our case."

"We have all that we need. I assure you of that," Nuss replied with confidence.

Dernbach began to speak, but Nuss lifted a hand at him, shushed him like a dog, and added, "I know my job well. You should trust me on this. We have all that we need. Now hurry. Let us move her. I have work to do."

The short trip out of one cell and into the other felt longer to Anna than her trek across the Alps. Nuss and Dernbach lifted her by her mutilated shoulders and dragged her over her broken feet. Once in the other cell, they set her with peculiar care onto her back and locked the cell door behind them as they walked away together. Nuss suggested to Dernbach that he return to his quarters and get some sleep. Dernbach, showing a degree of fragile deference uncommon in him, obeyed without protest.

Nuss joined Bubi in the main chamber of the palace. Bubi still showed signs of distress. That smooth, calm voice of Anna terrified him more than any beast in any tale he was ever told as a child.

"Come, my friend," Nuss ordered with a calm voice and a hand on Bubi's shoulder, "Come to my room and we will drink and calm ourselves."

They went together and Nuss poured wine for them both. He mixed a mild poison into Bubi's wine, not enough to kill the man, but enough to sicken him.

"Let us pray together," he suggested after they both sipped from their wine, "that God will protect us from the effects of the witch's incantations."

Bubi shook. He was not sure what he had heard from Anna's lips as he hoisted her with the rope. His worst fear was confirmed by Nuss — that the calm voice of Anna during such intense torture could only be an appeal to the Devil, an incantation, a curse, some malignant rite aimed at the torturer. Bubi began to cry.

"Fear not, my brother," Nuss assured him, "God is with us."

They sat together in prayer and thought. Their prayers were identical, but their thoughts were very different. Nuss

299

watched Bubi for signs of the poison. It began with beads of sweat on the brow, followed by chills and nausea. It all came upon him in rapid succession. Bubi looked at Nuss with the eyes of a terrified child. Nuss led him to his own bed and told him to wait there and pray.

Nuss went quickly and directly to Dernbach's room and begged the abbot to come quickly to the aid of a Christian in need. Dernbach dressed quickly and followed Nuss back to Bubi. When they arrived, the torturer had worsened. He had gone much paler with a hint of jaundice.

"Prince-Abbot, please," Bubi begged in a weak but desperate voice.

Dernbach knelt beside the bed and Nuss followed in kind. The abbot led a prayer against evil, a prayer extracted directly from one of his many texts on witchcraft. Nuss and Bubi recited their responses on cue. Dernbach gave his blessing and returned to his room. Nuss dozed briefly on a chair beside the bed.

In the morning, Bubi was improved. He still showed signs of having been very ill. He had vomited in the night and Nuss dutifully changed the bedding and wiped Bubi clean.

"God has responded to our prayers, my faithful friend," Nuss told him, "You are much improved. The witch's evil is being pushed from you by the Angels."

After allowing Bubi a pause for reflection, he added, "Now you must serve Christ as he has served you. You must come with me today to testify against the witch who cursed you."

Bubi began to shake, but Nuss assured him, "She cannot hurt you. God has already won that battle. God has done what only God can do. Now we must do what only we can do. We must cleanse this community of the witch who tried to deliver you to her master."

Bubi shakily sat up. A look of determined commitment overtook the terror on his face. He promised that he would do what must be done, with faith and without fear.

The gallery and the bench filled. There was an exuberance about the room. Family, friends, neighbors, even the judges believed that the trial would end early that morning and Anna Koob would return to her husband and son. Many times over the preceding decades Jost waited excitedly to lay his eyes on Anna, never so much as that morning. He could almost feel her hand in his. But the chair in front of the bench sat conspicuously empty.

Anna slept through a series of wild dreams, some exciting and some horrid. She slept with a strong sense of accomplishment. She survived the torture and confessed nothing that Nuss or Dernbach could use against her. She did not awaken to Nuss or Dernbach, not to Bubi or the jailor she had seen before. She awoke to two strangers entering her cell carrying two long poles. The poles were connected in the center by a small platform. Anna could not walk, and Nuss wanted to hide the signs of torture as much as possible from the court and gallery. The men set the poles down beside Anna. They sat her up and dragged her onto the platform. They lifted the poles by the ends and raised Anna off of the floor.

It was a jostling struggle to maneuver the poles up the stairs and carry Anna into the courtroom. She had slept little more than an hour that night and every twitch of her body enlivened the brutal pain in her feet and shoulders. She could not lift her arms, but to keep from tumbling off of the little platform, she gripped the sides of it with her hands. Each tilt, each shake, each jerk of the poles engaged her shoulders. She moaned and squealed with every clumsy step of her chauffeurs.

Anna's anticipated entrance into the room was not what Jost and Christoph expected. Neither of them understood at first why she was being carried on two poles and a small platform. Their minds struggled for an explanation. Albrecht had no such struggle. He knew that she could not walk. Her feet dangled beneath her, still bound by the wrapping. A small circle of blood showed at her left ankle. Other than that tiny piece of evidence, there was no way for the people in the gallery to know that she could not hop from the platform and spring to her place behind the banister rail.

Albrecht sat beside Jost. Jost leaned to him for an explanation of the spectacle before them. Before he could ask, Albrecht told him, "She has been tortured. We will know soon how she did."

Every conversation in the room, every sound, the light from the windows, everything Jost's senses perceived pushed down on him oppressively. He began to hyperventilate. He grabbed Albrecht's hand and squeezed with all of his strength. Albrecht pulled himself free of the grip and rubbed the back of Jost's head with a long-held, "Sssshhhhhh."

"I have great faith in the strength of your wife," he spoke confidently, "Her mind is freer than her body. I do not believe she would have succumbed."

Jost perked suddenly, whispering back, "Yes, she can easily take her mind away."

"We will know very soon," Albrecht concluded as Anna was transferred to the chair.

The men who carried Anna lifted her by the armpits. It felt to her like a line of nails were being hammered into her, shoulder to shoulder, up her neck, and down her back. But she made no sound. She curled her lips into her mouth and bit them as hard as she could without drawing blood. She did not see her husband and son as she was jostled into the room, but she knew they were there. She believed that she would soon be in their care and saw no reason to torture their hearts with an agonizing scream.

Once Anna was finally settled, the court brought the room to order. Dernbach entered in his clerical robes, followed by Nuss and Bubi. Anna was surprised to see her torturer before the court, surprised more to see how drastically altered he appeared. Bubi was pale. His eyes were dark and sunken. He looked like he hadn't slept or eaten in a week. He walked beside Nuss, supported by the arm as he dragged his feet with each step. He was the very portrait of a man in distress, yet there was a determined confidence in his sunken eyes.

Despite all that was done to her the previous night, Anna felt compassion for Bubi. When she saw him walk in front of her, she whispered, "Dear God, what has happened to you?"

Bubi heard her but was terrified of another curse and turned his head hard away from her. Anna said a quick prayer for his recovery. It was interrupted by Nuss addressing the court.

"Witches come at us in various ways," he began, "Satan works his way into our lives. Last night we applied some pain to this woman, to compel her to honesty. She was honest! She revealed her nature at its fullest."

The introduction hooked the attention of every ear. Hardly a breath could be heard. After a dramatic pause to raise anticipation, Nuss continued, "This witch did what witches do. She tried to destroy this good man and deliver him to Satan."

Nuss took a step away from Bubi and gestured to him. Bubi cowered in Nuss' shadow until a member of the court said, "For heaven's sake my son, say what you have to say."

Bubi slowly lifted his chin to the bench and answered the judge directly, as if he and that one judge were the only ones in the room, "Well…, I was… applying pain to this woman."

He stopped there and cringed, waiting for Anna to rise from her chair and strike him down with another curse. His fear was authentic and obvious to all who watched him.

"Go on," Nuss encouraged.

"She was crying…, because…, because it hurt. But then she stopped crying and started talking. It was like she couldn't feel anything anymore."

"What did she say?" the judge asked.

"I don't know. They were strange words."

The judge leaned forward on his elbows and pressed Bubi, "How were they strange? Were they in another language, like French?"

"No sir. They were not French. I know what that sounds like. It was no language men speak. It was Devil talk."

Bubi dared to turn his head toward Anna. When he caught a blur of her image in the very corner of his eye, he snapped in terror back to the judge, again displaying in full earnestness his fear of the woman behind him.

"What makes you say it was Devil talk?" The judge asked.

"Her voice changed. It wasn't her voice anymore. It was lower, almost like a man, and she cursed me."

The gallery saw a mix of reactions. Some gasped. Some shook their heads in disbelief. Albrecht inhaled deeply. His confidence in Anna's strength turned irrelevant. He saw where this was going.

Nuss asked, "What happened to you?"

"After she spoke her strange words in that strange voice, I got sick. I got really sick and was going to die." He pointed to Nuss and Dernbach and added, "But these men saved me."

All of the judges were as intrigued as the one Bubi addressed directly. One of them asked, "How sick were you? How did these men help?"

"I was going to die, but Mister Nuss and the Prince-Abbot kneeled by my bed and they prayed for me. They prayed that God would defeat the witch and return me to my family. I'm better now. I got better."

Bubi gathered the courage to turn and face Anna. He stood facing her for a few seconds, then turned quickly back to the bench, shivered, folded his arms defensively in front of his chest and said, "That witch cursed me. I got real sick. These men prayed for me. And God saved me from the witch."

Bubi began to cry. It could not have been faked. Tears rolled down his cheeks and he sobbed heavily. Nuss walked him from the room. Nobody moved and nobody spoke until Nuss came back into the room alone. He resumed his position between Anna and the bench. He lifted a hand to Dernbach and asked the abbot to tell what he witnessed.

Dernbach was not an evil man. He was a man of faith and truly believed himself to be working for the salvation of God's people. But he had by this point sunken scalp-deep into a mire of fanaticism so that he was blind to all light, to all warmth, and to righteousness, no matter how near to his eyes it might be. His heart was buried so deeply in the task of proving guilt that it was entirely blind to all signs of innocence. Those traits that had kept Anna first in the thoughts of so many, that sprang her name spritely from so many lips as they spoke their daily prayers, were invisible to the abbot's eyes. He had tried witches for many years, at first in search of truth, with some standards to check his zeal. But times had changed, and science grew in weight against him. He slowly turned from any judicial standards to unadulterated fearmongering with the sole purpose of burning women and stoking hysteria.

He took three bold steps toward Anna, truly believing that she had cursed Bubi into sickness, but fearing no evil. The floor was once again his. He seemed to swell to twice his size, and Nuss shrunk back to his subordinate position beneath him.

"It was just as the man said," he addressed the court while looking at Anna, "This woman suddenly stopped the cries of a woman and spoke calmly in a voice that was not her own. She spoke a melodic incantation in a devilish language. It haunted me, I tell you. I have never felt anything like it. The room seemed to get colder. I felt like her words were reaching into my chest. We moved her to her cell and left. Mister Nuss woke me later and told me that our friend, Bubi, was ill. I went to him and saw a man hanging to life by the weakest grip. He was stricken suddenly from health to the edge of death. The man that caused the witch pain was falling into death. I blessed him. We prayed together for his recovery. As you can see, God responded to us and saved that man from the witch's snare."

Heaviness settled over the room. No matter which side they were on, the people in attendance choked on it. It filled their noses and clogged their throats. The lightness that bounced from the walls before Anna was brought in was pulverized beneath it.

Forgetting the extent of her injuries, Anna tried to rise and speak. She leaned forward and put weight on her feet. She let out a short but sharp, wincing cry before falling to the back of the chair. She regathered herself and spoke as plainly as she could. There was distinct fear in her voice that altered the way she sounded as she said, "I spoke no devilish incantations. To take my mind from the mutilation of my body, I recalled a book I once owned."

"What book?!" a judge asked aggressively.

"It was from the Kingdom of Mavari, in Southeastern Africa."

The judges had turned against her. Dernbach's job was finished. The judge continued his job and pressed her with hateful bias, "You recited your curse from this book of African witchcraft?"

Jost could no longer contain himself. He exploded from his seat and ran halfway to Anna. He faced the bench and shouted, "It was no book of witchcraft. I bought it myself. *I* gave it to her. It was a book of philosophy, nothing more sinister than that."

"Did you read it?" one of them asked Jost.

Jost shook his head.

The same judge continued, "Can you recite any part of it now?"

"No," Jost answered honestly.

"My poor man, you too are a victim of this woman. Nobody here blames you for the harm you have caused with your *gift*."

"You do not know what you are saying," Jost shouted insistently, "I know what I bought and I know what I gave my wife!"

Nuss stood and ordered a guard, "Lock this man in a cell until he calms. He has no evidence to share with this court."

The guards took Jost to the dungeon and locked him in the cell where Anna had been kept. His removal from the room devastated Anna. The air around her turned sour and closed in on her. The pain of her cruelly inflicted wounds surged in her brain, and the confidence in her future waned. Her son was in the room. Albrecht was in the room. But it was with Jost that she had survived so much, and only with him that she could survive this. Terror took up every inch of ground that Jost left behind.

Still facing Anna, Dernbach lowered his chin and looked at the floor. He slowly lifted his head and, looking over Anna, addressed the gallery, "We all saw poor Bubi. There was no deception in him. He hardly had the strength to leave this room without assistance. He left shaking in fear of this woman and her unearthly powers. There is no cell that can cage her curses, no dungeon that can bottle her wickedness. She must be removed from your community the way all witches are removed from the righteous. She must be destroyed in flames."

Dernbach walked to the side wall, turned to face the bench, and folded his arms in front of him, as if to tell the judges, "You know what you must do." There was little deliberation. The judges whispered among themselves, with many more nods than shakes of the head. There was fear in their eyes. It was clear, and they avoided looking directly at Anna. These were not men used to fear. They were desperate to end it. They huddled very briefly. They whispered, not to keep their deliberations secret from the gallery, but to keep them secret from Anna, from the "witch" they feared.

The judges resumed their previous positions and their previous lofty postures. They announced that sufficient evidence had been presented, that Anna's devilish incantation in the dungeon was a witch's curse to punish her torturer, and that if not for the diligent prayers of Dernbach and Nuss, Bubi would have died. They ordered Anna to be executed by fire immediately. Anna heard them and lost her ability to draw breath.

Chapter Thirty-Two:
Brighter Than the Flames

JOST WAS LOCKED ALONE IN THE CELL with no way of knowing what was happening in the courtroom above him. His mind was too frantically abuzz to take notice of his surroundings. He began to pray for his wife. As he did, he calmed. When he opened his eyes again, he took notice of all that surrounded him. He looked into the neighboring cell and saw the rope and pulley. He saw the chair with the straps. He saw the blood that still pooled around it. He was separated from his wife, helpless to intervene. But he was little more than an arm's reach from her blood. The blood did not sicken him. It did not anger him. It was of Anna, and he wanted to touch it, to have it nearer to him.

Jost sprawled on his side and reached between the bars. Anna's blood was just out of reach. Part of him knew that he would never touch her again, and his desire to reach her blood, to have any part of her in contact with his hand grew feverish. He strained and he struggled before giving up, leaning his head against the bars, and crying like a child.

Preparations for the execution began immediately. The judges sent for the executioner, and the wood was being piled before the gallery of the courtroom was cleared.

The same two men who carried Anna to the chair lifted her from it. It had all fallen apart so quickly. She was in too severe a state of shock to pay much mind to her torn shoulders or shattered feet. The judges wanted her out of their sight as soon as possible. They ordered her to be locked in a small room adjacent to the courtroom to wait until the executioner was ready for her.

Albrecht could not bring himself to look at Christoph. He turned away with his head down and walked with struggling steps from the palace, as if walking through a thick bog. He did not pray. He did not think, plot, or plan. He simply walked. Once he was outside of the palace, in the streets of Aschaffenburg, his surroundings made him think of the past. He thought about his youth, when he was dispatched to investigate a strange phenomenon about a young lady who seemed magically healed by a little girl. He thought intensely about his experience with Anna, sitting on her bed and having his eyes opened by her. Sickening pity almost overwhelmed him.

Christoph was not so foolish as to follow the mandates of his instincts and rush the guards that escorted Anna. He wanted to fight them all, throw his mother over his shoulder, and run from Aschaffenburg in any direction. Instead, he simply begged one of the judges for a pen and a piece of paper. The judge's compassion for Christoph was authentic and he gave what was asked along with a prayer and a blessing. Christoph impatiently received the blessing, then he took to writing. He knelt on the floor in front of a chair in the gallery and he scribbled away on the paper. When he finished, he left the palace in search of Albrecht.

Albrecht turned back toward the palace. He saw Christoph at the entrance. Christoph handed him the letter he had written, turned away from the palace, and walked out of sight. The letter read,

Brighter than the Flames

Dear Father Albrecht,

My younger years were filled with stories about a Jesuit Priest who met my mother years ago. He saw her as none had seen her. He gave her a gift that changed the course of her life and made her the woman she is and the mother she is. On her behalf, I ask one more gift of that same priest. I ask that you help my mother now. Interfere in every way you can. Do what you must to stop this nightmare and return my mother to us. I beg this of you. If you can free my mother and return her to her place of prominence over our table, I will honor you with all that I have for the rest of my life.

Faithfully Yours,
Christoph Koob

Albrecht had no power to heed Christoph's request, but he could press his influence to see Anna and speak to her. He entered the palace and demanded to speak with Anna.

"She has the right to see me, to see her priest and receive my prayers," he insisted. The palace guards let Albrecht into the room where Anna was being held.

Anna was seated on the floor against the opposite wall. She was ghostly pale, and her eyes darted back and forth in furious thought. Albrecht walked to her. When he drew near, her mind cleared. Her eyes settled to look at him.

Albrecht stood in front of her. They stared at each other in silence for a few moments, until Albrecht finally spoke, "I find it both comforting and unsettling how comprehensively human beings are in the hands of fate. Of all the times in history and all the places on Earth you could

311

have been born, fate put a woman like you before men like these. I feel a new age on the horizon, one where you would thrive and receive the admiration you deserve. But here you are, in the ruthless clutches of a cannibalistic age, while a much gentler age is just a few breaths away… a few more breaths, I'm afraid, than fate has granted to you, my friend. Through one half of my mouth, I curse fate for its cruelty. Through the other, I thank God for his heavenly vision, with the assumption that your pain serves some heavenly purpose that is beyond me. I must believe that, for you are undoubtedly a tool of God, if ever I have known one."

The words were not scripted with some rhetorical purpose. They were not designed and rehearsed to bring Anna comfort. They were the wild effusions of a heart not sure how to feel and a brain not sure what to think. Those two organs shared one thing in common — they both knew unequivocally that the proceedings were a travesty, and that Anna Koob was as righteous as she was innocent of her charges, and that a rare and beautiful light in a dark world would soon be extinguished, to the immeasurable detriment of mankind.

He knelt beside her and bowed to kiss her cheek. Her face was crusted with tears that had dried and no longer had the strength to flow. His lips felt soft to her and touched her with admiration and compassion. For a flash of a moment, the kiss gave her visions of being held by her mother.

He knelt erect and promised her, "I will be as near to you as I am allowed to be. My eyes and my prayers will be on you."

He stood and walked to the exit, turning to her one last time and expressing a final thought, "You do not travel to God's hands today. You are in his hands *already*, and he will hold you until your soul is free, then raise you to his face."

His words were not spoken to the walls. They reached her and affected her. He stood still, stared at her, and allowed his words to saturate. He knew when they did. With her eyes locked to his, Anna's lips forced a slight smile that pushed crusted wrinkles across her parched cheeks. He made the Sign of the Cross, turned to the door, and walked away from her. He made his way to the city square and took a position as near to the execution site as the guards would allow him.

A few minutes later, the same two men came for Anna. They brought the two poles and platform they used to carry her from the dungeon to the courtroom. They had no care for her comfort and jostled her mercilessly. This time, they tied her lap to the platform, much more tightly than was needed to keep her from falling off. They carried Anna to the city square, near the fountain where she met Maria Echter decades earlier. Anna could not believe what was happening to her. Her mind spun so quickly that she could not form a coherent thought. Memories from all parts of her past flew at her with picture, sound, smell, and touch. Her life was passing before her, passing through a gauntlet of terror and pelting her like sleet in a strong wind.

Once Anna was out of the palace, guards released Jost. He asked them how things had transpired. They did not answer him. They escorted him in silence from the dungeon. Jost saw the empty gallery. He begged the guards for news. They escorted him from the palace and released him into the streets like releasing a bird into the wild. They went back into the palace and left Jost with no idea what was happening.

It was December 19, and the air was cold. It enlivened Jost's senses and returned his wits. He saw people from the gallery walking toward the city square. He caught up with them in time to see the wood piled high. A crowd had formed and Jost could not see beyond them. He yelled for Anna. He yelled for Christoph. He even yelled for Albrecht. The archbishop's guards had cleared a safe circle around the wood. Jost made his way to the front of the crowd. There was no more need for inquiries. The stage was set for his wife's execution and Anna's fate was all too clear to him. He looked around and saw Anna on the opposite side of the wood pile. He shouted to her, but his voice could not carry through the crowd. It wouldn't have mattered if it did. Anna's mind was still swept in the swirling, pelting, piercing memories that flew at her chaotically.

Christoph heard Jost yelling and worked his way to him. It was a strange mix of people in the crowd. Many had come directly from the palace, knowing well what was happening. Of those, the majority of them did not know how to feel. When they awoke that morning, they were Anna's friends and supporters. They were ready to help her celebrate her freedom. But many of them were terrified of the story told that morning by Nuss, Dernbach, and Bubi. They saw Bubi's sunken eyes and his shaking hands. They were slow to believe the accusations against Anna, but fear has a decaying effect on loyalty.

Many in the crowd left their homes and businesses when they saw the bustle in the street. They saw the preparations being rapidly made for an execution by fire, and they drew near to satiate their curiosity. Christoph paid none of them mind. He was deaf to the comments and deaf to the cries. He wanted only to be with his father.

With fake hope that flaked and peeled from his facade, Christoph told his father not to worry.

"I have given a letter to Father Albrecht. He took it and read it. He will put a stop to this."

Jost was a frayed and battered man. He dared not hope, but dared not give up hope. He could not form words in his mouth. He only gripped his son tightly by the upper arm and kept his eyes on Anna.

Anna was taken from the poles, and for a few minutes, she disappeared from Jost's view. A tall ladder was set flat on the ground in front of the wood pile. Anna was laid upon it, about 20 feet from the bottom. Two men lifted the top of the ladder to the height of their hips. The executioner was on hand. He forced Anna's arms behind her and between two of the rungs. Her hands were bound together with a rope that wrapped around the front of her waist. Her ankles were bound separately to the sides of the ladder.

Two large stones were placed at the feet of the ladder to keep it in place as they hoisted it erect with a rope tied to the top, hoisting Anna twenty feet into the air. The men who tied her down held the sides of the ladder to keep it from falling. Once the ladder was upright, Anna's weight was on her shoulders and pain snapped her from her fantasies. She screamed, hushing the chatter of the crowd. Anna pushed upward from her bound ankles and relieved the pressure. The crowd nearly silenced, watching her struggle. When her strength left her, she dropped her weight onto her shoulders again and let out another scream. Many gasps came from the crowd.

Jost yelled Anna's name, and many people turned to stare at him. Even to those who did not know them, it was clear that he was her husband. Such pain echoed from his voice. Some people patted his shoulder. Some rubbed his arm. Some stared in horrible compassion. Some stared in morbid fascination. Jost flicked them away like flies. He had drawn Anna's attention and she looked directly at him.

Christoph's eyes drifted to the left of his mother, where he saw Albrecht standing. Albrecht stood as he promised he would, as near to her as he could. Christoph began shaking Jost, yelling, "There he is. He is going to stop this." But Albrecht did not give any orders. He did not wield the authority of his order. He simply stood with his hands clasped in front of him, looking up to Anna.

The stones were moved to the other side, so that the ladder could be lowered over the fire. The executioner kept the rope and walked around behind Anna so he could release her slowly into the flames. Dernbach was nowhere to be found, but Nuss, delighted in his victory, played a prominent part. He brought the torch himself, carrying it like a trophy from behind the ladder. He lit the wood and the fire grew.

Anna saw the fire in front of her and lost all concern for the pain in her shoulders. She wiggled and squirmed and let out a staccato whine that carried over the crackle of the rising fire to be heard clearly by all in attendance. When the flames went high enough and hot enough, Nuss gave the signal, and the executioner started lowering Anna toward the flames. Anna stopped squirming and held stone-still. She was not yet over the fire and not near enough to burn. But she most certainly felt the heat.

She started screaming. It was not the scream of pain, but the scream of terror. Nuss signaled to the executioner to lower Anna farther. He watched Nuss closely as he obeyed. Nuss kept his hand up in a fist. The executioner released more rope and Anna lowered above the fire. The flames did not touch her, but the rising heat was searing. Anna's scream turned from one of fear to one of pain, shifting dramatically higher in pitch and doubling in loudness. The scream took control of the air and declared itself from the walls of every building. Jost yelled her name again, but he could not hear his own voice over Anna's blistering shriek.

Nuss opened his closed fist, and the executioner held his rope still. Anna was directly over the still-growing fire. The flames licked at her feet, but her dress started smoking and her hair curled upward and withdrew. Her cheeks, chin, and nose blackened and smoldered. Pieces of her dress fell from her into the fire.

Anna's piercing scream suddenly gurgled as she vomited through her blackened lips. The sound was so pathetically horrid that even the executioner recoiled. He lost his grip on the rope. What was left of Anna Koob plunged with the ladder into the bonfire, sending ash and embers high and wide. Christoph's eyes were wide as he stared at the rising flames, smoke, and ash. He prayed that his mother was already dead and not burning to death inside of the fire. A single piece of ash fell onto his right sleeve and clung to it as if it wanted to never let go. Not knowing if the ash had been part of the bonfire, the ladder or rope, or part of his mother, he defensively cupped his left palm over it to protect it from the breeze. He kept it protected in that way and stared into the fire. Once all doubt of Anna's death was gone, he turned to the river and followed it alone toward Kleinostheim.

Jost did not notice Christoph walking away. He stepped dangerously and uncomfortably near the fire. He had been just a few inches from Anna's blood when he was locked in the cell, and now he stood again unable to touch her. It was not bars that kept him from his wife this time, but fire — savage, murderous fire. He dropped to his knees and leaned in, scorching his own face until Albrecht lifted him to his feet and walked him backward.

Jost did not know it was Albrecht's hands that pulled him to safety. He did not know that anyone had touched him. His reddening eyes gazed forward at the bonfire, somehow still hoping that Anna would walk from the flames, take him by the hand with a smile, and escort him home with stories and quotations. Albrecht and a few others turned Jost away from the fire and set him in a carriage to home. Jost mumbled to himself between sobs. Albrecht could not tell if Jost was talking to him, to God, or to Anna. He said nothing in return, paid the carriage driver from his own purse, and watched with love as it drove away.

Christoph escorted the piece of ash on his sleeve all the way home. He talked to it, saying the things he wished to say to his mother. By the time he reached the eastern edge of Kleinostheim, he conversed freely and lightly with his mother, as if she walked beside him. When he got home, he did not know that his father was already there. He removed his shirt, taking great care not to disturb the flake of ash, and secured it in a chest. Only after the chest closed did the full truth of the moment strike him. It struck him hard, and he dropped to a seat on the floor and yelled for his mother.

Jost was in bed. He had not moved since he entered the house, walked directly to his room, and fell into a tight ball. Christoph cried for his mother for more than an hour. When he had no more tears to expel, he thought about his father. He knew the extraordinary sort of love his parents shared. It was his primary source of pride in them. When his thoughts abandoned his own loss and turned to what was suffered by his father, he learned a new form of sorrow, one darker, deeper, and malignant.

He found Jost still curled in a ball in bed. He did not know what to say. As much as he loved his mother and suffered her pain as she was lowered to the flames, he loved his father and suffered *his* pain. Christoph rubbed Jost's head and kissed him repeatedly, saying nothing, but expressing love beyond what all human languages could coordinate to express. Jost was utterly broken. Aside from his physical appearance, he would not have been easily recognized by his acquaintances. The shattered remains of a once vibrant man curled like a helpless infant in his son's arms.

Christoph slept that night beside his father, expecting some revival in the morning. Jost did not improve. He did not eat or drink. The following evening, night, and morning were the same. Jost soiled himself and showed no signs of notice. He stared at the wall with hardly a blink to show that he still drew breath. Christoph watched him decline over the next few days. He turned thinner and paler. Christoph changed his soiled clothes and linens, and begged him to rise and face the tragedy as a family.

Anna Marie was heartbroken. But she was strong and nurturing for the young man she loved. She spent a few hours every day helping Christoph tend to Jost. She was disturbed at how quickly and easily her village went on with life as if Anna Koob had never lived there. She even managed to pull her parents to compassion. Her mother cooked for Christoph, who otherwise would have eaten little more than Jost. Anna Marie and her family were a true life-line for Christoph. The infant embers of his passion for her kept some warmth in what was a frigidly miserable time in his life. Together they force-fed Jost and kept him a steady inch from the grave.

Father Albrecht had a strong sense of justice, of what was fundamentally right and wrong. He viewed Anna's death as a tragedy, but through thick academic lenses. Albrecht's heart had long lived in the shadow of his head. He had an academic relationship with everything, allowing few swells of emotion. As he sat on his bed on the night of the execution, his mind could make no sense of what had happened, and it yielded entirely to his heart. Albrecht tried to pray for Anna's soul, but with the first thoughts of her, he burst into violent sobs, thinking nothing and feeling intensely.

As the swell subsided and his thoughts sobered, he thought about the woman Anna had been and of the husband and son she left behind. The cruel pinching of his heart was a sensation new to him and he felt a dark, hollow, achy, mournful moan reverberate inside of him like a forlorn spirit in an empty cathedral. Guilt stalked him relentlessly. He asked himself by the hour what he could have done or said differently that might have placed Anna Koob back in the arms of her husband. The truth is, Albrecht lived too much in the pages of dead philosophers and not enough in the treacherous world of living people. He was well-read on the tragic history of mankind, but

Anna's death was not ink on paper. It was branded into his heart with fire.

He struggled increasingly to reconcile his thoughts and his feelings, and come to grips with the tragedy in a way that would allow him to proceed with his life. But each day for a week he felt hollower and hollower, darker and darker. He resolved to write a letter to Jost, to relieve himself, however minutely, of one portion of his guilt. He sharpened a pen and dangled it over paper with no idea how to begin. His heart swept his mind away.

He thought about the child he had met many years earlier. With flawless clarity, he envisioned her bounding back into her room with the family Bible, and quizzing him with the common sense of righteousness. Jagged-toothed regret gnawed at him from the inside, manifesting as sharp, debilitating cramps that buckled him over. But his thoughts were not on *his* pain. He thought of Anna, and of those first moments of burning, when the sensations were freshest. Many times he reminded himself of the futility of such thoughts, and he tried to turn his mind elsewhere, to Jost and Christoph and the letter he wanted to write. Again and again, he failed in that effort, and he forced himself to live and relive Anna's pain and fear.

He thought about the report he submitted on the case of Marie Echter, and how he could have more plainly shown the beautiful truth behind the miraculous recovery. He thought about the many years that passed neglectfully without contact with her. He regretted not being there at her first trial, where the right argument could have buried the case too deeply to be revived so many years later by Dernbach. Guilt swelled so severely within him that his heart, not his head, took control of his fingers and he wrote his letter to Jost.

Albrecht could not bring himself to deliver the letter by hand. The last letter exchanged between them was Christoph's final appeal to save his mother. Albrecht could not face them. But he had the letter delivered by trusted hands and it reached Christoph, addressed to Jost, two weeks after Anna's death. Christoph stared at it for several minutes before opening it, not sure if it would do his father good or harm to hear it. He decided that it was not his decision to make. The letter was addressed to Jost, and Jost should know what it contains. His condition could hardly be worsened by it. So Christoph sat beside Jost's bed and read the letter aloud.

> *Dear Jodocus,*
>
> *I have no idea how to begin addressing you. In my blindness, I did not see what part I was playing in this unspeakable tragedy. I only tried to understand an extraordinary woman who appeared as quite Godly to me. My eyes are open now and the path between meeting her when she was just a girl and standing near her at her end is as plain to me as the paper I write on.*
>
> *Although my share in your loss is just a tiny portion, it places more weight on my shoulders than can be overcome. To relieve that weight, I have turned to fervent prayer and to a stronger faith in the will of our God. Included in those prayers and in that faith is that you and your son will also seek peace in the Lord's hands. No tragedy can be solely mourned if it causes us to move closer to God.*
>
> *Nobody stood nearer to Anna when she died than I did. I would have stood much closer were I able. My*

senses witnessed an atrocity at the hands of my Church. Please know this. While my ears heard Anna's screams and my throat choked on the smoke, while my eyes were stained by the brightness of the fire, my spirit saw through it to a woman I only then came to understand. My spirit saw Anna's spirit, which shone brighter than the flames that took her from you.

From what I have come to understand, I am not the only person profoundly affected by Anna, or vastly improved by her influence. She left this world a more beautiful place than she found it, having brightened and enriched every life she encountered.

I cannot imagine your despair or the depth of your loss. But I can assure you of this. The whole world has lost that bright spirit, and a much darker world mourns with you. I mourn with you now and for the rest of my life, as I will remain always,

Your Affectionate Brother in Christ,

Albrecht

Christoph did not know what to expect when he opened the letter. It is safe to say that he was apprehensive and held his anger at the gates, ready to release it. He certainly didn't expect the letter to elevate him as it did. It taught him nothing of his mother he did not already know, but it gave him a glimpse into her effect on the wider world.

He folded the letter carefully along its original folds and held it with one hand against his lap, staring at it and pondering its broader truths. When he finally raised his eyes, he saw Jost standing in front of him, gazing fixedly at his wife's son with adoring eyes. Christoph stood and embraced his father. They sobbed heavily in each other's arms, and when the sobbing subsided, they pulled from each other with matching smiles of gratitude. Just then, Anna Marie came by with food for Christoph. She was delighted beyond expression to serve it to Jost as well. The three of them ate together on Jost's bed.

They walked hand-in-hand through Anna's house, where Anna's books sat still as she had left them, to the kitchen, where Anna's ingredients filled Anna's jars on the shelves Jost made for her. They thumbed through Anna's papers and found a special recipe. With trial, error, and eventual success, they brewed a perfect batch of Anna's Happy Tonic. As they sat at the table and received that signature brand of healing that only Anna could provide, they were again a family. They missed her. Oh, Good God how they missed her. There was a conspicuous and bitterly stinging absence, but that Anna was with them and they felt her nurturing attentiveness, there can be no doubt at all. Spiritually, she was as much in their company, as much in their hearts, as ever she had been, and her healing presence lost none of its potency after her death. In their rich mutual remembrance of her, she healed them as she had healed so many.

Christoph married Anna Marie less than a year later. Jost revived fully and expanded the wealth and status of his estate. As a landowner, he took his rightful position on the bench of the local lay court, determined to protect innocent women from Anna's fate. In spirit, Anna sat on that bench with him, speaking her words through his voice.

Much blood was spilled between the flames of 19 December 1603 and the Enlightenment that washed away the hateful misunderstanding that swept Anna Koob from the world. Through it all, Jost and Christoph, Christoph's wife and children, and all of their descendants mixed the Happy Tonic, altering it slightly with each generation, but keeping alive Anna's spirit, though her name and her story have fallen into obscurity. Now I invite you, my readers, to pour a brew of whatever makes *you* happy. Think of the story you have just read, and raise your mug or glass to the many women who have brought our species out of darkness and paid dearly to do so. Raise your glass to Anna Koob.

Postface

I DID NOT SET OUT TO WRITE A FEMINIST BOOK. I just wanted to tell the story of an ancestor and pay her the respect she deserves, but my research and reflections exposed themes that appear universal and tragically perpetual. Perhaps dynamic women are no longer being executed in flames. They are being scorched in other ways. More than four hundred years after Anna's death, women are called weak for displaying human compassion, and they are diminished for it. They are scorned for their ambitions and demonized when not dainty and submissive, and they are diminished for it. In many cultures still, women are assumed to have a lower capacity for understanding. The common sense of feminine sensibilities and the silent stoutness of feminine strength is deprecated by a masculine society. And still, as Christoph noted so long ago, the atrocities of our species are born of rampant masculinity.

We will not reach our potential until the feminine comes in balance with the masculine and begins to press upon our collective sensibilities its signature traits. When that happens, there will be nothing lost by men. Human life will finally rise to the surface and float high in balanced tranquility. As it does, I pray that we remember — we float on Anna's ashes. We float on Jost's tears and Miray's blood. We sit atop an ocean of human suffering. I pray that we remember Anna Koob, and every woman who pushed her qualities upon us at tremendous personal cost.

www.ingramcontent.com/pod-product-compliance
Lightning Source LLC
Chambersburg PA
CBHW051635050726
47502CB00011B/515